LB

D1531772

THE PUZZLE KING

This Large Print Book carries the
Seal of Approval of N.A.V.H.

THE PUZZLE KING

BETSY CARTER

THORNDIKE PRESS

A part of Gale, Cengage Learning

GALE
CENGAGE Learning

Detroit • New York • San Francisco • New Haven, Conn • Waterville, Maine • London

GALE
CENGAGE Learning™

LIBRARY OF CONGRESS CATALOGING-IN-PUBLICATION DATA

Carter, Betsy, 1945–
    The puzzle king / by Betsy Carter.
      p. cm. — (Thorndike Press large print reviewers' choice)
    ISBN-13: 978-1-4104-2256-9 (alk. paper)
    ISBN-10: 1-4104-2256-9 (alk. paper)
    1. Jews—Germany—History—1933–1945—Fiction.
    2. Immigrants—New York (State)—New York—Fiction.
    3. Families—Fiction. 4. Large type books. I. Title.
    PS3603.A7768P89 2010
    813'.6—dc22   2009041287

Published in 2010 by arrangement with Algonquin Books of Chapel Hill, a division of Workman Publishing Co., Inc.

Printed in the United States of America
1 2 3 4 5 6 7 14 13 12 11 10

For F.E. and M.E.

PROLOGUE

On a March morning in 1936, an American woman in her forties named Flora Phelps stood in line at the American consulate in Stuttgart, Germany.

For these times, in this place, this was an extraordinary fact. But Flora gave the people in line even more reasons to stare. For one thing, she was beautiful. While they all wore drab, ill-fitting clothes and the weariness of terrible times on their faces, Flora wore a floral-patterned silk dress that accentuated her ample curves. The raspberry-colored cloche she wore drew attention to her eager brown eyes. Vanities such as this had all but disappeared in Germany.

She carried an envelope and a bundle wrapped in brown paper tied up with twine. Anyone who saw the way she held the package, with both arms around it, understood that whatever was inside had everything to do with her visit here on this day.

When it came her turn to speak with the consul, he was immediately taken with her. Flora was as charming as she was beautiful, and it wasn't long before she and the consul were engaged in a conversation that went far beyond the parameters of his station. The talk turned to Flora's relatives. Flora was born to a Jewish family in Germany, and, as a young girl, was sent with her older sister to America, where she lived in a prosperous suburb with her aunt and uncle. Her other relatives stayed behind. Only a miracle would get them out of Hitler's Germany now.

Dire times breed unexpected heroes. Flora was one of them.

PART 1

New York City:
1892

Three years to the day after Simon Phelps was born, his father died unexpectedly. Simon's mother told him it had to do with a vision his father had right before his death: "He saw you being snatched up in the claws of a giant bird and taken away. He ran after the bird with his hands grasping at the air hoping to save you, but you were already lost to him. The stones of sorrow set heavy in his heart until, eventually, they crushed him."

Simon had no memories of his father, only a black, formless guilt that his birth was responsible for his father's death. Sometimes he would try to reach back into memory and draw a picture of him, but all that surfaced was the image of a small man disappearing underneath the weight of large stones. He sketched everything before him — his mother cooking, his sister braiding her hair, the maple trees at the botanical garden — and he drew other things that existed only in his imagination. He hoped that by re-creating what he saw inside his head, the image of his father would untangle and present itself to him.

Before she sent Simon away from Vilna, his mother bought him a notebook and some colored crayons. Only a mother who understood how much her son relied on his imagination would indulge in that kind of extravagance.

The family got by with little. She supported her seven children by taking in sewing: jackets, dresses, and pants with seams so worn that the wind blew through them. Of course she made all their clothing, which was passed down from one child to the next.

The future seemed as bleak and tattered as the clothes she tried to mend. It took months for her to scrape up the eight dollars it would cost to send Simon, her youngest and, in her mind, smartest, child to America, where she was certain he would find a better life. Vilna was no place for a child, not now, in 1892, when a knock on the door at the crack of dawn or in the middle of the day could mean that any boy over twelve would be taken away and sent into the army. It could be months or even years before his family would hear from him again. Or maybe never, if he was Jewish.

She promised him that she and his six brothers and sisters would follow. Someday, she told him, after he'd made some money and had a house, he'd be able to afford to bring them to America. "You must be brave for all of us," she'd said, turning her face away from his. To herself, she repeated the prayer that God would help him find his way. Her God would reunite them soon. She had to believe that.

Because he could take only what he could carry, she agonized over what else besides the notebooks and crayons she should pack in his satchel. She made the choice to include her apron because she wanted something he could touch and smell, and for her own selfish reasons, it gave her comfort to think that at night he might roll the apron into a ball and rest his head on it. The thought of how it felt to run her fingers through his wavy hair before he fell asleep hurt her heart, so she moved on to worrying about more practical matters. She stuck in a few coins she had saved because she'd heard that he could trade them in at the money exchange when he got to Ellis Island. She also packed a brown-and-white checked sweater vest that she had knit for him.

For weeks before he left on his voyage,

she told him things about America. Of course, no one who had gone there had ever come back to Vilna, so everything she told him was based on rumor, scant pieces of knowledge, or what she wanted to believe was true. "You must dress well in America, everyone there does," she said. "It is important that you go to school and get an education. With an education, you can do anything. And it's important to keep your chest warm and stand up straight."

Simon's mother was not a typical Litvak mother. She was a warm, embracing woman, stout and tall for her generation. The last time he saw her, he was just tall enough so that when he leaned into her, his head nestled in the crook of her arm. He was nine years old.

At nine, Simon was a runt of a boy, the kind who could easily have been swallowed up by the squalor and homesickness that consumed him. When the first-class passengers would throw nuts and oranges down below to steerage, he refused to get on his hands and knees like the others in order to grovel for the prizes. Instead, he'd turn away and put his hands over his ears to tune out the laughter from the people above them. It wasn't as easy to ignore the stench of rotten

14

food, sweat, feces, and urine that stung his eyes and clogged his throat. It was so crowded that when passengers got seasick, more often than not they would lean over and vomit on another passenger before they could make it to a window or landing. When his own stomach ran sour, Simon searched for a place to be sick in private. Only once had he lost control and puked on someone else's shoes, and the memory of it, years later, still made his face go red.

At night, he slept on one of the wooden bunks lined up two in a row with no mattresses, with whatever blanket he could find. Simon would be so wedged in between the other unwashed bodies that at least once a night a meaty arm fell on his chest or someone rolled over on top of him and all but smothered him. The cries and moans of the others were so palpable sometimes he couldn't be sure that they weren't his own. When he thought no one was looking, he would reach into his valise and pull out his mother's apron. It was the kind that ties around the waist, and it had blue and gray roses and a white ruffle around the bottom and hip pocket. His mother had worn that apron every day, and he could imagine her wiping her hands on it after cutting up a chicken or quartering an apple. He would bury his head in the apron and retrieve its history of cinnamon and onions. Breathing deeply, he could also smell yeast and paprika. For those few seconds, he was back in his mother's kitchen in Vilna.

His mother was right about the notebook. During the dreary days on the boat, he filled both sides of every page with colorful drawings of his fellow passengers. He'd focus on a few characters at a time and make up stories about them. The Fatso family slept near him, and although all they ate was the rancid food and watery soup that everyone else ate, they seemed to get bigger and bigger as the days went on. He sketched them all as roly-poly characters who gobbled up chairs and whole lambs and anything else in sight. "They made farts that smelled of gefilte fish," he wrote under one picture. Under another: "My stomach's going to explode."

He thought he would make some drawings of the Screamers, a man and woman and their dimple-cheeked daughter, who was about six or seven. He recognized the Screamers from Vilna, where they had brought his mother clothes for mending. Little Rita hadn't stopped sobbing since the moment they had boarded the ship; at night, her cries were commanding enough to cause the thin planks of wood to vibrate beneath him. In the daytime when she howled, he could see her eyes, wide and fear filled. Her mother would yell at her father to make the girl stop, and the father would shout terrible things back: "I am pulling out my hair. If this child doesn't shut up, someone will go overboard: her or me or all of us."

One morning, Simon came upon the wailing Rita. She was sitting at the edge of a crowded bench and looked as if she might fall off at any moment. He drew a picture of her with a happy face instead of a teary pouting one. In his version, she wasn't sitting on a bench but was nestled in the limb of a tree on a sun-filled day in front of a pretty house with flowers all around it. And her dress wasn't the soiled white frock she wore every day — it was pink and clean. She had a big purple bow in her hair, just like the one his sister wore the morning he went away. He tore the sketch from his notebook and handed it to her. Rita stared at the picture with disbelief then looked up at Simon. "It's you," he said.

That night, before she went to sleep, he gave her something else. He'd made a drawing of her with her mother and father, and once again he saw it through his prism of

17

sunny days and pretty houses. Only this time, he carefully tore the picture into odd random shapes and wrapped them up in another sheet of paper. "It's a puzzle," he told her. "Try to put it together." Rita and her mother and father pieced together Simon's gift, and that night she slept quietly.

After that, Rita rarely left Simon's side. She came with him when he snuck upstairs to where the first-class passengers were taking their morning coffee on deck. They eavesdropped on their conversations, and, for both, it was the first time they heard English spoken. Their movements, it seemed to Simon, were rigid, and when they spoke, they'd move their heads mechanically from side to side in a way that struck him as funny. That's where he came up with the character Mr. Machine, whom he drew at stiff right angles. It was Rita's idea to have his head shaped like an upside-down pot. They'd have Mr. Machine grinning a toothy cartoon smile and saying things like "Please tanks you" and "Mine name es Walthur."

Sometimes they'd creep into the bowels of the ship and watch one of the ship's stokers, a small man with shiny balloonlike muscles. He became the inspiration for Strongman, a character with no neck and throbbing biceps, which Rita insisted that

Simon emphasize by drawing wavy lines around them. Strongman would pick up first-class passengers and dump them into the ocean. One of his victims was a skinny woman with pointy features carrying under her arm a tiny dog with the same angular features. As Strongman hoists them into the choppy waves, the two of them are screaming, "Yap yap yap!" and wagging their tongues. Another Strongman victim was a young boy flying through the air, his shirt-tails flapping around his ears and a wurst shoved down the front of his pants.

The water in the pictures varied. It was blue or greenish or calm or stormy. Sometimes the characters in the background were vomiting. On this boat, time melted into a perpetual gray twilight wrapped around the rhythm of the water and the intervals between seasickness. Only Simon, the Fatso family, Strongman, Mr. Machine, and Rita lived in a world of pastels. On their last day at sea, Simon gave Rita a farewell present he had made for her. It was a series of consecutive drawings stacked one on top of the other and tied together with a piece of string from his own luggage. He showed her how, if she flipped the pictures quickly with her thumb, she could see his happy version of Rita in her pink-and-white dress with the purple bow in her hair jumping up and down with the word "America" coming from her lips. On the last page, in the bottom right-hand corner, he printed his name.

As the ship pulled into New York Harbor, Simon's colors became muted and his images more specific and less buoyant. He drew the ship's bow cutting a *V* through the gunmetal waters of the harbor. The brick and limestone New York skyline was sharp and angled, a far cry from Vilna, with its sensual silhouette of rolling hills, gothic church spires, and turreted castles.

Just before he stepped off the ship and onto the river barge that would ferry him to Ellis Island, Simon took his vest from his satchel and put it on. He would enter America well dressed. He would stand up straight even as he was ordered into a line with the rest of the children who were traveling alone. He watched the faces around him grow taut, eyes receding with fear. He had not come all this way to be intimidated by these tall and well-fed Americans who were barking directions in English. Compared with the sharp corners of his language, this one sounded lifeless and lazy. There was no urgency to it.

He looked straight ahead as a man held

down his tongue with a wooden tongue depressor and studied his tonsils. He tried not to flinch when another one took a metal buttonhook, turned up the upper lid of his eye, and shone a light into his eyeball. This was the moment everyone dreaded. For one thing, it hurt. But more significantly, if one of the inspectors found even a trace of trachoma, a highly contagious eye infection that could cause blindness, they'd send you right back home on the next lice-infested boat. And before you knew it, America would become a fever dream that belonged to somebody else.

Maybe it was the severity of his rimless spectacles, or the gray aura around his eyes, but Simon looked older than his nine years. When he went to the money exchange, the man behind the counter didn't call him "sonny" as he did the other boys. Instead, he said, "Good luck, young man," and handed him back twelve American dollars. With his satchel in one hand and notebook in the other, Simon stepped off the ferry that took him from Ellis Island into New York City, a place that was more vivid than anything he could have dreamed up in his own sketches. People were waving handkerchiefs, calling out foreign names. Some were crying. He listened for his name and waited to see a familiar person. But there was nothing; no one.

The families walked in huddles, embracing and laughing and occasionally throwing little children up in the air. He trailed behind them as they headed east, away from the river and the piers. The leather soles of his boots were thin enough so that he felt every step of the cobblestone terrain. It was early spring, and although there were no flowers anywhere, the buds on the trees were heavy and green, and when the sun shone down on him, he could feel its warmth beat back the chill of his fear. He stepped over the orange peels and wiped away the dust that the horses on the horse cars had kicked up into his eyes. The air was tart with the smell of garbage and manure. He made his way past young boys and old men hawking everything they could fit onto their decrepit pushcarts. "Knives sharpened here," they shouted. "Ripe melons for sale." "Potatoes, fresh from the earth." The words, so new and circuitous with their open vowels and jaw-snapping consonants, sounded more to him like animal cries.

The old wooden shacks and brick row houses here were as shabby and tumbledown as the ones he'd left behind. He kept walking because that was all he knew to do. Every now and again, he reached his hand into his trouser pocket to make sure the twelve dollars was still there. He was so tired that he thought he might sit in a doorway and close his eyes, just for a few minutes. But he knew that a sleeping boy with a satchel by his side and twelve dollars in his pocket was prey, so he kept on going. There were houses that would take him in and give him a pallet to sleep on in a room crowded with others. They talked about that on the ship. Someone wrote the English words on a piece of paper for him, "Boarders, ten dollars a month." He just had to find a sign whose words matched up.

It was getting late and the sun was low in the sky. He looked back toward the harbor and watched the sky change from a pale yellow into a blood red. Light shimmied off of the glass windows like fire and everything was touched with gold. He felt embraced by the light. It was not his mother's embrace, but it had a feeling of warmth, of something he might learn to love. His heart beat fast and his stomach growled so loud with hunger that he was certain that everyone could hear him coming.

At last, he saw the letters whose shapes he had memorized: "B-O-A-R-D-E-R-S eight dollars" a month. Close enough. He would stay here.

The number 262 was painted on the lintel above the entrance. In Vilna, he would have taken the steps two at a time, but this was not home. Slowly, he pulled himself up the stairs and pushed against the wooden front door. Save for a bowl of light coming from a gas lantern in the lobby, it was completely dark. He dropped his satchel to the floor and shouted, "Hallo." He heard voices from above and footsteps on bare wooden floors. "Hallo," he shouted again, trying to sound more authoritative. "Hallo."

After the third try, he heard a woman's voice call down to him. Her words were a garble but her tone was unmistakably annoyed. *"Ja, ja,"* she said, as she made her way down from upstairs with slow, heavy footsteps. He noticed her hands, red and gnarled, tightly gripping the mahogany banister. Her eyes were cloudy and she squinted, trying to make out his form in the darkness. When she did, the edges of her voice softened. *"Ein Kind,"* she said, then said it again, as if she were speaking to someone else. *"Ein Kind."*

He pulled out his twelve dollars and waved it in the air. *"Hast du essen?"* she asked, pretending to lift food to her mouth with a fork. He rubbed his stomach to indicate that he was hungry. *"Komm,"* she said, beckoning him upstairs. *"Müss essen."*

The old woman knew what she was seeing. He was not the first young boy to arrive hungry and alone on a stranger's doorstep. There was an unspoken fellowship in this neighborhood: *They come, just as we came, and whatever food we have, we share. We can always make room for one more body. But we don't have to like it.*

There were two rooms and twelve people in this apartment. They all spoke at once, each in a different cadence and accent. It sounded to Simon as if dishes were breaking. An old man yelled at a young boy, then turned and pointed at Simon. A lady about his mother's age, though shorter and rounder, placed a pot of borscht and some freshly baked bread on a table. The others rushed for the food, making no pretense at politeness. He waited to see if anyone would offer him some soup or bread, but no one bothered. He took his place next to a girl who seemed to be his age. She pushed him aside and broke off a hunk of the bread for herself. He tore off another piece of bread and ladled the beet-colored soup into his bowl. All the while, a thick, fleshy teenage boy kept asking him a question. "Outside?"

he'd say. "Wanna go outside and take a piss? Piss. Piss. Even foreigners have to piss."

Simon gulped down the soup as the boy's eyes stayed fixed on him. When he finished, the boy, frustrated at Simon's lack of comprehension, motioned him to follow. They went down the back stairs to a little unlit yard. Simon recognized the acrid odor of urine before he saw the hole in the ground. The boy unbuttoned his trousers, took out his penis, and aimed straight for the hole, about a foot away. "That's better," he said, shaking off the last drops. "C'mon, you gotta have to piss by now. Stand here." He pointed to a spot right next to where he was standing. "See if you can get it right into the hole."

Simon did as the boy had done; only he held his penis so that the trajectory of his urine formed a fine golden spray before it met its destination. The boy slapped him on the back. "That's the way to go," he said.

As they headed back up the stairs, Simon worked his lips silently and then tapped the boy on the shoulder. "Piss," he said, shyly.

"That's right, piss," said the boy.

"Piss," said Simon again, and then again, proud that he had just learned a new word of English.

It was a cold evening, but the room that

Simon shared with seven other people was hot. There were no windows and the only air there had already been breathed by other people. But that was okay. He had a full belly, a roof over his head, and for the first time in many weeks, he was not rocking and pitching and fighting back nausea. Tonight he would sleep, and tomorrow he would look for a job.

NEW YORK CITY:
1894

Mr. and Mrs. Eisendraft, the old couple who rented out the rooms at 262 Eldridge Street, took Simon under their wing and never raised his rent beyond the original eight dollars a month. They enrolled him in the same public school their son attended, the boy who'd initiated the pissing match. His name was Aaron, but when Simon tried to say "Aaron," his tongue would trill over the *r* and it would come out sounding more like a command. "Never mind," Aaron said one day after Simon had stumbled over his name a few times. "Just call me Pissboy. That way you'll always remember me."

Simon immediately got work as a newsboy. Up at 3:30 each morning, he'd be at Newspaper Row to pick up that day's bundles by 4:15. He'd stand out on Delancey and Orchard in the punishing sun or the numbing cold, and there he'd stay until every newspaper in his stack was gone. "Getcha

New York Sun, only two cents." "Fire on the Bowery, read all about it." He learned the language of the city while his mind's eye captured its contour and nuances.

His pictures filled the apartment at 262 Eldridge Street. In the rooms without windows, he hung sketches of windows looking out to sunlit skies with birds in the trees. For the kitchen, he made drawings of the pushcart vendors and of peaches and bananas and the other exotic fruits he'd discovered in America. He drew real likenesses of the people in the apartment, not caricatures with exaggerated features and swipes of brushstrokes. In Simon's pictures, Mr. Abner's mole above his right eyebrow looked as smooth and pink as it did in real life, and the purple veins in Mrs. Futterman's nose were as clear and visceral as the coarse hairs sprouting out of Mr. Selig's ears. Simon's drawings were almost obsessive in their exactitude. He drew fast and constantly, as if he was trying to make the pencil or crayon keep up with the images that played in his head like a zoetrope.

The others at 262 Eldridge Street called him Rembrandt, although with their Yiddish, Hungarian, and Russian accents, it came out with too many *r*s at the beginning. He nodded and accepted their compliments with a smile. "What a polite boy," they said. "How remarkable for a child to be that sensitive to adults. And no parents, to boot." Mostly, he looked serious and old for his age, but sometimes, when his blue-gray eyes were open wide behind his rimless glasses and his mouth was round and slightly puckered, it was easy to look at Simon and find the face of a helpless child.

What they couldn't see was how Simon was locked up inside. Unlearning one language while claiming another, he owned few words to give voice to his feelings. All he could do was travel through his eyes, tracing the lines and flows of what he saw in his head. Like the other people at 262 Eldridge Street, he was from somewhere else that didn't want him. He was stuck with them in this little house, all of them as poor as they'd been before they got here. Only now there was no America to look toward. Simon hoped that he would find his place, that he would be one of the lucky ones whose pictures he had seen in the newspaper: the ones who found a foothold in this world. In that way, he felt separate from the other people in the house, and even, at times, disparaging of them.

These people. They talk all the time. They talk in the language of the old country. And what do they talk about? They talk about noth-ing. They talk about food and money and the work they do, and they talk about each other. They will never be Americans if they don't learn to speak English the way Americans do. They never go anywhere, just to their jobs and back. The same four blocks every day. I will learn to speak so that no American will be able to tell that I am not one of them. I'll talk about the crimes and the fires and the prize fights and I'll go to far away places like the Bronx and Brooklyn. I won't end up here like the rest of them. God will put me in jail for having bad thoughts like this, I know He will. But when my mama and my sisters and broth-ers come to America, they have to have a house and money. I promised.

On the wall in the place where he slept were two drawings that Simon had made the day before he left the ship: one of his sisters and brothers, and one of his mother. Often, he would close his eyes and try to conjure up his father, but the image would never come to him. He'd envisioned pieces of each fam-ily member then put them together as best he could. In the drawings he made, the lines were faded or creased with age but the forms were unmistakable and the strokes were the broad and simple ones of a child's hand. These were the only pictures that lacked the concentration and fluidity of the others.

In one of them, two girls and four boys of varying heights were standing in front of a house. One of the boys, the smallest in the group, had a pronounced cowlick. A girl with pigtails held on to a doll with only one eye, which appeared to have been made from a button. The other girl was slightly stooped and did not have the same smiling face as the rest of them. A purple ribbon around her long hair culminated in a bow that was far too showy and carefree for the rest of her. It was clear that Simon took time drawing the pattern of the bow: different sized squares with different shadings that suggest a particular plaid. The house was lopsided. There was no sun, no grass, no trees.

The picture of his mother showed her with a big bosom, soft smile, and hair knotted on top of her head. She was wearing a striped dress underneath an apron with roses, and she was holding a child, a stick figure, by the hand. Most of the picture was scribbled, except for the fingers of the mother and child, which were intricately drawn and tightly entwined. The two hands were darker than the rest of the picture, as if by bearing down on the charcoal, the young artist could make them indelible. Sometimes at night when he thought everyone was asleep, Simon would press his cheek against the wrinkled paper and stare into its charcoal folds, trying to draw out of them a new fact or forgotten moment. Then he would try to pray. It was so simple when his mother did it. She'd press her palms together, lower her eyelids, and talk to God as casually as if she were talking to a next-door neighbor. "Oh God, help me see my way clear to cleaning up this mess of a house." "Dear God, save us from persecution and poverty." She'd ask for the simple and miraculous with equal intimacy.

As she did, Simon would close his eyes and press his palms together. He'd think about how he craved the noise of his six brothers and sisters and the way his mother smelled like mint and cloves. In the dark silence, he could hear their voices, each a different timbre, and in his brother Jurgis's case, a slight lisp. He searched for words, but he had nothing to say to this God, this old friend of his mother's. He didn't have the words for the longing and fright that lived like worms in the pit of his stomach and startled him out of sleep each morning. It was as if the part of his brain that held language had room for only so much, and as the new words moved in, the old ones moved out. Until the transition was complete, he'd keep it all to himself.

What the world saw was a boy as clean and shiny as a lacquered box. In daytime, in public, he learned how to keep the worms at bay. Each morning, before he left for his job as a newsboy, he'd spit-shine his shoes, slick down his hair with some coconut oil he'd found in the bathroom, and run the palm of his hand over his shirt and trousers to straighten any wrinkles.

When he finished selling the newspapers, he'd walk to school. Often, he arrived there before the teachers. There, he'd hunch down in a corner of the schoolyard and pull out his sketchpad or his grammar book. At around seven-thirty, Mrs. O'Mara, his teacher, would show up. "Well, Mr. Early Bird, here you are again. You'd better come inside before you turn to ices, ay?" Every morning, it would be the same words. Something about the way she said *ices* made this the best part of his day.

Mrs. O'Mara wore her red hair piled on top of her head with tiny curls escaping down the sides of her face. Her cheeks were pink with rouge and, possibly because she wore a corset, all the plumpness from the rest of her body was squished up into her soft round face, which was filled with anything but ices.

She seemed tall and grand in her green gabardine coat and brown ankle-high boots. Simon always smiled up at her, though he never said anything back, afraid his English would come out muddled. He heard it all the time: twists of the tongue that sounded clumsy and ugly. Not him. Sometimes the class would sing "Yankee Doodle." Afraid that he'd stumble over the word *Yankee,* Simon never sang along, even though he'd find himself humming it when he was alone. Only when Mrs. O'Mara had them stand up, face the flag, place their hands over their hearts, and recite the Pledge of Allegiance did he speak out loud. And then he took great care to enunciate his words, arcing the *r*s in "America" and coming down hard on "justice for all."

What he lacked in words, he made up for with his drawings. He drew pictures of the other kids in the class with gaps where their baby teeth used to be, and others with freckles just the right color brown. He drew a picture of Mrs. O'Mara using only rose-colored crayons. Her mouth was the shape of a heart.

One afternoon, Davey Mullett, a skinny

kid with twine-colored hair and yellow teeth, said to Simon: "You draw so good, did you learn it from your father?"

With uncustomary boldness, Simon answered: "My father is died."

"And your mother?" asked Davey. "Is she died, too?"

"My mother lives in another country," said Simon. "She and my brothers and sisters live with her. Soon they will come to America."

It was the kind of answer that could have gotten Simon into trouble: a punch to the stomach, cruel taunting. *Sissy boy, misses his mama.* Simon had seen other boys beaten up for lesser crimes. In this neighborhood, someone always seemed to want what you had even when you had even less than nothing.

As if to authenticate his story, Simon turned to a blank piece of paper in his sketchpad and drew a beautiful woman with long yellow hair and six perfect children standing before a red house high on a green hill. Then he took a black crayon and drew the outline of a seventh child with no features and no color. He held the picture up to Davey. "That's them," he said.

"Who's that?" asked Davey, pointing to the shadowy outline.

"That's me."

"Could I have the picture?" asked Davey.

"Sure," said Simon, ripping the page from the notebook.

Davey Mullet wasted no time in telling the other kids. Sometimes, he'd ask Simon for a particular picture he'd drawn and Simon always gave it to him. Davey Mullet never said as much, but it was clear from the way he and the other kids treated Simon that, while they thought a boy with a dead father was a big deal, a boy with a dead father and a mother living in a foreign country was even bigger. The boys thought he was heroic and lucky not to have any parents to boss him around. The girls wanted to mother him. One day, Christina Ryan, a pale, skinny girl with sad, walnut-shaped eyes and long, wavy brown hair, waited for Simon after school. "Can I walk with you?" she asked. Christina was more than a year older than he was and lived down the street from him. Her father owned the milk cart, which he would push around the neighborhood shouting, "Milk here, milk here, fresh from a cow's teat. Milk here, milk here, fresh from a cow's teat." Mrs. Futterman said that the milkman was coarse, but Mr. Selig said, "Yeah, but you buy his milk, don't you?" He'd heard the boys make crude jokes about Christina, who was curvier than the other girls in the class.

Simon walked down Orchard Street with Christina, aware that she towered over him by at least a head. She stared straight ahead; he had a tight, concentrated smile. It wasn't often he walked with a girl, particularly a nice-looking one. He walked slowly to make sure everyone in the neighborhood could see him.

The next day, the same thing happened: Christina waited after school and asked if she could walk with him. Again they walked in silence.

On the third day, the news of it reached 262 Eldridge Street. "So, I hear you have a sweetheart?" said Mr. Selig, as they sat down to a dinner of roasted chicken. Simon could feel his face get hot. Pissboy looked up from his soup. "She's got bazooms out to here," he said, cupping his hands in front of his chest. Mr. Selig slapped his hand and tried to hide his smile. Simon would always remember that gesture, Pissboy holding his hands as if they were weighted down with grapefruits — not because of its coarse nature but because after that Pissboy punched him in the arm and called him a "stinkin' piece of shitball," just as he would have any of the other boys.

The next day in class, Simon drew a picture of a girl with brown wavy hair, big wide eyes, and oversized cherry breasts. Mrs. O'Mara happened to walk by just as he was finishing it. She stood over him and stared at the picture, squinting as if she was trying to take it in. "You have real talent. You could be an artist someday." Then she did a strange thing. She knocked on Simon's head as if she were knocking on a door. "You're all head," she said. "But heart, where's your heart?" She did the same tapping gesture on her own chest. "Why don't you put that drawing away before someone's feelings get hurt?" Shame dragged over Simon as he crumpled the picture into a ball and threw it into the trash.

"There's a place uptown where they have beautiful pictures from people all over the world. Do you know where I mean?"

Simon shook his head no.

"It's way uptown, on Fifth Avenue. It's called the Metropolitan Museum of Art and it's filled with paintings and sculptures, beautiful art by people who knew about heads and hearts. It's real pretty up there with all the mansions and Central Park. Sometime you could take the Third Avenue El to Eighty-sixth Street and take a look."

Simon thought that if Mrs. O'Mara believed that they were beautiful pictures, he would like to see them.

"I've never been there," he said.

"Maybe I could take you there this week-end," she said.

Could this be possible? What would the other kids think if they found out he went to a museum with his teacher? The other boys would never let him hear the end of it. He'd go, of course, but he'd tell no one. Chances of him bumping into anyone way up there were next to nothing. He tried to imagine what it would be like to travel on the El with Mrs. O'Mara and walk with her through those fancy streets. Simon decided not to risk having her change her mind by expressing his disbelief.

"I would like that fine," he said.

"Okay then." She smiled, as if she could read his pleasure. "I'll meet you here in front of the school at eleven on Saturday morning."

Everything about that day at the museum stayed fixed in his mind. Aside from the sculptures, he was mesmerized by a Giovanni Bellini painting called *Madonna and Child.* He studied the way the Madonna's fingers caressed the child's curly red hair and how she stared sidelong from the canvas as if to ward away intruders. Her lips were soft and forgiving. He thought about his mother. Then, in this place of beautiful paintings, he tried again to conjure up an image of his father. Still, nothing came.

My father is lost to me, he thought. And as he often did when the reality of that loss sat heavy inside him, he consoled himself with the promise of seeing his mother again soon. He glanced up at the painting. Would anyone but his mother ever caress his hair this way or kiss his head or regard strangers with a suspicious eye when they came too close? Standing before the mother and child in this painting made him feel like an intruder. He was nobody's child, and that was the saddest feeling he'd ever had. Mrs. O'Mara put her hand on his arm. "You miss your mother, don't you?" she asked.

No one had touched him in an intimate way since he left home, and the feel of her fingers on his arm was familiar and soothing. He could feel tears come to his eyes, and he fought them back by turning to the Frans Hals painting across the room, *Portrait of a Woman.* Even that, a painting of a pleasant heavyset woman, reminded him of how his mother used to sit with her hands folded on her lap. "Is this the Metropolitan Museum of Mothers?" he said, trying to sound casual.

Mrs. O'Mara started to laugh. She put her hand over her mouth to squelch the sound of it, but despite her efforts, she made little snorting sounds. Simon started laughing as well, harder and harder until tears ran down his cheeks, which made Mrs. O'Mara laugh even harder. In order to steady herself, she put her hand on the wall right next to the Hals painting. That's when the uniformed guard came over to them and said, "Please, you are disrupting the other visitors. And madam, I'll have to ask you to remove your hand from the wall."

The pretentious way the guard said "madam" stirred them up all over again. "We'd better get out of here," said Mrs. O'Mara.

Back in the street, they could see Central Park, forestlike in its expanse, and the sprawling lawns of the brick mansions on Fifth Avenue. As they walked east toward the Third Avenue El, the lawns got less gracious and the homes got smaller. Simon could feel himself getting farther and farther away from what seemed like a safe place. For however long they'd been in front of those paintings, he'd been home and happy and somebody's child. As they walked, he tried to re-create the feeling he had inside the museum. He called Mrs. O'Mara "madam" mimicking the high-falutin tone of the guard, and he brought up "the Museum of Mothers," but by the time they got back to Eldridge Street, he'd put a distance between himself and her, afraid that one of the other boys might catch him walking with his teacher.

That night, he tried to draw the women of Bellini and Frans Hals but all he could come up with were red-haired women who looked like Mrs. O'Mara.

NEW YORK CITY:
1900

Even though he'd been in the country for nearly eight years, Simon Phelps still hadn't gotten used to the way things in America would appear to be one thing and then inexplicably change to another. For example, here it was late in September. A cold rain had been falling steadily for a week. The puddles in the streets were filled with shiny dead leaves. Simon had taken to wearing his warmest woolen sweater, and even so, he had to rub his hands together and walk doubly fast in order to stay warm in the early morning chill. And then yesterday, the last day of September, the sun came out and the air smelled young and fresh. It was as if July had momentarily skipped around the corner, and now it was back. The peak of summer coincided with Yom Kippur that year, and in synagogues all over New York, rabbis had moon-shaped sweat stains under the arms of their long black robes.

Simon normally paid no attention to Yom Kippur. He knew that Mr. Abner and Mrs. Futterman, the oldest people in the house, would fast on this day. Each year, they'd come home from synagogue just after the sun set. They always looked pale and their hands would shake. The other people in the house would be waiting for them, and Mrs. Eisendraft would prepare a celebratory meal of chicken soup, gefilte fish, herring, a challah, and roast chicken. "It wasn't a bad fast this year," Mr. Abner would say, tearing off a piece of the challah and using it to sop up some chicken fat from the bottom of the pan. "Not bad at all."

Mrs. Futterman would barely make it up the stairs on her wobbly legs. "Bring me a chair," she'd cry out. "I'm getting too old for this. I'm sure God, or whoever thought up this fasting business, just meant for us to atone a little, not to die."

Mr. Abner and Mrs. Futterman always invited Simon to join them in the synagogue, and every year he would conjure up an excuse, like he had to go to school or he didn't have a suit. He wouldn't have gone had Pissboy not said to him two days earlier that, according to the Torah, he was a man now. "You're seventeen," he'd said. "You've been a man for four years. How're you going to get God to give you what you want if you don't repent for your sins? You're old enough to have sins, aren't you?" Pissboy punched his shoulder, and Simon wished he had something to confess to the older boy: a fight, a girl, a petty crime.

"Aw come on," Pissboy continued, "don't tell me you're pure as snow? I seen you with Christina, I seen the way she looks at you. You gonna tell me nothin' ever went on? Never stuck your hand underneath her shirt, never let your hand *accidentally* slip between those creamy thighs of hers?"

Pissboy was eighteen now. When his shirt was unbuttoned you could see a crease of fat sitting as a necklace would under his chin. Like many pudgy boys, he held his arms bowed and his hands in a beseeching position, which gave him an odd penguin-like gait. Already he'd lost two teeth to fights with other boys in the neighborhood, and more than once Simon had seen him stuff a bloodied or torn shirt into the trashcan outside the house.

A few weeks earlier, Pissboy had told Simon that he was going out to hunt down some souvenirs and asked if he would he like to come. When Simon told him that he really didn't understand what he meant by souvenirs, Pissboy shook his head and put his hand on Simon's shoulder. "You know, I'd call you a mama's boy, but you don't even have a mama," he'd said. "So that either makes you a sissy or some oddball foreigner. Nothing that can't be fixed with a little guidance from someone who knows the ropes. Know what I mean? Come with me. I'll show you some souvenirs."

He took Simon down to the basement. In a dark corner, behind the washboard and underneath a wooden bench, was a wad of old rags. Pissboy scooped them up using both hands and carefully unwrapped them. Simon could see that he was holding something small and round. Whatever it was, it picked up the narrow band of light that shone through the basement window. A thick link chain slipped through his fingers and in the palm of his hand he held a gold pocket watch. "Lookee here," said Pissboy, holding the watch close to Simon's face. "This is no fake. Heavy as a rock. She's a real beauty, isn't she?" Carefully, he placed the watch on the bench. Simon noticed the initials on the watch cover: GMC. He didn't know anyone with those initials.

Pissboy unfolded another rag. This time he pulled out a magnifying glass. The glass was beveled and the handle and rim were made of pewter. "Ever see one of these?" he asked, placing the magnifying glass into Simon's hand. The handle fit perfectly into Simon's palm and felt cool in his grip. "Go ahead, look through it. You won't believe it." Simon always carried some paper and a pencil in his back pocket because he never knew when he'd see something he wanted to sketch. He pulled out the wad of paper and drew some swift lines across it. He examined them under the glass. Seen this way, the pencil lead formed tracks and branches and spidery gullies on the paper, which itself was knobby and textured. Simon could have spent hours looking through the magnifying glass but for Pissboy, who was watching over his shoulder. "Never had anything like it, have you? I'll bet you want one of these."

Simon held the glass at arm's length and ran his fingers around the edge. "It's a beautiful thing," he said.

"See, that's the point," said Pissboy. "I've got lots of souvenirs like this, things you want but you never think you can get. But if you're clever enough, you can get whatever you want." His head jerked as he winked, "Know what I mean?"

Simon knew exactly what Pissboy meant. There was something he wanted. He wanted money so that when his family came to

America they would be able to buy a house. He wanted to know that his family was safe in Vilna, because in all the years that he'd been in America, he'd heard nothing of them even though he'd written to them innumerable times. He wanted to see them again, and he would do almost anything to get that, even if it meant going into a strange synagogue and making amends to an unfamiliar God. He thought he'd used up all of his wanting on them, but that was before he saw Pissboy's magnifying glass.

On this Yom Kippur morning, Pissboy stood before him in a suit that was too tight across his chest to button and a shirt whose sleeves hung way below his fists: hand-me-downs, most likely. Only his cufflinks, almond-shaped onyx stones, looked new and expensive and sharper than all the rest of him. They were obviously another of Pissboy's souvenirs.

They walked the two blocks to the synagogue together. From the outside, it might have been another tenement on Chrystie Street. The synagogue was on the second floor: a large unimposing room with wooden straight-back chairs, a podium, and a hand-carved walnut case in the front of the room, where the scrolls of the Torah were stored. They took seats near the back. The rabbi and cantor chanted in Hebrew, and the people in the audience followed along in the prayer books, moving their lips as they read. The exotic words they sang sounded ancient and impenetrable to Simon, yet they provoked in him such a palpable longing that he closed his eyes so as to move out of its way.

As he stood there in his self-imposed darkness, a memory, long forgotten, was being dislodged. He could feel himself rocking back and forth. But he wasn't the one who was rocking. It was a man with a beard. The beard smelled fusty and was tickling the side of his cheek. He was in the man's arms, and the man was chanting words that sounded like these words. He was a little boy, little enough to be held in his father's arms as his father prayed and sang and rocked back and forth. He could feel his father's warm words in his ear and smell his breath, stale and sour. It must have been this same Yom Kippur service, and it must have been the last one his father would live to see.

Simon became aware of the wooden seat rail of his chair banging against the back of his knees. How long had he been swaying like this? How many years back in time had he traveled? He opened his eyes and wondered if Pissboy had noticed anything out of the ordinary, but Pissboy was staring down at his shoes and absentmindedly jiggling the coins in his pocket. Simon looked straight ahead at the rabbi, who stood with his back toward the congregation before the walnut cabinet. As he touched his finger to the doors, they swung open slowly. Simon could see the red velvet cloth that lined the ark and the golden Hebrew letters embroidered on the Torah cover.

The rabbi wrapped his arms around the Torah, lifted it from the ark, and carried it to the podium. Simon felt as if he were seeing all of these things for the first time, and yet he was seeing them again. Again, he could feel a man's arms around him, holding him as tenderly as the rabbi held the Torah. A pleasurable warmth shot through his body, and for the first time since his father had died, he allowed himself the thought that he was once a father's son.

At the end of the service, when it came time for the Kaddish, the prayer for the dead, the rabbi asked all who mourned to rise. Without thinking, Simon started to stand. Then he paused. He looked at the others who had come to their feet. Most were old, with shiny cheeks and wrinkled skin where hair no longer grew. He would leave the praying to them, he thought, as he sat back down. Their voices were croaky and tired. Some closed their eyes; others bent forward.

Yis'ga'dal v'yis'kadash sh'may ra'bbo,

The prayer had a somber cadence.

b'olmo dee'vvro chir'usay v'yamlich
    malchu'say,

The words sounded as if they were weighted down with stones.

b'chayaychon uv'yomay'chon . . .

Simon wondered if they were the same stones that had crushed his father's heart and killed him.

He'd never understood how sadness could stop a man's heart. His mother had a flair for making things more dramatic than they were, and when she told him that his father died from stones of sorrow, he assumed that she was exaggerating. But now, as he sat so close to Pissboy that he could see the dots of perspiration beading his upper lip, he felt a pressure in his own heart that was heavy and absolute. Only Pissboy's proximity kept him from crying out.

Instead, he closed his eyes again and

52

brought back the memory of his father. He let himself smell his father's beard, an earthy, grassy smell. He imagined his father's strong arms around his tiny chest. He had no cause to recite the mourner's Kaddish. His father was more alive to him on this day than he had ever been. And so he mustn't think of his mother and sisters and brothers as dead. They were still back in Vilna, and he would see them soon. If he didn't believe these things, then what did he believe? What other reason did he have for working so hard? Why else come to this synagogue?

He was seventeen, and Pissboy was right, he was old enough to have sins. He knew exactly what they were. He remembered how Mrs. O'Mara had told him he was all head, and how she'd said to him, "Where's your heart?" Why did he always think such mean thoughts about the other people in the house? They were good people, and they'd been kind to him. But their lives were small and suffocating. None of them, it seemed to him, could see beyond the present. Same with the kids at school; it's not that he thought that he was better than they were but he just didn't want to grow up to be a policeman or a fireman the way the rest of them did. And Pissboy, he thought, was a sorry case: stealing the things he couldn't afford to buy. There were words for the way he felt. Although he didn't know what they were, he guessed that this God, who was writing people into the Book of Life on this most sacred of Jewish holidays, would find him lacking for having passed those judgments on the people he knew.

What Simon did next could not exactly be called praying. He imagined that he was holding on to a large balloon. The balloon was filled with his mama and papa and brothers and sisters and sins and wishes and everything else he'd thought about in the synagogue on this afternoon. He let the balloon go and watched it until it floated out of sight into the sky. Maybe it would bump against the gates of heaven and pop open at the feet of God.

That afternoon, as Simon left the synagogue with Pissboy, the sun was dropping into the Hudson River, leaving licks of purple in its wake. "Pretty boring, wasn't it?" said Pissboy.

"Not so bad," said Simon.

"I'm so hungry," said Pissboy. "I kept thinking about the roast chicken and mashed potatoes. And the vanilla ice cream with Himbeersaft. The best thing about this holiday, as far as I'm concerned." Pissboy licked his lips, just imagining the ice cream melting under the sweet raspberry syrup. His mother kept the sauce hidden throughout the rest of the year. Pissboy had searched all the cupboards, and once even went through the drawers in her armoire. But she was sneaky that way, always shoving a box of the best butter cookies under her bed, or wrapping some prized marzipan in one of her scarves and tucking it behind a stack of books. Pissboy was on to her secrets, but even he wasn't wily enough to figure out where she hid the Himbeersaft each year after the Yom Kippur dinner.

As Pissboy daydreamed about his favorite dessert, Simon noticed a white hill of flesh where Pissboy's stomach was bulging through his shirt. "Race you home," said Simon. "If you win, I have to get you a whole bottle of Himbeersaft; if I win, I get to choose one of your souvenirs."

"Holy smoke, are you kidding?" Pissboy jumped at the offer. This would hardly be any kind of contest. Skinny Simon with his wire spectacles was no athlete; Pissboy had never even seen him run. Pissboy spent his life running from neighborhood bullies or streaking down alleyways with his souvenirs tucked under his shirt. He was already envisioning where he'd hide his own bottle of Himbeersaft. It would have to be somewhere where his mother couldn't get her hands on it. "Okay," he shouted. "On your mark, get set . . ."

Simon, confident that he could outrun the fatter, older boy, clenched his fists together, bent his knees, and tucked his head down. In Vilna, he used to run through the hills for what seemed like miles. He ran for no particular purpose other than that it felt so good to watch the clouds skim by and feel the stones and roots of the trees under his feet. When he ran, the world seemed an expansive place with no obstacles. Since he'd come to New York, Simon had hardly run at all. New York was all edges and boundaries, and besides, there was no place to run other than the few blocks to his paperboy post. And then he only ran in the early morning frost, to beat the other boys and get the largest stack of newspapers. That wasn't the kind of running you did for fun.

"Go!"

Simon and Pissboy ran past the Jews in their black hats and wool suits walking slowly home from the synagogue. They ran through the narrow streets, past the old knife sharpener, who was packing up his pushcart, past the other tenements, where young children were still sitting on the stoop and the smell of onions cooking in chicken fat floated out from the windows. The early evening light softened the buildings' edges and cast the city in shadows. For the few moments before the sun sank into the river, Simon could believe he was running through the rutted hills toward his home in Vilna.

But the silhouette of underwear and a lady's dress waving like flags from a clothesline stretching from one window to another across a small courtyard brought him back to New York City, to America, where things would appear to be one thing and then inexplicably change into another. On this summery Yom Kippur day, the memory of his father had been restored to him. And he'd learned something from Pissboy that he would never forget: that you didn't have to be dishonest to get what you wanted, as long as you were shrewd.

It was dark by the time Simon reached the front door of 262 Eldridge Street. Hardly out of breath, he could hear Pissboy grunting behind him. He leaned against the front door, wiped his glasses with his shirt, and waited for Pissboy to come so close that he wouldn't be able to miss his smile and hear him say, "Sorry about the Himbeersaft, but since I won, I'll take the magnifying glass."

"You stinkin' piece of shitball," said Pissboy.

Simon took the magnifying glass to work with him the next day. His boss, Arthur Wade, would surely find some use for the instrument; at the very least, he'd find it a handy tool for composing the tiny type that ran on some of the show cards they were designing.

Just over three years earlier, Arthur Wade had wandered into Simon's life on the afternoon of the great Corbett-Fitzsimmons fight. For the weeks leading up to St. Patrick's Day, the papers were bloodthirsty with anticipation of the upcoming fight between Bob Fitzsimmons and Jim Corbett, the heavyweight champ. Fitzsimmons, an Englishman who had come to America via Australia, was the middleweight champion and gave away fifteen pounds to Corbett. With his skinny legs, short neck, small head, and strapping shoulders, Fitzsimmons reminded Simon of the ancient sculptures he'd seen at the Metropolitan Museum of Art. He had stood before these heroic figures — the runners, the discus throwers, the gladiators — and felt their strength and brazenness. Now these figures had come to life in the real-life persons of these fighters. The size of his sketchbook paper was not large enough to contain them. He needed a bigger canvas, where he could draw them life-sized just as he imagined them. Only the slabs of sidewalk outside his building offered that kind of space. All he'd have to do would be to clear away the newspapers, horse manure, and rotting vegetables, and then he could draw from here to Orchard Street.

While Corbett was the bigger man, it was Fitzsimmons — with his square chin, piercing blue eyes, and broad chest — who was every boy's fantasy of a brawler. Day after day, Simon would use the chalk he had bought with his paper money to copy the images from the newspapers onto the blocks of cement. It was the middle of March, and occasionally gentle gusts of warm air would nudge winter's grip, and the men would take off their woolen jackets, push up their shirtsleeves, and gather around the chalk drawings in front of 262 Eldridge Street. They regarded the boundaries of the drawings like a street marked off with police tape, and no one dared to step on a single line of the sketches. Their conversation knew no such boundaries, and the men battled with each other for who could be the most insulting.

"Fitzsimmons is a bum, not even an American."

"He's a pipsqueak. Corbett'll bust his head open."

"Corbett's a rich boy sissy."

"He's got a head like a rabbit. You know what they say about guys with small heads, don't you?"

And so it went until the day of the big fight, which took place in a packed amphitheater in the frontier town of Carson City, Nevada. Every sports reporter west of the Mississippi was there, as was the legendary lawman Wyatt Earp. The newspapers would have a field day reporting fact by bloodied fact. In the fourteenth round, Fitzsimmons landed a left-handed blow under Corbett's heart. He followed that with a jab to his face. Corbett sank into the ropes, hoping they would support him. His hair fell across his face as he tried to keep himself upright; the blood mixed with sweat spreading across his features. His ears swelled like mushrooms; his eyes turned upward until all you could see were the whites. Fitzsimmon's face looked haunted. After one minute and forty-five seconds in that round, Corbett sank onto his left knee and the referee declared Bob Fitzsimmons the new world heavyweight champion.

More than a thousand people had gathered at City Hall Park, where bulletins were posted blow by blow. But anyone who came to 262 Eldridge Street just hours after the fight saw the final moment come to life, come to larger than life, in concrete and chalk: Corbett on his knee, balancing on his right hand, struggling to stay aloft; the referee counting down, jabbing his finger like a pistol in the air; Fitzsimmons, looming over his wounded opponent, his arms akimbo, his brow furrowed, looking more like a worried parent than a new world champion. While Pissboy ran back and forth delivering periodic updates, Simon spared no detail.

That day, the clouds loomed low in the sky, their gray pockets stuffed with rain. The threat of a storm created a sense of urgency about the chalk pictures on the sidewalk and word spread quickly to as far away as the Upper East Side about the boy on Eldridge Street who'd captured the already famous countdown.

Simon was on his hands and knees on the sidewalk, starting to make another drawing of the referee holding up Fitzsimmons's gloved fists in victory. A heavyset man in a gray gabardine suit and a white linen shirt kneeled down next to him. "So you're the kid that's been drawing all these pictures," he said, losing his balance and pitching toward Simon.

"Yes, that's me," said Simon, instinctively moving backward.

The man placed his hands on the sidewalk in order to steady himself. "Your pictures are real good, particularly that one." He spoke in a wheezy voice and pointed to the one of Fitzsimmons scoring his knockout. "I'll buy that one off you for five bucks."

Simon was still on all fours. He drew himself up to his knees and was now the same height as the gentleman crouched down next to him. "Five bucks?" Now it was Simon's turn to lose his balance. He was fourteen years old and to him five dollars was a small fortune. It was nearly half the money he'd brought from Vilna.

"Yeah, you draw me that exact picture on paper, and I'll pay you five bucks. I'll make a poster from it. Plenty of people are keen for it."

Simon paused, trying to figure out if he'd ever seen such a thing as a poster. The man mistook his silence as hesitation. "Tell you what, give it to me by tomorrow and I'll give you a penny for every one I sell. Not bad, eh?"

"I'll do it," said Simon. "Five bucks and a penny for every one sold."

"I'll come back tomorrow," said the man. They shook hands.

When the man came back the following day, Simon handed him the drawing. The man held it out in front of him and studied it for a long while. Then he reached into his pocket, pulled out five dollars, and handed it to Simon. "I don't hate this," he said. He rolled up the drawing, careful not to crease it, and walked away.

The man hadn't told Simon his name; Simon hadn't told him his.

Maybe the man sold a thousand posters or maybe he sold two. Either way, Simon never received another penny for his drawing.

Arthur Wade was the man who'd bought Simon's picture. He'd come around again this past summer and asked people around Eldridge Street if they knew where he might find the kid who'd drawn all those pictures of the fighters on the sidewalk. Everyone told him the same thing. "Go find the *Spazierer*, he knows everything."

"What kind of name is that, *Spazierer?*" asked Arthur Wade, spitting out the syllables of the word for dramatic effect.

63

"Spaz-i-er-er." They said it slowly and phonetically. "It means 'the stroller' in German."

"How will I know him?" asked Arthur Wade.

"You'll know him by the way the sun has made his skin nearly black," they said. "You'll know him because he walks up and down Eldridge Street all day. That's what he does."

In a neighborhood filled with sallow people who worked indoors as many as eighteen hours a day, the *Spazierer* wasn't hard to find. Stooped over and leaning against a bamboo cane, the spazierer slowly made his way from one end of the block to the other and back again, from seven-thirty in the morning until the sun went down each day. Some said he was a crazy old man who had nothing better to do with his time than to patrol the streets. No one ever asked him who he was or where he came from, nor could anyone ever remember how it happened that the women set out bowls of porridge for him in the morning and pots of boiled cabbage and potatoes at night. This was simply how it had always been.

It was a steamy afternoon when Arthur Wade found the *Spazierer* making his way down the street. Despite the clinging humidity, the *Spazierer* wore a black cape and a black derby. His long white hair and white mustache glistened against his dark craggy skin. His legs were bowed and his eyes were so blue they were nearly silver. "You mean Rembrandt, don't you?" he said, in answer to Arthur's Wade's question. "He lives over there." He lifted his cane and pointed in the direction of 262. "What's your business with him?"

"My business with him is my business with him," said Arthur Wade, who wasn't given to explaining himself to anyone. As he headed toward 262, he heard the *Spazierer*'s footsteps behind him. "Listen, buster," he said, jabbing a finger in the middle of Arthur Wade's crisp white linen shirt. "I wouldn't go knocking on strange doors if I was you."

Arthur Wade had a practical streak in him that outran his pugnacious one. *This peculiar old fellow could be useful,* he thought, brushing off the spot on his shirt where the *Spazierer* had just poked him. Best to play his cards right. "I'm looking to offer that kid a job," he said in his raspy voice. "As my apprentice. I run a lithograph shop." The old man shook his head, as if he were considering the offer for himself. "He's not home now," he said. "If you come back at six-thirty, he'll be here." He turned around and resumed his shuffling.

At precisely 6:30, Arthur Wade knocked on the door at 262 Eldridge Street, and by 6:32, Simon had agreed to show up the next morning at the Arthur Wade Lithograph Shop on Lexington Avenue and Twenty-ninth Street. For the next fourteen months, Simon had spent nearly every moment of his spare time at the shop, sometimes coming home as late as eleven at night. He loved being an apprentice. It meant that someone had chosen him above everyone else. It meant that he could quit his newsboy job and that he got paid to draw. He told Christina that when he studied the word *apprentice* through squinted eyes, it looked to him like *a prince.* "That's what I feel like," he'd said. "Imagine, earning ten dollars a week to draw sketches." He didn't mention that he also had to make Mr. Wade's coffee, throw away his garbage at night, and wash up his dried wads of spitting tobacco.

"You are my prince," Christina had said. She squeezed his arm a little too hard. It was the kind of thing she usually did in public. It made him uncomfortable, how she tried to claim him in physical ways, always grabbing his elbow or ringing her arm through his. She had taken to call him

"My Prince" or "the Prince." Pissboy told him this was a girl he could go all the way with. Simon didn't doubt it, but something held him back. Maybe it was that boys two or three years older than he was were getting married at eighteen or nineteen, and having babies and pinching pennies just to make ends meet, and it seemed that was how it would always be for them. Or maybe it was the way Christina did fluttery things with her tongue when they kissed that made him think about moths flapping around in his mouth. When they got that close, he could feel her breasts against him like small squishy birds. No, more like mice. He thought about how he would draw the mice with their sharp noses and inquisitive little eyes. Something was wrong with him. All head. No heart. Why couldn't he just feel things the way other people did? Why did he always piece together how his feelings would look? Pissboy was right about one thing: He sure was an oddball foreigner.

It was a good thing Arthur Wade kept Simon as busy as he did; there was no time to worry about things like that. Mostly, when Simon came into the office — actually a back room painted dark blue that faced into a sunless courtyard — Arthur Wade would dangle a sheet of paper over his head, holding it as if it were a dead cockroach. Then he'd say something like: "P.U. See if you can turn this piece of crap into money." Simon's job was to do preliminary sketches or scripts for Arthur Wade. "Just give me a rough copy, I'll do the rest," he'd told Simon. "I'll throw in twenty-five cents extra for anything you do that our customers end up using."

Businessmen paid Arthur Wade to design show cards advertising their products. They would write the words they wanted him to illustrate, or depending on the client, they would give him an image and ask him to write the words. "See what you think, Wade," said one of those customers, Mr. Hofsteder, one afternoon, handing over his copy. "I'm hoping you can do something with it." Arthur Wade read the wispy script on the page and looked up with a big smile. "Mr. Hofsteder, it is an honor for me to work with you. This will warm the hearts of everyone who reads it."

Hofsteder was a flat-nosed man with slits of brown eyes that seemed to sink into his raw-boned cheeks. The more Arthur Wade flattered him, the wider Hofsteder's tobacco-stained smile became. Arthur Wade offered him a cigar then told him a joke whose punch line he whispered. Simon saw him look in his direction and heard him say something about not wanting to upset the Yid. Simon was sure he misheard, that Arthur Wade must have said that he didn't want to upset the kid. Mr. Hofsteder's cheeks flushed as he glanced at Simon, and then he punched Arthur Wade in the arm. "You're a corker, Wade," he said. "Have you heard the one about . . . ?" And there was more whispering.

As soon as Hofsteder walked out the door, Arthur Wade turned to Simon and said in his wheezy voice, "Now there's the kind of sucker who's going to make me a rich man. Here, see what you can whip up out of this little turd."

"MY PAPA IS GOING TO BUY ME A PAIR OF STANDARD SCREW FASTENER SHOES. HE SAYS THEY ARE THE BEST IN THE WORLD." As Simon stared at the slogan, he could picture the kind of little girl who would wear Standard Screw Fastener Shoes and brag about her papa. She was beautiful, with little pudgy hands that came together in the prayer position and a mouth that was soft and full.

"Here's a doozy," said Arthur Wade, late one afternoon. He'd scrawled on a sheet of paper: "Beautiful lady . . . let us help you keep beautiful . . . Ellis Stone Beauty

Shoppe." "Make a masterpiece out of that one, Rembrandt." For this ad, Simon imagined Mrs. O'Mara, ten years younger. He drew a woman with cropped red hair. Her head was thrown back so that her neck and throat, a dusty pink, easily took up a third of the drawing.

Eager for the extra twenty-five cents, Simon would occasionally ask Arthur Wade if any customers had bought any of his drawings. His answer was always the same. "Nah, nothing yet. Those cheap bastards don't know a good thing when they see it. But don't worry, one of them will bite soon and then you'll be rolling in dough."

Often Arthur Wade would disappear for a couple of hours in the afternoon. By the time he came back with breath smelling like gasoline and eyes glassy and unfocused, Simon would have completed his drawings. Things he could never express in words came pouring out in his images. Drawn from old memories or present yearnings, they had nothing cynical about them. Arthur Wade would hold the drawings out in front of him to view their precise lines and rich colors. He'd spit out a wad of tobacco; often he'd breathe uneasily, making a sipping sound as he inhaled. Sometimes it got so bad he'd have to sit down and double over before he could gulp some air back in his lungs. When he could finally talk again, he'd say the thing he always said: "I don't hate this."

Then he would tuck Simon's pictures in his pocket, taking care not to fold them, and never mention them again.

On Sundays, Simon would take a dime from his earnings and walk over to Essex Street with Christina, where they would each buy a pickle from Gus the Pickle Man. All week long, Simon would crave one of Gus's garlicky pickles. He loved how the crispy sweet-and-sour pickle made the back of his tongue tingle, and best of all, if he bought a pickle at ten o'clock in the morning and sucked and bit at it slowly, he could make it last well into the afternoon. Sometimes there'd be a line in front of the large wooden pickle barrel. But on this morning, a nor'easter was ripping down the coast and there was no line at all. Horses strained against the harsh winds and people walked down the streets with their arms in front of their eyes to shield them from garbage that swirled around them. Gus the Pickle Man stood by his barrel, the captain of his ship, shielded only by the wooden overhang of the barbershop next door. As soon as he saw Christina and Simon coming, Gus stuck his arm into the scummy brine. He narrowed his eyes and looked into the distance as he searched around the bottom of the barrel for just the right pickle: not too spongy but not too hard. Gus never spoke to his customers, yet he knew his regulars: He knew exactly who liked sweet and who preferred something more peppery. When he finally caught the two he wanted, he wrapped each in a piece of paper and handed them over.

The wind was so strong that it smeared pickle juice across their cheeks. Still, they walked through the rain savoring their Sunday treat. The few people outside acknowledged each other with a wave or nod. Eldridge Street was deserted but for one slight figure bucking against the weather. His white hair blew willy-nilly around his head almost as if someone had shaken loose feathers from a pillow. He wore a black cape, which flapped in the wind, and held a black derby hat under his left arm. As soon as he caught sight of Simon and Christina, he began to wave his other arm in the air. It was the *Spazierer,* gesturing urgently.

"Hello," he shouted. "Hello Simon Phelps, please wait." Simon had never spoken with the *Spazierer,* and he was taken aback that he even knew his name. "Simon Phelps," he yelled again, this time even louder, "I have something to show you that may be of interest." Because of his bowed legs, the *Spazierer* had a precarious walk and it seemed that only his cane prevented him from tipping over to one side or the other.

He was slightly out of breath by the time he caught up with Christina and Simon, and he took a few moments to wipe his face with a handkerchief. Then he reached into his pocket and pulled out a clipping that had been ripped from a newspaper. "Do you recognize this?" he said to Simon, pointing at an advertisement on the page. Although the image was smudged with raindrops, it was clear enough for Simon to make it out: a little girl with bright blue eyes and long wavy hair holding a bottle of Hall's Vegetable Sicilian Hair Renewer. The bottle was about one-third the size of the girl, and Simon could read the print on the bottom of the page: "Keeps the scalp healthy. THE PEOPLE'S FAVORITE." Underneath the advertisement, in a small familiar script, the artist's name was written: Arthur Wade.

But these were Simon's words. This was his little girl. Arthur Wade had picked this particular drawing off of Simon's desk, and in his usual late-afternoon sodden voice had said, "You people can get awfully sentimental, can't you?" before slipping it into a folder. Now, here it was, reproduced in a newspaper. Arthur Wade had never mentioned that it would be published. Whenever Simon had asked if any of his ads had been sold, Arthur Wade had always given him the same answer about "the cheap bastards."

"The *New York Telegram*," said the *Spazierer*. "Yesterday and today. He didn't tell you, did he?"

"Not yet, sir," said Simon, convinced that this was just an oversight on Arthur Wade's part.

"Didn't get paid an extra cent for this, I'll bet."

"Not yet, sir," he repeated.

"It's not my business, but I'd watch out if I were you. That man will make a fortune off of you and you'll never see a penny of it. He assumes that people like us are just grateful for the work. It would never occur to him that you would speak up and claim what is rightfully yours." Simon recognized the *Spazierer*'s accent as similar to his own.

"Thank you," said Simon, shoving the newspaper clip into his pocket. "Thank you for showing me this. I'll see to it, I promise."

The *Spazierer* reached over and patted Simon's cheek. His palm was callused and

74

scratchy. "You are a good boy," he said. "But sometimes being good isn't good enough."

As the *Spazierer* ambled off into the rain, Simon became aware that his own breathing was heavy. His arms were frozen and his legs were wobbly. Suddenly, the smell of the garlic made him want to vomit. He threw his half-eaten pickle into the street. "Stinkin' piece of shitball," he shouted.

Christina came toward him. "What's the matter with you?" Her voice was whiny, almost pleading. He didn't have the words for Christina, much less for himself. If he were to sketch how he felt at that moment, he would show a man with billowing cheeks and a purple face. No, that wasn't quite right. This anger wasn't diffuse and purple. It was white and pure and traveled a straight line.

That night, as he lay in bed, Simon knew it was pointless to try and figure out what he'd say to Arthur Wade the following day. Now that he was fluent in English, words would pop up unexpectedly in his conversation. If he could see them, he could say them. Words like *skidoo, clapboard,* and *gizmo* were so visual to him, it wasn't as if he was learning a new language as much as it was verbs, nouns, and adjectives making themselves known to him. When he thought about Arthur Wade and his boozy breath, the image came easily: the man was a stinkin' piece of shitball if ever there was one.

The following afternoon, Simon showed up at the Arthur Wade Lithograph Shop three hours early. He'd found it impossible to sit through school that afternoon, and at lunchtime, he told his teacher he was leaving because he was sick with a stomachache. The stomachache was real enough, but it wasn't because he was sick. His stomach was tied in knots; he could see it clear as day. He just wanted to confront Arthur Wade and be done with it.

Even in midday, the Lexington Avenue office was dark and airless. No sunlight filtered into the courtyard, and even if a sliver or two did make it through, the soot encrusted around the windows would surely have blocked it out. So it seemed to Simon that Arthur Wade was sitting in the darkness when he walked through the door. He saw only his back, his wide shoulders, and the creases in his fleshy neck. His head was bent forward. Simon thought he might be studying his shoes, but then he heard gurgling noises and little whistles. Arthur Wade was sound asleep and snoring.

Later, Simon thought how easy it would have been had he just snuck up behind him and clobbered him over the head with a chair. But in his wildest imagination, he never thought it would come to that. He scraped his heels and banged the door shut. Arthur Wade still didn't wake up. He walked around and stood in front of him. His mouth was slack and he was drooling down the front of his white linen shirt. Simon was surprisingly thrilled at how repulsive he found the sight of him and let himself wallow in that feeling for a few moments before he tapped him on the shoulder. "Mr. Wade, wake up," he said. "Wake up, I want to talk to you."

Arthur Wade's eyes popped open and he shook his head. For a moment, he was startled and didn't seem to know where he was.

"Oh Christ, kid, you scared the hell out of me," he said, wiping the spit off his chin with the back of his hand.

"I have to talk to you, Mr. Wade."

"What time is it?" Arthur Wade looked at his watch. "Aren't you supposed to still be at school playing potsie with the rest of the children?"

"I left early because I have something to say to you." Simon reached into his pocket, pulled out the Hall's Vegetable Sicilian Hair Renewer ad and held it up. "You never told me this ran in the newspaper. What about it?"

Arthur Wade shook his head again, only this time he was wide-awake. "What about what? What are you asking me?"

"You owe me money, twenty-five cents. That's what you said you'd pay me if any of our clients used one of my ads."

"You're joking, aren't you?" said Arthur Wade. "But while you're standing there, do you mind getting me a cup of coffee?"

It was as if Arthur Wade hadn't heard a word he said. Arthur Wade was still the boss and Simon thought he should bring his boss the coffee. But if he did, then they'd be right back where they started: boss and subordinate. Right now, Simon didn't feel like the subordinate. This wasn't about work. The man had made false promises and taken credit for Simon's work. He said awful things. So what if he was the boss? He was a bad man. A liar. A thief even. Let him get his own coffee.

Simon stood impassively, the ad still in his hand.

"I guess you didn't hear me so let me speak a little louder. I'D LIKE A CUP OF COFFEE."

Simon didn't budge. "You owe me money," he said.

Arthur Wade rose to his feet and gripped Simon's shoulders with both hands. Two red moons broke out on each of his cheeks and his breathing became uneven. "I don't think you know what you're saying." He was pausing between words now. "Do you know how many little bastards like you would give their eyeteeth to be working at a joint like this?"

Simon tried to pull away from his grasp. "But you said twenty-five cents for every picture that a client used, and this one got used. There's no getting around that."

With his right hand, Arthur Wade grabbed Simon under his jaw and squeezed hard. He tried to say something, but his words came out as coughs and hollow honking sounds. He loosened his grip on Simon and finally found his voice.

"Stupid, money-grubbing kike," he said.

Then he said it again.

The advertisement shook in Simon's hand. He tried to hold his mind steady. He was searching for something, something specific in his memory. He took mental inventory of all the sketches he'd done, the characters he'd created.

Oh wait, there it was.

The chalk lines from the breaks in the pavement were as vivid as when he drew them more than three years ago on the day of the Corbett-Fitzsimmons fight — the drawing that Arthur Wade had bought for five dollars to turn into a poster.

A penny for every poster sold, that's what he had promised him then.

Simon's intention was to throw a left jab under Arthur Wade's heart just as Bob Fitzsimmons had done when he knocked out Jim Corbett in the fourteenth round. As Simon was taking his swing, Arthur Wade leaned over to try and catch his breath.

"What the hell?" he cried as his words collided with Simon's fist.

Arthur Wade heard a snap in his head, felt a sharp pain in his mouth. It tore up through his nose and into his eyes. The blood was warm and salty in his mouth. He ran his tongue over the place where his front teeth used to be. It felt like broken glass. When he spat out blood, it was flecked with pieces of enamel. One drop spattered on the newspaper clipping that Simon had dropped to the floor.

You're fired! He tried to shout, but nothing came except the honking noises he had made earlier.

He sat down and sucked in some air.

Finally, he caught his breath enough to try again. "You're fired!" The words sounded feeble and full of air. And by that time Simon was well on his way down Lexington Avenue.

New York City: 1905

For her first trip into New York City, Flora Grossman brought two leather valises and one hatbox containing her latest purchase, a pink silk hat with a black velvet trim. She threw her bags on the seat across from her and pressed her face against the glass window when an unfamiliar voice startled her out of her daydreams.

"Excuse me, miss, I certainly don't mean to impose on your time or give cause for alarm, but I cannot help but notice your hands. My trade being the reading and interpretation of the human palm, I am in a position to recognize a strong and richly detailed hand when I see it. And, if I may say, even though you are so young, I can see a worldliness about you and a life experience that is far beyond your imagining at present. May I?" he asked, making a slight bow while extending his arm to the vacant seat next to hers.

Flora was fifteen and had been in America for nearly four years, long enough for her to have practically lost her accent. "Sure, be my guest. Sorry about all my stuff," she said, pushing her bags to one side. "I'm visiting my big sister for a couple of days, and I couldn't decide what to bring, so I brought everything."

"I can see that is so," he said, plopping his lanky six-foot frame into the seat. "Ah, these bones get weary." He leaned his head against the back of the seat and closed his eyes for a few moments, all the while rubbing his temples. Then he opened his eyes, stretched forward, put his elbows on his knees, and stared at her for a few moments. "Your accent. I can't quite place it. You're not from around here."

"Germany," she said, "I came over with my older sister. I live in Mount Kisco with my aunt and uncle, who aren't really my aunt and uncle — she's my mother's second cousin, but we're very close. My sister is the one I'm going to visit. She just moved to the city."

He nodded, folding his hands in front of him. "I don't mean to trouble you any further, but I wonder if you would you be so kind as to let me study your palms?"

Flora stared down at her hands, turning

them over and examining them as if it were the first time she had noticed them.

"Why would you want to study my palms?"

His voice resonated like a trombone. "Please believe me when I say that I have not seen hands like yours since Lilly Doucet's. Of course, you've probably never heard of Lilly Doucet, as she was well before your time, but you must take my word for it, she was a rare one and in possession of a keen and able intellect, most particularly unusual for a female."

"Lilly Doucet, I've never heard of her," said Flora, still staring at her hands. "It sure is a pretty name. Was she beautiful?"

"A beauty she was," said the man. "Not unlike yourself, if I may say. I should add that were you kind enough to grant my request and allow me to read *your* palm, I would dispense with my usual fee and perform my services gratis. Free of charge."

"Sure, why not?" said Flora, extending her hands then pulling them back immediately. "Ooh, they got a little dirty from carrying all these bags. Sorry."

"Makes no difference to me."

"Well then, here they are." She held her open palms before him, and he looked at them for a long while, moving his lips and making notations in the air with his finger. Then he whistled through his teeth. "Take my word for it, Lilly Doucet has nothing on you. This is as remarkable a palm as I have seen in many years."

The man's words flowed in a silky cadence Flora had never heard before. She stared at his long snaky fingers so black they were almost blue. She'd never met a Negro before. When he smiled, his teeth seemed as white as piano keys. She wondered if Negroes had more teeth than other people, because his smile seemed to go on for octaves.

"Tell me my fortune," she said, twirling one of her blond curls around her finger. "I want to know everything that's going to happen to me."

He laughed. "That's what you think now. But believe me, in my business, a little information goes a long way. I'll tell you what you need to know."

The man traced the line across the top of her palm under her fingers. "This is where I can see into your heart," he said. "I can read your loves, adventures of the soul. . . ." He clicked his tongue against the roof of his mouth then followed the crease at the edge of her palm above her thumb that traveled in an arc toward her wrist. "Your life line," he said, then stretched her fingers with his left hand and ran his finger up in a straight line up from under her wrist to just under her middle finger. She was aware of how small her hand was in his, and how dry and calloused his skin felt. When he was finished, he rested his head in his hands and closed his eyes. "Oh my," he said, his eyes still shut.

"What do you see?" Flora placed her hands over her heart. "Will I fall in love? Will I travel the world? Oh please, tell me my fortune."

The man opened his eyes and put his hands on his knees. "You will live a long rich life, that is for sure."

Flora smiled at this news. "And what else? What do you know?"

"Young lady, I can only say this, and I hope you will listen well."

"Yes, I'm listening," she said, the smile still on her face.

"You must hold on," said the man. "That's my advice to you. Hold on, and never forget who you are."

"What do you mean, 'hold on'?" she asked. "Hold on to what?"

The man got up from his seat. "That's what I have to say. Thank you so much for your time. I am most obliged." He made a slight bow and began to walk down the aisle.

"Wait," she shouted, "wait one more moment. I didn't even catch your name."

"It wasn't meant to be caught," he said with a smile, and he strode down the aisle of the train then pulled open the heavy door that led him to the next car.

Flora had the feeling that she was falling. It was the same disoriented sensation she'd felt when she'd taken a spill in her kitchen back in Germany years earlier. Her mother had asked her to reach up to a shelf in the cupboard and bring down the jar of flour she needed to make pastry dough. She'd picked the jar from the shelf and had taken a step backward. Somehow, she lost her balance, and her feet went out from under her. The fall seemed to take forever — long enough for her to anticipate that she'd be hurt, and probably badly. When she landed on her tailbone, the glass jar smacked against the kitchen floor and splintered. One of the jagged pieces gashed Flora's right leg from behind her knee down to her calf. She remembered sitting on the floor, blood and flour and broken glass all around her. She felt nauseated and faint from the pain in her tailbone, and she remembered little else except her father shouting at her not to move. He'd lifted her out from the bloody mess on the floor and carried her into the bathroom, where he put her down into the tub and began washing her wounds.

Right after that, her father got sick. Her mother said it was influenza, but Flora was convinced it was her blood that had infected him. Three months later he was dead, and though she never told anyone that she carried this guilt, every time she looked at the scar that ran like a scimitar down her leg, she could see her father's taut face and feel the gentleness of his hands as he swooped her up on that day and cleaned out her cut.

Unconsciously, she rubbed her hand down her right leg as the train slowed down and slid into the tunnel under Grand Central Station. All around her was darkness. The cars shuddered and clacked, and she could smell the sulfurous smell of metal wheels grinding against metal track. Even though she was seated in her rattan chair on a train coming into New York City, Flora felt as if she were back in her old house in Germany. She could feel herself falling. Falling and wondering how bad it would be.

She gathered her matching red-and-white valises and stepped off the train. Flora studied the crowds of people milling around the emptying train. The Negro man was gone, but she saw women in muslin dresses so sheer that she could make out the shapes of their breasts underneath. She watched as porters unloaded crates filled with oranges and bolts of satin, and down at the end of the vast platform, she could make out the form of an organ grinder with a monkey on his head. The monkey wore a banana hat strapped under his chin and jumped about collecting silver coins from anyone who would pay. New York. Already it was as exotic as she hoped it would be.

With all that was going on around her, Flora almost forgot to search for her sister, although Seema would be hard to miss in any crowd. At nearly five-foot-ten, she towered over most other women and an awful lot of men. With her long black hair ("shiny like a seal" was how their Uncle Paul described it) and green eyes with gold flecks, Seema was the most striking of the three Grossman sisters. Margot, the youngest sister, had the makings of a real beauty: full lips, soft almond-shaped eyes, and the grace and swiftness of a fawn. But years of worry had weighted her down and drained her complexion of its natural rosiness.

What Seema didn't have naturally, she made up for with her flair and elegance. She was lean and angular, with lips that sloped and peaked like sand castles. Her poppy-red lipstick was vivid against her creamy

white skin, and though Seema laughed it off
when her friends nicknamed her Seamless,
that pretty much summed her up. Flora was
heading toward the organ grinder when she
heard a familiar smoky voice calling behind
her. "Hey Chatterbug, where are you going?"

When Flora first came over to live with
her aunt and uncle, Uncle Paul nicknamed
her Chatterbug because, he said, she'd talk
to anyone, even the ladybugs who lived in
the backyard. He called Seema CeCe and,
although his wife's name was Hannah, he
called her Harry. Hannah called him Ziggy,
because she claimed he looked more like a
Ziggy than he did a Paul. Aunt Hannah and
Uncle Paul shared code words that could
summon up a memory in a heartbeat.
That's how it was with them. They had
private jokes and secrets and did whatever
they could to reinforce the clubbiness of
their family. They lived in a colonial-style
corner house in Mount Kisco surrounded
by privet and linden trees that smelled like
sweet lime blossoms on a summer day. Their
family was very close. Paul and Hannah's
daughter, Ruth, grown now and out of the
house, still wore her mother's gold baby ring
on a chain around her neck, and never a
week went by that they didn't receive a

funny note or drawing in the mail from their son, Lev, who had recently moved to Chicago.

To Aunt Hannah and Uncle Paul, the world was split evenly between takers and givers. Takers tended to be "pretentious," and "imbecilic," two of the first words Flora learned when she came to America. Givers were "civic minded" and "generous," and although they would never claim that they were the latter, Aunt Hannah and Uncle Paul were the ones who insisted that the girls stay with them when Flora's mother first brought up the idea of sending her daughters to America.

Seema grabbed Flora's bags and pretended to be bogged down by the weight of them. "You've brought everything but the kitchen sink." Seema had been slower to master English than Flora, and she was still delighted with herself each time she came up with an American aphorism or slang phrase. In Seema's case, it only added to her allure. Flora hadn't seen her sister in four months, and each time she did she seemed even more beautiful than the last. Young men were always trying to help her choose the correct word and get rid of the Teutonic sludge in her accent. But young men were always trying to help her with everything, and Flora knew it would only be a matter of minutes before some eager fellow with glowing cheeks and a hopeful smile would come up to Seema and offer a hand with the luggage.

Flora laughed, so happy to see her sister after all these months. "I didn't know which dress to bring, so I brought four of them."

"So, you are turning into a fashion plate, are you? Well, I'm sure all of them will turn heads."

Flora walked beside Seema. Even amid the crowds in the dimly lit station, Seema glowed. She laughed and tossed her hair. One young man did come up and offer to take her bags, but Flora could tell that with his shabby suit and dirty fingernails he didn't stand a chance. "Thank you, but I can manage," said Seema, not even meeting the boy's gaze. Flora straightened her spine and tried to keep up with her sister's brisk pace. She wondered if she would tell her sister about the strange man on the train. No, not while Seema was shining all of her attention on her.

A whole weekend with Seema. She wished she could make the next two and a half days last forever. Seema was working as an au pair for the White family. He was a wealthy banker, an old friend of Uncle Paul's, who had three children and lived in one of the new brownstones on Fifth Avenue. Although Seema had been with the White family since the winter, this was the first time Flora had ever visited. When Flora had asked Aunt Hannah and Uncle Paul if she could go in and spend the weekend with her sister, the two of them had pretended to be in a fix about whether or not to allow her go. "I don't know," said Uncle Paul with mock seriousness. "Two beautiful young women alone in the big city could be catastrophic. What do you think, Harry?"

"Flora's only fifteen. Can she really take the train by herself? Maybe it will be too much for her, Ziggy."

Back and forth it went like that until they finally, and with great fanfare, decided that yes, she could go. "On one condition, Miss Chatterbug," said Uncle Paul. "You mustn't talk to anyone on the train. New York City isn't like Mount Kisco, where you can count on people's good intentions. And when you're with Seema, just keep your conversation between her, you, the Whites, and their children. Can you promise us that?"

Flora had said of course she would. "Besides, what do I have to say to total strangers?"

"Young lady, I would never worry that you lacked for conversational topics," Uncle Paul had answered.

It would be out of the question to ever tell Aunt Hannah or Uncle Paul about the strange man on the train, thought Flora, as she and Seema walked out of the station and onto a street that was wider and filled with more people and buildings than Flora had ever seen in one place.

Flora had heard about the horse-drawn trolleys that carried people up and down the streets of New York City, and now she and her sister were grabbing on to the metal handlebars and hoisting themselves onto one that would take them to the Whites' house on East Sixty-first Street. The two horses pulling the trolley clopped along in a steady rhythm; the wheels squealed on the tracks below. As the sisters rode uptown, Seema kept talking. She told Flora how Mrs. White would get dressed up three and four times a day and go out for social engagements. She talked about the bedroom she had in the back of the Whites' house and how she had decorated it with magazine pictures of girls in beautiful dresses with lace insets and pearl buttons. And she told her about Lulu, the family dog, who had become her closest friend. Flora tried to listen but could barely pay attention for all there was to see: the red brick train station with its copper cupolas, the cobblestone streets, the conductor in his official-looking uniform who stood at the back door holding a large gold pocket watch in his hand. Had Seema become so familiar with this amazing spectacle that she didn't even notice it anymore?

"Here we are," said Seema, as the trolley came to a bumpy halt at Sixty-first Street and Fifth Avenue. "Come, we go in the back way." It was a grand house, different from the one in Mount Kisco. This one was made of limestone, and the way the sun hit it just so, it looked as if it were covered with glinting specks of diamonds. Seema pushed open the back iron gates, which were taller than Flora and were topped with ornate curlicues. As soon as Seema stuck her key into the lock, they heard a loud, piercing bark. Flora backed away. "Oh, don't let that scare you," said Seema. "It's Lulu. She's happy to see us."

Her aunt and uncle's house smelled like fresh air, or like basil and rosemary and whatever else Aunt Hannah was cooking. This house smelled like leather and wood and had the faint odor of yesterday's fire. It was dark inside, and as Flora's eyes were adjusting to the lack of light, she felt something cold and wet press against her knee. "Down Lulu," said Seema. But that was after Lulu had placed both paws on Flora's breastbone and knocked her to the floor. Lulu drooled on Flora and stuck her nose under her armpit. "Get her off me," she screamed.

"Nothing to be scared of," said Seema, bending down to pet Lulu. "She's a German shepherd, a landsman. She wouldn't hurt a flea."

"A fly," said Flora abruptly. "She wouldn't hurt a fly is how they say it. And I don't care if she's from Kaiserslautern, she's drooling all over me and smells awful."

Seema put her arms around Lulu's black-and-russet neck. "Ach, Lulu darling," she said. "Don't worry, everything is okay. You stay with me now. Okay?"

There was something about the way Seema cooed at Lulu, the way she talked about the Whites and studied the pictures from the magazine that made Flora think Seema had changed. Flora stood up, brushed herself off, and made sure the anger was out of her voice before she spoke again. "C'mon, Seema, show me your room. I'm so sweaty, I'd love to splash some cold water on my face."

Seema led Flora down the back hall past the Whites' hulking mahogany furniture and wood-paneled rooms with Tiffany windows and Persian rugs on the floor. As Seema pushed the door open, Lulu ran past the two of them and jumped on the narrow cot that was pushed up against the corner of the small, sweltering room. "This is the only room where she gets to be on the furniture. The Whites are very strict about that," said Seema, pushing Lulu to the foot of the bed and placing Flora's suitcases atop her linen sheet.

Seema closed the door and the air inside the room became even more still and clammy. "I have a surprise for you," she said, turning to Flora. Maybe it was the way she'd lowered her voice to a whisper that made Lulu sit up on her hind legs and widen her liquid black eyes. Both dog and sister leaned toward Seema as she revealed her secret. "We're going to a dance tonight. It's at the New Irving Dance Hall on the Lower East Side. The other girls who work here go every week. I've never been, but I've decided it's time we go."

"A dance?"

"Shh," cautioned Seema. "Keep quiet."

"Why? No one's here."

"Just in case. Aunt Hannah and Uncle

Paul would be so displeased if they knew I took you to a dance. Or to the Lower East Side. It's not really a place for people like us."

Flora noticed how Seema's face changed as they walked into the New Irving Dance Hall. The eyes of every boy in that hall were on her, pleading and caressing. Seema glanced at all of them, settling on none of them. Flora wondered was it her imagination or was Seema swaying in a way she had never seen before, as if she were balancing a large package on one hip, then the other. Her mouth melted into a hint of a smile. She must have realized the effect she was having, but she just tossed her hair and kept walking. Seamless indeed.

Flora followed in her wake, feeling that each of her steps was landing with a thud. Why had she agreed to come here in the first place? Unlike Seema, who had the air of someone who'd spent her whole life going to dances, Flora had no idea how to act in a place like this.

She followed Seema to the corner of the room, where the rest of the girls were lined up, whispering as they studied the boys standing at the other side of the room. The room was so large and crowded with people that it was impossible to see from one end to the other. The girls wore their best dresses and fancy bows in their hair. Some boys wore knickers, others long pants. Everyone's face was scrubbed. Only the ground was filthy with peanut shells, spilled beer, and globs of spit. Flora had to sidestep a cockroach, and her shoes stuck to the floor. Best to look up, she thought. Besides, she didn't want to miss a thing.

In the center of the room stood a man in baggy trousers holding a silver triangle in his hand. "Okay, all of you Romeos, shut up for a minute and listen to me," he shouted.

The man had one of those accents that Uncle Paul liked to mimic. "Shaddup ya little creeps," he'd say, talking as if he had a cigar dangling from the side of his mouth. Only this man wasn't pretending. "So here's how it goes. When I ring the bell, the gentlemen will go over to the other side of the room and ask one of these fine ladies to dance. And ladies, if any of these gentlemen don't suit your taste, just give 'em the brush off. Remember, this ain't no barnyard, so be polite. And no running. Ready?"

He hit the silver triangle with a metal beater. The pings were still reverberating in the air as at least eight boys lined up in front of Seema. Most of the others lagged behind and only a handful stood at the feet of girls they knew, sisters or cousins or girls who had caught their eye earlier. Flora watched her sister scrutinize her admirers the same way she'd seen Aunt Hannah squint her eyes and examine the chickens that hung at the butcher's. Seema looked away, her mouth twisted with displeasure. None of the chickens measured up. The man in the center of the room kept striking his triangle until, finally, everyone paid attention.

"Okay, that didn't turn out so good. We're gonna try somethin' else. The Mirror Dance."

A murmur floated through the room. Some of the girls were smiling. The Mirror Dance was a favorite.

"Any of you smarties out there don't know the rules?" Flora raised her hand. "Not me, sir. I never heard of the Mirror Dance."

There was some tittering. Then another hand shot up. "Me neither," said a slight boy in the back of the room. "I've never heard of it." He cast a quick glance at Flora. She noticed his hands, delicate and slender.

"Come on up here, young lady," said the man. "I'll show you how to play."

He pulled a wooden chair into the center of the room. "You sit here," he said, pointing to it. "Good, now take this." He gave her a yellow hand mirror. "Hold it up so that you can see what's happening behind you. When the music starts playing, some boy will come and look over your shoulder into the mirror. If you like him, nod your head yes and get up and dance with him. If you don't, shake your head no, and the poor bum'll go back to where he came from."

Flora positioned the mirror so that she could see behind her shoulder. A brass band struck up a melody that most in the room seemed to know. Boys started to whistle; a few girls tapped their feet. Because the mirror was so small, Flora could only guess by the amount of rustling and footsteps behind her that there was some commotion. In the glass's reflection, she caught sight of a boy with a wide face and a shiny pair of gold cufflinks. The boy was sweating and gesturing to someone behind him who Flora could not see.

Slowly another boy came into view. He was short and slim and wore silver-rimmed glasses. She recognized his hands, the same elegant fingers that had waved in the air moments earlier. He wasn't handsome. He had pursed lips and heavy-lidded eyes, and his face stayed tense and earnest all the while that his fat friend was coaxing him forward. Clearly, he wasn't having a good time.

101

Impeccably dressed, he had a steady gaze behind those glasses and he looked older than many boys in the room. When he saw that Flora noticed him, he smiled thinly. *It's not the kind of thing he does often,* she thought.

The boy with the thick neck was pointing at Flora. By now, everyone in the room could see what was going on. A few boys began clapping in rhythm to the music. More joined in, but when the boy in the glasses stuck his face right behind Flora's shoulder so she could see him, and only him, the room turned quiet. Flora knew this, and slowly, and almost imperceptibly, moved her head up and down until it was clear she was nodding yes. There was a short burst of applause and a few cat whistles. As Flora put the mirror down on the chair and got up to dance with the boy, she caught Seema's eye. Did she raise her eyebrow as if to say, *He's not our type,* or did Flora just imagine that?

The boy put his hand on the center of her back; she held him around the waist. There was nothing tentative about his grip. She had danced with a few other boys before and always felt as if she were being sloshed across the floor. This one was different. He wasn't graceful but he danced with energy and determination.

Flora whispered in his ear: "You must be a regular here, you know all the steps."

"Not really so," he said. "This is my first time."

"How did you get here?"

"My buddy. He said that all work and no play made me a dull boy. Or something like that."

"You work? You don't go to school?"

"No," he said. "I left school many years ago. Now I work in the design business."

"You're an artist?"

"No, more an inventor than an artist. I design window and store displays. How did you get here?"

"My sister Seema brought me. I'm sure you saw her."

"No, which one is she?"

She pointed to Seema. He barely gave her a glance.

There was something about his formality and the way his vowels curled slightly that made her realize he was an immigrant. Rather than ask too many questions, Flora told him her name and offered up information about herself.

"I've been in this country nearly four years, and I've never met an inventor."

"Where are you from?" he asked. "Oh,

and my name is Simon."

"That's a nice name. My name is Flora Grossman. I'm from Germany. A small town in Germany."

"Did you come here with your parents?"

She told him how she had come over with Seema, leaving her mother and her younger sister, Margot, back in Kaiserslautern.

The band started to play a sentimental ballad.

Her cheek fell naturally against his collarbone; she could feel his heart beating.

"I drew a girl who looked like you when I did an advertisement for Ellis Stone Beauty Shoppe."

His palms were dry, not sweaty like so many boys. He didn't hum along to the music; instead he made a kind of soft inverted whistling sound. It could have been annoying, but coming from him it was endearing.

She could feel her breasts against his chest and it made her blush.

On the other side of the room, she saw Seema dancing with a blond boy. They held each other so closely they seemed like lovers rejoined after a war. Flora could see that the boy was handsome. He wore a three-button cutaway with a vest underneath that looked as if it were made of expensive fabric. She could tell by Seema's smile and the way she searched the room with her eyes to make sure people saw her that she was pleased to be dancing with this handsome, fashionable man.

Flora didn't want anyone to see her and her young man. The way his mouth was so close to her face when he talked that, now and again, his lips would brush against hers, and how he'd intertwined her fingers between his — it was just between them.

"What about your family back in Germany?" he asked.

She told him all there was to tell. "And what about yours?"

"I left Lithuania when I was nine. My mother and sisters and brothers are still there. I'm hoping they'll come to America soon."

Then he was quiet. Flora tried to think of something to say, but his step became awkward and he turned his head to the side, which made her feel as if she'd been intrusive and had assumed an intimacy that wasn't there. When the music stopped, he dropped his hands to his side, bowed slightly, and thanked her for the dance. She went to the back of the room where all the girls were standing and he went to where the boys were.

She thought about asking Seema whether or not she should apologize to the boy for being too nosy. Seema would probably say something like, *Forget about him. There are more fish in the sea.* But Seema was so cozy with her new boy that Flora couldn't think of interrupting. So she sat on one of the folding chairs and watched the others.

After some minutes, she noticed the boy, the one with the fat neck, who had coaxed Simon toward her. She worried that he might ask her to dance. She didn't feel like dancing with anybody right now. Then she saw that he had a folded up piece of paper in his hand. He seemed flustered as he stood before her. "Here," he said, shoving the note at her. "He asked me to give you this."

The way he rushed his words and vanished before she could thank him made her frightened to see what the message contained. She opened it slowly. There was no note, just a hastily drawn sketch of a bespectacled boy with his hand over his brow staring across what appeared to be an ocean. On the other side was a mother with six little boys and girls waving at him. Underneath were the words: "Me and my family." It was signed, Simon.

On the back of the drawing, Flora wrote,

"I'm not an artist but I am a chatterbug and I'm sorry if I was also a nosybody."

She hoped she could find the fat boy and ask him to give the note back to Simon, but he was nowhere in sight, so she made her way through the crowd until she found him herself. Simon was heading toward the door, and she had to run to catch up with him before he left. She tapped him on the shoulder. When he turned around she said, "Here," and she handed him her note. He held the paper under his nose and scrutinized it as if it were the Constitution.

"A chatterbug is what?" he finally asked.

"Oh, you know, someone who talks too much. My uncle says I'd talk to anybody, even the ladybugs in the backyard."

He smiled, and something happened to his face that Flora hadn't seen before. The sternness was gone, and for the first time, he looked more like a boy than a man.

"Well, if you're a chatterbug, then I'm a blockhead for not knowing what that meant," he said. "So I guess we're even."

"I guess we are," said Flora, trying to think of something else to say but worried that again she would talk too much.

Simon took up the silence. "You don't by any chance happen to like magic shows?"

"I don't know," said Flora raising her

eyebrows with surprise. "I've never been to one."

"How about you go with me to see the Great Mysterio?" he said. "Tomorrow, at the Fourteenth Street Theater. It starts at three o'clock and I could meet you there."

"Okay, that would be fine," said Flora.

Later that night, as they left the dance hall together, Flora was bursting to tell Seema about Simon and the magic show. But Seema beat her to it. "I saw the two of you," she said. "He's not particularly attractive. And what does that mean, he does window displays? Doesn't sound very clever to me. Honestly, Flora, I don't think he's our type."

Flora didn't know she had a type. Nor did she know what it meant to do window displays. Maybe Seema was right. Maybe Simon wasn't that clever. He seemed nice enough though, so what harm could it do to go to the magic show?

Simon looked smaller and crisper in day-light. The night before, she had thought his eyes were blue; in the sunlight, they were more of a steel gray. She also hadn't noticed how large his ears were or the faded ink stains on his hands.

She'd chosen for this day a light green cotton chemise with a scoop neck and tiny

108

glass red buttons running down the front. She wore a matching red hat and shoes. "You're certainly getting all dolled up for a magic show," Seema had teased her that morning.

But when Simon saw her, he said, "You look so pretty," immediately dispelling her worry that she had overdressed.

"Thank you, you look very nice, too."

"Well, my clothes are nothing much," he said, "but at least I'm clean."

It was a bad joke, but it set them off into easy conversation as they found their way to their seats in the theater.

"This may be a bunch of hooey," Simon whispered as the lights went out, "but I like to try and figure out how they do it."

For the next two hours, they watched Mysterio turn rabbits into ducks, make dollar bills flutter onto the stage from nowhere, and use his telepathy to guess the birthdays and pocket contents of various audience members. He performed a dowsing trick, using a chicken wishbone to detect the Canadian nickel from a hatful of American nickels. And he finished with his famous vanishing-girl act, where he placed a beautiful woman inside a cabinet on the left-hand side of the stage then padlocked it shut. With a clap of his hand and a "presto," he conjured up the same girl in a cabinet on the right side of the stage. The audience gasped when he unlocked the first cabinet and the woman was gone.

Flora sat forward in her seat, which meant that Simon could watch her at the same time as he scrutinized Mysterio's every move. When it was over she cheered with the rest of the crowd and rose to her feet.

"It was something, wasn't it?" he said as they headed toward the door.

"It was more than something," said Flora. "It was the most amazing thing I've ever seen. How did he do those tricks?"

"Are you really curious?" asked Simon.

"Oh you smarty, do you really know?"

"I'm only guessing, but did you notice in the dowsing trick how he put on his leather gloves before he performed it? Canadian nickels are magnetic. I'll bet he had a magnet in one of the glove fingers."

Flora considered his words. "Okay, that makes sense. But the vanishing girl: Even you can't figure that one out, can you?"

"Probably not." Simon smiled. "But consider what can be done with trap doors and twins."

He walked her all the way back to the Whites' house on Sixty-first Street, where they stood by the tall iron gates in the quiet night air. "How can I get in touch with you?" he asked. She gave him Aunt Hannah and Uncle Paul's address. "They have a telephone but I don't know how to reach it."

"Don't worry," he said. "I'll find you."

Flora thought that if Simon tried to kiss her, she wouldn't mind. It might have happened right then if Lulu had not bounded toward them barking as if they were waving machetes.

"It's only Lulu. She's very friendly," said Flora. "Actually, I don't know if she's friendly, but that's what people always say about scary drooling dogs."

"She looks okay to me," said Simon, rubbing the top of Lulu's head. He told Flora how he used to hawk newspapers in the street. "It's a surefire way to learn things about men and dogs," he said. "To tell which ones mean you harm and which ones don't."

"And what do you take me for?" asked Flora, turning her chin toward him.

"I take you for a good dog," he said. "A very good dog."

Two weeks later, an envelope arrived for Flora. Inside was a carefully wrought sketch of a boy with a perfectly cubed head wearing a round pair of glasses. Compared with his head, his arms and legs were tiny and spindly, and he was looking up at a beautiful girl with yellow hair, a red hat, and red buttons on her dress. On top of the drawing, in a perfect script, was written: "Mr. Blockhead and the lovely Miss Chatterbug." On a separate slip of paper was a note to Flora:

If I come to Mount Kisco, can we take a walk in a park where there are no dogs? Simon

Flora folded up the drawing and tucked it into her purse. Seema was wrong, she thought, smiling to herself. This was a very clever boy.

NEW YORK CITY: 1909

On this morning, the sun was hidden and the sky was the color of putty. Seema was awakened in an unfamiliar bed by the sound of bus brakes squealing and someone shouting obscenities. *Too early to be morning,* she thought, rolling over on her other side. As she was about to tuck the blanket under her chin, she opened one eye long enough to glimpse the clock that sat next to the bed. It was 7:25.

Just a few more winks. She shut her eye against the headache that tightened like a crown around her head. If she lay still for just a few more moments, she could slow the heaving in her stomach. But it was time. It was late. So she got up slowly, putting one foot after the other on the icy stone floor. *Scheisse.* Another day. No, not just another day. This was the day. The one she'd been planning and dreading for the last ten months. Seema parted the curtains and looked out. On the street, people walked fast, with their heads bowed and their eyes fixed on the ground. Move through it, that's all you could do in this kind of cold. Seema shivered and grabbed hold of the window-sill, steadying herself against the nausea that rode up inside her.

Scheisse, she thought again. Leaning against the wall, she made her way back to bed, then she got under the covers and went back to sleep.

The next time she awoke, the light coming through the parted curtains made her squint. This day seemed more manageable than it had two hours earlier, and if there was one thing Seema had learned in the past couple of years, it was how to get through a day no matter how miserably it lay at her feet.

She turned on her side. The sheets were rumpled and the covers thrown back. She shut her eyes, waiting to remember who had slept in that bed with her, and putting together the pieces of the night before. He was a handsome boy. A college boy. He told her that the light in her eyes danced like the moon over the Riviera on a summer night, and it made her laugh.

"There's a line I haven't heard before."

The way she said it, with her slight German accent and the boldness that comes from being beautiful, made the boy love her even more. He took her to a dance hall not far from where the Whites lived in the East Sixites. There they drank gin. He held her closer and ran his hands over her hips. When she made no protest, he moved his hands lower until they cupped her behind. He whispered into her ear that she was the kind of girl who was special and needed the kind of boy who knew how to take care of her. His voice was rough and husky and he danced her to the corner of the room.

"Another gin for the road," he said. This would be her third or fourth — by now she'd lost count. She sat on a bar stool, crossed her legs, and sipped her last drink of the night. The boy ran his hand up and down her calf and reached beneath the lace leg of her bloomers, making his way up to her thigh. He smiled as if he were stroking the chassis of an expensive automobile. She smiled, too, as she studied his square jaw and cornflower-blue eyes. He was a fine-looking boy. A gentile, of course.

Seema pulled the covers around her and sat up in the bed. It was after nine o'clock. No more time to waste. Uncle Paul and Aunt Hannah would have been up for hours. And Flora. God only knows but that

Flora was probably driving them crazy by now what with all her jabbering about her hair and her dress. "You only have one wedding day in your life," she'd said to Seema, "and that day ought to be perfect, don't you agree?"

Flora was nineteen, still a girl. She looked up to Seema as an older woman, as a mother. At twenty-one, Seema was a woman many times over. But as she never tired of telling Flora, "I am not your mother. You have a mother. She's my mother, too, and when the time is right she will come here."

Even as she said these words, Seema knew that would never happen. Her mother would not come to America. Her sister Margot would not come to America. Whenever Seema had broached it in a letter, her mother would write back, "You can't uproot an old tree." Her mother, Margot — they were both old trees who'd sunk their roots into the German soil to which they would cleave until the day they died. In truth, it would be fine with her if she never saw her mother again.

But this was a day to put thoughts like that out of her mind. If there was any day in her life she would try to be motherly toward Flora, this was it, even if Flora was marrying that earnest Jewish fellow who

116

looked like a tortoise.

Seema held the woolen blanket around her shoulders as she picked up the clothes that were scattered around the floor. She couldn't, for the life of her, remember how her shoes had ended up on the dresser, but there they were, with her stockings stuffed neatly inside of them and an envelope propped up against one of the heels. Inside were five dollar bills and a note that read:

The evening was spectacular but alas has come morning and the pursuant tasks at hand. Don't take the enclosed funds as any more than an expression of my delight and deepest desire that you find your way home in the most convenient manner possible. I shall see you again soon, my lovely.

One thing that drove Seema crazy about these college boys was their highfalutin use of language. "Pursuant." "Convenient manner." What did all this mean? But she was glad for the cash. She had exactly an hour and a half to get home, change her clothes, and hop on a train at Grand Central in order to get to Mount Kisco by early afternoon.

She shoved the money into her purse,

slipped her dress over her head, and pulled on her stockings. Last night's clothes looked duller, felt heavier, in daylight. The inside of her mouth was dry and the sour taste of gin still lingered in the back of her throat. She went into the bathroom, where there was a single toothbrush. She'd shared more than that with the man last night, so using his toiletries didn't seem like such a big deal. She brushed her teeth, washed her face with cold water, and put on the lipstick and rouge she carried with her in her bag. She was about to walk out the door when the thought struck her that she should leave a note or some memento for her young man. Seema couldn't help but smile as she reached up under her dress, pulled off her bloomers, and placed them carefully on the middle of his pillow.

Snowflakes the size of tears bounced against the windowpane as the train shuddered toward Westchester. Seema rested her head against the cool glass, hoping the chill of it would dull the ache above her eyes. Mount Kisco, Mount Kisco. The name played in her head to the rhythm of the train. Mount Kisco. Those were the first words she had ever spoken in English. Before she and Flora left Kaiserslautern, they would talk about Mount Kisco with Margot, each of them giving a different face to Kisco, who must have been a great enough man to have a mountain named after him. Seema had envisioned Kisco as tall and bony with a thick black beard and a slight hooked nose — exactly the kind of man she would never be attracted to now.

But oh the dreams they had about Mount Kisco. The Grossman sisters took a piece from every fairy tale they had ever read and came up with a Mount Kisco where the sun always shone, where the flowers were round and plump, and where the houses were as big as castles. Aunt Hannah would be beautiful, with long blond hair and cherry red lips. Uncle Paul would be handsome and suave like the king's son in "Rapunzel."

Seema tried to conjure up a vision of her thirteen-year-old self. Newly arrived in America, she was afraid to speak English and became convinced that the reason her changing body was betraying her in such confounding ways was because she was a foreigner. That was before she had any inkling about the way she really did stand apart from other girls. Sometimes older men would hold her in their gaze for a few moments too long, and she would look away, discomforted by their intensity.

119

Shortly after Seema came to Mount Kisco, Aunt Hannah and Uncle Paul invited a couple over for coffee. Mr. and Mrs. Holt had a daughter who was Flora's age and Mr. Holt owned the new furniture and carpeting store in town. Mr. Holt was about two heads taller than Seema and had brown stained teeth. She couldn't remember how he looked, only the feeling of him as he came into Aunt Hannah's kitchen to help Seema carry out the coffee cups and blackberry pie. When she picked up the pie, he stood behind her and put his arms around her. "That's a mighty heavy load for a little thing like you," he'd said as he pressed himself against her. She'd frozen in place while he took the pie from her and held it above her head. She didn't know what had happened, only that it made her feel queasy and like she wanted to cry. After that, every time the Holts came to visit, Mr. Holt would find a way to be alone with her, and the same kind of thing would happen. Once, he came into her bedroom while she was brushing her hair. "Let me help you with that," he'd whispered, taking the brush from her hands and running it through her hair. Just then, Flora walked in. Mr. Holt's voice suddenly got loud and deep. "Seema was just using me as a guinea pig to show off her new hairstyle, weren't you Seema?"

Because she and Flora were still new enough to the country to believe that everyone in America was touched with magic, Flora didn't seem to find Mr. Holt's behavior unusual. But instinctively Seema knew it was best to keep what she knew of Mr. Holt to herself.

The snow was falling harder now, and it seemed as if the train were traveling through a cloud. Seema pressed her thumb and middle finger to her brow. Her mind was webbed with so many secrets. She remembered a morning shortly after her father had died. It was cold and snowy, like now, and the windowpanes were opaque with frost. She, Margot, Flora, and their mother were huddled around the kitchen table. As her mother studied the three of them, Seema noticed the lines around her mouth, newly inscribed by her widowhood. She could still hear the hurt in her mother's voice as she stared out the window up at the sky: "What kind of God leaves a woman alone with three children?" she said to no one in particular. "My days as a woman are over now. But you girls, you have it all ahead of you." Then she went around the table and pinned a future on each of them. Flora, "my merry one," would always have men dancing around her, "like a maypole." It might take her "shy, peculiar child," Margot, a longer time to find a husband, but when she did, he would be as "loyal and true blue as she was." Then she turned to Seema. "My unknowable one," she said harshly. "She doesn't even bother to chew her secrets; she just swallows them whole." It was the first time she remembered thinking how much her mother disliked her.

Now, as she replayed that morning in her mind, three things leapt out at her: Her mother was thirty-four when she declared an end to her days as a woman. She wondered if her mother had ever seen an actual maypole. And she knew that had she ever confided to her mother about Mr. Holt, she would have somehow figured a way to put the blame on her. What kind of God, indeed?

She thought about Flora, the merry one, with her clear brown eyes and the easy way she had of talking to people. No unchewed secrets in her history. What must that be like? She was such an innocent, and now she was getting married. "Shy and peculiar," Margot had outfoxed them all by being the first to marry at eighteen, just two months earlier. That left Seema as the spinster in the family. Everyone assumed that she would marry soon. But she was in no hurry. She liked going to dance halls, meeting handsome new men. The way things were now, she understood what men wanted from her and, frankly, she wanted little more from them. A husband would expect her to wash his clothes, prepare his food, care for the children — all the things she was doing for the White family, but at least they paid her. She never talked about her life to her family, and she wondered what, if anything, they knew about her.

Her mother's letters were brief and infrequent; she rarely asked about Seema. From time to time, Aunt Hannah and Uncle Paul would make some comment about the bloom coming off the rose or fruit being too ripe, but then they'd turn it into some kind of a joke and they'd all end up laughing as if they were in it all together. And Margot? She couldn't even imagine what Margot would think of the life she was living here.

She wondered what Margot was doing now. She imagined her puttering over the window box that overlooked the yard behind their house in Kaiserslautern. She could see the curve of her back as she bent over the bright red flowers, smelling their sweet leaves and cupping a blossom in her hand as if it were a soft-boiled egg. Margot kept the window box filled with geraniums, even during the coldest months. She doted on these flowers as she did on her collection of tiny porcelain owls and the assortment of hatpins she kept on the table by her bed. "It could be worse," she'd say when anyone teased her about her quirky hobbies. "I heard about a man in Hamburg who kept two snakes in his room for five years before the police found him out. *That's* what I call an eccentric hobby."

Seema had the gorgeous hair and sexy bearing and Flora had the curvy feminine body, but it was Margot with her winter-pale skin and long slender legs who was the real looker. She was the youngest, and as far as Seema knew, she'd never had any more unhappiness than the usual theatrics that play out in a young girl's life. Yet even as a child, Margot was inclined to extremes. She collected stories from the kids at school and later from newspapers and magazines. The more bizarre, the more she favored them: the little Indian girl born with eight limbs whom everyone thought was the reincarnation of the Hindu goddess of wealth and prosperity, Lakshmi; or the man in Brussels who weighed 850 pounds and couldn't get out of his house until the fire department came and broke down his door. Along with stories, she collected symptoms. God forbid any of them got a rash or a cold. Margot would become convinced they were on their way to malaria, pneumonia, or some other dreaded disease. From as early as Seema could remember, Margot had that hairline furrow in her brow, which grew deeper as she got older. She remembered how their mother would rub her finger on that spot between her eyes and say, "It's a shame. You're such a pretty girl, if only we could clear your head of all that nonsense and make your worry go away."

When Aunt Hannah and Uncle Paul first suggested that the Grossman girls come to America, there was never a question of whether or not Margot would go with them. She'd read about the hooligans in the Gas House Gang in New York and the Indian massacre at Wounded Knee, and that was all she needed to know about America. "No, thank you, it's not for me," she'd said.

Right before Flora and Seema left, Margot began to get violent headaches. Sometimes she would take to bed for days at a time and lie in the dark, a damp cloth over her eyes, her skin so translucent that her temples and arms were a map of veins. The merest sound made her flinch. Seema remembered how their mother would tiptoe into their room and whisper, "Would you like a bowl of soup, *mein Schatz?* Something to warm your stomach?" Margot was convinced she was going blind, which was another reason she gave for not going to America. Who would take care of a blind young girl except for her mother? No, she'd stay right here in Kaiserslautern.

Margot was the only one of them for whom their mother had a pet name. Maybe it was because Margot was the most like her and had inherited her nervousness and streak of melodrama. Whatever the reason, the two of them were emotionally tethered. One day, when the sisters were very little girls, a bird flew into their house and couldn't find its way out. The bird was shiny with a black head and a black beak — a crow, Seema realized now. It swooped and zigzagged and made piercing caw-caw-caw cries as their mother chased it with a blanket. When its wing glanced Margot's shoulder, she began to shriek, "A bat! A bat!" Someone at school had told her about a vampire bat in Budapest who had sucked all the blood out of a child while he was sleeping, and when his mother came to wake him up the next morning, he was dead. Seema shushed her and whispered, "It's not a bat at all, it's really the wicked witch from "Hansel and Gretel," and if you aren't quiet right now she's going to pick you up and eat you alive."

Margot gulped back her tears and froze in place. The air went out of her and she crumpled to the floor. Her mother dropped the blanket she was using to trap the bird, turned on the balls of her feet, and slapped Seema across the face. "You are the cruelest child I have ever known," she shouted, before kneeling down to hug Margot. "It is your job to protect your little sister, and if you ever do anything like this again, your punishment will be worse."

Seema was glad her mother was thousands of miles away.

As she got off the train in Mount Kisco, Seema rubbed her fingers over her right cheek, where she could still feel the fire of her mother's handprint. Out of the corner of her eye, she saw Aunt Hannah, who was wrapped up in her brown wool cloak and hugging herself to keep warm. She was the only person waiting at the station on this frosty morning. Seema quickened her step and put a smile on her face as she braced herself for Aunt Hannah, a small but effusive woman with a big hug.

"Seema, finally you're here. I thought you'd be on the last train," shouted Aunt Hannah. She spread her arms, and the cloak billowed, making her seem twice her size as she swaddled Seema in her wooly embrace. "Now everyone's here. Ruth and Lev came last night. Flora's been waiting for you all morning. She looks absolutely radiant. Oh, you girls. You must miss your mother so on a special day like today. Uncle Paul and I want you to know that we are your family and couldn't love you more if you were our own children."

Seema tried to turn her face away from Aunt Hannah, afraid that the liquor was still on her breath. Their cheeks touched. Aunt Hannah's skin was smooth and cold. She thought about the man last night and his stubble and the red scratch marks he'd left on her cheeks. If Aunt Hannah smelled gin or noticed any nicks on her face, it didn't distract her from her chatter. "It's so sad that your mother and Margot couldn't be here. But, of course, it's such a long and expensive trip. Oh, but let's not dwell on the negative. There are so many happy things to talk about. Flora. What a dream she is in her dress. She even found some gardenias for her hair. And Simon. We are so lucky to have Simon in the family. He's shy. A little hard to get to know. But a fine man, don't you think?"

No, Seema didn't think he was a fine man. He was quiet. Moody. Unassertive. Not the kind of fellow who could walk into a room full of people and make himself known. He was one of those pale Jewish types who lived in their heads. Seema hated men like that. By now, she believed she could size them up right away: soft damp hands, indecisive, always measuring their words. And worst of all, she knew that they would love her in a tentative, trembling way.

Not like the man from last night, who smelled of fine leather and tobacco and called her "sugar." Jewish men spoke a jagged English or, like Simon, used oddly formal language when they talked, which, in his case, was hardly ever. The men she liked had straight noses and wore suits that were hand tailored. They didn't dress in clothes that were too big for them or chew with their mouths open and smell of onions. When the men she liked made fun of the Jews with their hooked noses and stooped shoulders, she laughed along with them and never told them that she was a Jew herself. Why should she? No one ever asked.

Aunt Hannah kept talking about the wedding: the leg of lamb for fifty; the bottles of French wine Uncle Paul had stored in the cellar; how beautiful the synagogue looked, particularly the chuppa, which was decorated with gardenias to match the ones in Flora's hair. Seema smiled secretly, imagining the look on the faces of all those men if they could see her inside a synagogue.

As they drove up the circular driveway, Seema could see Uncle Paul standing on the front porch, already dressed in his black tuxedo pants. When the car stopped, he ran around to the passenger side of the car and opened the door. "CeCe," he shouted. "Let me take a look at you." He grabbed her bag and helped her out of the car. "You are a sight for sore eyes," he said, standing back and taking in the full image of his niece. "Quite a sight indeed."

If anyone would notice that she was drawn and slightly hung-over, it would be Uncle Paul. He'd keep it to himself at the time, and then, maybe months later, he'd drop it into a conversation. For now, he just asked, "You working hard, honeybunch?"

"No," she answered flatly. "I'm fine. I'm excited about Flora's wedding, that's all. Really excited."

"Yeah, well, no one's as excited as Miss Chatterbug," he said. "She's had us going since early this morning. Honestly, Simon must be a very patient man. Either that, or he has no idea what he's getting into and he'll be dead within six months. C'mon inside. Your sister's eager to see you."

For the past ten months, Seema had barely tolerated Flora's giddiness. Flora the scatterbrain, she thought, was always in a tizzy about something and now it was this. But today Seema would exclaim about her sister's dress and the gardenias, and she'd embrace Simon. And who knows, maybe she'd even manage a couple of tears at the ceremony. So she was taken aback when she opened the door to Flora's room and found her sitting on her bed, dressed in nothing but her chemise.

"Hey Mrs. Phelps," said Seema, sounding as upbeat as she could. "*Finally,* the big day. You must be so excited."

"I am, I really am," said Flora, crossing her legs and resting her chin in the palm of her hand. But her voice was anything but excited.

"So why the long face?" asked Seema.

"I don't know if I can do this. It's just so much."

Seema sat down on her sister's bed and put her hand on her knee. "What do you mean, so much? You love him, don't you?"

"Oh yes," said Flora. "It's just that . . . you're the only one who will understand this. I'm nervous about the love part."

Seema squeezed her sister's knee. "Oh sweetie, I know a little something about that. Don't worry, it's surprisingly easy. There may be some awkward fumbling at first, but you'll figure it out. Everybody does. And once you get the hang of it, it's not bad."

Flora looked at her sister as if she were seeing her for the first time. "Noooo," she shook her head. "I'm not worried about that part. It's the love part. I mean the real love part. The thing is, you don't just wake up one day and know how to love somebody. You have to learn it somewhere. Look at Ruth and Lev. From the moment they were born, they knew that Aunt Hannah and Uncle Paul loved them the best, and every day they got to practice it. Simon's been on his own since he was nine. I never really knew our father, and Mama is — well, I'm sure she loves us in her own way — but she sent us here when we were so young, she really didn't have time to love us in that way. Uncle Paul and Aunt Hannah love us. But that's almost like secondhand love, because they feel sorry for us, and they had to take care of us. And you and me, we love each other, but in a faraway kind of way. Neither of us has ever had someone who loves us the most and would do anything for us. What if Simon and I have children someday and we don't know how to love them? It's so awful, the thought of that."

Whatever she said now would matter for a long time, so Seema thought hard before she spoke. Flora was right about one thing: Nobody had ever taught them to love. When their mother shipped them off to America, she told them it was because of how much she cared about them that she was making this big sacrifice. But to them it felt like rejection and abandonment. They both understood about survival, about being polite in order to ingratiate themselves to strangers. Flora, more than she, was charming and shrewd about appearing more helpless than she was so that people would want to help her. For her part, she knew about letting herself be admired. She understood desire. But love? The kind of love that meant giving yourself completely to another without expecting anything in return? That's what Flora was talking about. What did either of them know about that?

Seema bit her thumbnail as she thought about these things. "You're right, we're not like Ruth and Lev," she said. "Every love is different, even though I think they all require a leap of faith. You have to let yourself trust somebody even when it feels like the scariest and least likely thing to do. This is something I think is easier for you to do than it is for me. You and Simon already know how to make each other happy. You tell each other what's in your heart, and I'm assuming there aren't many secrets between you. You're creating your own kind of love. You're already doing it. I think that's the best two people can do."

How long had it been since they'd talked about private things? Flora leaned against Seema's back. It was the kind of cozy gesture that she wouldn't have thought about twice when they were children in Germany. But since they'd come to America, their relationship had changed enough so that she wouldn't presume such an intimacy.

"I know," said Flora. "But what if we're not good at it?"

"I didn't know if I'd be able to take care of Lulu," said Seema, "but now I don't think twice about it."

"Lulu?" laughed Flora. "Lulu's a dog who slobbers all over you and leaves muddy paw prints on your bed. That's kind of different from a man who wears a coat and a tie and a tiepin to work everyday, wouldn't you say?"

"That's my point, you nitwit," said Seema. "It doesn't matter that Lulu's a dog. I love her and I'll do what I have to do to keep her safe. Maybe that's the most love I'll ever have for anybody, but it's real and no one's had to teach me how to do it. I know Simon's not a dog, or at least I don't think he is, but I guess that's how it works."

She raised her eyebrow and Flora elbowed her playfully in the ribs. Their faces were close enough together so that she could smell her hair. It smelled sweet and talcy, just as it did when she was a little girl.

Flora jerked away and studied Seema's face from a distance. "What's this?" she asked, running her fingers over the red marks on her face.

Seema covered her cheeks with the palms of her hand. "Oh these silly chicken scratches? They're nothing. I was just playing around."

"Playing around with what, some scissors and a knife?" asked Flora.

"You're being a little overly dramatic, don't you think?" she answered, the tartness back in her voice. She looked at her watch. "If we keep on blabbing like this, the wedding will be over before you even get there.

Don't you think you ought to get dressed?" Flora kept her eyes on her sister's cheeks as she got up off the bed and went to her closet.

The dress was made of ivory lace over a satin floor-length sheath with a high collar and what must have been a hundred Jacquard buttons that ran from behind the neck to below the waist. The sleeves were long, with one little button at each wrist. Seema had not seen the dress before. "It's beautiful," she sighed. "I can't wait to see it on you. Just one thing, though. By the time Simon gets all those buttons undone, you could both be very old people."

Flora giggled and put the dress back in the closet. She sat down on the bed and rested her head on Seema's shoulder. "I wish Mama and Margot could see me," she said.

"I know you do," said Seema. "I wish Margot were here, too."

Flora was a shaky bride. Aunt Hannah and Uncle Paul walked down the aisle on either side of her, but she was trembling so badly that the leaves from her gardenias cascaded dramatically to her shoulders. There was a wispy smile on her face. It looked as if at any moment she might burst into tears —

or wild laughter. The piano player cranked out a lugubrious version of Mendelssohn's *A Midsummer Night's Dream,* but people craned their necks and sighed nonetheless.

Pissboy stood in the back of the synagogue, where a draft of cold air seeped through the spaces between the two old wooden doors. The women hugged their shawls tighter around their shoulders, but rivulets of sweat collected in the creases of fat around Pissboy's neck. He eyed the sapphire ring on Mrs. Futterman's finger and the fox stole around Mrs. O'Mara's neck. *Easy pickings,* he thought to himself, then forced his attention back to the front of the synagogue, where his friend stood, looking scared and more serious than ever in his long black waistcoat and black embroidered yarmulke.

Pissboy saw marriage as a dead end. He'd done well for himself on the street, and a wife and children would only cramp his style. He shoved his hand in his pocket and wrapped his fingers around the silver and ebony cigarette case he had just acquired. It felt cool and substantial, which comforted Pissboy and reassured him that the life he had chosen for himself was the right one. He rubbed his thumb around the smooth ebony inlay. Simon was an odd duck, he

137

thought. He'd probably like being married.

Seema stood at the front of the synagogue holding the gold band that Flora would slip onto Simon's finger. Little Flora was all dressed up in her gown and her rouge and white gloves. She looked older than her nineteen years, yet she still had the sweetness of a child about her. Seema used to think that Flora was her mother's reward for having endured her. Whenever their mother would reprimand Seema for some unkind act or word, she would add, "Why can't you be more like Flora?" Despite that, Seema adored her younger sister. She remembered baby Flora's feet. They were so tiny, her toes all one size. When she'd take a little foot into her mouth and pretend to chew it up and swallow it, Flora would writhe and giggle. The foot was sweet and squishy in her mouth, like an éclair.

Simon was watching Flora behind his spectacles with a look Seema had never seen in a man's eyes before. It wasn't lust. It was more raw and agitated than that. Whatever it was, Flora seemed to tame it as she came closer. His lips were parted slightly and he kept taking deep gulps of air. Flora stopped shaking, and as she got closer to Simon, his breathing steadied. Her face relaxed into a genuine smile and their eyes hooked into each other's. A kind of peace fell over the synagogue. Even the piano player must have felt it as she released the final chord of the "Wedding March" into its natural, exhilarating crescendo. It wasn't any one thing that made Seema start to cry, but when she did, the salt from her tears stung the marks on her cheek, which reminded her of the man from the night before, which for some reason only made her cry harder.

"Take off your glasses."
"I see badly without them."
"Take them off anyway."
Simon slipped the glasses from behind his ears. All he could make out was a blur of pink and the exquisite roundness of the woman who stood before him. The candle on the dressing table was sending flickered shadows across the bed, and the floorboards creaked every time he shifted his weight. Flora ran her fingers through his hair, making concentric circles on the base of his skull with her forefingers.
"Your hands feel so soft," he said.
She pulled his head toward her and he rested it on her bosom. He could feel her heart beating underneath the lace. Neither of them was breathing.
"Come, let's sit down," Simon said, tak-

ing her by one hand and sliding his glasses back on with the other.

A blue chenille spread with pink and yellow flowers covered the bed. Aunt Hannah and Uncle Paul had paid for their honeymoon at this New Rochelle inn called the Lavender House. Uncle Paul said it was the place where all the "lovebirds" went after they were married. Simon tried to ignore the smell of stale perfume drifting up from the pillows, choosing to believe that he and Flora were the only lovebirds ever to stay in this little room. But there was evidence to the contrary: the framed needlepoint on the wall, which said, "Love Makes a House a Home," and the freshly cut white roses that the owners had discreetly placed in a silver vase on the dressing table.

Flora and Simon sat down on the bed and laughed uneasily as their knees bumped together. Simon stared up at the needlepoint then took off his glasses for a second time before putting his arms around Flora. "*You* are my home," he said. "I am so very happy."

She leaned her body into his until their hips were touching. He began to unbutton the one hundred Jacquard buttons on the back of her dress. "You're locked in here," he said, putting his glasses back on. "So unlock me," she answered, shimmying out of the dress. That left only her chemise, which was far more forgiving and less protective of the parts it was meant to hide. He kissed her in places he had never been before. She tasted like licorice.

Often, he had drawn the taut muscles of prizefighters and the milky flesh of characters like the Fatsos. But until now, he had never held a real body in his hands. He had never understood its warmth, the way it hummed and yielded, or the power it had to make him want to bury himself in it until he wept. For nearly twenty years, Simon had not allowed himself the luxury of tears. Even when the voices of his mother and brothers and sisters snapped his dreams apart at night or teased his memory in the day, he always pushed the sadness down. If he didn't, he imagined, it would burn through him. Now, as he and Flora lay back on the perfumed pillows, he could feel his throat tighten with desire and his eyes fill with tears.

"Take off your glasses."

She was the only one who ever asked him to do that, the only one to see him as he was. "Take off your glasses." In the years to follow, those four words became their code for wanting each other.

He felt Flora was his destiny, a wondrous

quirk of fate. What else would explain why he had allowed Pissboy to take him to the New Irving Dance Hall that night and what drew him to Flora during the Mirror Dance? He could never get over that a beautiful woman like her would fall for a plain-looking man like him. He used to tease her by telling her that he came from a family of toads. "I am the ugliest man in the world, and I have ended up with the most beautiful woman in the world. If there is a God, then He has a preposterous sense of the absurd, don't you agree?"

Whichever God put the two of them together was secure in His knowledge that opposites attract. Flora was taller than Simon, and while he was a man of straight lines and spare dimensions, she was all circles and curves. She moved slowly and fluidly, with hips that swayed like the tide. He had a brisk stride. With her thick, curly blond hair and eager brown eyes — Simon liked to describe them as the color of fresh pumpernickel — she put people at ease immediately. He was the standoffish one — a nice enough fellow, but hard to know. His head was small and his ears were large and floppy, so he wore hats only on the coldest days. She loved hats and did them justice. They reveled in their differences. The origins of their names said it all: Flora was the goddess of blooming vegetation, while Simon was an obscure form of *cement.*

But the same fate that brought him Flora had also impulsively snatched up his father and separated him from his mother and siblings. And so he remained wary of it, always keeping one eye out for its spidery footsteps. Those who didn't know him thought him earnest and dour. Even those who thought they knew him well would say of him that only Flora could make his eyes light up and the clouds on his face part. He carried an umbrella even when the sun was shining, and he always had a spare linen handkerchief neatly folded in his inside pocket. Like any man who is skittish about fate, he tried to be prepared for anything.

KAISERSLAUTERN:
1910

She lay on the bed, the stiff linen sheets twisted around her fingers. The sticky mess between her legs smelled like iron. Her knees were pulled up to her chin and she squeezed her eyes shut. Her husband sat by her side. "Just a little more, Margot. It will be over soon," he said, dabbing a cold cloth on her sweaty forehead. Her face was the color of old snow, and there were small lines etched down the sides of her mouth that he'd never seen before. She made a sound that came from deep inside her. It wasn't so much a human sound as the heaving sound of something being unearthed, something that was never meant to move.

She felt cold and clammy, and while she could hear her voice cry out, it felt separate from the rest of her. The last thing she remembered was tasting her own breath; it was sour and pungent. Gratefully, she gave herself up to the darkness that rocked her and carried her far away from the pain.

Then it was over. The child that was not meant to be bled out from inside her. When she opened her eyes again, the pain was gone. She reached for her husband. It was reassuring to feel the coarse hair on the back of his hand and his sturdy knuckles. He cupped her hand in both of his and brought it to his lips. "Sleep now," he whispered into her fingers. "Next time we will do better, I promise you."

The child, unformed and mistaken, was nevertheless intended. It had lived in their minds and daydreams, and to not give it a name was implausible. So they called her Gilda, and though they rarely said the name out loud, Gilda lived on for them as the ideal. They knew it made no sense, so they kept it as a secret between them. Only Margot's mother dared to talk about the dead child. And then it was to bemoan the fact that none of her daughters — two of them lost to her now in America — had borne her grandchildren. "My Margot is the only one of them who has the motherly instinct," she would say in a sorrowful tone.

Although one year later the pain came from the same place, this time it was pain with a purpose. And pain with a purpose, she said later on, was bearable, because it wasn't all there was. Frederick had kissed her on the forehead and called her "my brave little woman." That night, he made her a beef-steak all her own and said it again. "My brave little woman, this will help you get your strength back."

They named this baby Edith. She had large eyes like a squirrel's and a chin that jutted out enough so that you could wrap your index finger around it. Their mother wrote to Seema and Flora in America:

> She is a beautiful baby. Frederick says she is a real Ehrlich and looks like his side of the family. But let me tell you, she is Grossman through and through. Flora, she looks like you did when you were born. Finally, I am a grandmother.

From the moment she drew her first breath, Edith was a happy child and a child who intuitively understood that her survival depended on not fussing too much, even when her diaper was dirty. She smiled easily and gave off a sweet vanilla baby smell. Her parents called her their gift from God. But while they bounced her in the air and gave her endearing nicknames like *Liebchen,* the two of them wondered in the silent ways in which families share their secrets whether little *Liebchen* could ever usurp the place held in her parents' heart by a seedling whose name was spoken only in whispers.

In 1910 in the western German town of Kaiserslautern, there was no language for the troubled spells that afflicted Margot, even before the death of her firstborn. For no apparent reason, her eyes would suddenly fill with tears, or her stare would become distant and frozen. After hearing a secondhand story about a hurt child or a fire in Frankfurt that killed dozens, she would become engulfed by a sadness that would take her far away. Frederick said she lived too much in her imagination; the doctor said it was melancholia. Whatever it was, it became as much a part of the Ehrlich family as the shadow of Gilda.

Edith grew up with her mother's melancholia looming over her when she went to sleep and beckoning her inside when she went out to play. From early on, she knew how to make her laugh pleasing and her jokes lighthearted. "My sunny one," her mother called her, as if there were another. Sometimes Margot would hug her so tight that Edith could feel her mother's boney landscape. "You are my sunny one," she'd say. "What did I do to deserve one with this easy disposition?" When she was old enough to understand her mother's words, Edith would try to find a lighthearted retort. "It was your lucky day, I guess." One time she said, "God made a mistake. He meant for me to born into a rich family in Berlin." Her mother's eyes darkened and she stared past Edith. "That would have been His second mistake. Careless, don't you think?"

PART 2

YONKERS:
1915

The way things went during their first six years of marriage made it hard for Simon and Flora to imagine that their lives together would be anything but peaceful. Simon made enough money in the window display business to afford a small Tudor house not too far from where Aunt Hannah and Uncle Paul lived in Mount Kisco. Flora took up gardening and became active in the sisterhood of the synagogue. Each morning, Simon would commute to his office on East Twenty-ninth Street. Because he was a junior partner at Adler, Broder, and Phelps, he had no window next to his work table. His view was the bland green wall on which he had hung a map of the United States. It was better that way. So much of Simon's life went on in his imagination that watching the traffic outside or the change of light and weather would only be a distraction.

Until Simon Phelps got his hand into the

window display business, storefronts had the usual flat scenery and mannequins. Lately, window-shoppers did double takes at coffee beans popping out of their cans and sexy ladies swinging their legs back and forth showing off their side-buttoned shoes. He borrowed from memory as much as he did from his fantasy life. Many of the characters he drew as a boy showed up in his early window displays. There was Strongman streaking across the storefront with a bar of Fels Naptha laundry soap in his hands, and Mr. Machine rigged up by special wiring to bob up and down over the new Smith Premier typewriter.

Even Flora didn't know the extent to which Simon invented his own world. Because he took the 7:15 train into work every day, getting a window seat was easy. He'd stare out the glass and begin what became a daily daydream. He'd check in with family as if they'd seen each other yesterday. With Europe at war, he tried not to think about what might be happening to them. Instead, he'd imagine what his mother planned to cook for that night's dinner and what the younger children would learn in school that day. Sometimes he'd think in Lithuanian, sometimes in English. Other times, there'd be no words, only smells and sounds and the feeling of familiar skin and clothes. In that way, and through his work, Simon was able to keep his family alive.

For one of his new clients, the Hoover vacuum cleaner company, he devised a model of a woman rolling the new contraption back and forth under the banner that read, SWEEPING CHANGES. Though the woman he created was more slender and modern looking than his mother, he gave her his mother's apron, the one that he'd kept all these years that tied around the waist and had blue and gray roses with a white ruffle around the bottom and hip pocket. He'd brought the apron to work with him, telling himself that it would be helpful to have it on hand while he re-created it for his Hoover lady. But in truth, he liked keeping it tucked away in his bottom drawer, where he could look at it whenever he wanted, run his hands through it, and use it to evoke the smells from his boyhood kitchen.

It seemed impossible that he was still uncertain about his family's fate. Word had gotten back to him about the outbreak of typhus in the region where they lived. Also, there were the pogroms: the vicious attacks on homes and businesses that decimated the Jewish population. And of course, the war itself, which sent waves of new immigrants to New York. Whenever he could, he would meet with immigrants who had recently arrived from Vilna and ask if they had any news of his family. One, a man roughly the same age as his brother Isaac would have been, stared at him before answering in a halting broken English, "There are so many who are gone, it is hard to keep count." He even tried to hire a private detective to go there and search, but he was unable to find anyone either.

Simon kept his family alive the only way he knew how, by using their faces as characters for his window displays. For a store that sold Buster Brown shoes, he used a smiling girl with pigtails. A little boy with a cowlick became the centerpiece of a window advertising vacations in Palm Beach, Florida. But it was his display for the Gillette razor that caught people's eye and put the name of Simon Phelps on the lips of every advertising man in New York City. He had figured out how to mechanize a cardboard robot that sat in drugstore windows and sharpened razor blades. Until then, nobody knew that cardboard could do more than contain pottery jugs or nutritious wheat cereals. But Simon saw life in the mud-colored paperboard. He gave it color and found new ways to bend it and cut it.

So it was no surprise when he and Flora received a hand-embossed vellum invitation from the Lithographers Association of New York requesting their presence at their annual masquerade ball. This year, the Lithographers Association, or LANY, as they called themselves, was holding its party at the ritziest hotel in town, the Waldorf-Astoria. For a young man like Simon to be invited meant that the most prominent members of his profession recognized his talent. There was no question that he would have to attend. Even so, the idea of it made him ornery. "Why should I stand around with a bunch of self-congratulatory men holding up silly masks?" he asked Flora.

"Because they just might invite you to join."

"You know how I feel about clubs. I'll never belong to any of them."

For the umpteenth time, he told her how, in the eyes of the world, he would always be a Jew. "A Jew is a Jew first and foremost," he said. "And in this country, no matter what else I do, I will still be a foreigner — masquerade ball or no masquerade ball."

Flora resisted the impulse to roll her eyes. He was obsessed with being a foreigner even though he'd lived here for more than two-thirds of his life. "But you're an American now. What's more is, you've tossed your hat into this advertising business and you've worked awfully hard at it. How unlike you it would be not to finish something you started. Of course we'll go to this ball. And you know what? We'll have a good time. Think of it this way, you'll be wearing a mask, so no one will be sure who you are anyway."

"Sure," said Simon, suddenly taken by the idea of creating a different persona. He took her hand. "But now I'm thinking that I don't want to be just another guy in a white half-mask. I want to be John Barrymore. Do you think I can be John Barrymore?"

"Of course you can." Flora laughed. "No one's stopping you."

Simon saw how funny it would be if he, the short and nearsighted foreigner, could somehow figure out how, for that night, he could become the swaggering, handsome, and very non-Jewish actor John Barrymore.

For the next couple of weeks, he studied photographs of Barrymore. He memorized his features: his patrician nose, the twist of cruelty on his lips, the cleft in his chin. He was a man whose earnest gaze and blue eyes revealed little of his nature, other than he seemed to stay inside himself. In that way, he was like the hand-carved wooden Indian that stood outside the tobacconist store in Yonkers. Simon visited the statue several times, running his hands over the concave planes of his face and squinting back at the Indian's unflinching stare. And when he was ready to draw, he could feel the creases on either side of John Barrymore's mouth when he smiled, and how the thick arches of his eyebrows lifted imperceptibly when he was curious or amused.

The night before the ball, Flora and Simon were sitting at their kitchen table. Flora had prepared a roast chicken and some rice. Simon was just about to tuck his napkin into his shirt when he snapped his fingers and opened his eyes wide. "Oh wait!" he said, as if a new thought had just flown into his head. "I have something to show you." He folded up the cloth napkin, set it next to his fork, and excused himself. "Start without me," he shouted to Flora from the living room. "I'll be right back."

Flora was poking the chicken thigh in front of her. She had a tendency to under-cook chicken. The last time she made it, Simon had refused to eat it after he cut through a pink rubbery thigh and a stream of blood oozed into his mashed potatoes.

"Flora, nobody likes rare chicken," he had said.

When he returned to the kitchen, she was still stabbing at her meat. "How do I look?" he asked, his voice sounding as if someone's hand were covering up his mouth.

She glanced up. "Good God!"

"What do you think?" he asked.

"John Barrymore! You look like John Barrymore!"

He pulled the cardboard mask from his face. "Does it work?" he asked, holding it up in front of Flora.

"Let me see that," she said, wiping her hands on her apron and grabbing it from him.

He had fashioned a mask from a single sheet of pliable cardboard that fastened behind the ears with elastic and curved around the entire face. On the mask, he replicated John Barrymore's features with tempera paints. He cut a flap for the nose and crafted peepholes for the eyes that were actually cut into the shaded part of the lower lid so that Barrymore's fixed blue-eyed expression was not sacrificed.

Flora put the mask over her own face. "How do I look?" she asked.

"Funny, you look like John Barrymore, too, only your physique is more pleasing than his." He grinned as he picked up his knife and fork and cut into the chicken breast on his plate. The white meat was moist and supple and nearly fell off the bone. Although he had impeccable manners, Simon still ate with the anxiety of someone who had known hunger. He used his knife and fork to scrape off every shred of meat on the bone and made sure not to leave a grain of rice on his plate. He also ate fast, poised over his plate as if he were expecting someone to snatch it away. "Slow down," Flora would urge. But it was as futile as telling a man on fire to lower his voice.

"That was delicious," he said to Flora when he finished eating. "I think you've mastered chicken."

"And you've mastered John Barrymore," she said, leaning across the table and rubbing her hand up and down his forearm. "Why don't you take off your glasses?" The question always made him flush, and he did so now as he squeezed her wrist and answered, "There is nothing that I'd rather do, I think you know that. It's just that John Barrymore and I have a lot of work to do before tomorrow night."

For several reasons, Simon Phelps became

the talk of the LANY ball the following evening. First of all, there was Flora. While most of the women that night wore their hair swept up, Flora let her saucy blond curls fall around her white mask. Behind it, her brown eyes gleamed like amber against the teal satin gown she wore that accentuated her statuesque figure. The members of LANY could be forgiven if they stopped and stared. She was a real looker, at least three inches taller than her husband, and she couldn't keep her hands off him. Those are the kinds of things that engender respect, and curiosity, in other men. None of them would have guessed that the earnest young Mr. Phelps would be married to a woman like that.

Then there was Simon's mask. Everyone was handed a papier-mâché half-mask when they entered the ballroom at the Waldorf. The men's were black, the women's were white, and they all were attached to wooden sticks. At first, no one seemed aware of the face behind Simon's mask. Then someone did a double take and nudged someone else, who pointed him out to another, until everyone in the room noticed that Simon wore the face of John Barrymore. The resemblance was downright eerie. Instead of the usual peepholes for the eyes, there were John Barrymore's eyes. Not only that, but until then, no one had seen masks that weren't made of wood or papier-mâché. This one was pliable and fitted the face perfectly. People began to gather around Simon. Someone rubbed his finger across Barrymore's bushy eyebrows. Someone else reached beneath the flap and tweaked Simon's nose.

When the orchestra announced that they were playing the last dance, Simon handed out twenty copies of his John Barrymore mask to twenty random men in the room. Inside each mask, in an elegant script, he had written the words: "Face it, Adler, Broder, and Phelps will get you noticed!"

That night, when they came home from the Waldorf, Flora held onto Simon's arm as he opened the front door. "You were a sensation tonight," she said.

Still wearing his John Barrymore mask, he answered her in a throaty baritone he thought appropriate for the actor: "And you, my dear, were the most beautiful woman in the room. The belle of the ball, if I may say."

Flora took his cardboard apple cheeks in her hands and in her own throaty voice said, "Take off your mask."

This time, Simon didn't hesitate. Both of

them took the stairs two at a time.

Their house in Yonkers had three bedrooms, two of them just waiting for the children they knew they were going to have. Sometimes, when Simon wasn't home, Flora would stand in one of the empty rooms and envision the nursery. Often when she was in the local Woolworth, she'd wander into the baby clothes section and pick up a snowsuit or a crocheted blanket and hold it in her arms imagining how it would feel with their child bundled inside. She'd already picked out names: Kate or Rose if it was a girl, Sam, after Simon's father, Samuel, if it was a boy.

Six years into their marriage, Flora was twenty-five and Simon thirty-two. Flora was still not pregnant, though not for lack of trying. Each time her period came, she'd feel betrayed and ashamed. "Maybe this is God's way of telling me I don't deserve a child," she confided to Seema. "Or maybe I'm not womanly enough." Margot had gotten pregnant twice. And here she was, the picture of health, barren. She hated herself for thinking that. It was nothing personal toward Margot. In fact, she had a warm spot for the child Edith. Everyone said how much alike they looked and she felt an odd connection to the girl, even though she'd not yet met her.

Wanting a child was the furthest thing from Seema's mind. She'd had her own brushes with motherhood and they were anything but sentimental. Last summer, after she was three weeks late, she suddenly got violent cramps and started bleeding heavily. She was out with a group of friends at a roadhouse on the New Jersey shore and had to go lie down on the cold stone floor in the washroom. After about ten minutes, she felt strong enough to wash up and rejoin the group. They hadn't even noticed her absence. She spent the rest of the afternoon pretending nothing was wrong and stealing backward glances to make sure that the blood hadn't soaked through to her skirt. Then, in the fall, a friend of hers nearly died after douching with lye in order to flush out an unwanted baby. She'd watched pregnant women, their bodies stretched and distorted, wobbling down the street like overstuffed clowns. No sir, there was nothing about motherhood that appealed to Seema.

"You are so beautiful now," she said to Flora. "But you have children and just like that —" she snapped her fingers "— your complexion is pale, you have dark circles under your eyes, your prettiness is gone.

And that's not all that goes. I see the way Simon stares at you. Do you think he'd look at you like that with two brats hanging off you? Do you know what having children does to your body?" Seema ran her hands around the curves of her breasts. "I'm two years older than you and I still have my shape. If I had children, by now I'd be a fat old horse. No man would give me a second glance."

Flora studied Seema's face. She noticed the lines around Seema's mouth: faint, but the shape of disappointment. "I'm sure Simon would love me, even if my belly was fat with babies," she said.

"I know something about men," said Seema. "I wouldn't count on it."

Still the babies didn't come. Simon and Flora never spoke about it; they just filled the bedrooms. Flora moved her sewing machine along with a box for threads, needles, and buttons into one of them. She added a trundle bed with a calico spread for Seema, who would come to stay with them when she needed a break from her job and friends. The other room became Simon's office. It was where he kept drawings, window displays, and drafts of proposals that he was sending to the U.S. Patent and Trademark Office. Things had changed on East Twenty-ninth Street. Now he had the big office that looked out onto the street. Still, there wasn't enough room for all of the ideas that crowded into his imagination. They came faster now: the characters, the memories, the gadgets for advertisements. Living in his head as he did, Simon often had trouble separating the real world from the one he was creating.

Only Flora, licorice-sweet and welcoming, was able to straddle both. Always Flora.

KAISERSLAUTERN:
1921

Edith's father, Frederick Ehrlich, was in the butcher business. He'd worked at the same store since he'd gotten out of the army in 1917 after taking a superficial wound to his left shoulder. All that Edith remembered from his time away was how her mother would sit staring out the window, as if she expected him to come up the path at any moment. That and how she'd hug Edith to her and say, "You must always be proud of how your father serves his country."

Back home, his job was to grind the meat that was used to make sausage and wurst. Frederick always had about him a vaguely sweet smoky smell that Edith thought suited his personality. He was round with pink soft cheeks and a shiny bald head. He was not a handsome man, but with his amiable smile and strong barrel chest, he was not unpleasant looking either. When he spoke, he did so with a tempered voice and words chosen to be soothing: "Edith, can you be so kind as to bring me a sweater" or "Margot, maybe it would be nice if we took a little walk this afternoon and got some air."

Her nature was more like his, and she had the same crook in her nose as he did. Otherwise, she resembled the Grossman side of the family. She had her mother's high forehead and unruly auburn-colored hair. Her mother kept hers knotted up in a bun while Edith wore hers loose, her curls seeming sometimes to spring out of her head. Both of them were tall and thin and had eyes that, in the sun, turned the color of moss. Edith had a rosy complexion and a flock of freckles around her nose. Her mother's skin, in the past years, had become translucent and drawn with worry.

Although they were only three living in the small stone farmhouse at the edge of town, Margot's melancholia took up the space and attention of a truculent fourth. They felt blessed by Edith's cheerfulness, which kept them afloat for the first ten years of her life. Then, right before Christmas of 1921, the trouble came.

As Edith walked to school on a Thursday morning that December, she blew air out of her cheeks slowly so she could watch cloud shapes form in front of her. There was a light snow falling and the earth felt soft beneath her feet. She'd woken up that morning feeling warm and a little light-headed. Not wanting to alarm her mother, she said nothing of it. Now, as she spat out air puffs, her throat caught, and she began to cough a rumbling cough that sounded like something coming out of a squeezebox. She felt so dizzy she thought she might fall to the ground. When she tried to catch her breath, the cough erupted again. There was a sharp pain in her ribs that made it difficult to take in more air. If she could only make it to school she'd feel better. She'd get warm and would be able to sit down. By the time she finally did get there, her legs felt rubbery, as if all of her energy was draining through them. She slumped down in her desk without removing her coat. She couldn't stop shivering or coughing. She'd cough until she ran out of breath, then suck back as much air as she could get into her lungs before the pain in her ribs seized up again.

After a while, the sound of her cough was the only thing that filled the quiet classroom. Exhausted by the pain of trying to breathe, Edith crossed her arms on her desk and cradled her head in them. She fell into a woozy sleep until the touch of her teacher's skirts against her ankles roused her from it. Fräulein Huffman leaned over. "You're not feeling so well, are you?"

"No, no, I'm fine," said Edith, embarrassed to be noticed in this way. She sat up. "Really, I'm —" But the cough intervened. Fräulein Huffman placed the back of her hand on Edith's forehead. It felt cool and reassuring, and Edith wished she would keep it there.

"You're burning up," the teacher said. "I think we need to send you home." She put her hand on Edith's shoulder. "Come now, let's get you on your way."

Edith knew she was supposed to stand up, but all she wanted to do was go back to sleep. She was ashamed of how weak she felt and hoped no one noticed. Slowly, she pulled herself onto her feet and tried to smile. "Stranger things have happened," she said. It was the other half of her thought that somehow she would make it home, though right now it was impossible to imagine.

Fräulein Huffman walked Edith into the hall. Edith leaned against the gray wooden door that led into the classroom. Her eyes fixed on the peeling paint and nicks in the wood. It seemed a world unto itself, so vast and textured. Surely, she could rest here for a while.

"Are you sure you can get home by yourself? I can have one of the other children walk with you."

Fräulein Huffman's voice came in and out like the wind.

Edith heard herself answer, "I do this every day." She tried to smile again.

A more observant teacher might have seen the strain in Edith's face or the glassiness in her eyes. But Fräulein Huffman was young and eager to please the headmaster of the school. She wanted to be seen as mature and steady under fire, not as someone who would panic just because a child had a cough. "Would you like some hot tea before you go?" she asked.

"No thanks," said Edith. "No hot tea."

"Okay then. Walk slowly and stay as warm as you can."

Edith followed the same path she took every day. It was exactly a mile and a half and took her through the forest and past a pond, nearly frozen now, that was part of the Schultz farm. After the pond, all she'd have to do was cut through the Frau Schultz's front yard, and within a few minutes, she would be home. There was an old evergreen on the property that was rumored to be over one hundred years old.

Even on this cold January morning, its generous limbs were raised toward heaven. Covered with snow, the tree looked embracing, and Edith thought that if she could lie down in it for only a minute or so, she would surely have the energy to make it the rest of the way.

She curled up in a ball, her head resting on one of the branches. Snow fell onto her cheek. It was cool against her hot skin, just like Fräulein Huffman's hand. Maybe it was Fräulein Huffman's hand.

That was the last thought she had before she fell asleep. She lay in the snow for nearly an hour. When Frau Schultz found her, she thought her young neighbor had frozen to death. She shook her, but Edith wouldn't budge. Her face had a blue cast to it; only the tip of her nose was red. There was no one around to help lift her, so Frau Schultz ran to the house and grabbed a woolen blanket. She wrapped Edith up, and when she still wouldn't move, Frau Schultz used the blanket as a sled and dragged her to the front of her house. There, Edith opened her eyes and looked around. "Come child," said Frau Schultz, placing her arms around her waist. "You must try and get up now. We'll do it together." Edith started coughing and sat up. The cough brought color to her cheeks. She spat up tiny flecks of blood that looked beautiful against the white snow. All she wanted to do was go back to sleep, but she managed to stay awake just long enough for Frau Schultz to half drag her to the bed.

Frau Schultz covered her with a quilt and left her there long enough to run across the yard and fetch Margot. "She's at my house, asleep now. I'm afraid she's not very well," she said, deciding not to mention the blood. "I'm sure once she gets some rest, she'll be fine. So let's go to my house and bring her back here together, shall we?"

Margot tried to stay calm but all she could see in front of her was the face of a stillborn girl. She grabbed her wrap off the brass hook and followed Frau Schultz out the door. It wasn't until she ran past the fence separating the two properties that she realized how snow was sloshing between her toes and her feet were becoming numb. She'd forgotten to change out of her slippers. God could take her feet, both of them, for all she cared. He could take her hands, her arms: she could bear that. She could not bear losing another child.

Frau Schultz had rushed out forgetting to close her door and Margot could see Edith's silhouette before she even reached the house. She was so still. As she came closer, she could see her face, drained of color. Margot left her slippers by the door, knelt by the bed, and took Edith's cold hand into her own. There was life in the hand. She placed her fingers on the pulse in her neck and felt its tentative beat. Frau Schultz put some water on the fire while Margot stroked Edith's brow. "I put some schnapps in the tea," she said handing Margot a cup. "It would be good if she could drink this."

As she sat at her daughter's bedside, Margot's eyes sank into her pale skin. Strands of her hair escaped her bun, floating like ribbons against the late morning sun. "Here, my *Liebchen,* drink this." She pulled Edith up by her shoulders and held the cup to her lips. "Come on, just a little." Margot was not the sort to bargain with God — theirs had been an uneasy relationship. But at that moment, she gave herself over to the possibility of mercy and miracles. "Let her live," she offered, "and I will let Gilda's memory rest in peace."

Edith opened her eyes and sipped the drink. When she had drained the cup, her mother asked if she felt strong enough to go home. Edith said that she did, and with the help of Frau Schultz, Margot swaddled her in the blanket.

They made an odd duo on that frosty

December morning: Margot in her slippered feet shuffling across the snow with her arms around her daughter, who was wrapped, ghostlike, in a brown woolen blanket.

It was pleurisy that caused the cough and fever. Dr. Mueller told Margot and Frederick that Edith would have to go to the hospital. She lay in the hospital bed for a week, her fever getting higher and the cough deeper. The doctor prescribed morphine for the pain in her ribs. "Morphine for a young girl," said Frederick, who had seen plenty of suffering in the war. "It doesn't seem right." Dr. Mueller was slumped and skinny and, except for his black mustache, looked like a man trying to disappear. When he called Margot and Frederick into his office at the end of the week, he spoke with the deliberation of someone used to giving bad news. "It is urgent that we operate as soon as possible," he said. "She is filled with infection and if we don't go in and clean it out, she will surely die."

Frederick grabbed Margot's elbow. Margot pulled her arm away. "If an operation will save her life, then of course that's what we'll do," she said.

During the eight hours that it took for the

doctor to clean up the pus and infection in Edith's ribs, Margot and Frederick sat on a backless bench outside the operating room. Frederick had brought a leather bag filled with bread, a few pieces of cheese, wurst, and flasks of coffee. In this dark place, where the sounds of rolling gurneys echoed off the walls and the narrow windows caged the noon light, Margot found comfort in the familiar packages with their garlicky offerings. They passed the time talking about their daughter's future — she would learn to play piano, take the baths at Baden-Baden, swim in the lake — and built a wall around the possibility of anything but a positive outcome. By the time Dr. Mueller emerged from the operating room, in their minds' eye, their daughter was the picture of health. Dr. Mueller pulled a cotton mask from around his mouth. His eyes sagged and his voice was more dolorous than ever. "Well, she made it," he said. Edith and Frederick rose to their feet at the same time, waiting for the inevitable "but."

"But we had to remove one of her ribs. It was rotten with infection. Don't be overly concerned, she's got twenty-three of them left."

Frederick and Margot exchanged looks. A rib? They had never considered something might happen to one of Edith's ribs. They'd worried about her lungs, naturally, even her heart and her liver, as these parts were indispensable. But a rib? There were two dozen.

One less egg in the box, thought Margot.

Frederick had seen plenty of ribs in his time. A cow without a rib, or a pig without a rib, he could imagine that. They would lean heavy to one side. "Will she be misshapen?" he asked the doctor.

Dr. Mueller rubbed his eyes. "Ah, I wouldn't call it misshapen. She will, without proper attention, become slightly stooped the way we old folks are. There will be a significant scar on her back, but there is no infection left in her body, and she will be healthy."

Edith's scar was significant. It was on the left side of her back where the second rib would be. It looked like a mouth sucking in its lower lip — an upside-down smile. Edith missed three months of school. While she was gone, the local Catholic church sent her a basket of yellow daisies. Tucked inside was a small cross made from twigs. It was such a simple and pretty design that Edith kept it by her bedside. Some of Frederick's co-workers took up a collection and bought her a quilt from a lady in the next town. The children in her class made cards for her with pictures of butterflies and chocolate cake and girls with smiling faces. Underneath their drawings, they wrote messages about her bravery and how they yearned for her to come back. But none of them came to visit her, because their parents worried that maybe Edith's pleurisy was contagious. On her first day back, she wore the same blue woolen coat she'd worn on the morning she'd fallen sick, only now her arms dangled from the coat's sleeves and her knees jutted out inches below its hem. Even in the classroom, she kept her coat wrapped around her shoulders. The weight she'd lost during her illness gave her nose and jaw a hawklike prominence.

The other kids regarded her with curiosity and kept their distance. She smelled different, had the pallor of someone who'd been locked away in a hospital. She'd had surgery and nearly died. What she knew and they didn't accounted for most of what frightened them about her. Also, it was the second week in April, and no one was wearing winter coats anymore.

Fräulein Huffman had stood up when Edith entered the classroom and had given a little bow. "So you have decided to rejoin us. We are very happy to have you back."

The night before, she'd decided to bake a cake for Edith's return. She'd told herself that she wasn't doing it out of guilt. Any teacher would do that for a student who'd been so ill. She imagined that when she presented Edith with the cake she'd be surprised. Maybe it would even make her forget how her teacher had released her into that snowy December day.

Fräulein Huffman waited until the morning had rolled into routine. Then she reached into the clothing closet and pulled out the package. "In honor of Edith's return to our class and in celebration of her good health, I have baked a cake." She smiled at Edith, and Edith smiled back. At the moment that Edith's eye met hers, Fräulein Huffman lowered her eyelids and looked to the floor again.

Pig eyes, thought Edith, who knew about reading eyes. On a good day, her mother's hazel-colored eyes were bright and focused and held her gaze. On bad days, her mother's eyes reminded her of the pig.

Once, Edith had visited her father at work. She'd wandered into the yard where there was a pig lying on the ground, legs trussed, waiting to be slaughtered. The pig's eyes were half closed and lifeless, as if he had already surrendered. Just then, she could hear her father shout to one of the other workers, "Are you crazy to let the child in here?" In a gentler tone, he said to her: "Come Edith, this is no place for you."

Now, as she looked at Fräulein Huffman standing before the cake with eyes dull and forfeiting, Edith wanted to say something that would lift the heaviness from them. She took off her coat and stood beside her desk. "Sometimes when I was sick, all I wanted to do was sleep," she said. "Now I'm so glad to be back in school with everyone." The children stared back at her.

Edith sat back down and hugged her coat around her shoulders. The children clapped. Until that moment, she'd been so pre-occupied with her own behavior that she hadn't noticed that at least half of the kids in the class had shaved heads. How large their ears looked. Only Fräulein Huffman stood impassive, twiddling a few stray hairs that had escaped her bun.

At recess, Emmy, her best friend in the class, waited for her in the back of the classroom. "Are you really fine?" she asked Edith.

"I'm tired," said Edith, letting down her guard. "Tired's okay. Everyone's tired some of the time. Right?"

Emmy nodded. "Are you in pain or anything? I mean, you're walking kind of funny."

Edith straightened her back, aware that she was favoring her left side. "It hurts here," she said, pointing to where her rib was missing. "It's kind of like a drawing, empty feeling and it hurts when I straighten up."

Emmy put her hand on her own ribcage. "I can't imagine," she said.

"My father says I'll be stooped over for the rest of my life unless I fix it now. So every day he has me walking with a cane that I hold behind my back like so." She picked up the blackboard pointer and put it behind her back, resting it in the crooks of her elbows. She walked in circles around the back of the classroom. "It'll get better as I heal," she said.

Edith realized she was talking too much. But it had been ages since she had been able to speak to someone her age. During the three months she'd been ill, all they talked about at home was her health. Sometimes, her father's boss, Gustave Reinhart, would give him some prized muttonchops at the end of the day. "The marrow is nourishing," he would say. "Give it to the girl." At dinner, Margot and Frederick would pick at the meat then pile their bones on Edith's plate and watch intently as she sucked out the fatty tissue. One of them would comment on how much stronger she was and the other would say, "I can see you getting better already." Of course she was eager to be back with other ten-year-olds.

She stopped walking and placed the pointer back on its shelf. "God, I'm just babbling on and on, aren't I?" she said to Emmy. "Tell me what's new here, what's new with you. What about the hair?"

Emmy ran her hands through her hair, which was barely a patch of fuzz. "Lice," she said. "There was a lice scare when you were gone. We all got checked for them. The headmaster said that Jews get lice more than other people so that all Jewish kids in the class had to get their heads shaved. The eight of us started something called the Baldies Club."

Edith had noticed the others with the short hair, all of them Jewish. They reminded her of dandelion seeds. "Why would Jews have lice more than other people?" she asked.

"Fräulein Huffman says there's something about Jewish blood," said Emmy. "Lice like Jewish blood. She said that there's research to prove it. Anyway, the Baldies Club is fun.

We have a secret handshake and wear gray woolen caps. Sometimes we meet after school and take hikes together or go to somebody's house. It's fun."

That night, as Edith and her parents ate dinner, she told them about her first day back at school. "They must have missed you terribly," said her father.

"I missed them, too." Edith paused. "Pappa, what do you know about lice?"

Her father scratched his head. "They live in the hair," he said. "During the war, they were responsible for a lot of typhus. Why do you ask?"

"Well, it's just that, while I was gone, there was a lice scare, and Fräulein Huffman said that Jews have lice more than other people, so she made all of the Jewish kids in the class get their heads shaved, and now they have this club called the Baldies Club. So I was wondering: Is it true that lice like our blood better than other people's?"

Her mother turned to her father. "Don't be bothered by such nonsense," he said. "You hear this kind of thing all the time; it's just ignorance, nothing that should trouble you."

Before he went off to war, Frederick had convinced Margot to turn over to the German government the one heirloom she'd inherited from her grandparents: a pair of gold candlesticks in the shape of entwining serpents. At first, she'd hesitated: "It's all that I have from them." "That's the point," he'd said. "Think how proud they would be to know they've helped in the war effort." He was a devoted patriot, and nothing — certainly no schoolgirl gossip — could shake Frederick's belief in his country.

Edith saw her mother's unease and tried to change the subject. "Anyway, tomorrow's some big assembly and we're all supposed to wear gray woolen caps. Pappa, do you have one?"

"You go look with your father," said her mother. "I'll clean up here."

Edith watched as her father pulled things from the shelves of his armoire and rummaged through an old hat box. "This must be some assembly," he said, carefully placing everything back into the armoire. "I have nothing even close. Could you perhaps make a hat?"

"Sure," said Edith. "I'll figure out something."

That night, after her parents went to bed, Edith sneaked into her mother's sewing box. She moved aside the remnants of beige muslin her mother had used for making curtains and rummaged around the spools of purple, green, and yellow thread — colors that none of them wore. Underneath the wooden darning egg, she found what she was looking for: a pair of silver scissors that had belonged to her grandmother. They were in the shape of a crane, with the blades forming its beak and the handles its long stalky legs. The scissors were no larger than her hand, but they would do the trick.

Her mother loved to sew, and she made all of her clothes by hand. When she sat at her Pfaff, her foot bearing down on the pedal as if she were tapping along with a popular song, her fingers came alive and she was as at ease as she ever was. The thought of it made Edith smile as she tucked the scissors into the pocket of her dress and carried them into her room. She sat down on her bed and, without looking in a mirror, began grabbing clumps of her hair in her hand and cutting them off. She clipped away all of her curls, then cut more and more until she could feel her scalp, soft and spongy. She chopped away as much hair as was possible to cut. After twenty minutes or so, she ran her hand over her nearly bare, thatchy scalp. There were ridges and dents on the back of her head that she'd never known were there.

It would startle her parents to see her this

way in the morning, so she swept the chunks of hair into a paper bag and hid it under her bed. Then she took the red plaid woolen scarf that her mother had kept wrapped around her neck while she was sick and wound it around her head. As she lay down, she could feel the wool bristle against her naked head. She fell asleep wondering how she'd look with her hair all gone. *I'll look like everyone else in the Baldies Club,* she thought.

Her father was the first to step into her room the next morning. Edith's back was to him, her head sunk into her pillow and the scarf pushed behind her ears. At first, he didn't notice anything different, but as she stirred he saw the back of her head, smooth but for some stubble and wisps of hair. Seeing his beautiful daughter lying there like an old man, he wanted to scream. Hadn't she suffered more than most people do in a lifetime? She couldn't know that her hair had fallen out overnight. He must break the news to her gently.

"Edith," he whispered, rubbing her shoulder. "Edith, wake up." He sat on the edge of her bed. She rolled over on her back and looked up at his worried face. She put her hand up to her head and felt that the scarf was gone. "It's okay, I know," she said to her father.

He folded his hands in his lap. "You mustn't worry. It's a common thing when someone's been so sick. It will grow back, to be sure."

Edith sat up. "It didn't fall out, Pappa. I cut it off."

"Why would you do such a thing?"

"The others are bald," she said. "If I hadn't done it, I'd be the only Jewish kid in school with hair."

He stroked her cheek. "This is a terrible thing, what they tell children these days. You mustn't let that kind of foolishness go to your head." He paused and smiled. "Well, it's safe to say it's already gone to your head."

"Yes," said Edith, banging her knuckles against her skull. "It has gone to my head. Or whatever's left of it."

"Your mother," he said. "You must find a way not to startle her."

"Okay, but what shall I tell her?"

"The truth," he said. "Tell her that you did it so you could make a show about what Fräulein Huffman said about Jews and lice, that this was your way of pointing out her foolishness."

"But it wasn't," said Edith. "I did it

because the other Jewish kids in the class had to shave their heads. If they were going to do it, so would I."

Her father leaned forward. "My Edith, I don't know whether what you've done is stupid or brave, but you will certainly make an impression on Fräulein Huffman. Come now, I have to go to work. You have to face the music."

Edith pulled the woolen scarf from under her pillow and wrapped it around her head. She would give her mother time to get used to the change. She dressed and came into the kitchen, where her mother was boiling water.

"Did you sleep well?" she asked.

"Oh very," Edith answered. "Listen, I don't want you to be mad at me, but last night I did something that you might find a little, um, strange."

Her mother turned and saw her daughter sitting at the kitchen table, the woolen scarf tied around her head. "Are you cold?" she asked. Edith shook her head no. Her mother looked again. "You have a new hairstyle. Come, take off the scarf and let me see."

Edith put her hand on top of the scarf and held it to her head. "I suppose I have a new hairstyle," she said. "Though it's not really a hairstyle at all. I mean, I guess it is a style, but not of hair." Edith pulled off her scarf. Her mother stepped closer. "God in heaven," she cried. "What did you do to yourself?"

As Edith explained, her mother's eyes narrowed with a ferocity she had rarely seen. "Listen to me," she scolded. "We are not wealthy people. Your father works hard at the store, and I do my best to keep up a good home for you. We can't afford for you to do crazy things because you think they're faddish or will keep you in good standing with the rest of your classmates. People like us have to be careful." She shook her head. "There are these disturbances from time to time, but you mustn't let them get in the way of your life. It's nothing that you have to worry about. Believe me, no one could ever accuse us of being religious Jews."

Edith wondered what her mother meant when she said, "People like us have to be careful." She gathered up her books and coat. "Don't worry Mama, I won't get into any trouble."

Outside the air was still crisp but without the bite of winter. It was the kind of morning when women threw open their windows and men pushed up their jacket sleeves. So people noticed Edith as she walked to school, still wrapped up in her blue winter coat and a woolen red-plaid scarf tied around her head.

With Frederick and Edith gone, Margot began to straighten up the house. As she made up Edith's bed, she discovered spidery strands of hair scattered about her pillow. She thought little of it until she went to clean underneath the bed. That's when her broom struck something that moved easily as if it weighed nothing. She gasped as she pulled the item from under the bed and saw that it was a bag stuffed with her daughter's curls.

Staring at the hair, Margot thought back to how terrified she'd been to try and have another child after Gilda. She believed that getting pregnant again and giving birth to Edith was the boldest thing she'd ever done. She remembered Frederick kissing her and calling her "my brave little woman," and how courageous she'd felt. Then she thought about how sick Edith had been and how hard it must have been for her to go back to school. She'd never complained about any of it. This business of her cutting off her hair was foolhardy, of course. But Margot understood that it was Edith's way of ingratiating herself with the others. The school couldn't possibly be singling out Jews like that. Anyone could get lice; it was the most common thing in the world. It must be the teacher. She was young and new and maybe a little stupid.

Edith was feeling anything but courageous as she made her way toward school that morning. Inside the classroom, she took her seat. As she had the morning before, she kept her coat wrapped around her shoulders. She removed her woolen scarf and deliberately kept her head down so no one would catch her eye. She waited for the other children to stare or laugh, but nothing happened until noon, just before lunch. Fräulein Huffman poked her on the shoulder and said, "You stay put for a moment. I want to speak with you." Edith remained in her seat as the classroom emptied.

"So, what's this all about?" asked the teacher, folding her arms in front of her chest.

"What's *what* about?"

"Don't play innocent with me, you know exactly what I'm talking about."

"Oh this," said Edith, touching her scalp. "I knew you would want to check my head for lice. I thought I would make it easier for you."

"Young lady," she said, staring at the top of Edith's head. "Are you trying to provoke me?"

"No, I'm not."

But Fräulein Huffman kept talking, as if she hadn't heard what Edith said. "Because if you are, it won't do you any good. The school has its policies and there's nothing you can do to change them. It is only because you have been ill and I am a forgiving person that I am not reporting you to the headmaster. But let me tell you, should you pull any more shenanigans like this, I will have no problem taking you to his office in person and demanding your expulsion. Is that clear?"

"Yes, Fräulein Huffman."

"Good then," she said. "We understand one another."

When Edith got home from school that day, her mother was waiting for her with a cup of tea and some of her favorite butter cookies. They sat down together at the kitchen table.

"So how did it go today?" asked her mother.

"Well, I am a member of the Baldies Club."

"And what did Fräulein Huffman have to say about your hair?"

"She said she thought I did it to get under her skin," Edith said.

Her mother's eyes softened as Edith

related the teacher's words. Then Edith let the tears come. "She was so mean. She hates me. I know she does."

"You are not the kind of child one can hate," said her mother. "It might be that Fräulein Huffman is scared about something in her own life. For all we know, she feels guilty about sending you home on your own that morning."

Edith's tears plopped into the tea. "I know she hates me and she hates all the other baldies. But I don't understand why."

"Some people are just like that," said her mother. "You can't take it personally." Then she got up and walked into her bedroom. When she returned, she kept her left hand behind her back.

"I found the bag of your hair under your bed this morning," she said, taking her seat. "And while I don't necessarily think you did the right thing by cutting off your hair, I think I was able to put the hair to good use."

She pulled her hand from behind her back.

At first, Edith didn't understand what she was seeing. It was a small pillow made from muslin in the shape of a heart. Across the heart, in bright green thread, was embroidered the word "Courage."

Edith recognized the muslin. It was the

same material her mother had used to make all of the curtains that hung in the house, the same beige material she'd found in her mother's sewing box the night before.

"My hair," cried Edith, getting up from the table and throwing her arms around her mother. "You made me a pillow filled with my hair!"

"I don't know who's a bigger fool, you or me," said her mother, hugging her back.

Edith rested her head on her mother's shoulder, and her mother rubbed her cheek against her daughter's head. It felt soft and tender, like a flower bud. Like a newborn baby.

■ ■ ■ ■

PART 3

■ ■ ■ ■

CONEY ISLAND: APRIL 1923

The seagulls flew along the horizon and were nearly indistinguishable from the flock of clouds that scuttered across the sky.

"Those birds, they're so loud and angry," said Flora. "What's all the fuss about?"

"Food. Territory. Pecking order. What's it ever about?" said Simon.

It was the first temperate day of April, a Saturday. Flora and Simon, as they did every year at this time, marked the change of season by a drive down to the beach at Coney Island. She looked smart in her summer navy-blue suit, a pair of spectator heels, and a new plum-colored hat with white petals. He looked distinguished in his gray, double-breasted, light wool coat and felt fedora. They nodded at the other couples strolling the boardwalk that day, all of them infused with the promise of spring.

They watched the gulls, eyes closed and chests puffed as they perched on pilings and let the sun bathe over them. When Flora and Simon came to a nearby bench facing the ocean, they sat down and pretty much did the same as the birds. The sun seeped through their clothes and warmed their bones, which had become weary with the cold winter months and the worries that they carried. Simon let his head drop against Flora's shoulder and fell into a half sleep. Her softness became his mother's arms. She was covering him with blankets so gently it was as if the lapping sea were embracing him. Flora placed his fedora in her lap and kissed the top of his head. He smelled like camphor and brine. She noticed his graying sideburns and how his hair was thinning on the top. He was only forty, still a young man. The thought that they could have forty more years together, that she would be there when his hair was white and the top of his head bald and smooth, settled over her and made the world seem smaller and safer than it had in a long while.

Flora hadn't heard from Margot or her mother in nearly two months. The mark had become so devalued in Germany that sending a letter to America cost nearly a billion marks. In her last letter, Flora had suggested that Margot and Frederick let young Edith spend the summer with her and Simon.

Edith was still recovering from her pleurisy, and her parents thought that the fresh air and open lawns of Yonkers might be good for her. Besides, the news out of Germany was alarming. There were reports in the newspaper that middle-class parents were allowing their daughters to hire themselves out as prostitutes so long as they were paid in butter. Adolf Hitler's National Socialist Party was doing field exercises and parading down the streets of Munich. Meanwhile, people were starving, and Hitler was using the desperate economic conditions as an excuse to pound away at the upper-middle-class Jews and Jewish "financiers." In America, the wealthy automaker Henry Ford was publicly and financially supporting Hitler's party. Reportedly, there was a photograph of him on the wall of Hitler's office. True or not, Simon bought a Buick that year instead of a Ford, which would have cost him half the price.

"Simon and I are no political experts, and we don't know what to believe from the newspapers," Flora wrote in her best German. "But for certain we know that, should you allow Edith to come, we would do everything in our power to make sure that her stay is exceptional. We urge you to consider our offer."

Edith had been only ten years old when they had visited Margot in Kaiserslautern two years earlier, but Flora and Simon had fallen in love with her. She was bright and funny and, like Flora, loved clothes and even had a predilection for modern hats.

Flora smiled as she thought about that. If she'd ever had a daughter, she would have liked her to be like Edith. Daughters become best friends, and she missed having a best girlfriend. She and Seema saw each other about once a month now. Seema had a steady boyfriend: Oliver Thomas, one of her blue-eyed boys, as she liked to call him. She lived in a fancy apartment house on Park Avenue, and she and Oliver gave lavish dinner parties. She was still pretty, but in a way that was more mannered and brittle. When she laughed, she threw her head back so that the alabaster nub of her throat was all you could see. She smoked cigarettes that dangled from Bakelite holders and she called everyone "darling." Flora was sure that Seema didn't intend to make her feel like a hick, but each time Seema called Simon "that cute little man" or where they lived "your cozy little house," Flora couldn't help but feeling somewhat diminished.

The sky suddenly became overcast and the air chilly. Simon woke abruptly, as if someone had snatched away his blankets. They sat on the bench staring out at the ocean when they caught sight of some boys on the shore. They were laughing, throwing stones at the gulls, who were still stirring up a ruckus. Flora thought she saw one of the stones nick one of the gulls' wings, but she couldn't be sure. All she said to Simon was, "I wish those boys would quit doing that." He took her arm and they left the bench, continuing their stroll down the boardwalk at a slightly brisker pace.

When the wind stirred up and the sky got molten, they decided to turn around and head back. As they neared the bench where they'd been sitting, Simon was first to notice the gull. The other birds were gone now, and his solo cry sounded plaintive as he spiraled toward the water. One of his wings was outstretched like a leg in a cast. The wing was first to hit the water and he landed gently, as if in a parachute. Flora saw what Simon was seeing and the two of them stood on the boardwalk, speechless and helpless. The gull was silent, too. He kept turning his head to look at his broken wing, opening and closing his orange beak as if with disbelief.

Gamely, he tried to lift himself out of the water, but his flapping became weaker. He was beginning to list to one side. "Stupid kids," shouted Flora, turning away. But the boys were well out of earshot, way down the shore, still throwing stones at the sky. They had hit their mark here and didn't even know it.

Simon kept staring out at the water.

"Make them stop," cried Flora, so agitated that she was walking in circles. "We should do something."

Simon buttoned up his jacket and turned up his collar. "You're right, we should do something," he said, as he watched the gull sink out of sight.

KAISERSLAUTERN:
APRIL 1923

"Oliver Thomas. What kind of a man has two first names? Not a Jewish man, I think."

Flora and Simon finally received a letter from Margot two weeks after the walk on the beach. She'd written it on onionskin stationery in a disjointed hand. It was dated March 12, 1923.

You say she lives in a house with marble floors and crystal lights that hang from the ceiling. It is not something I can imagine. Is this Oliver Thomas a nice man? Will they be married? Frederick is so kind. Without him my life would be vacant. I hope Oliver Thomas is good to Seema.

The situation in Germany is hard but we are fine. We eat well. Always meat once, sometimes two times a week. Frederick works hard. Germany will recover soon and be stronger than ever. When I told Edith that you and Simon wanted her to come to America, she jumped up and down and said how much she would like to come. It's hard for me to believe that she has not yet met Seema. I think Seema would get a kick out of her lively young niece who, by the way, is healthy and does well in school. She is a strong-willed girl who goes her own way. We would like her to come to America to visit with you and Simon when the time is right. She has such good memories of your visit here and cherishes the jewels from her Aunt Flora.

Margot finished the letter by saying:

Sometimes I look at Edith and wonder if we were ever that young and without cares. It is hard to imagine now. She has her whole life ahead, and her nature is more like yours than mine, which for her is a fortunate thing. Edith and Frederick send their best regards. We speak of you and Simon often and still have some of the peanut butter and Juicy Fruit gum that you brought from America.

Your loving sister,
Margot

Margot wondered if Flora would guess how

long it had taken her to write that letter. Writing did not come naturally to her, nor did the casual, cheerful tone she tried to affect. It was important that she not reveal the truth. Frederick would not have allowed it. The cold made her fingers so numb that she could barely grip the pencil. Her words looked like a litter of matchsticks. She hoped that her worries had not slipped through.

The situation at home was frightening. Frederick still had his job, though Rinehart had cut back his wages. Businesses were closing every day. She knew people who had lost everything. She'd report one apocalyptic story after another to her mother, who would brush her off by saying, "You don't have to believe everything you hear." At night, Frederick would reassure her: "Whatever happens, people always need to eat meat. Germany without wurst? It's not conceivable, is it?"

But that was the trouble: everything was starting to be imaginable to Margot. She didn't know whether Frederick was pretending to be calm or whether he honestly believed that all this would pass. His was such a good heart that perhaps it rejected the kinds of negative thoughts that occupied her. What would happen if Frederick lost his job? What if they couldn't afford to put food on the table? What if they froze to death? Edith was so thin that her hipbones practically jutted through her skin. She was twelve and as flat-chested as she had been at ten. Her hair had grown back, only it was thinner now, and there were spaces where you could see patches of her scalp. Margot found it hard to look at her own daughter; the sight of her only stirred up more worry. What if she got sick again? What if, this time, they didn't have enough money or food to take care of her?

She'd tell herself that she was being overly dramatic and that her mother was right, she was too gullible. Then she'd repeat what Frederick often said: This was Germany, and Germany would never let her people break in such awful ways.

She hadn't lied to Flora about the meat. They did eat it sometimes twice a week. Frederick would scavenge pieces from the neck or hindquarters of a pig or cow after they'd wrung all they could from the animal. Sometimes what he brought home was little more than bone or gristle. But no matter: he would wrap it in brown paper, place it in the center of the table, and declare, "Tonight we eat like kings." Margot would boil the scraps with potatoes, onions, paprika, and anything else she could find that would add up to a meal. Edith and Frederick would eat so fast that sometimes they used their fingers to scoop food into their mouths. Then they'd rub their stomachs and start the game. "Mmm, wasn't that the best *Rind-fleisch* with red wine sauce and mushrooms you've ever eaten?" Or "That raspberry cake with the dark chocolate icing was exactly what I had in mind for dessert." It was a game that hungry people played.

On the night that she wrote the letter to Flora, Margot had lashed out at Edith and Frederick after they'd finished a make-believe menu of sauerbraten and noodle pudding: "I am cold and hungry and so sick and tired of these silly games. Surely you see what's going on! Am I not the only one who is frightened?"

"We are all here now," said Frederick evenly. "At this moment, in this place, you and Edith and I are together and healthy. We are blessed, Margot. Don't you see that?"

Later that night, Margot bolted up in bed, her nightclothes soaked with sweat. She'd been dreaming of a man who used to live on the other side of Frau Schultz. He was sleeping, face down, in the street. One foot was bare and swollen and leaking pus.

She wanted to give him bread or some money, but she had neither. She thought he might be dead and tried to call for help. That's when she woke herself up, trying to cry out.

She wanted to wake Frederick so that he could comfort her, but as she moved closer and studied his face, she thought as she had so many times that, in sleep, he had the startling sweetness of a child. She wouldn't disturb him. Instead, she lay next to him, trying to synchronize her quick heart to his slow breathing. What seemed like hours passed until the chalky light of morning filled the room. Bad dreams were all she had to show for this sleepless night and her head throbbed behind her temples. She got up with Frederick and went with him into the kitchen, where he lit a fire.

They boiled water for a cup of what was passing for coffee these days. He took one of her feet in his hands and rubbed it in front of the fire. When it got pink, he put it down and picked up the other one. This was how they started each day. On this morning, after he massaged her feet and they poured a second cup of coffee, she pulled her hair back from her face, clasped her hands behind her head, and said, "Frederick, I've come to a decision. The time is right now. Edith should go and stay with Flora and Simon this summer."

New York City:
May 1923

The skies of New York were filled with crosses. That's what Seema noticed when she moved to the city over twenty years earlier. Every time she'd look up, there'd be the cross of St. James, the cross of St. Thomas, or the gilded cross of Trinity Church soaring over the harbor. In those years, when she worked for the White family, the only doors that were open to her were back doors. The crosses were a comfort to her. It was inspiring, the way they withstood the sun and wind and harsh winters of New York. She loved the way they looked against the early evening sky, and when robins perched on them in the spring.

She got to know each one of them by their distinct characteristics: The limestone one that hovered over the Episcopal church on Forty-third Street was dignified despite being covered with soot; the one atop the Baptist church downtown was fussy and spindly, unlike the no-nonsense iron one on top of the Lutheran church on Madison Avenue. Her favorite was the roughly hewn wooden crucifix that seemed to bear all the weight of the Catholic church on Park Avenue. Sometimes these crosses welcomed her with their outstretched arms; other times, hands on hips, they turned her away. Either way, they never failed to move her.

On bright days, the sun would bounce off the heavy bronze doors of Saint Patrick's Cathedral on Fifth Avenue and turn them gold. But it was the flickering lights of the votive candles by the entrance that always drew Seema inside. She loved the smell of the melting wax and the incense and how the light refracted through the stained-glass windows seemed to melt down the sides of the walls. It was dark, and it was the quietest place in New York City.

When Seema took the Whites' ten-year-old daughter to Saint Patrick's during one of their walks, she told her, "This is the kind of a place where you can listen to your heart." But the girl was not interested in what her heart had to say. She spent the whole time fidgeting and flipping through the pages of the prayer book looking for pictures. Seema told her that if she would be quiet for just a few more moments, she would buy her a present. So the girl barely took a breath until it was time to go.

At the back of Saint Patrick's Cathedral was a little shop that sold assorted medals and statues of Jesus and Mary Magdalene. The girl pulled Seema toward the shop. "Here, I want my present from here," she demanded.

"No. This isn't the kind of store one buys presents from," Seema said softly.

"You promised. You said if I was quiet . . ." Her shrill voice resonated in this house of whispers. Rather than make a scene, Seema followed her into the shop.

Next to the cash register was a row of wire baskets. Each one contained rosary beads. They were divided by materials — silver, glass, wood. The girl stuck her hand into one of the baskets and pulled out a crystal rosary. "I want this one."

Seema had noticed people in church rubbing their fingers over the beads and moving their lips in prayer. It felt so intimate, the way they'd sometimes lean over and kiss them. Now she picked up the crystal beads and held them in her hand. They were cool to the touch and heavy. She ran her fingers over the brass cross. All the times she'd looked at crosses, she'd never actually touched one, though she'd memorized their contours. She squeezed the cross tightly and brought her closed fist up to her cheek. She looked to see if the little White girl had noticed, but she was too busy wrapping another rosary, this one made of wood, around her fingers. "This is the one I want," she said, spinning it in the air like a lariat. "I like this one best of all. Please, you said I could have it."

Seema bought them both. The White girl spun her beads around for a few days then threw them over a doorknob. "Watch this," she said to her sister one morning, grabbing at the beads then yanking them so hard that the chain holding them together broke. The beads spilled onto the floor, rolling under chairs and behind the bed, and stayed there until years later, after the Whites moved from that house and when the new occupants, finding pieces of wood and a small brass cross scattered about, dumped them in a bag with the rest of the trash.

But Seema held onto her rosary beads long after she left the Whites. In the winter, she tucked them into her coat pocket and would close her hand around them the way other people did with a rabbit's foot. In summer, she hid the beads in her purse. When she was alone in the bathroom of a restaurant, or in the dark of a movie theater, she'd stick her hand in the purse to reassure herself that they were still there. Seema never considered herself a Catholic. She had no interest in the religion itself. The beads were reliable and familiar, and that was the point; they could have easily been a child's top for all that the symbolism meant to her. But it was the way her fingers wrapped around the cross and the perfect symmetry of its design that reassured Seema that some things in life were permanent. That it was sure to shock anyone who found her, a Jewish girl, secretly clasping a cross in her pocket only added to her mystique.

Oliver was an Episcopalian. His father had been one of John D. Rockefeller's boys, and now Oliver was a banker. He was also married, a fact that Seema kept to herself. He'd put her up in the Park Avenue apartment so she would always be nearby. That's what he said when he told her he would never marry her. He didn't say that men like him never married women like her, but he didn't have to. She knew that his wife was also an Episcopalian, that they'd grown up together in a small town outside Hartford, that they'd married one week after he graduated from Princeton. Their children were named Cornelius and Ginny, short for Virginia, and that was all she needed to know.

They had an understanding. He could tease her about anything — her accent or the funny way she held her knife and fork — and she would laugh along with him, lucky to be at the party. But under no circumstance could she ask about his wife or children. He would take her to the best speakeasies in town and introduce her to his buddies from Princeton. She was not to mention her relatives in Germany. If anyone should ask, her name was Seema Glass, not Seema Grossman. And if he was to boast about how this beautiful woman catered to all of his whims, she was to laugh and throw him a look that said his boasts were true.

Oliver insisted that there be a library in the Park Avenue apartment, though neither of them found reading books to be particularly interesting. There was a formal dining room, a master bedroom suite, and a living room that looked down Eighty-third Street and had a view of Central Park and the Metropolitan Museum of Art. When they first looked at the apartment, Seema said she had no idea what she would do with all of those rooms. Oliver winked at the real estate agent and ran his hand over Seema's stomach in a way that made the agent look away. "Don't worry, sweetie," he said. "We'll figure out something."

He was funny, Oliver. He made people around him feel as if they were at a party even when they weren't. If Seema didn't always understand his punch lines, his booming laughter immediately roped her into the joke. Despite his robust personality, everything else about Oliver was thin: his pinched nose; his lips, which sometimes disappeared into his face; his eyes, which could be brown or green depending on the light; his blond-gray hair, a color that has no name; and his body, so long and reedy that it seemed to fold in the middle. Only his head, square as a die, was thick. Or maybe it just looked that way because of his small ears and goggle-shaped rimless spectacles.

Rich men didn't have to be handsome to be considered attractive. Whenever they spoke, no matter what they said, people leaned forward to catch their words. It was no different with Oliver. Once people knew who he was, they hovered around him; even those who knew him well tended to be acquiescent and eager in his presence. Seema felt honored that he had chosen her, and he indulged her in ways that only a man of his wealth could. He loved the way diamonds shone against her throat and how

Dom Pérignon made her kisses tangy. "Where would you be without me?" It was a question he asked many times, and she would always answer, "I'd be nowhere without you. Certainly not on Park Avenue."

But his money wasn't the only thing she found alluring. She liked that she could wrap her arms around his lithe body and the way his cool fingers felt against her skin. In public, he would slip his hand under the waist of her skirt or brush her ear with his tongue as he whispered something to her. She'd blush when he'd pat her on the rear end and linger there a little too long. He was bold and unashamed about his desire and unpredictable in his lovemaking. Sometimes, he'd curl up next to her and put his head on her lap. Other times, he'd pin her down by the wrists and furiously pound his body into hers. It excited her — the sounds they made, the welts and scratches they found on each other after — and she could never get enough of him. He nicknamed her "Seema Glass, Sweet Ass," and sometimes he called her that in public.

On a rainy Sunday afternoon in early May, Seema brought Oliver to lunch with Flora and Simon at Aunt Harriet and Uncle Paul's house in Mount Kisco. For months they had been asking to meet "the famous Oliver Thomas," and when he agreed to go with her, she couldn't figure her way out of it. She tried to convince herself that Oliver would be his usual boisterous self. "I'm great with people's relatives," he assured her. "I'll have them eating out of the palm of my hand." He was swell with his Princeton friends but it was hard to picture where he and Simon would find common ground.

For lunch, Aunt Harriet served pot roast and a cucumber salad along with Margot's kugel. It got them to talking about how ill Edith had been and the desperate situation in Germany. "We're hoping she'll come here for the summer. It would do her a world of good, don't you think?" Flora had asked the group.

"She'd be crazy for Coney Island," Simon said.

"Poor little Edie," said Uncle Paul, already giving her a nickname. "We'd spoil her rotten. We'd take her to the Hippodrome and all the stores on Fifth Avenue." Seema glanced over at Oliver, waiting for him to show some interest. But Oliver sat silently with both elbows on the table, staring at the kugel. Foam from his beer washed over the lines of his mouth.

On the way home, she said to him, "You

were so quiet. Is everything okay?"

His eyes narrowed. "That was a funny little group of people."

"That's my family," she said, somewhat startled.

"I'm your family, sweetheart. Without me, you'd be living in some cute house in the middle of nowhere eating *krugel,* or whatever you people call it."

"I guess Cornelius and Ginny eat steak and caviar then," she said without thinking.

The rain was falling harder now, and in the darkness it was difficult to know exactly what happened next. Maybe a deer ran in front of the car, or the car in front of theirs had stopped abruptly. Whatever it was, Oliver slammed his foot down on the brake.

Seema lurched forward and hit the bridge of her nose on the dashboard. Her nose felt numb at first, but when she moved her head even a little, she could feel pain fill her face. The blood trickled, then gushed. It was thick and vivid and the only color she could see on this dark night. She leaned her head against the leather backrest and tried to staunch the bleeding. Something felt terribly out of place. "Broken," she said in a clogged voice.

He didn't reach over to comfort her, just stared at her and handed her his handkerchief.

After that is when Seema started to bring crosses home.

By the time Edith came to visit in early June, nearly a dozen of them were hung around the house. At first, she placed them unobtrusively: one propped up against a volume of Stephen Crane's *The Red Badge of Courage,* another in her dressing room, between two bottles of French cologne. Seema didn't pray to her crosses. Prayers imply hope for change, and at this point in her life, that wasn't a possibility. The crosses made her feel less alone. There was a miniature mother-of-pearl cross next to the icebox in the kitchen and a wooden one shoved into a shelf above the liquor cabinet in the pantry. Oliver noticed the filigreed one from Spain. "You a Catholic now?" he'd asked.

"No, I just thought it was pretty," she'd said.

"As pretty as a horse's ass," he'd answered.

Seema was good about remembering to hide the crosses before Flora visited. It used to be that she and Flora had no secrets from one another, but now it was different. Flora never told Seema how she thought it was her own fault that she and Simon couldn't have children, how she believed that the same bad blood that had killed her father was now poisoning whatever chance they had of making a baby. Seema didn't tell Flora that Oliver was married or how she worried that having her twelve-year-old niece around would disrupt her life with him. And now there were the crosses. Some things were too hard to explain, even to a sister. So, to be on the safe side, just before Edith came to New York, Seema went around the house and collected them, hiding them in the lavender tin box where she kept her nail polish, lipstick, and other makeup. She slid the box into a cabinet next to the toilet. No one would ever think of looking there.

YONKERS:
JUNE 1923

Margot rehearsed how she would say it, like a child learning her lines in a school play. She wanted to be able to tell Edith that she would be going to America for the summer in a way that made it sound like an adventure. "The child mustn't sense that we are trying to be rid of her," she said to Frederick. Mostly, she worried that Edith would pick up on her own fear, that by sending her across an ocean to a foreign country she was letting another child slip away.

So she practiced with Frederick until the words came out effortlessly. Late one afternoon after Edith came home from school, Margot was ready, though Edith was tired and hungry and had deep pockets — like wounds — under her eyes. "How was school today?" Margot asked, her voice lifting.

Edith stretched out on one of the kitchen chairs and yawned. "Emmy's father lost his job last week. They told him that business

222

was slow in the grocery store so they had to let people go, but Emmy says that because he's Jewish, they don't want him there anymore. She says they'll have no money and her mother is afraid they'll starve. Emmy says her father has been sitting in his room since it happened and won't do anything. She said that we should be careful, that Pappa could lose his job for the same reason, but I said that he'd been there for so many years that they would never let him go, even if he is Jewish. That's right, isn't it?"

Margot took a deep breath. "Oh *Liebchen,* don't become a worrier like your mother," she said. "Of course Pappa will be all right. He is the best wurst maker in the country. Can you think of Germany without wurst? It's not imaginable. Besides, let's not dwell on sad things. Let's talk about happy things, shall we? We have a surprise for you. Aunt Flora and Uncle Simon want you to come and stay with them in America for the summer. They have even booked passage for you on a ship that leaves for New York on June 2. You'll live with them in their house in Yonkers. Isn't that the best surprise?"

Margot searched her daughter's face for a hint of what she was feeling, but she saw no clue.

"Does Pappa know?" Edith asked.

"Of course he does. We've talked about it many times. We both think it would be good for you to have a change. American food is healthy, and we want you to get stronger. We know how much you love Flora and Simon and they are so eager to have you come. And finally, you'll get to meet your Aunt Seema. Can you imagine, Edith, New York City?"

Edith raised her eyebrows. Their world had gotten darker in the past few years. Suddenly there was a crack and light was streaming in.

"I don't understand. What did you say about New York City?"

"You heard me. I said Flora and Simon would like you to visit them this summer and Pappa and I think you should go."

Edith's first impulse was to throw her arms around her mother's neck and say, "Yes, I shall start packing now!" But she drew back, knowing how that might hurt her feelings. "I don't know anyone who's been to New York City," she said. "I can't imagine being away from you and Pappa, but yes, I think I would like to go."

"We'll miss you, it goes without saying," said Margot, trying to sound casual. "But New York City? An offer like this doesn't come along often."

"No, it doesn't, does it?" said Edith.

"So it's decided then," said Margot.

"I suppose it is."

Margot knew that her daughter was kind of an actress. She intuited who people wanted her to be and without any effort became that person. It came from a lifetime of anticipating and pleasing, and it served her well. Although Edith's face was impassive, Margot had to smile when she noticed how her daughter kicked her leg back and forth, like a metronome, under the table.

Early on Wednesday morning, Simon and Flora set out in their car from Yonkers to Pier 60 in New York City. Their conversation was full of optimism. Simon tried to name all the colors that made up the new greens of spring. "The blues and yellows and oranges," he said. "This is God's palette . . . when He's in a good mood." Flora tried to prepare Simon for having a twelve-year-old around. "She's somewhere between a girl and a young woman. Talk to her as an equal until she bursts into tears or runs to her room. That's when you have to go back to being the adult. Be as kind and encouraging as you can."

"You don't have to tell me how to act

around children," he said. "You remember I grew up with plenty of them." It was a painful memory and he quickly changed the subject. "Do you think we have enough food in the house?"

Their shelves were stocked with canned peaches, jars of peanut butter, and tins of sardines and tuna fish. They'd pick up some milk and some fresh whipping cream at the dairy to go with the cake Flora had baked. "Children that age eat an awful lot," said Flora. "Do you think we should have something for her for when she gets off the boat?"

"No, I'm sure they gave her plenty of food on the boat."

"Yes, but it can take a long while for a ship to pull into a port."

Simon took Flora's hand. "Miss Chatterbug," he said, "you're nervous, aren't you? It will be all right. Edith will be fine. Do you forget how famously the two of you got along when we were in Kaiserslautern?"

Flora nodded. "I love her like a daughter, but she's not my daughter. There is a difference between your own and someone else's. That you and I never had children — it's the disappointment of my life."

"You would be a great mother," said Simon.

"And you, a model father. It's my fault."

"It's nobody's fault."

"There's something about my blood," she said, running her hand over the scimitar-shaped scar on her leg. "It's what killed my father."

The first time she told Simon the story of her father and the tainted blood, Simon tried to comfort her by explaining how it was impossible that her blood could have infected her father in that way. "It's enough that you miss him. To blame yourself only adds to the sadness," he had said.

He hadn't realized that Flora thought her blood had something to do with their inability to conceive. He swallowed hard. "Flora, I won't listen to this nonsense about your blood." He pulled the car over to the side of the road and turned off the engine. "There are so many reasons people can't have children. I'm seven years older than you. For all we know, it's my fault."

Flora's voice got small. "You're yelling," she said. "I've never heard you raise your voice like that."

"I find the word *fault* awful. We're not doing anything wrong. It's nobody's *fault* that we don't have children. God knows we've tried every damn trick in the book. If I were a more religious man, I'd say it's God's will and that He has other children in mind for us to care for. We make our families where we can. In the end, whether they are our blood or someone else's, what does it matter? Our families — whoever and wherever they are — live in our hearts. If I didn't believe that . . ."

She leaned her head on his shoulder. "I believe in you. I believe in you and me."

"Sweetheart," he said, his voice softening, "I love you so much. We have a wonderful life together. Let's not dwell on what we don't have and let's enjoy what we do have."

"All right then," she said, placing her hand on his knee and looking up at his taut face. "Why don't you take off your glasses?"

"Okay, my gorgeous one," he said, ripping his glasses from behind his ears. "I'm all yours."

Flora shot him a look of mock astonishment then checked her wristwatch. "Ach, if only we had a little more time. But we should probably get this car back on the road and pick up our niece."

Flora was the first to spot Edith on the deck. She was tall and stringy, and her hair was flying in many different directions. There were dark shadows under her eyes, and it seemed to Flora that Edith had grown at least a foot since she'd last seen her. She looked older than her twelve years — a different person from the little girl Flora had met a few years before.

Simon took out his handkerchief and started waving. Flora stood on her tiptoes and shouted, "Yoo-hoo, Edith." When she finally spotted them, Edith smiled tentatively, lowering her head until her chin nearly touched her collarbone. She was carrying a duffel and wearing a white jacket over a periwinkle dress that looked as if it had been slept in for days. *I know this isn't what I should be thinking at a moment like this,* thought Flora, *but I need to buy her some nice clothes. Fix her hair. Get some food in her.*

There was little of the child left in Edith. She had the milky eyes of an old person and a slight stoop in her carriage. As they drove back to Yonkers, Flora tried to talk with her in German. *"Wie geht es deine Familie?"* she asked. Edith nodded, said *"Gut,"* and kept staring out the back window. "What news of my sister, *meine Schwester.*" Again Edith nodded and mumbled, *"Gut."* Edith had picked up English quickly when they'd visited her in Kaiserslautern, so Flora wasn't sure how much she understood. *Oh my God, what have we gotten ourselves into,* she thought and shot Simon a look that said the same thing. For the next forty-five minutes, they traveled in silence.

When they arrived at the house, Simon carried Edith's bag into Flora's sewing room. She had moved her sewing machine into the other bedroom and had bought a bedspread covered with peonies and a lamp whose wooden base was carved in the shape of a cat. She'd framed some of Simon's drawings and emptied the closet for all of Edith's clothes. If Edith noticed the girly flourishes in her room, she didn't say. Flora said, "You must be starving," and made her a bologna sandwich and poured a glass of milk. Edith took one bite of the sandwich, then put it on the plate and pushed it away. It went like that at dinnertime, too, when Flora tried to feed Edith a breaded veal cutlet with mashed potatoes and canned peas. For the next few days, every time Flora would set down food — fruit, cheese, chocolate cake, apple pie — in front of her, Edith would take a bite or two and then turn it away. Sometimes she said, *"Nein, danke."* Other times she said nothing. Mostly, all she did was sleep.

On Saturday morning, after Flora had made scrambled eggs with fresh chives from the garden and fried potatoes, Edith covered her mouth with her hands and refused to take a bite. "I give up," cried Flora. "I'm not trying to poison you." Edith froze. Her eyes widened. Simon turned abruptly toward Flora, who put her head in her hands and shook it. "I'm sorry. I'm sorry I lost my temper, but really, I'm at my wit's end. You're going to starve to death if you keep on like this."

Something about Edith's wild eyes was familiar to him. He remembered the little girl Rita from the boat, and the way she would scream, particularly late at night. "She's scared," said Simon, gently squeezing Edith's shoulder. "This is probably more food than she's had in six months. She'll come around. Make what she's used to."

That afternoon, Flora baked a chocolate walnut cake — an old recipe of her mother's. She went to the butcher and bought kosher salami, the closest thing to wurst she could find. She also bought a loaf of black pumpernickel bread, some vegetable soup, and a jar of orange marmalade. At dinner, as Edith ate the soup with the bread, Flora unconsciously imitated Edith each time she opened and closed her mouth to chew. Simon smiled, feeling the same pride as she did. From then on, they did what all families do: talked while they ate and now and then sampled things from one another's plate.

On Sunday, Simon drove them to the part of Nyack that looked over the Hudson River. He explained to Edith that in this river, unlike in most rivers, the current flowed both ways. They stood at the river's edge long enough to watch a barge go by. Flora thought she saw a giant bluefish, and Edith threw rocks into the water — overhand, not like a girl — each time trying to out-distance herself.

On the way back to Yonkers, they went past a horse farm. Flora and Simon had stopped here often to watch the horses, sometimes to feed them, and now there were new foals. Simon pulled over and got out of the car. He walked up to the fence, propped his elbows on it, and leaned in. Then he turned and beckoned for Edith and Flora. They tiptoed toward him and listened as he clicked his tongue against the back of his palate making a *clock-clock* sound. The mare, silky chestnut with a coal-black mane, flicked her ears as if shushing away a fly. Simon kept on until the mare put her head down and walked slowly toward him, her shaky-legged colt trotting close behind. When they reached the fence, Simon stuck out his hand and patted the mare on the bridge of her nose. He looked at Edith and raised his eyebrows, as if to ask, *Want to try this?*

Because of the work her father did, Edith's only experience with animals was with dead ones. She hesitated at first and then let Simon take her hand and place it on the horse's nose. It was cold and wet, with a bridge that was hard and bristly. Edith rubbed it again, this time on her own. The horse tucked its head and butted Edith's arm as if trying to snuggle underneath it. "She likes you," said Simon. Edith smiled and Simon winked at Flora as the two of them headed toward the car. Edith lingered behind and tried to copy the *clock-clock* sound, but the mare and her colt wandered to the farthest side of the meadow.

On Monday morning, Simon left for work before Edith was awake. It would be the first time Edith and Flora would be alone, and still, Edith had barely spoken a word. "What if she doesn't talk to me?" Flora asked Simon.

"You'll think of something," he said.

When Edith woke up, well after ten, Flora was ready to make her some hot farina. "No please," said Edith, holding her hands up as if to say, *Stop.* They were the first words of English she'd uttered since she arrived.

"Toast then?" said Flora, holding up a

piece of bread and pointing to the toaster.

"Toast then," said Edith.

The toast popped out of the toaster blackened on both sides. "Oops, burned it," said Flora.

"Oops, burned it," repeated Edith.

The two of them looked at each other in surprise. Flora started to laugh. Edith smiled, not sure if Flora was laughing with her or teasing her. Flora pointed to the butter and then to the toast. "Butter for the toast?"

"Butter for the toast?"

"Good," said Flora. "We'll speak English."

"English," said Edith.

Flora nodded. She understood that Edith wanted to be American while she was here, not a foreigner. She remembered that when she had come to America over twenty years earlier, she'd felt the same way. So for the next few days, Flora concentrated on making Edith an American girl. She bought her two frocks, a pair of white linen trousers, and a new cloche. She took her to the beauty salon, where she got her hair cut in a short, fashionable bob. All the while, she spoke to her in English, and Edith would either repeat Flora's words or answer back with her own.

At home, Flora played songs like

"Swanee" and "I'll Build a Stairway to Paradise" on the phonograph. When she put on a record of the latest hit, "Yes! We Have No Bananas," Flora started dancing. Her hands flew in the air. She turned her knees and toes inward, kicked her legs up in the air, shifting from side to side to the music. Edith laughed at the crazy sight of her aunt. Flora laughed, too, but she kept dancing. "It's called the Charleston," she said, breathless. "It's a popular dance."

Edith began tapping her feet and swaying in place without even realizing it. Flora extended her hands and Edith took them, falling into her own knock-kneed version of the dance. When the record was finished, Flora lifted the phonograph arm. "One more time." Again, they danced to the banana song, and when it ended, Flora flopped onto the couch while Edith ran to the phonograph and cried, "One more time."

Over the next days, Edith still had trouble digesting the peaches, French toast, and farina that Flora put before her, but her appetite for any American experience was insatiable. She spent a day walking with Flora, looking at the skyscrapers and running her fingers over the limestone bases of the buildings. When they rode the subway,

Flora had to nudge her so that she'd stop staring at the Negro men who often sat across from them. She loved the smell of the exhaust fumes from the buses and how, when they stood at Thirty-fourth Street and Fifth Avenue, they could look uptown and see nothing but a ribbon of people moving up and down. She gobbled up the language and spat it back as fast as Flora could feed it to her.

Flora talked to her in the overly pleasant way that people with no children talk to other people's children. "How's your mother's health?" she'd ask.

"She is good. She comes to America," Edith would answer, knowing how unlikely that was.

"And your father?"

"He is good, too. He works hard."

Flora never pushed and Edith never told the truth, afraid that if she admitted how frightened her mother was, how she worried about her father, then this new world of Flora, Simon, and New York would somehow deflate. They understood each other, and neither dared to ask the questions that really preoccupied them.

Why was Edith was so thin? Was she getting enough food? Did her parents have enough money? Was Margot still taking to bed with her terrible headaches?

Why didn't Flora and Simon have children? Why had Flora left her mother and sister alone in Kaiserslautern? Did Flora have any idea what her mother would say if she saw the house in Yonkers with its wood-paneled den and sweet honey locust bushes in the front yard? And what about Simon? Where was his family? Why didn't he ever talk about them?

As long as these questions remained unasked, both of them could fill in the blanks as they wished and keep their worlds in order.

By Edith's second week in New York, Simon noticed that the dark circles beneath her eyes were fading. "I have a surprise for you," he said one night just after coming home from work. "Baseball. You know about baseball?" Flora pretended to swing a bat as he spoke. "Baseball," she said again. Edith had no idea about this baseball but nodded anyway and said, "Ah, baseball."

He reached into his vest pocket and pulled out an envelope. "What I have here," he said, waving the envelope in the air, "well, let's just say that what I have here is something most New Yorkers would give their eyeteeth to have." Flora pointed to her own canine teeth, but Edith couldn't imagine what teeth had to do with eyes, or what this baseball was. Simon continued in his overly dramatic voice. "What I have here are two tickets to Yankee Stadium for Saturday afternoon. And we all know who plays in Yankee Stadium . . . the Great Bambino!"

"Oh Simon," cried Flora. "How on earth did you do that? Edith, you are in for the treat of a lifetime."

Yankee Stadium had opened in the Bronx only two months earlier. The Yanks' Babe Ruth, the baseball player with the mighty body and hound-dog face who flew around the bases on short spindly legs, was a New York sensation. He already had ten home runs this season, an unheard of amount in so short a time.

Simon turned to Edith. "I have a friend who has a friend. How could our esteemed guest from Kaiserslautern visit New York City without seeing a baseball game? It just wouldn't be right." Flora gave Edith a look and shrugged as if to say, *I can't believe it either. Isn't he amazing?* Then she threw her arms around Simon and kissed his neck. Edith enjoyed how easy they were in front of her and how they seemed to please one another effortlessly. Simon was always telling Flora how beautiful she looked; Flora would tell Edith what a clever man he was.

238

It made Edith sad that they didn't have children of their own.

Edith couldn't imagine how she would ever describe Yankee Stadium to her parents. It was oversized in the way that things in America were. But the colors — that's what fixed in her memory. The sky, framed by the stadium's decks, seemed bluer than a child's drawing, and the clouds were so full they looked as if someone had blown them up. The packed bleachers reminded her of her mother's embroideries, each person a different needle prick of color. Simon had tried to explain the game to her, which seemed unnecessarily complicated and beside the point compared with all the other distractions. People ate peanuts and threw the shells on the floor. There were more Negroes in the stands than she had seen in her life.

In the third inning, Babe Ruth hit a ball so high it disappeared into the clouds. People yelled and stomped their feet so hard Edith worried that the stadium would crack. Simon jumped from his seat, cupped his mouth with his hands, and screamed, "At-taboy, Babe." The announcer said over the PA system that there were nearly fifty thousand people in the stadium that day.

Edith guessed that was more people than in all of Germany. After the seventh inning, the crowd stood up and sang "Take Me Out to the Ball Game." They all knew the words, and when they sang, "Let me root, root, root for the Yankees," they raised their voices and pumped their fists in the air. Just before the end of the game, Babe hit another homer. Edith jumped to her feet with Simon and, together, they cried, "Attaboy, Babe." They turned to each other and laughed. Simon thought, *So this is what it would be like to have a daughter.*

Edith had felt joy before, but it was always something quiet and private. She had never seen it splayed out before her this way with thousands of other people apparently feeling as she did. Life in Kaiserslautern was filled with muted greens and browns and hushed voices. After this day, her America was loud and gaudy and permeated with the blazing white lights of the electronic scoreboard in right-center field. Although she never would quite understand the rules of baseball, she became a diehard Yankees fan nonetheless.

New York City:
July 1923

Could there ever be anything more dazzling than Yankee Stadium? That would be impossible, thought Edith. But that was before she was introduced to her Aunt Seema on Park Avenue a few days later. First of all, there was the doorman in a gray coat and matching cap. His sleeves were too long, the coat hung below his knees, and the cap hid most of his face. Only the sweat that dribbled down his forehead and clung to the tip of his nose gave away his discomfort at wearing a wool coat and cap on this sweltering morning. "We're here to see Seema Grossman," said Flora.

"Grossman. Grossman." The doorman studied a leather-bound notebook that he kept behind a mahogany podium. He ran his fingers up and down the column of names, while shaking his head. "I'm sorry, madam, but I don't think we have anybody of that name in this building." He spoke in

241

a formal, overly enunciated English, which seemed to irritate Flora.

"Grossman. Seema Grossman. She lives on the sixth floor." Her voice was filled with bees. "I am her sister, and I've visited her here many times before."

He raised his head suddenly and Edith could see how the sweat stained the rim of his collar. "Ah, Grossman. You mean 6-A. We have her down as Seema Glass." He picked up an earpiece and pushed some buttons on a switchboard. "Who shall I say is calling?"

"You shall say it is her sister, Flora *Grossman* Phelps, and her niece, Edith." Flora's mouth tightened as she waited for the doorman's reply.

Edith would have kept staring at the doorman and her agitated aunt, but the mural behind them suddenly caught her attention. It was a painting of statues. One of the statues was of a naked young man. Naked! She'd never seen a naked boy before. Only once had she glimpsed a penis, and that was when she had sat opposite her friend Franz in a rowboat last summer. He had been wearing shorts and his legs had been spread as he rowed the boat. Suddenly, there it was, a reddish purple blob like an overcooked knockwurst lying not two feet away from her face. Poor Franz, he had just kept prattling on and on about his trip to St. Moritz and how he had learned to ski, never suspecting that the reason Edith's face had become flushed had less to do with the Alps and everything to do with knockwurst.

Then, it had felt like worms in her stomach. She had been afraid to stare for too long. Now, she could stare all she wanted. The penis in this painting was more streamlined, more elegant than what she had seen in the rowboat. It pleased her to look at it and she wished she could get a little closer. Just then Flora nudged her. "Art. Do you like art?" she said, not seeming to notice how Edith was blushing. "We'll have to take you to the Metropolitan Museum of Art sometime. C'mon now, it's a little stuffy down here." She turned and glowered at the doorman. "Let's go up and see Seema."

The elevator rumbled and shimmied and Edith, who had never ridden in one, clung to the brass railing. Flora paid her no attention and kept tapping her foot as if she were keeping time to some song in her head. When they reached apartment 6-A, Flora jammed the bell several times. From the other side of the door came the sound of someone running and an eager voice shouting, "Hold your horses, I'm coming, I'm coming." Then a svelte figure wearing a clinging long coral silk robe and apparently not much underneath answered the door. Her fingers were pale with a perfect crescent moon on each buffed nail. The smell of cigarettes and lilies and something bitter gathered around her. She had black shiny hair and green eyes. But it was her lips that Edith noticed first, thick lips that fanned out into a cherry red smile — just like an American movie star.

So this was Seema.

"What's this 'Miss Glass' nonsense all about?" Flora demanded, before they were even inside the apartment.

"It's simpler to spell Glass than Grossman," said Seema. "Besides, people have trouble pronouncing Grossman. Oliver and I thought we'd make it easier for everyone."

"Oh really? Gross Man. How hard is that to say?"

"Flora, it's no big deal, honestly." She placed her hand on Flora's shoulder and gently pushed her aside. "And you're Edith," she said, her voice rising. "I am so happy to finally meet you." She studied Edith as if she were looking at her own reflection in the mirror. "It's odd, you resemble Flora the most, yet everything about you looks familiar. You don't look so bad for someone who's had whatever that was you had."

She is perfect, thought Edith, who did not yet know the English word for "seamless."

They might have stood at the door all morning if Flora hadn't said to Seema, "Aren't you going to invite us inside?"

"Oh, of course. I was just staring at our niece. You didn't tell me she was so pretty. She does have a lot of Glass — I mean Grossman — in her, doesn't she?"

Was that a slight smirk on her face? Edith couldn't tell.

Flora placed them back to back. "The two of you are about the same height, both of you skin and bones. She's got my eyes. Her hair is more like mine than yours, though all of us have the same brainy forehead. How about that? I think she's got your nose."

Seema flinched. She hadn't gotten used to her new imperfection. She studied Edith's nose. It was definitely a Jewish one. She wondered if hers gave her away as concisely.

Flora continued, "Lucky girl, she's inherited her mother's gorgeous long legs." Now it was Edith's turn to start. Her mother seemed so old and unstylish compared with her two beautiful sisters. She wondered if they knew how consumed she was with worry, how shrunken her world had become. "She comes to America," she said, hoping they would believe her.

Flora ignored the comment, as she was in a hurry to move on with her plan. "I'm going to let you two girls catch up on the last twelve years by yourselves. I'll just be in the way." She laughed, trying to disguise her relief at escaping. She would go downtown and window-shop, buy herself a new hat maybe. She could use the break: Edith had not left her side in the weeks since she'd arrived. Children took up an awful lot of time; she hadn't quite realized that.

Seema was alarmed at being left alone with Edith. What would they say to each other? How much English did Edith understand? She didn't know a lot about Edith other than that she'd been sick and had to have her rib removed. Pleurisy, or something like that. She would ask about Edith's life and hope that Edith wouldn't ask about hers. "Come, let's sit down," she said, pointing to the couch. But Edith remained standing, looking out the window straight across Eighty-third Street. She pointed to the large building on the edge of Central Park. Seema craned her neck. "That's the Metropolitan Museum of Art," she said. "Art." She raised her voice and spoke slowly. "Do you like art?"

Until twenty minutes earlier, Edith had never thought about art. But that was before she'd seen the mural. "I like art." She grinned. Buoyed by the passion in her niece's voice, Sema ventured, "What else do you like?"

Edith gestured as if she was swinging a tennis racket. Then she made swimming motions with her arms. She lifted her left arm. "Not good," she said, then lifted both arms to show how she could only raise the left one to about three quarters the height of the right one. "Pappa says I get crooked." She stood up and walked around the room stooped over. Seema shook her head and laughed. Edith exaggerated her movements, placing her hand on her back and lurching around the room like a hunchback. Seema laughed harder as she tucked one leg underneath her.

Edith knew she was going on too much. Between meeting a new person and trying to converse in English, she was nervous, and when she got nervous, she fell back on what she knew how to do best, which was to ingratiate herself. She was particularly eager to delight this woman. What could she tell Seema that Seema would find interesting?

The Baldies' Club! That was some story. The trick was to tell it in a way she would understand.

She knew the English word for school, and as she talked about Fräulein Huffman, she puffed out her chest and pursed her lips together. "Oh, Fräulein Huffman, your teacher. I get it," said Seema.

Then she ran her fingers through her hair as if they were crawling bugs. Going back into her Fräulein Huffman pose, she made a chopping scissors motion with her hands. This was becoming like a game, and Seema grew excited as she deciphered Edith's clues. "Your teacher," she shouted. "She cut your hair!" Edith repeated the crawly bugs gesture and Seema guessed that it was lice. Only after Edith repeated the motions and said the words *"Das Juden"* a few times did Seema also understand that it was the Jewish children who had to shave their heads. "So you were bald?" she asked.

"Yes. Bald. All the hair gone. My mother makes a pillow from my hair." Then she pointed to the hurt spot on her back and walked her funny walk.

"And your rib," said Seema, running her hands over her own ribs. "Well, you must have been quite a sight." It was a dumb remark, but she was so taken aback by what she was hearing, she didn't know what to say. She hadn't heard about the hair or the lice and wondered what else she didn't know.

Edith kept on. She pointed to the same spot on her back that she had articulated earlier, and then to Seema.

"Do I want to see your scar? Is that what you're asking me?"

Edith knotted her brow.

"Scar." Seema made a slashing motion against her stomach. Edith got up and took a pad and pencil from the nearby desk. She handed it to Seema. "Scar," she said, indicating she wanted Seema to write it. So Seema printed the word and handed it back to her. Underneath "SCAR," Edith drew a picture of a girl with a smile on her face. The she drew an arrow pointing to the smile and wrote, "*Mein* scar." Again she pointed to the place on her back and said, "I show you."

Seema studied the picture. "I see, so your scar is a smiling face." She reached over to an ebony box on the coffee table, opened it, and pulled out a cigarette. She bent her head as she lit a match, cupped her hand around the tip of the cigarette, and inhaled. Her glossy black hair fell in front of her face and her movements were slow and silky.

When her robe fell open revealing her knee and most of her thigh, she didn't pull it closed. Edith had never seen a woman this mysterious and beautiful. Although her mother was also slim, she carried herself heavily, as if bundled in the doorman's oversized coat. Her mother had often told her what a beauty Seema was and that she "had a way with the men." Edith never knew what that meant, but sitting here this close to her, she felt privileged. Seema caught Edith staring at her. She tilted back her head, exhaled the cigarette smoke, and said, "Sure, I'd love to see your scar."

The way Seema looked at her, not straight on but out of the corner of her eyes, made Edith think of the mural she had seen downstairs. *Things forbidden,* she thought. *Her eyes have seen things forbidden.*

"I show you," Edith repeated. She got down on the floor on all fours and put her head on the Persian rug, preparing to do a headstand. The carpet tickled her scalp and smelled of cigar smoke. She was wearing one of the chemises that Flora had bought her, and as she kicked her long legs up in the air, she became aware of the chemise slipping over her body. She would be naked but for her knickers, though it was not the kind of thing that would embarrass her.

Since her illness, she'd gotten used to all sorts of people seeing her undressed and prodding her in private places. Besides, Seema was a relative. So she stood straight as an exclamation point as her chemise gathered around her head.

Seema hadn't considered what she was asking Edith to do when she said she'd love to see her scar; she had merely been trying to make conversation. Now this young girl was standing upside down before her. Seema stared at her scrawny ribcage. And her arms, whispers of flesh so slight Seema wondered how they could support her. Edith kicked her legs back and forth. Her face turned purple.

Seema's eyes wandered to Edith's back. She had the smooth skin of a child except for the left side of her back, which was the color of bananas. Embedded in the banana skin was a red gouge and sloppy Xs that looked as if someone had used a shovel to hack out a piece of her back. This was not what Edith had described. It looked gaping and toothless: nothing smiley about it.

Seema tempered her voice. "Yes, I see it," she said. "Very impressive. And the head-stand. I don't believe I've ever seen anyone stand on their head for so long."

Edith allowed her legs to fall to the floor.

251

She straightened her dress and ran her hands through her hair. "Is good?" She pointed to the picture of the smiling face she had drawn. "Jah?"

"The real McCoy," said Seema. "A smiling face if I ever saw one." Seema's laugh was tense. There was something about this young girl and the shabby things that had been done to her that made Seema want to cry. She felt a swift kick of shame for allowing Edith to show her nakedness, her ugly wound. Life had borne down hard on Edith, yet she seemed unaware of it. There was no self-pity or sadness about her. In fact, she was joyful, someone who could see the colors in blackness and make jokes out of misery. Seema imagined the doctors butchering her — one of their charity cases — as they chatted among themselves and took as little time as possible. A poor girl. A Jew girl at that. Seema could picture it all too well and it made her heart hurt.

"I have scars, too," said Seema, wanting to return Edith's intimacy.

Edith lifted herself off the rug and moved closer to Seema. "You? Scar?"

For a moment, Seema dropped her elegant pose on the couch and slumped back into the pillows. She considered what she was about to do and wondered if Edith was old enough to understand. She didn't want to frighten her. More than that, she worried about whether Edith might judge her. "Well, they're different kinds of scars. You might not really call them scars. They're more like secrets. My secrets. Things that nobody knows about me, things nobody has ever seen."

Everything involved with trusting another person went against Seema's nature, but for some reason, she felt safe with Edith. The girl seemed kind, not the type to look for the flaws in others and then ridicule them. If she did what she was about to do, the two of them would be even. She would reveal something about herself. Not the slapdash work of a surgeon, but something personal that she'd never meant for anyone to see.

Seema took Edith by the hand and led her into the bathroom, where she knelt down in front of the cabinet next to the toilet. Edith couldn't imagine why Seema had brought her here. All she knew was that there was urgency in Seema's voice and that she held her hand too tight, as if she were rushing a child across the street. One month before she'd come to America, Edith had begun to menstruate. Even though her mother had told her that all girls her age menstruated, Edith found the sight of the reddish brown bloodstain in her pants as terrifying as it was mortifying. With the same fervor that she had begged her mother not to tell her father, she prayed that Seema would not pull something out of the bathroom cabinet that would have to do with menstruation or any of the other private things that women kept hidden in their bathrooms.

For a moment, it seemed as if her prayer would go unanswered, as Seema pulled from the cabinet a lavender tin big enough to hold the secrets of all womanhood. She put the tin in her lap then handed something to Edith, who was standing by the porcelain sink. It was a cross, made out of stone the color of a blackboard. Then she handed Edith another, this one green, and another, mother of pearl. Seema kept her head down as she handed Edith one cross after another. When she was finished — there must have been twenty of them in all — Seema lifted her face. "There they are, my scars. My secrets. Now you'll really have something to write home about, won't you?"

Edith didn't understand what Seema said, only that her voice got gruffer and she kept studying Edith's face. Edith remembered the basket of yellow daisies the Catholic church at home had sent to her when she was sick. A cross made from twigs had been tucked inside it. She had liked the twig cross because it had reminded her of the forest, so she kept it by her bedside. When her father noticed it, he'd snatched it away. "We don't keep these kinds of things in this house." It wasn't like her father to be so harsh. Although she hadn't understood why, she had felt ashamed at the time. Now, as she watched her Aunt Seema act so on edge, she thought that she must feel the same way.

Seema watched Edith study each one of the crosses. "Ahh," she nodded at the mother-of-pearl cross and the one made out of black onyx. *"Sehr hubsch."* At others, like the one made out of painted tin, she shook her head and said nothing.

In this way Edith and Seema became friends. Edith recognized the sadness that filled her aunt. It was silent but constant, like the cigarette smoke around her. Edith carried her sadness in silence, too, but hers had definition. What they shared was the belief that their grievances were an indulgence to which they were not entitled. Edith hid hers behind her cheerfulness and friendliness. Seema chose other ways to keep hers under wraps. It snuck into her laughter, girlish but brittle, and her eyes, alluring yet distant. She was different from her mother, who, it seemed to Edith, had cause to be anxious. Edith couldn't imagine what would make a woman like Seema this disappointed. Yet as different as they were in age and personality, there was an immediate intimacy between them that happens when two people look inside each other and see shadows of themselves. Seema was confident that Edith would never mention her collection of crosses to anyone. Certainly, Seema would never talk about Edith's headstand.

The summer of 1923 was a summer of firsts for Edith. She tasted a tuna fish sandwich, ogled the naked Greek boys at the Museum of Art, sipped a martini at a picnic with Seema and her friends; washed a car with Uncle Paul, and bought a brassiere with Flora. Nearly every Sunday, they'd drive to Mount Kisco for dinner at Hannah and Paul's. Lev and Ruth were there once and treated her as if they'd known her forever. Simon said those dinners were the closest thing to Thanksgiving. And then there was the magic.

Late on the first Saturday in July, Simon announced that they would be going to a special celebration. "Have you ever seen magic up close?" he asked Edith. When she said no, he told her that she was about to see a spectacle that she would never forget.

Edith looked quizzically at Flora, who shrugged her shoulders and said, "Don't look at me. Your uncle's the magician."

They drove to a park right on the Hudson River, where hundreds of people were already sprawled out on blankets. Children ran barefoot in the grass while the adults pulled sandwiches and bottles of wine from the oversized wicker baskets that they'd brought with them. Flora, Simon, and Edith sat as close to the water as they could. The sun was starting to set, leaving in its wake plumes of purple, yellow, and orange. They unpacked their own wicker basket and ate the feast that Flora had prepared: fried chicken, potato salad, coleslaw, baked beans, and a blueberry pie. It was almost dark by the time they finished and as Edith scraped the last of the blueberries from her plate Simon moved closer to and whispered, "Are you ready?"

"Ready for what?"

"You'll see," he said.

Just then, the band started to play brassy marching songs. The people on the blankets clapped their hands to the music; some sang along. A sound like a gunshot rang out

257

before the sky exploded into neon yellows, pinks, blues, and purples. Edith jumped. Was someone shooting at them from the river? Had the sunset imploded?

Simon put his arm around her. "Happy Fourth of July," he said, watching as her jaw hung open and the reflection of the pyrotechnics sparkled in her eyes.

Later, as they waited in traffic with the rest of the crowd, Simon explained that nearly 150 years ago, on July Fourth, the United States had signed a document making them independent from the British. "There's nothing Americans are more proud of than their freedom," he said.

"What about baseball?" asked Edith.

Simon laughed. "That's my girl." She smiled a purple blueberry smile back at him. Something tugged at his heart. It was the same feeling he had whenever he thought about his mother or his sister with the purple bow.

But miraculously, this child Edith was sitting right next to him.

NEW YORK CITY:
AUGUST 1923

An autumn chill blew in through Seema's
living room window as she and Flora sat
and talked on the last Thursday in August.
The day before, Edith had sailed back to
Germany. They had all gone to see her off
at Pier 49: Flora, Seema, Simon, Aunt Hannah, and Uncle Paul. The women cried, and
so did Edith. Simon dabbed his eyes with
his handkerchief and made a point of
mentioning his allergies. "He's a softie at
heart," Flora said to Seema, "though he'd
prefer to keep that to himself. But Edith
and he . . ." she stared as if she were fixed
on an image straight ahead. "Well, it made
me see what a good father he could be. The
two of them had something special between
them. Neither of them said anything, it's
just one of those things you know when you
see it. She could make him laugh and tease
him out of his serious moods. She followed
him like a puppy and hung on to his every

word. You know how guarded Simon is — a picket fence around him when it comes to human emotions. Sometimes I think that he doesn't let himself get close to other people because he can't stand the thought of losing them. But Edith . . ." She held her hands over her heart. "She just wormed her way in there. Like a daughter. Do you know what I mean?"

Seema bit into a piece of praline candy. A morsel lodged in her teeth and she tried to pry it out. So like Flora, Miss Chatterbug, to keep talking no matter what. Seema loosened the gob then handed the box of candy to Flora. "You ought to try this," she said. "Oliver brought it back from New Orleans."

"Simon told her that when she was sixteen, she should move to America and work for him," Flora continued. "He said he'd teach her everything she needs to know about business and numbers and all that. Says she has a real talent in that direction, he can tell." She broke off a piece of candy as she talked and seemed to swallow it whole.

"He told her that we'd go visit her in Kaiserslautern before that. Have you thought about going back there, Seema?" She snapped off another piece of the candy and, this time, chewed it more slowly. Just for a moment, it diverted her attention. "What did you say this was?"

"Praline," said Seema, studying the cocoa-colored box. "Oliver brought it back from New Orleans."

"It's good. A little too sweet, but I like the pecans."

"Even Oliver liked her," said Seema, grabbing the conversation away from Flora. "At first he wasn't that interested in meeting her."

She quickly corrected herself. "What I mean is that he was so busy with work. But then, one night when she stayed over, he happened to come by. You know how people always get polite and reserved around Oliver? Edith didn't. She acted as if she'd known him always. Asked him rude questions like how come his hair was so stiff and where did his father work. He was charmed by her. Thought she was pretty." Seema blushed and tried to hide her smile. "He said we looked alike."

The two of them talked until the sun set and they found themselves sitting in Seema's darkened living room with an empty box of praline candies. They talked about things they hadn't discussed in years. Flora confided to Seema that, while she was proud of Simon's success, it sometimes made her feel irrelevant. "I am a nobody. I am nobody's mother. I love being Simon's wife, of course, but I need something more. Something of my own."

And for the first time, Seema spoke freely about Oliver. "I know you don't like him. None of you do. He was so, well, you know, reserved that time he came to Aunt Hannah and Uncle Paul's. But he makes me laugh, Flora. He's an educated man and people respect him and that makes me feel important. So he has things about him that aren't perfect, but he thinks I'm beautiful, and let's be honest, I couldn't afford this lifestyle without him."

The two women studied each other in the dark. "With his help, I can even afford electric lights," she said.

But neither of them moved to switch one on. They didn't want to break the mood and stop the conversation. It was the most intimate they'd been since Flora's wedding, fourteen years before.

"I see that," said Flora. "He makes you feel like a somebody. That's good. But I don't understand why you use the name Glass? Is that his idea? Does he think Grossman is too Jewish?"

"Oh, don't be a silly," said Seema, falling

into the condescending tone Flora hated so much. "Oliver and his friends have nicknames for everyone. That's just the way they are."

Seema leaned over as if she were going to tell Flora a secret. "I'll tell you what Oliver calls me if you don't repeat it to anyone. He calls me 'Seema Glass, Sweet Ass.' Isn't that funny? I mean, darling, really?"

Flora thought about "Sweet Ass" and all it implied. She'd fallen in love with Simon when she was so young that it was exuberance more than sex that fueled their union. She was certain that he loved her. And there was sex in their marriage always, plenty of it. But "Sweet Ass" was dirty, vulgar in a way that was strangely arousing to Flora. She wondered what it would be like to have a man regard her *that* way. Simon always told her how beautiful she was, how he loved her womanly body. He said she was so "warm and giving in the lovemaking department." But it all sounded so clean and almost clinical compared with "Sweet Ass." She wondered how she'd react if a man talked to her that way.

But she wasn't that kind of a woman. Even if she spent a fortune for hats at Wanamaker's or could figure out how to imitate her sister's walk or girlish way of speaking, it was the last thing in the world that she would ever be. Seema was a real seductress. Her presence demanded comment, just as a chord progression insists upon resolution. Men were always whispering things to her, giving her sidelong glances. How could they not? Even her choice of language was exciting. *Isn't that funny? I mean, darling, really?* Words like that from the lips of a woman like Seema could go to a man's head.

Oliver was no looker, but judging from the strange way Seema smiled whenever she talked about him, well, Flora had to believe that he was awfully good at other things. He had the presence of other men she had met who were not attractive but squeezed her arm with enough pressure or laughed with a kind of self-assurance that made her think they might be dangerous. Not in a cloak-and-dagger sort of way but in the way that they understood things about women and their bodies, and what they would or wouldn't do.

Flora thought about telling Seema that Oliver made her uncomfortable and that she didn't think it was very polite of him to call her "Sweet Ass." But if she did that, she ran the risk of sounding prudish, which was the last thing she wanted to do. So she said, "I suppose it's better that he call you 'Sweet

Ass' instead of 'Gross Ass.' "

Seema raised her eyebrows in mock surprise. "Flora Phelps, how naughty."

Flora persisted. "But does he make you use the name Glass so his friends won't know that you're Jewish?"

Seema shook her head. "That's the problem. Jews make everything about themselves." She spoke the next words with an exaggerated Brooklyn accent: "This one wouldn't serve me a drink at his club because he hates Jews, or that one wouldn't invite me into his home because he's an anti-Semite." Her voice rose as she went on. "Why does it always have to be about that? Maybe Oliver likes the name Glass better than Grossman. And you know what? I don't blame him. Grossman sounds undignified, like someone just off the boat. Glass is far more refined. Oliver and his friends are of a certain class. They prefer things to be elegant. If changing a few letters in my name pleases him . . . well, that's the least I can do."

By now it was too dark in the room for Seema to see how Flora's face had reddened or for Flora to notice how Seema's fingers shook as she lit another cigarette. They sat in silence. Flora stood up, placed her hands on her hips, and looked out the window.

Seema studied her sister's body silhouetted against the waning light. She had filled out over the years and was beginning to have the same sturdy bearing as their mother. Seema got lost in a stream of memories about home and might have remained mired in them but for one thing. She thought about how Oliver would describe women who were built like Flora and her mother as having "a peasant's body." She bit her lip so she wouldn't smile, and just like that she snapped out of it.

KAISERSLAUTERN:
FALL 1923

It was a bittersweet homecoming for Edith. She could see her parents from the deck of the boat — not their faces, just their rigid silhouettes at attention. Even as Edith ran to them, they held their solemn expressions. She saw that her mother had dotted her cheeks with rouge and was wearing a silk blouse with a high-ruffle collar. She thought the blouse might be new until she noticed the yellow ribbon of a sweat stain around the neck and some finely stitched patches on the sleeves. Someone with broader shoulders and longer arms had inhabited this blouse before her.

Her father was smoking a cigar, something he did only on special occasions, and was wearing a bowler hat and a newly grown mustache. He also looked as if he'd dressed in someone else's clothing. She hugged her mother first, taking care not to squeeze too tight. Aunt Flora's hugs were warm and fleshy, and Edith sank into her body without the worry of crushing her. Her mother seemed lighter, as if her bones were filled with air. When she kissed her mother's cheek, Edith had to bend over slightly. Either she'd grown or her mother was more hunched over. Her mother must have noticed it too, because the first thing she said was, "They fed you well in America." Her father took a puff of his cigar. He might have looked like a prosperous cigar-smoking American man had it not been for the buttons of his topcoat, which seemed as if they might pop off each time he inhaled.

"Pappa, the mustache," she said, "it looks very *deluxe.*" The remark pleased him.

"After all the fancy people in America," he said. "I didn't want you to come home to your old fogey Mama and Pappa. So it's not displeasing to you?"

"I love it," she said, throwing her arms around him. She never had to worry about crushing him. The acrid smell of his cigar reminded her of how Seema's carpet smelled when she'd done the handstand, and her eyes smarted with the memory.

Never mind that. She'd had ten days on the boat to think about it. America was not hers. She was just a visitor. Nobody in her school had ever been there. As far as she knew, nobody in Kaiserslautern had ever been. She was the lucky one, so to wallow in homesickness for a place that was not home — well, it just wasn't her right. She was happy to see her mama and pappa, and it would be nice to go back to school and be with people her own age.

The house seemed small and dark. After the big Victorian in Yonkers with its bay windows and rolling backyard, she'd expected that it might. The smell of her mother's freshly baked chocolate walnut cake only slightly masked the dank odor that came from years of windows being shut and the earth seeping through the floors. It was the same chocolate walnut cake that Aunt Flora had made when she'd first arrived. At Aunt Flora's, the syrupy sweet smell had curdled her stomach and made her homesick. Now, it reminded her of America. Stupid girl, she thought, gulping down tears and turning her attention to her mother. "Mmmm, the cake smells *marvelous,* Mama, it really does." She had promised Uncle Simon that she'd keep practicing her English so that, when she came back, she'd have no trouble working in his office. *Marvelous.* She could hear how Seema would say it, like butterscotch rolling around her tongue.

"I don't suppose it's anything like the food your Aunt Flora made for you," her mother said, as she placed the loaf on a freshly pressed doily in the middle of the table.

The cake was expensive. Chocolate. Eggs. Butter. Black walnuts. Whiskey. Sugar. Her parents had probably stashed away money for weeks in order to pay for the ingredients. When Aunt Flora had made the cake, she'd thrown the extra black walnuts into the trashcan. In Germany, they were as valuable as gold nuggets, the kind of thing one had to pay for dearly on the black market. Edith could envision her mother crushing the nuts using their old iron hand grinder, the same kind her father used to grind sausage. It would be hard for her, and her veins, like blue wires, would strain beneath the sallow skin of her forearms. Edith felt guilty that her parents were trying so hard. "No one makes this cake the way you do," she said.

Frederick and Margot weren't the kind of people to ask questions directly. Questions were intrusive, and they were uncomfortable probing. Instead, they spoke in generalities and waited with hungry ears for whatever their daughter chose to tell them.

That was another thing Edith liked about America. People there said what they had to say and didn't talk in code. She knew that her parents wanted to know everything about her trip but would never ask. So she would tell them what she thought they wanted to hear: how it looked inside of Aunt Flora and Uncle Simon's house, what Aunt Hannah and Uncle Paul had made for lunch, the afternoon she'd spent at Yankee Stadium, the fireworks. There were only three things she wouldn't talk about: the statues she'd seen at the Metropolitan Museum of Art, Seema's crosses, and how, now that she was home, the first thing she intended to do was learn to smoke just like her Aunt Seema.

By the time Edith finished describing everything, they had each had a piece of the cake. "Have some more. I know it's your favorite," said her mother, shoving the platter toward her.

The moist cake melted in Edith's mouth. The walnuts gave it a grainy texture, and the shot of whiskey cut down on the sweetness. "Flora's cake was gooier than this," said Edith, her eyes fixing on the hand grinder. I don't think she used a hand grinder, so you couldn't taste the nuts as much. Did I tell you that everything in Aunt Flora's kitchen was yellow? Corn yellow she called it. The floors were tile, the chairs . . ."

Margot turned to Frederick: "She misses them," she said, as if she'd forgotten that Edith was sitting between them. "Of course, it's natural," he said. "After such a great adventure, so far from home. I'm sure they treated her like a queen. It isn't every day that a girl from Kaiserslautern gets to go to New York City. It's okay, Margot," he said, stroking the worry crease between her eyes. "She knows where she belongs." He turned to Edith. "Don't you, *Liebchen?*"

Edith managed a smile.

"Yes, but she's still lonesome for them, I can see that," her mother said, still talking to her father. "I have a thought. She should send them each a present with a note, something personal that will always remind them of her."

"That's a good idea, Margot. Why don't you tell her? She's sitting right here."

It was a funny remark in a home whose walls held little laughter.

Edith floated out of her memory bubble. "I like that. I think they'd like that, too."

They discussed the gifts for days, as if they were about to make a presentation to the chancellor. Aunt Flora was stylish and liked pretty things. A hat was out of the question, as she already had an armoire bursting with them. It would have to be something light that wouldn't cost a fortune to mail. They decided on a tea towel. Edith would cross-stitch a bright yellow sunflower onto it, the same yellow as everything else in the kitchen. They thought they might send Uncle Simon a pen or maybe some fine onionskin paper for his drawings. But that was too obvious. Surely Uncle Simon had all of the pens and paper he could want.

Edith told them how Uncle Simon was always making sketches for other people: things he'd drawn hastily on napkins or backs of matchbooks. Right before she left America, he'd given her a blue felt bag. Attached was a note that said: "Do not open until you are in the middle of the ocean."

Inside the little bag were puzzle pieces. She was alone in her cabin on the boat when she first pieced them together, and what she saw made her cry. But when she showed it to her parents, she laughed, taking care to mask the pride she felt about the puzzle's message. It was a drawing of the three of them: a voluptuous Aunt Flora wearing a hat with feathers that reached to the sky; a serious Uncle Simon, half the height of Aunt Flora, dressed in a suit, tie, and giant round glasses, his puckered lips taking up most of his face; and between them a red-cheeked Edith kicking up her heels. With her hair in the new bob and a toothy grin on her face, she was holding the hem of her red, white, and blue dress and apparently dancing the Charleston. Underneath, he'd written, "Flora, Simon, and All-American Edith."

"I think Simon would be happy if someone drew him something for a change," said Edith. "I'm going to make him a book."

That settled, it was time to talk about Seema's gift. "We saved the most difficult for last," said her father. "She has everything."

"She has everything but one thing," said Edith. "I know what to send Seema."

It took nearly two weeks to sew the tea towel and prepare the booklet of drawings. When it was time to pack the presents, her mother pulled out some old newspapers she'd been saving. Her father brought home brown paper from the butcher shop and strong cord. Edith wrapped the booklet and the tea towel. Then she went to her room and brought out the little muslin heart-shaped pillow her mother had sewn for her after she'd cut off her hair. "This is for Seema," she said. Her mother held the pillow in her palm. Some of the embroidered letters of the word "Courage" were faded. Margot looked at it quizzically. "Why would Seema want this old hair pillow?" she asked.

Edith shrugged. "She just would. That's why."

The three of them brought the package to the postmaster and told him it was going to America. "America. Of course," he said, as if he'd been in on the planning the whole time.

When the parcel reached Flora and Simon nearly a month later, the cord was frayed, though it still held its knots. The lettering on the address was faded, and the brown paper was pocked with yellow blotches that could have been coffee stains or somebody's tears. "This looks as if it came from hell," said Simon, before he noticed the Kaiserslautern postmark. When they realized it had come from Edith, they sat down in the sunroom and placed the package between them. Slowly, they untied the cord and removed the paper without tearing it.

Flora read aloud the note on her gift: "For your beautiful corn kitchen." There was no note attached to Simon's gift: a booklet of a few pages stitched together, each with simple black-and-white sketches. There was one of a girl and a man at a baseball game shouting "Attaboy, Babe," another of a girl and a man and a horse with *"clock-clock"* written beneath it, and the last of a girl and a man watching the sky explode and "BANG BANG BANG" splashed across the page. On the cover, in a loopy script, was written: "MAGIC UP CLOSE FOR UNCLE SIMON FROM EDITH."

Simon stared at Flora, then studied the pictures again. He wasn't accustomed to getting gifts. Flora always gave him something for his birthday or for Hanukkah, but he knew it was a chore for her. He was a finicky man with particular tastes and, more often than not, what she got him was too flashy, and though he tried to act grateful, he could never be convincingly exuberant. Only once before had someone given him the perfect present. And that was the notebook and crayons his mother gave him when he was nine, right before he came to America.

"Not bad," he said, swallowing. "She has real promise."

Flora rubbed his back. "She must have learned it from you."

Seema's gift tumbled out last. They shook and squeezed it. A pillow. The note on it read: "I always remember our time together."

"Sweet," said Flora, scooping up the paper for the trash.

Out of curiosity, Simon unfurled the

newspaper wrapping and spread the old sheets out on the floor. Flora noticed how he pressed his lips into a straight line, the way he did when he was angry.

"Did you see this?" he asked, bending down to look closer. He pointed to a cartoon on one of the pages. "It's grotesque," he said, jabbing the drawing. Flora got down next to him to study the cartoon. She saw that one of the characters was a man with a hooked nose, a bald head, and stooped posture. "An idiotic caricature," he said, ripping out the drawing and balling up the rest of the paper.

"What are you going to do with it?" she asked, not quite understanding what she'd seen.

"I don't know," he said, folding the cartoon into neat squares. "But I'll tell you this. Germany is no place for Edith."

■ ■ ■ ■

PART 4

■ ■ ■ ■

NEW YORK CITY:
1928

His mother's apron still hung in the pantry. It was yellowed and threadbare now, its onion-cinnamon nectar long replaced with the fusty odor of something needing to be thrown away. Simon still had the old checkered vest that she had sewn for him before he'd left Vilna. Sometimes when he was undressing for a bath, he'd reach into the armoire and pull it out. Because he was a slight man, he could still slip his arms into the armholes. He didn't even try to stretch the vest across his chest for fear of unraveling it. Instead, he'd stand in front of the mirror in his undershorts and silk socks, the vest bunched up around his nipples like a doll's clothes, praying that Flora wouldn't walk in just then. He'd keep the itchy vest on as long as he could stand it. Then he'd strip down and sit in the bath reading the tiny welts the vest had raised on his chest — each one a scratchy hieroglyphic from the past.

At work, he kept an accordion file in his bottom desk drawer marked in his fine handwriting: FUTURE PROJECTS. The ink on the words was smudged with fingerprints from his busy hands always hoping to find something new. The accordion file, so fat now it threatened to pop its pleats, was filled with old sketches of familiar faces, scraps of paper with dashed half-sentences, articles, sketches, and photographs torn from newspapers and magazines. Simon hoped they would add up to something someday, offer him a clue about his missing family. His compulsion to compile clues became his passion. Late at night, when everyone else had gone home, he'd often clear his desk and lay out the bits and pieces in front of him. There were phone numbers of people who knew people from Vilna, drawings of every item he could conjure from his childhood home (each detail, like the filigree on his mother's silver napkin ring rendered with precision), every newspaper piece in which the word *Vilna* appeared. He'd arrange them in alphabetical and chronological order. He'd make lists, outlines, timelines, new pictures. Yet as patient and as logical a man as he was, the timelines always had missing years and the lists were filled with questions that never got answered. Even the drawings had blank spaces where the face of his mother or one of his siblings might have been.

By now, Adler, Broder, and Phelps had become Phelps and Adler after Broder, a forty-seven-year-old amiable fellow with gray hair and a paunch left his wife of twenty-three years and took up with an eighteen-year-old girl he'd met when she came to the office one day to deliver sketches for the Sunshine Biscuit advertising campaign. The story was that the girl was pregnant and that Broder had taken her off to the West Indies so she could have the baby in private, away from the brouhaha that had been kicked up by their union. But that's not the way Flora heard the tale from her friend Myra, who was in the sisterhood with her at Temple Beth David of Yonkers. Myra was friends with the first Mrs. Broder, who told her that Mr. Broder's new wife was, first of all, not his wife at all, and second, not the least bit pregnant. Trudi Broder had apparently snorted to her friend Myra, "That man hasn't been able to arouse his member in years. And if he did, I seriously doubt he'd know where to put it."

Flora was breathless when she repeated this story to Simon. "So what do you think?

Do you think Broder made it all up so his friends would think he was, you know, a real stud, or was it just an excuse for him to disappear?"

"Oh for God's sakes, Flora, with all that's going on, do you really want to waste your time worrying about this sort of nonsense?"

"It's not nonsense," she answered. "This is a man you've known nearly half your life. You've been with him, ten, eleven hours a day for twenty years — you figure it out. You've spent more time with him than you have with me. And then he goes off on this lark, which may not even be a lark at all, and you aren't concerned or even mildly curious? Are you really that above it all?"

Flora and Simon bickered infrequently, but when they did, she had no problem blurting out whatever was on her mind. More often than not, he would snap back at her, then immediately feel repentant. She never begrudged him his success and the fame that came with it. He was talented and a hard worker and earned everything he had. It just had all come so fast, like a train materializing out of the fog in a great huff and gone again before you can whisper its name. That's how it felt to Flora: as if she were the one who'd been left behind at the station. Flora still kept the first drawing Simon had ever given her folded up in her wallet: "Mr. Blockhead and the lovely Miss Chatterbug." It wasn't nearly as skilled or detailed as his current work, but every time she looked at it, she felt the wholeness of their marriage, and for that reason, she loved it the best.

Phelps and Adler had grown so much that they moved to their own building downtown on Bond Street. Simon had more than seventy patents for window displays and paper toys pending with the U.S. government. When *Forbes* magazine or *Advertising Age* needed a quote from a smart businessman, they often turned to Simon, who had become known for his terse yet pointed remarks and his fine haberdashery.

What he lacked in God-given good looks, Simon made up for with aplomb and dignity, and though he was spare, he carried himself as a man twice his size. He had all of his shirts and suits hand made by a Lithuanian tailor on the Lower East Side and always wore a silk tie and a sterling silver tiepin with a tiny diamond on the tip. His name and face had become so familiar in the press that they affectionately called him "Dapper Simon Phelps." When his picture and a quote from him showed up in a wire service story that ran all over the country, Flora teasingly asked him if there was any muckraker he *wouldn't* give an interview to.

"I want my name and face everywhere I can get it," he said.

"You're kidding, aren't you?"

"No, I'm not. I'd even have my face plastered on billboards if I could figure out how to do it."

"Am I to think that all of this fame and money has gone to your dapper head?"

"You know me better than that. Suppose just one person sees my name or picture and says, 'Isn't that the boy from Vilna?' and that one person can lead me to another person who knows something about my family, then all this would be worth it."

He had made nearly a million dollars. The way things were going with the business expanding from window displays to advertising designs, games, and now puzzles, it was pretty much guaranteed that he would make millions more. They still lived in the same house in Yonkers, though now they had a cook and someone who came in to clean two times a week. Flora had an ankle-length beaver coat and diamond earrings that could light a moonless night. They gave dinner parties for people like Gerard Lambert and Albert Lasker when they were in town. Lambert, from St. Louis, had recently put halitosis on the map with his chiding ads for Listerine: "Always a bridesmaid, but never a bride." And Lasker, out of Chicago, made smoking a desired way for women to lose weight with his "Reach for a Lucky instead of a Sweet" campaign.

As a boy, Simon had shaped his vision of America from newspaper headlines and photographs. But these days he found that advertisements gave him an even clearer picture of Americans. He understood that they adored modern gadgets: the record player, the meat-slicing machine, anything that glittered and went fast. Cleanliness was a virtue; women wore revealing lace robes and silky undergarments and were always available for romance yet were still expected to get dinner on the table; children were as guileless and iconic as the Baby Jesus; and men in their leather driving gloves and fedoras were always roughing it in fine suits or preparing for important outings. Beyond all else, Americans loved their dogs. Simon absorbed all this and developed a marksman's instinct for coupling the right image with the right emotion. Smart consumers could spot a Phelps and Adler ad anywhere.

James Walter Thompson himself had put Simon's name up for membership at the

Granite Club. The club was in one of the townhouses down the street from the new public library building on Fifth Avenue. Thompson had told him it was where New York businessmen took clients for lunch. It was the kind of place where a man could sip a whiskey, smoke a cigar, and sink into an overstuffed chair. When Simon visited the club for his interview with several of its board members, it was below freezing outside. A warm fire in a stone fireplace greeted him as he walked through the heavy oak doors. Upstairs, he had been taken with the oil portraits of distinguished members — including Theodore Roosevelt — and the rich smell of leather-bound books.

The interview had taken place in the dimly lit director's office. An umbrella that had been propped up on the windowsill held the peeling window open. Lithographs and photographs of famous golf courses filled the walls. The director was a slim, immaculately dressed man well into his seventies. He had fine white hair and shook Simon's hand firmly, pressing his thumb into the spongy part between Simon's thumb and forefinger. Four other men, members of the admissions committee, sat in a semicircle around the walnut chair with the ornately carved back in which Simon sat.

The men laced their fingers together and nodded with interest as Simon fielded questions about what kind of business he was in, what he foresaw in the Machine Age, and whether he thought America would continue to prosper.

At one point, he even pulled out a scrap of paper and drew them a sketch of how he imagined the robots of science fiction might look in the future. His answers made the men sit up and listen. The questions went along like that until the director, in a voice so casual it seemed like an afterthought, leaned forward and placed his bony hand under his chin. "This is all very fascinating. So tell me, if I may ask. What kind of a name is Phelps?"

Two of the men crossed their legs at the same time. Another cleared his throat. All of them looked somewhere else rather than into Simon's eyes.

"Jewish," he said, imagining the word splattering across their faces. "It's a Jewish name. Lithuanian Jewish to be exact. Comes from the Lithuanian name Filips. I think that will be all for today. Thank you for your time, gentlemen." Simon stood up, grabbed his brown felt hat from the hat rack, and walked out. When he'd gotten down to the lobby and put the hat on his head, it fell well below his ears. He'd taken someone else's hat, someone with a head the size of a possum, which meant he'd have to go back upstairs and face those men again. In his anger, Simon took the stairs two at a time. The men were still seated around his empty chair, as if they hadn't yet realized he'd left. He placed the oversized hat on the rack and took the one that belonged to him. "Stinkin' shitballs," he said under his breath, and he stuck the hat on his head. It had been Piss-boy's favorite phrase. At the time, Simon had found the phrase crude. Now it brought a smile to his face, as he realized that Piss-boy had been the first person he knew who'd intuitively grasped the basic tenets of advertising: See it. Say it. Feel it.

By the time he'd gotten back to Yonkers that evening, Simon had composed a letter to the *New York Herald Tribune.* He'd written about his interview at the Granite Club and how, as a foreigner to this country, he'd learned to interpret codes: "When a man asks another man, 'And what kind of a name is Phelps?' particularly when the man being asked the question has the residue of a foreign accent and the kind of nose that suggests something other than a direct bloodline to the Mayflower, that man must assume his interrogator is not asking an innocent question."

He'd said that he'd wished this had been an isolated incident rather than more evidence of the "underlying bigotry that threatens to corrode the city's institutions" and lamented that "the longer we ignore these manifestations of hate, the greater the risk grows that they will eventually destroy the democracy we hold so dear."

His indignation in full throttle, he'd signed the letter, "Simon Phelps, Citizen of the United States, Jewish Citizen of the World."

He'd read the letter one more time before he got off the train. He'd rewrite it when he got home and maybe take out the sign off. It was too much. Why give them ammunition?

Flora often wondered how Simon could go through a day at the office plus nearly three hours of commuting and never come home with a wrinkle on him. His shirt was always buttoned to his neck, and his silver tiepin was always exactly in the same spot as it was when he left in the morning. She still washed his shirts, so she knew that he rarely sweated. Only the ink stains on his fingers and occasional smudges of blue or black that rubbed off on his shirt gave a hint of his work. But on the night he'd come back from the Granite Club, Simon had stormed through the front door with his top button undone, his shirtsleeves pushed up above his elbows, and the swampy odor of a man who'd been chased.

"What happened to you? Did you walk home?" Flora had asked, greeting him at the door.

"I'm not in the mood for jokes, Flora."

"Well, then, I'm not either, darling. Shall I get you a Manhattan?"

Lately, bits of Seema had crept into Flora: "Darling" and the trill in her voice when she said "Manhattan." It irritated him, these affectations, but he would mention it to her later, after he'd had the Manhattan and put his feet up.

She poured herself a glass of sherry and they sat in the sunroom, where Simon described what had happened at the Granite Club.

As he told her how the man had asked about the name Phelps, he threw his hands up in the air and knocked over his Manhattan. The drink spilled onto the red-and-orange diamond-patterned Persian rug under his chair. Flora ran to the kitchen to get a dishtowel. She got on her hands and knees to blot up the whiskey and vermouth when she noticed she was using the towel that Edith had sent her. "It's amazing how she got the yellow just right," she said. "I don't think whiskey stains rugs, do you? But you know what, I've been thinking we could certainly perk up this room a little. A new carpet wouldn't hurt, something a little more modern maybe."

Usually, it amused Simon how easily derailed Flora could become. But that day, he found it annoying. He wouldn't tell her about the letter or how he'd gone back and cursed the man under his breath. She'd only have said that the letter was overwrought and he was overreacting. Silently, he fought back. *Well, at least someone in this family has one foot in the real world. Okay, I'll take out the part about Citizen of the United States, Jewish Citizen of the World, but that is all.*

Simon stared at his wife. As he often did, he stepped back and watched his thoughts as if they were panel after panel in one of those newspaper comic strips. Flora would be a round character, beautiful with a wide smile and sparkling jewelry. She would have an adoring, and mostly out of the picture, husband and a madcap sister who lived in the big city. Flora would live in a glow of sweetness and innocence. He'd draw it like a pink cloud filled with goose feathers. It would hang over her head wherever she went and make her impervious to anything ugly or mean. During the day, she would have quixotic, pastel-colored adventures, but at night, no matter how far she'd traveled in the day, she'd come home to her husband: an earnest black-and-white fellow with the downcast demeanor of a beagle. In the last panel of the strip, they would always lie together in their bed — she with her pink cloud hovering, he with his eyes wide open and his teeth locked in a grimace. The husband's head would be oversized, so that his brain was visible. It would look like one of those new-fangled machines with pieces fitted together at right angles, and in big letters over the brain, he'd write: CLICKETY CLACK CLICKETY CLACK.

While Simon was creating his fantasy, Flora finished cleaning the rug and sat across from Simon watching the agitation play across his face. Now in his forties, Simon was becoming set in his habits. He'd taken to reading half the paper out loud, not really to her, but to some imaginary audience who would share his outrage when he'd yell, "Those morons, who are they kidding? Doesn't anyone pay attention to history? Look what's happening in Europe!" He was always preoccupied with something, whether it was the state of the world or his business. And then there was the obsession with finding his family. Always calling this one or that one who might have a connection to someone who knows someone. The endless scraps of papers and lists and envelopes filled with God knows what. She loved him for his devotion to them, yet pitied him for what she feared was their fate. All this worrying seemed to wear him down. By the time he came home at night, he wanted to do little else than put his feet up, read the paper, and fret about the state of the world.

Sometimes Flora envied Seema's glamorous life with its cocktail parties and evenings at the theater. Not that she wanted to go out every night, but once in a while it would be fun to get all dressed up and go out to a fancy restaurant or the opera. She thought about her looks. She was pretty, and because she'd never had children, she still had her figure, even near forty. But what good was being pretty and having a good figure if no one ever saw you? She noticed how men looked at her. It was not the way they looked at Seema, but with steady, appreciative eyes. It wouldn't last much longer. Seema told her that by the time a woman reached forty-five, all her sex organs started to break down. "They're no better than a scrap heap," she'd said. She'd told Flora that when that happened, women gave off an odor, a very subtle odor that only men could smell, even though they didn't always know that they were smelling it. The odor went to the part of their brain that was responsible for reproduction and gave off a chemical signal that let the man know her time had run out, that she was no longer capable of bearing his children. Because men were biologically put on this earth to procreate, Seema said, the chemical reaction in their brains caused them automatically to reject this woman. "It's sad," said Seema. "So many nice women over forty-five. But that's just how it works."

Flora never questioned how Seema knew all this, although it sounded like the kind of thing Oliver would tell her. By this logic, Flora had only seven years left. It seemed impossible that in seven years her sex organs would be a scrap heap. She'd forgotten to ask Seema if husbands could smell their wives' dying sex, or if it was just men who were out looking for women with whom to procreate. Would Simon be the only man she would ever know in that way? She wondered what it would be like to touch another man or go to bed with him before her time ran out. She daydreamed about spending a week in New York City with Seema. They'd go to speakeasies and dances and maybe a cabaret — anywhere that wasn't in Yonkers and didn't involve Phelps or Adler or any of the women of the Beth David sisterhood.

Even though it was the first week of November, New York was enjoying the kind of Indian summer that made people believe that they'd outwitted winter. Flora was in the backyard planting anemone and tulip bulbs. There were even new rosebuds on the bushes, and Flora was deciding whether or not to prune them or wait for cooler weather. Her train of thought was interrupted by a young male voice.

"Sorry to bother you, but are you Mrs. Simon Phelps?"

Flora wiped her muddy hands on her slacks. "Yes, I am."

"Then I've come to the right place," he said, handing her a yellow envelope.

It was rare to get a cable. She assumed it was for Simon. Maybe there was some good news about his family.

"Hope you get a good crop of whatever you're growing back there, ma'am," he said, heading back to his truck.

She ripped open the envelope and saw the

297

following words pasted side by side: OUR MUTTI IS DECLINING. COME IMMEDI- ATELY. MARGOT.

She could imagine how Margot must have agonized over those words. But why did she use the word "declining"? In the last letter Flora had received from Margot several months ago, Margot had mentioned that their mother was losing words, as many older people do. Margot had said that when she couldn't remember names, she'd make up unsettling substitutes. Frederick became the *Fleischmann* and Edith, *der Buckel,* "the hunchback" — a reference to the days right after her pleurisy surgery. In the letter, Mar- got had written that "our *Mutti*" can be so silly sometimes. At the time it struck Flora as odd. She knew there wasn't a silly bone in her mother's ferocious body. But Margot hadn't mentioned anything about "declin- ing."

Flora went inside and put the cable down on the kitchen counter. She needed to call Simon. No, she should call Seema first. Of course she and Seema would go to Kaiser- slautern right away. Simon wouldn't want her traveling with Seema. Seema wouldn't want to go at all. Maybe she'd call Simon first. Oh, but he would be too upset about her possibly missing Thanksgiving. Okay, she'd call Seema.

Seema answered on the first ring. Flora wondered what she did all day and why she would be that close to the phone at eleven o'clock on a Wednesday morning.

"I just got a telegram from Margot." Flora read her the message. "I guess that means we have to go to Kaiserslautern as soon as possible."

"Why do we have to go?"

"What do you mean, why do we have to go? Our mother is dying. That's why."

"I know our mother is dying. It's just that she's lived without us all these years, she can die without us, too."

Flora had tucked the phone under her ear and had been picking the dirt out from under her nails. But Seema's words made her stop and grab the receiver with both hands.

"Seema, what an awful thing to say. We have to go."

All Seema could think about was how harsh her mother had been to her as a child, and how, since she'd come to America, she'd heard from her infrequently, and then only to extol Margot's virtues as a mother.

"I don't have to go. I don't like that woman and I never have, you know that."

They'd had this discussion many times.

Seema would say, "She sent us away when we were little children so she could have her darling little Margot all to herself." And Flora would answer, "Yes, but she sacrificed a lot to send us here. You've got to be grateful to her for that much."

Usually, when the subject of their mother came up, Flora would let Seema's comments pass, but today she found Seema petulant and even cruel. Flora didn't disdain their mother the way Seema did, though whenever she'd thought about having children of her own, she'd hoped that they would love her unsparingly and that they would always live nearby. She understood why a mother would do what she did. But with that kind of time and distance between them, how could her children not be, at best, indifferent, and at worst, resentful toward her?

"Look Seema, we don't have time for this nonsense now. We're going and that's that. I'll find out when we can book passage and I'll get back to you."

"Christ, Flora," said Seema, "You really can be so annoying. Has Simon given you his permission to leave?"

"I haven't asked him yet. But of course he'll say yes. What's the matter? Are you afraid to leave Oliver alone in the big city?"

"Don't worry about him, darling, Oliver will be fine. He'll miss me, of course, but honestly, I don't expect to be gone that long."

Flora called Simon. He was always terrible on the phone. He had no time for chitchat and was abrupt and impatient. So she said what she had to say as plainly as she could.

"I just got a cable from Margot. My mother is dying and Seema and I are going to Kaiserslautern."

There was a sharp intake of breath on the other end of the line. "Oh God Flora, that's awful," said Simon. "I'm so sorry, that's really awful."

He seemed more upset than she did. "Of course you must go. I'll go with you. I'll call up the Hamburg American Line and book us all passage on the first boat we can get."

"Oh Simon," she said, "I knew you'd understand. And of course I want you to come. It's just that — how shall I say this? It's just that she's dying, but she's not dead yet. It could be days or weeks or, I don't know. Can you really miss that much work?"

She heard the rustle of paper and figured that he was looking through his calendar. "Hmm, there could be a problem. But I can't have you traveling alone."

"But I won't be alone. I'll be with Seema."

"I know," he said. "In some ways that's worse."

"Oh, you worry too much. I can take care of myself. And besides, we'll be on the boat for only a few days and then we'll be in Kaiserslautern. Even Seema can't get into trouble in Kaiserslautern."

"Pff, I wouldn't be so sure of that. Okay, so the two of you go and if you're there — God forbid — for too long, I'll come."

"Okay, that's good."

Again she heard the rustle of paper. "Flora, you'll be back in time for Thanksgiving, won't you?"

Of all holidays, Simon embraced this one the most. Each year they went to Aunt Hannah and Uncle Paul's and stayed for the entire day. Lev and Ruth would be there plus a crowd of friends and of people who had nowhere else to go. It always amazed Flora how, on that day, Simon, "Dapper Simon Phelps," would unbutton his collar and roll up his sleeves and play football in the yard, and how later he would throw himself into the game of charades, making funny faces, getting down on all fours, doing a little dance in place — anything to win.

"Ooh, I hope so," said Flora. "But it could be tricky. One week going over, another week coming back, and we're already in the first week of November. I don't know."

They were both quiet as they realized how long they might be apart.

Finally, Simon spoke. "Well, Flora, you'll do what you have to do."

"Yes, I will. And I'll come home as soon as I can."

Simon knew his feelings were irrational, but the thought of her going away made him dizzy with anxiety. The morning that she pulled her suitcase from the closet and placed it on the bed so she could pack, he became so nauseated that he had to lock himself in the bathroom. In his life, when you said good-bye to people you loved, you never saw them again. He and Flora had never been separated, and it was his intention that they never would be. It wasn't fair to burden her with his fears, so he tried to keep them to himself. But when he came out of the bathroom, he paced back and forth, scrutinizing every item she put into her suitcase.

"This would be a good time to talk to Margot and Frederick about having Edith come back here. Do you think it's out of the question that the two of them might come with her?"

"I'll certainly bring it up," said Flora.

"I'm sure I could help Frederick find work," he said. "And Margot. She'd love having you and Seema around to . . ."

Simon lost his train of thought.

"You're packing two hats. I don't see why you'll need *two* hats. You won't have time to wear both."

"A lace blouse for a funeral seems awfully fancy, don't you think?"

"And a suit no less! Are you planning to move there?"

Flora stopped what she was doing, sat down on the bed, and took his hands. He stood before her like a child, his head bowed. "Simon, sweetheart," she said. "I am coming back. I promise you, I'll be home as quickly as I can. I'll write you a letter every day so you'll know exactly what I'm doing. I hate this as much as you do. After this, let's promise that we'll never be parted again.

"I swear it," he said, squeezing her hand.

"I swear it, too," she said, squeezing back.

Seema would rather have died than have anyone watch her pack. She threw in several of the lacy peignoirs and camisoles that Oliver had given her. They were clingy and transparent, and it gave her a spiteful thrill to imagine Flora in her flannel bedclothes trying to pretend that she wasn't shocked by her sister's flimsy underwear.

She packed a few simple dresses from B. Altman, a couple of pairs of trousers, some sweaters, and six pairs of shoes. She threw in Edith's small "Courage" pillow because, while she was never certain why she had sent it, the gift spoke of an understanding between them and gave her comfort. Besides, courage was one of many things she would need for this journey.

She went into the bathroom, sat down on the cold tile floor, opened the cabinet, and pulled out the lavender tin where she kept her crosses. She couldn't take them all, so she'd have to pick one. She knew which one that would be: her favorite. It was the one made of two slivers of gold, slightly wider than brush bristles. She'd found it at Saint Patrick's in one of the racks in front of the pews, where the prayer books were kept. The catch was broken and she'd figured that it must have fallen from someone's neck as she knelt praying. It was so delicate, that cross, it could have even belonged to a young girl. Seema had wanted to do the right thing and get it back to its owner, but Saint Patrick's had no lost-and-found.

Unsure what to do, she had decided to

keep it. She'd gotten the clasp fixed and had worn it under sweaters or tucked into blouses whenever she could. She took that cross as a sign, a covenant, that as long as she was in possession of it she would do what she could to protect it and, by association, the young girl to whom it had belonged. In turn, whoever was watching over things like young girls and their prayers would keep an eye on her at the same time. It was the most she dared hope for. Well, she was making this dreaded trip, wasn't she, so that had to count for something. She took the cross and slid it into the back pocket of her suitcase.

She'd remembered the cigarettes, thank God, two cartons of them, and the flask. She couldn't imagine that Kaiserslautern would have cigarettes, much less rum. She wished she had another one of these as she poured the rum into the one she had. She slipped these into the back pocket of the suitcase as well. Oh, and one more thing. She went through the photo album she kept in her desk drawer. There were lots of pictures of her with Oliver. She finally settled on one taken at a lake somewhere upstate, though she couldn't remember where. It was just before sundown, and the golden light made them look like bronze statues. They were in profile and he had his arm around her. It must have been taken years ago, because her nose was still straight then.

On their first night aboard the ship, Seema ordered a bottle of champagne. Flora took a tentative sip, then another. Seema, well into her second glass, said, "Simon must be having conniptions that you're here with me alone. He's scared to death that I'm going to turn you into a loose woman."

Flora gulped her drink. "For heaven's sake, Simon trusts me completely. And you flatter yourself if you think he thinks you're the femme fatale you obviously think you are."

"Oh, that's peachy. Then I'm not going to worry about you at all." She opened her purse and pulled out a blue velvet case. "Take a look at this, a present from Oliver." She handed it to Flora. "Go on, open it." Inside was a sterling silver cigarette holder. It was long and fluted and engraved with a beautiful scroll design.

Flora studied the cigarette holder and absentmindedly bounced it in her hand as if she were weighing it.

"It's real all right," said Seema. "And you must read the darling note that came with it." She handed Flora a card with the navy initials O.T. embossed in the upper left-hand corner. Flora was surprised by his feminine curvy penmanship. "Go on, read it," insisted Seema.

Something to keep in your beautiful mouth until I see you again.

As Ever, Oliver

Seema smirked as her sister read the note. "He's a dear, isn't he?" she said.

Flora was embarrassed but refused to give Seema the satisfaction of showing it. "What a thoughtful gift," she said. "And not a cheap one either."

That evening set the tone of their crossing. There was the champagne at dinner and the inevitable well-suited men who would manage to find their way to the table and talk to both of them while always keeping an eye on Seema. Sometimes, Seema would dance with one of them, and there were a couple of nights when Flora would go back to the stateroom by herself and be sound asleep by the time Seema came back.

On their final morning at sea, Seema slept until after eleven, when Flora came in with a cup of hot coffee for her. Seema sat up in bed, her knees pulled to her chest so that she made a tent of her peignoir. She sipped slowly from the coffee, holding the cup in both hands. "Have you any idea how much I'm dreading this?"

"I can't say I'm looking forward to it myself," said Flora, who was starting to pack.

"All I remember are those tiny houses and the woods — like out of 'Hansel and Gretel.' I hope Edith will come home. And you'll be there, course. But everyone else, they're like strangers to me. And God knows what they'll think of me. Can you hand me a cigarette please?" Seema pointed to her suitcase. "Back pocket."

Flora pulled out a carton of cigarettes. Something hung on one of its corners. It was a gold chain with a cross. "What's this?" asked Flora, taking the chain in her hand.

Seema considered confessing to Flora about the crosses. But Flora would never understand. She would assume it had something to do with Oliver, just giving her one more reason to dislike him. So she lied and said that she had loaned the suitcase to one of her friends, a Catholic girl, and that she must have left it in there by mistake.

"Catholics are funny the way they wear their religion on their sleeve," said Flora, placing the cross back in the bag.

"I suppose so," said Seema, getting out of bed. "Guess I'd better start packing, too."

KAISERSLAUTERN: NOVEMBER 1928

It was raining when the ship pulled into Hamburg harbor late that afternoon. When Seema looked out, all she could see were the muted colors of the ship's hull and the pier piles that jutted out of the water at drunken angles. Mist covered the gangway as she and Flora made their way down. Seema caught her heel on one of the planks and her shoe came off. She leaned over and picked it up, but the crowds pushing forward left her no time to put the shoe back on. She hobbled down the rest of the way, her stockings ripping and mud oozing between her toes. The two sisters stood on the dock for a few moments, Flora looking around for familiar faces while Seema hopped on one foot, trying to wipe the mud from the other with a handkerchief she'd pulled from her handbag. That's how Edith found them when she came running through the crowd. "Here they are," she shouted to

Frederick, who was several paces behind her.

Flora put down her bags and threw her arms around Edith. "My, oh my, you've gotten so big," she said, grasping her by the shoulders and holding her at arm's length. "Let me take a look at you. You're not a girl anymore; you've become a young lady."

"A fat young lady," said Edith, patting her stomach. "At gymnasium they feed us nothing but starches."

In the five years since they had seen Edith, she had blossomed into a woman with full cheeks and a round milkmaid form. Edith knew her aunts would notice her weight gain right away, particularly Seema, to whom she directed her next comments. "But I've recently taken up smoking, which everyone tells me is the secret to losing weight. So soon, I'll be as skinny as you."

Seema stopped fiddling with her shoe long enough to wrap one arm around her niece's neck and kiss her on the cheek. "You're a beautiful young lady," she said. "Don't worry about the weight thing. We'll smoke together until you're thin as a rail."

That's when they all turned their attention to Frederick. Next to Edith, he looked sallow and caved in. He really was as skinny as a rail — nothing like the hearty young

312

man they remembered from their childhood. Flora put her arm around him and told him how good it was to see him again. Seema hugged him without getting her body close to his and kissed the air next to his cheek. The shoe still dangled from her hand. He asked about their journey, and they asked about his health. Edith asked about the shoe, and they all laughed as Seema tried to squeeze her dirty foot back into it. Then Flora shifted to speaking German. "So how is she?" she asked.

Edith and her father exchanged looks. "I'm afraid she is not so good," said Frederick. "Taking care of her mother has been draining."

It took Flora and Seema a moment to realize that he was talking about Margot, not their mother.

Frederick continued, "She's worn out. I'm so glad you're here to help her."

Seema tightened her grip on the handle of her suitcase. She'd assumed her stay would be short and never considered that she'd be asked to do more than sit by her mother's bedside.

"I must warn you," he lowered his voice, "your mother won't recognize you. She can barely speak and has all but stopped eating. Margot won't give up. She still cooks her soup and bakes her favorite bread. She talks to her day and night, as if she understands. Poor Margot . . ."

Edith interrupted, "She's very happy that you've come." Her voice lifted unnaturally. "So are we. Frau Schultz, the woman who owns the farm next door, has fixed up a room for you. Nothing fancy," she glanced at Seema, "but it's clean, and you'll be nearby."

Seema's stomach did uneasy flip-flops. She pictured a straw mattress and a dirt floor. Oliver had laughed when they talked about where she'd stay. "Well, wherever it is, it won't be the Ritz, you can bet your money on that," he'd said. She knew already that she would lie to him about the Schultz farm and make it seem more glamorous than it was.

The trip from Hamburg to Kaiserslautern in the Deutsche Bahn took nearly all day. Seema watched out the window and thought that everything looked more crammed together here than in America. In America, the mountains seemed to have recently burst through the landscape; the lakes and rivers looked as if they were puddles left behind by melting icebergs. The land here was tame, smoothed at its edges. It had been used up by too many farms and too many factories and too many wars. America's topography seemed youthful and suited Seema much more than the dusty roads and dull palette that lay before her.

As the train slowed down to pull into the Hanover station, Flora noticed an elderly man standing by the side of the road wearing a shabby suit and a sign around his neck. She understood enough German so that she could read what it said: I AM A PROFESSOR OF MUSIC AND I AM HUNGRY. BUY MY HANDMADE POSTCARDS. He held the postcards in one hand and in the other a hat with barely enough coins in it to buy a cup of coffee. Flora said nothing, nor did she mention the cripples they passed along the way: men who were missing a limb or two and hobbled along on crutches. It had been nearly ten years since she'd been in Germany. Things seemed so much more desperate to her now. She looked around their compartment to see if anyone else in the car noticed what she was seeing, but Edith was still talking in that falsely cheerful way about her roommate at gymnasium, and Frederick, who'd brought a basket full of cervelat and *Teawurst* sandwiches, kept urging everyone to eat. "Come now, girls, you must have a bite of something. You want to be strong for your sister, don't you?"

The sandwiches reeked of garlic and something sweet and smoky. Frederick spoke to them in a soft, coaxing manner, and the combination made Seema feel as if she might puke. She had the urge to say the meanest thing she could think of to Frederick. Her thoughts turned to Oliver, who was never at a loss for sarcasm, and she wondered what he would make of Frederick: a butcher, a peasant, who wore his devotion to his wife without shame. Just then, Edith turned to her as if reading her dark thoughts. "Seema," she said, resting her hand on her aunt's arm, "we're about to pass St. Nikolai Church. It's the tallest building in Hamburg and I think you'll find it beautiful. Look, here it is, coming up on your left."

Seema stared up at the gothic brick structure. The sun was on its way to setting and the light burned off the baroque cross atop its spire. A feeling of relief spread through Seema's stomach. It was the first thing she'd seen since arriving here that made her feel welcome, and she wondered if Edith sensed her pleasure. She knew Edith hadn't pointed it out to taunt her, nor did she think that Edith had ever told anyone about her secret stash of crosses. She brought her hand to her throat and felt for her gold chain. Of course, it was in the back pocket of her suitcase, where Flora had returned it this morning. That had been a close call, she thought. Flora seemed to accept her explanation of why it was there.

It was dark by the time they reached Kaiserslautern. Only the light from a crescent moon shone through the foggy sky. No one said anything as they got out of the cab, but if dread could speak it would have found its words in the heavy steps they took and the way they dragged their suitcases behind them. Inside the house, a candle flickered.

"Margot*schön,* we're home," Frederick whispered. He raised his voice when no one answered: "We're here, all of us." There was a rustling noise. A light went on and there stood Margot, her beautiful auburn hair mostly gray now, springing like cries of help from her head. She still had the beautiful long, slender legs, but she was paler and thinner than Seema or Flora had remembered, and her red and watery eyes looked like fresh blisters. Flora was wearing an olive green hat with a dashing ostrich plume and Seema had on her brown-and-white suit and what was left of the morning's makeup. The two of them took in the sight of their sister, trying not to let their shock show on their faces.

Margot patted her hair in place and took off the apron she'd been wearing. She hadn't thought about her appearance since God knows when, but now, caught in the stunned gaze of her sisters, she realized what a sight she must have seemed. She lifted her arms to hug her sisters and became aware of the pungent smell of her own perspiration. "Mutti and I are so happy you are here," she said, hugging her arms in front of her chest. "Come. Come in. I know she is eager to see you."

"Ach Margot," said Frederick, "these people are tired and thirsty. Let's give them some schnapps and let them relax a little. We'll sit for a while. You haven't seen each other in ages."

An awkward half hour passed as the three sisters and Edith sat at the kitchen table. Frederick took out a bottle of plum schnapps and poured them each a shot. Edith took up the slack in conversation. She told them how her mother had filled a window box with geraniums and how well they were doing. "Can we see them?" asked Flora, jumping from her chair, eager for the distraction. Edith showed them the flowers, and it reminded Flora of the present she had brought for Margot. She dug down into her bag and pulled out an egg-shaped porcelain object wrapped in tissue paper. "Do you still collect these?" she asked, handing the gift to her.

Margot unwrapped the tissue slowly. "Another owl? Yes, I still do. You remembered."

"Of course I remembered," said Flora. "How could I forget those little creatures of yours? You used to line them all up by your bed. You gave them all names and you would say good night to each one before we went to sleep."

The sweetness was still in Margot's smile. She rolled the blue-and-green owl in her hands and looked into its agate eyes. "He's beautiful. He looks like an Erich, don't you think?"

Seema hadn't thought to bring Margot a gift. Now she considered giving her one of her dresses or the sterling silver cigarette holder that Oliver had given her, but even in her moment of panic, she knew how completely inappropriate that would be. So she said the next thing that came to her mind. "Margot darling, I didn't bring you a present. I thought we'd go shopping, the two of us, and I'd buy whatever you chose — silk stockings, a leather handbag, pigskin gloves — something beautiful that's just for you." Flora rolled her eyes, and Edith squinted, unable to imagine how Seema's indulgent taste and her mother's simplicity would square. "That is very kind of you," said Margot, looking to Frederick, who was nodding his head.

"Margot," said Flora gently. "Before we go inside to see Mutti, tell us what we can expect."

Margot described how their mother's illness had begun. When the vision in her left eye started to blur, their mother would press her finger against the lid, hoping to rub away the shadows. All that happened was the eye went slack and the flesh beneath it sank into her cheek. Margot shook her head and hesitated. Frederick continued: "Soon after, the left side of her face became immobilized and she had to struggle to keep the eye open. She had difficulty speaking and the side of her mouth drooped. Chewing became a chore. She had neither the interest nor the energy to keep trying."

Margot broke in and described how their mother's body had shrunk. "She became so light I could have carried her if I had to." They had moved her into Edith's room after she left for gymnasium in Frankfurt. "Sometimes, at night, when I come in to check on her, I think for a moment that it's Edith as

320

a little girl."

Margot sighed at the thought of it. "We were so young when Papa died. Do you remember how afterward Mutti never cried?" Seema and Flora nodded. "I was seven at the time," said Seema. "I asked her why she didn't cry, and she said something like, 'I'm not *that* kind of a woman.' I didn't understand what she meant by *that* kind of a woman, do you?"

"She probably meant she wasn't the kind of woman who would fall apart," said Margot. "She couldn't afford to because she had the three of us."

"Maybe she meant she wasn't sentimental," said Flora. "Or at least if she was, she sure as heck wasn't going to show it."

"I remember, right after, I tried to get her out of bed one morning," Seema continued. "She pushed me away and turned her face to the wall and I thought that maybe she had become *that* kind of a woman."

Margot sat up. "She's done the same thing these past few months when I tried to get her out of bed. Two weeks ago, I brought her some water and she looked at me as if she'd never seen me before and said, 'Who are you?' That's when I sent you the telegram, Flora."

Frederick moved his chair closer to his

wife. "It's been rough. Now that the two of you are here, Margot doesn't have to be the lone soldier anymore."

Seema reached for the plum schnapps.

"Come, let's go see her," said Margot, who had convinced herself that her sisters were as deeply devoted to their mother as she was. She tiptoed into the room, sat down on the bed, took her mother's hand, and began stroking it. The other two followed. Seema sat at the foot of the bed, on the edge, making sure not to touch her mother. Flora stood and studied her mother's shriveled body. Already her skin was starting to fall away from her bones. Flora searched her face for something familiar, but age and disease had stolen all of that.

Margot cupped the owl in her hand and held it up to her mother's face. "Look what Flora brought me. Isn't he beautiful? I'm going to call him Erich," she said in a child-like singsong voice. "Didn't you have a distant cousin named Erich? Wasn't he the one who took you to the old castle wall? You were a very little girl then, and he dared you to climb to the top with him, and you fell and you twisted your ankle but you didn't cry and you kept climbing. You remember that, don't you?" She placed the owl on the table next to the bed. "I'll leave

him here tonight so he can watch over you."
She kissed her mother on the cheek. "Sweet
dreams, Mutti. And don't have nightmares
about Erich and the castle wall." She stood
up and said to her sisters, "I read somewhere that even if people are unconscious,
you should keep talking to them as they
might hear you. There was this man in Lis-
bon, I believe, who was asleep for seven
years. His family kept talking to him anyway,
and one day he just opened his eyes, looked
around the room, and said, 'Where have you
been?' These things can happen."

Seema jumped up and left the room as
quickly as she could. Flora stared at her
mother and at her sister. She felt pity for
the frail woman and for her youngest daughter, whose heart was clearly breaking, but
that was all.

Seema had one more glass of the plum
schnapps before walking next door with
Flora to the Schultz farm. Out here it was
dark, darker than any night she'd seen in
New York City. In New York, nights just
seemed like days with shadows. There were
never any stars. And even if you were up at
four in the morning, all you had to do was
look out the window to see that you weren't
alone. But here, it was barely ten p.m. and

there were no signs of life or light, only the smudges of stars in the sky and the cold musky air. Seema thought the air smelled as if there were wild animals nearby, and it made her afraid. Flora carried a candle, and Seema took her arm. In her high heels, with a few glasses of schnapps in her and her suitcase in the other hand, she was wobbly. "I hope this place is, you know, decent," she said.

Flora laughed. "You won't care tonight," she said. "We just need to get into bed and everything will be fine."

The Schultz farm turned out to be more than decent. Frau Schultz had fixed up a room for them off the kitchen. There were two beds with fresh linen sheets and goose-down quilts. There was a bureau, a fireplace, and a little table on which she had left treasures: chocolate, a loaf of bread, butter, and a bottle of milk. Seema sat down on the bed nearest the door. The pillows were fluffed and the room was toasty. In the fire's glow, Flora looked like a little girl, unpacking her suitcase and carefully laying her things in the bureau. Seema kicked off her shoes, took off her suit, peeled off her stockings, and dropped them to the floor. Without bothering to wash up, she got under the covers. Someone had taken the time to make it cozy here. She lay in the goose-feather cocoon and watched Flora as she readied for bed.

It was reassuring to have Flora so close by. It was even reassuring to have Margot next door. Seema felt warm and she hugged the quilt around her. She tried to remember the last time she had felt this taken care of and safe. It must have been when she and Flora were very little girls, right after they came to America and stayed with Aunt Hannah and Uncle Paul. An uninvited memory barged into her thoughts. Mr. Holt, Uncle Paul's friend. The things he did to her in the kitchen. She tried to shoo away the party crasher by turning her mind to other things. "Do you suppose if we had stayed here, we'd look the way we look?" she asked Flora.

"Do you mean, *Would we dress in clothes from B. Altman's and Wanamaker's?* I doubt it. If you mean, *Would we look as worn out as Margot?* I don't know."

Flora got into bed and kept talking. "Margot's always been high-strung, but I've never seen her like this. Thank God for Frederick. He's saintly, the way he takes care of her. I can't imagine what she'd do without him — well, you know, after . . ."

"Do you think she really believes that

Mutti can hear her and might even wake up?" asked Seema.

"I guess she's hoping that if she keeps at it long enough, she can jog her memory and bring her back to life," said Flora.

Seema sighed. "It's sad. That woman is as close to dead as a living person can be. How long do you think she has? One day? Two at the most? I predict we'll be home in a few weeks."

"People don't die on schedule," Flora said flatly. "We could be here for a while."

Seema heard the annoyance in her sister's voice, and suddenly she was a million miles from Frau Schultz's firelit bedroom. "This place isn't such a dump after all. But honestly, I'll last here about a week, at the most. Even if she doesn't die, I don't know how much of Margot's moping I can take. Frederick may be a saint, but truthfully, he's going to drive me crazy; the way he talks to Margot, as if she's a two-year-old. It's sickening."

"Seema, you've had an awful lot to drink. Why don't we just go to sleep now and talk in the morning?" Flora closed her eyes and turned away.

"Oh come on, don't tell me they don't drive you as crazy as they drive me," Seema pressed, wide awake now. "How is it that everyone is always trying to protect little Margot? Even Edith — and you know how I adore Edith. Poor Edith, sleeping in the same room as that woman. I could never do that. The smell alone . . ."

"For crying out loud, Seema, shut up. You don't know what you're saying. You've had half a bottle of liquor tonight."

"You're my sister," said Seema, her tone suddenly plaintive. "If I can't talk to you, who can I talk to?"

"How about Oliver?"

"I would rather die. To be perfectly honest, there's not much I can talk about with Oliver. I don't mean that I'd be ashamed talking about these things with him. It's just that he has specific tastes, if you know what I mean. I know he'd want me to be comfortable and he'd be concerned that I . . . Flora? Flora. Are you awake?"

Over the next week, and the one after that, the three sisters took turns sitting by their mother's bedside. When Seema suggested they call a doctor, Frederick shook his head. "It's too late for that," he said. "The one time the doctor came, he said there was nothing to be done." Now there was even less to be done as she'd mostly stopped eating. They were able to dribble water into her mouth and every now and again some milk. Every other day they would wash her. Margot would brush her hair and make sure that her fingernails and toenails were trimmed. The hardest part was when she soiled herself. They'd fashioned diapers out of old linen sheets, dishrags, and anything else they could find, but even then there was some leaking. And the smell. It was the stench of urine and feces and something rotting from within. While none of them talked about it, it was clear by the nasal sound of their voices that they each held their breath every time they were near her. At these times, Seema would usually find a reason to walk out of the room, leaving the chore of changing her mother to one of the others.

When Seema was off duty, she would take long walks in the countryside. If she walked south, she'd come to the Pfälzer Wald, the woods and the lake where Edith swam in the summer. Seema found comfort in the still water and the lithe beechwoods and in the thought that these things would go on forever. And when she'd had about enough of nature, she'd walk north to Café Konditorei, where she could have a cup of bitter German coffee, or something stronger, smoke a cigarette, and eat an éclair. The walls were a golden yellow, and the place always smelled of cigarette smoke and freshly brewing coffee. It wasn't like the frantic bars back home, where people knocked back drinks for sport and bragged about it. Locals sat here for hours reading newspapers, writing letters, or just talking with friends. They didn't come for show but for comfort and, as in Seema's case, because they didn't have a better place to go. It didn't take long for the owner to recognize Seema and to bring over the first cup of coffee without her asking. Now and then a strange man would look her way or even sit down for conversation. Once, when one of them asked her where she was staying, she said the Schultz farm. "Oh, that's next door to the Jew house, isn't it?" he'd asked. She didn't make much of it.

One evening, close to midnight, Seema was sitting with her mother. It was her turn and the others had gone to bed. The awful smell was all over the room. At first, she tried to ignore it, but it wasn't something that could be ignored. Several times she walked out, hoping the odor would have disappeared by the time she returned. But each time it stung her eyes and stuck in her throat until she gagged.

She closed her eyes and begged to find the strength to do what she would have to do now. Out of habit, she reached for her gold chain, and again it wasn't there. But she pretended it was, and she thought about the cross and the young girl she'd imagined had lost it and how she'd felt so protective of her. She looked at the figure lying in the bed, pitiful and even smaller than the young girl in her imagination, and she stopped thinking that this was her mother. She was another child, a helpless infant, and she thought to herself that no one with an ounce of humanity in them could deny an infant.

I can do this, she thought, as she pulled back the sheets. She cleaned her mother, tossed the soiled diaper in a bucket for Margot to wash, and fashioned another one out of an old dishrag. She did these things without holding her breath, and when she finished, she gently tucked in the sheets around her mother. She felt surprisingly protective, and she even allowed herself to realize that when she was a baby her mother must have done the same for her. It made her wince with forgotten comfort, but it didn't make her like her mother one bit more.

Late in the evening on Thanksgiving Day, Flora sat by her mother's bedside writing her daily letter to Simon:

> Right now I imagine you are sitting down to dinner at Aunt Hannah and Uncle Paul's. I close my eyes and wish with all of my heart that I were there with you. I hope that Aunt Hannah doesn't make that disgusting sweet potato dish with marshmallows, and that you get to carve the turkey instead of Uncle Paul, because I know that his sloppy carving drives you crazy. Here it is depressing and lonely and about as opposite from Thanksgiving as can ever be. I am so homesick it is hard to describe.

The thought of home seemed like a miracle to her, and impossibly out of reach. She allowed herself a moment of sadness, and even said out loud, "Oh Simon." It was in the silence that followed that she became aware of her mother's breathing, irregular and rattling. Flora dropped the letter onto the floor and ran to get the others. They came in, reluctantly, and stood around the bed, none of them knowing what to say. The sisters, Edith, and Frederick sat vigil until dawn blazed across the sky. Margot got into bed and lay next to her mother as the others sat on straight-backed chairs. Just before the sun broke through, Margot rolled over. She put her arm around her mother's shoulders and placed her head on her chest as her mother heaved and made strangled gurgling noises and finally made no sound at all.

"My poor Mutti," whispered Margot.

The next day, they buried her in the cemetery outside of town. Some neighboring families showed up, as did a few of the men who worked with Frederick. The local rabbi performed the service, such as it was. It took him only a few minutes to read the Twenty-third Psalm and recite the Kaddish. Frederick had warned them about what would happen next. According to Jewish custom, after they lowered the pine box into the ground, members of the family would each have to place three shovelfuls of dirt on top of it. It was a matter of honor, he said, to bury the dead personally rather than leave it to the grave diggers. Margot started at the thought. It was such a definitive act, one that made it impossible to deny what had just happened. When the baby Gilda died, they hadn't buried her at the cemetery. The people in the hospital had taken her. Margot never considered where they might have put her, but now her mind began to wander. Had they thrown her in a sack with other ruined bodies or body parts? Dumped her in the garbage? Dropped her to the bottom of the lake? Margot's body heaved and sagged as if she might scream. It came out as a moan. Frederick put his arms around her and helped her lift the dirt. "Don't worry, I'm here," he whispered.

Flora needed no help. She lifted three neat mounds and placed them squarely on the center of the coffin, then handed Seema the metal shovel. It was heavier than Seema expected, and she was unsure whether she'd be able to lift it at all. She felt as if she might fall down in the pile of dirt, or worse, on top of her mother's casket. She was trembling and light-headed, and she was crying. Seema rarely cried, and never in public, and she looked imploringly to Flora and then to Edith and Frederick, as if any one of them could help her, but no one moved to do so. Even after she managed to dump the three shovelfuls of dirt on her mother's casket, she continued to sob.

That evening, Flora, Seema, and Edith sat around the kitchen table eating some of the *Apfelkuchen* and *Streuselkuchen* that the neighbors had brought. Frederick poured Seema a glass of schnapps. "It's good for the nerves," he said, and this time Seema found his voice surprisingly soothing. Then he boiled some water for tea, stirred two tablespoons of honey into it, and placed it on a tray along with a slice of the *Streuselkuchen* and a piece of bread with butter and jam. He carried it toward Margot's room. "She hasn't eaten a thing all day," he said to nobody in particular. "She has to get something in her stomach."

Seema swallowed her drink in one gulp and poured another, while wondering what kind of a woman would solicit that kind of sympathy from a man. Then she pulled out a pack of cigarettes from her purse, along with the silver cigarette holder that Oliver had given her. The cigarette holder felt clumsy and cold in her hands. It wasn't of this place. Oliver wasn't of this place. She thought about the goose-feather quilt next door, the smell of coffee at the Café Konditorei. Since she'd been here, no one had called her "Seamless" or "Seema Sweet Ass," and no one seemed to care if she used the right fork, had the clever retort, or wore stylish gowns. As she thought about her life in New York, it seemed glamorous and expensive but not familiar or comfortable. Not like it did here.

She looked across the table and smiled at Edith, who smiled back. Seema thought that the weight her niece had gained made her look cherubic and filled with life. Then she remembered what Edith had said earlier about smoking to lose weight, and she offered her a cigarette. As they lit up, Flora waved her hand in front of her. She hated the smell of cigarettes and could be insufferable when anyone around her smoked. Seema blew a smoke ring in her sister's direction. Flora waved both hands and Seema gave Edith a look as if to say, *You do it now.* Both of them blew smoke right under Flora's nose. Seema knew it was mean to tease her sister this way, but Flora could be so demanding and exasperating. Edith and Seema made it into a game, and the more Flora gesticulated and grimaced, the harder they laughed. Laughing and smoking at the same time made Edith cough, which even made Flora laugh. When she stopped long enough to catch her breath and say, "This isn't funny, we just buried our mother today," the three of them started screaming with laughter. Seema's head fell to the table, and Flora buried her head in her hands. "Shhh," said Flora. "What if Margot hears us?" That set them off even more. Tears ran down their cheeks, and they had to hold their sides. They laughed like that until their throats were sore and the backs of their necks ached, and they had no more laughter in them. Seema couldn't remember the last time she'd laughed like that.

They were quiet now as she poured herself another drink and Edith took up a new cigarette in earnest. Flora placed her elbows on the table and folded her hands in front of her. She stared at her older sister, whose eyes were still swollen, and she spoke carefully. "So Seema, what happened to you at the cemetery today?"

Seema shook her head.

She thought about all of it: the joyless gray sky, the doleful rabbi who wouldn't look any of them in the eye, the tiny group at the graveside, her small and shrinking family. It wasn't any one of those things but it was all of them.

"I don't know. I guess it's that our mother is gone," she said. "Our mother has always been gone, but we always had a mother and now we don't. Does that make any sense?"

"Yes. It makes you feel off balance somehow," said Flora. "Like no one is in charge except us."

Seema turned to Edith. "You're lucky, you know your mother and father and you know you're loved by them."

"That comes with a price, too, believe me," said Edith.

"I'm sure it does," said Seema, rolling her eyes in the direction of Edith's parents' bedroom, "but you know your place with them. I have no idea who my mother really was and she had no idea of what my life was like. It never occurred to me that she wouldn't just keep going on and always be there. This was so surprising. So quick."

Seema pulled a handkerchief from her purse and blew her nose. Then she picked up her cigarette, though this time she blew the smoke away from Flora. "You're lucky, too," she said to Flora. "You have your place with Simon. He loves you and he really is your family."

"And you?" said Flora. "You have Oliver. Surely, he would say that you're his family."

Seema shook her head. She didn't say what she knew to be the truth. She was no more a member of the Oliver Thomas family than she was of the John D. Rockefellers.

They talked long into that night. Edith said she was worried about her mother now that her grandmother was gone. "Pappa is so patient with her. Sometimes I feel in the way here, like she's more his child than I am. I worry that, if something should happen to him, she would be lost."

"How's he doing?" asked Flora.

Edith shrugged. "You see how he is.

Cheerful, helpful. I think it must be a relief for him to go to work each day even though that place is horrible."

"You think the job's going okay?" Flora continued. "You know, with things the way they are?"

Once again Edith shrugged. "All I know is there's still food on the table."

Flora was playing with her napkin, twisting its corners. "Edith, let me ask you a question. I don't want you to answer right away, but I want you to think about it. The situation here, as I'm sure you know, is not so good. Simon doesn't think it's going to get better soon, and he's usually right about things like that. We've been talking a lot about it, and we would like to bring you and your parents to America. Now that your grandmother is gone and the rest of us are in New York, it would be a good time to come. Your mother would have company and we could all be together. Simon is certain he could get your father a job, and you could go to school at one of the universities nearby. I'm going to bring it up to your parents tomorrow."

"I could eat this cake all by myself," said Edith, nibbling at the *Apfelkuchen.* "That's the thing about being away at gymnasium. No one tells you what you can or can't do, so you do everything to extreme until you realize that you can't anymore. Look at me. I'm as fat as a horse, yet there's always more cake and potatoes and chocolate to eat."

"Oh darling, you look beautiful just the way you are. Just get the hair out of your eyes," said Seema, sweeping Edith's hair off her face. "Look at those gorgeous eyes. Who can see them behind all this?" You know what? I think you should cut your hair and have bangs. You'd look adorable. Don't you think so, Flora?" Seema went to pour herself another glass of schnapps but the bottle was empty.

Flora stared at the two of them as if they were speaking Chinese. "Has anyone heard anything I've been saying?"

"What? Were you saying something?" asked Seema.

Edith picked up Seema's taunting voice. "Oh, Aunt Flora, I'm sorry, I didn't hear what you said."

The two of them giggled. Flora was so earnest and persistent and so easy to tease.

"Do you think this is a joke?" Flora raised her voice and turned toward Edith. "This country is nearly bankrupt. Your mother is emotionally and physically exhausted. And I'll tell you something else: Simon and I don't think this is a great place for Jewish people to be right now. Your father could be out on the street at any second. And then where would you be? Is that really so funny?"

Seema shook her head from side to side and made an exasperated face. "Whoops, there she goes again. Edith, in case you hadn't noticed, your Aunt Flora and Uncle Simon are Jews on a mission. According to them, the whole world is anti-Semitic. With them, it's all about who's for the Jews and who's against them." Then, turning to Flora, she said, "Nobody cares that much, Flora. Really, nobody does!"

Flora was about to answer her when Edith broke in. "I'm sorry, Aunt Flora. It is very kind of you and Uncle Simon to think about bringing us to America. But you know my mother. She'll never leave this country, not even this town or this house. And Pappa, well, you know how he feels about Germany. Sometimes he'll say that Germany is having its growing pains, but that's as far as he goes. How do you say it in America? He's a German through and through. Me? I'd come in a minute if they would, but I can't imagine going without them."

Flora leaned back in her chair. "Have you ever seen pictures of New York City at Christmas? There are lights everywhere, and the streets are filled with people, and every store you go into is playing Christmas music. It's beautiful, like nothing you've ever seen before. We could all be in New York by Christmas. Together. That would be something. Don't you agree, Seema?"

Seema was staring at something on the floor and didn't bother to raise her head. She was thinking about how every year since she'd known him, Oliver had taken his family skiing in St. Moritz over Christmas and she'd end up spending the holidays sitting alone in her apartment on Park Avenue. She never wanted to admit to Flora or to Aunt Hannah and Uncle Paul that her married boyfriend was off with his family, so she'd decline their invitations and pretend that she and Oliver were going away together for some swanky holiday in Florida or Havana. Now the thought of spending another Christmas alone in that stuffy, overfurnished apartment lodged in her throat. When she finally answered Flora, it came out in a croak. "Christmas in New York stinks," she said. "And you know what else? New York stinks, and I'm never going back there."

New York City:
1932

So long as Flora Phelps could go shopping downtown, she claimed she would never have to go to Paris. At least that's how she would rationalize it to Simon after one of her shopping sprees. When he came home from work, she would have already laid out on their bed the extravagances she had hunted down on that day's foray into the city. Then, one by one, she'd try them on for him: dresses in lurid colors and clinging styles that accentuated her bosom and made no secret of the rest of her. He would lie on the bed, his hands folded beneath his head, and watch as she whirled and posed in front of him, the way the models did in *Vogue* and *Harper's Bazaar*. They would talk about the colors that complemented her skin tone or which skirt lengths flattered her legs. She got a kick out of the surprising matches he'd make between her dresses and hats and how he'd follow her with his eyes and say things like, "How is it that you are more beautiful than ever?"

Flora relished this ritual because it made her feel young and sexy. It was also one of the few times she could bring Simon into her world. If he judged her to be superficial or girlish or, heaven help her, too much like Seema, he never said so. Sometimes, he would pretend to scold her: "That one must have cost a pretty penny. At least when we go bankrupt, *you'll* go out in style." To which she would say, "It could be worse. What if I wanted to go to Paris every season for the latest couture? This way we only have to pay for me to go to Fifth Avenue and back."

She missed Seema. She missed talking about the latest fashions with her and their occasional shopping sprees. She even missed how Seema would chide her and say, "Don't buy that dress. It makes you look like a frumpy matron. Honestly, you can't be trusted on your own." It was just the two of them now, and for the first time in her life, Flora shared Simon's longing to have her family in one place.

In late October 1929, the stock market had crashed, and nearly everyone in the country had gone bankrupt. By December of the following year, more than half the stores downtown had been shuttered; their window displays faded and their mannequins developed a cover of dust. The mannequins that were still dressed wore the wool jackets and pumps of a season that seemed an eternity ago. On the streets where Flora's beloved millinery shops were tucked away, men and women, wedged together so tightly that no one could break in, waited in the interminable bread lines that snaked around the blocks. Many of the men in line dressed in their business suits, pretending for their neighbors — and sometimes their wives — that they were heading off to work in the morning. Even so, their clothes hung on them as heavily as their desperation.

A few lucky ones, like Flora and Simon, didn't lose everything because they had stashed money away in places other than the stock market. In Simon's case, he'd remembered how J. P. Morgan brought together financiers and banks to bail out the ailing market in 1907. Ever since then, Simon had always kept his money in J. P. Morgan's bank.

Old habits die hard, and despite the dire economic situation, Flora continued her trips downtown, taking care to hide the magnitude of her purchases. Someone would tell her about a milliner on the fifth floor of a walk-up around the corner from Macy's, where she'd find a perfect hat with a large silk rose. Or she'd go uptown to Bergdorf Goodman and buy a pair of blue-and-white spectator shoes or a jacket with a mink collar and mink cuffs to match. Instead of carrying her goods in the fancy wrappings and hatboxes they came in, she would bring with her a string bag and other unmarked bags, so she wouldn't call attention to her luxuries.

But she and Simon also bought for others, a fact that helped assuage her guilt. Through the Beth David sisterhood, they gave clothes and money to Jewish families who had nothing. And that Christmas, Simon donated enough books, toys, and games to the Yonkers schools so that each child was guaranteed a present.

Because people still craved cigarettes and found money for soap and razor blades, Phelps and Adler stayed in business and even managed to remain solvent for the next two years. By now, they had earned a reputation for being modern and innovative and at times even a bit crackpot with their use of invisible ink and mechanized window displays. Anyone looking to bend the rules and rewrite the language of advertising was likely to find his way to Bond Street. So it was that Earl Lambert came to call on Simon in the spring of 1932. A man of considerable wealth but few words, Lambert had inherited the Lambert Pharmacal Company from his father. A tall New Englander with a spoon-shaped face and brown eyes, Lambert sat across from Simon's desk in a wooden chair that was too small for him, and for the entirety of their twenty-minute meeting, he never stopped fussing. He used the pinky of his right hand to rummage in his right ear. He swayed his foot back and forth, hitting the leg of the chair each time. He bit the inside of his lip and blew air inside his cheeks until they looked like balloons. When Simon told Flora about him later, he referred to him as "Mr. Fidget."

"I'll give it to you straight. Pro-phy-lac-tic, our toothbrush subsidiary, is in the soup," said Lambert, slapping his left hand on Simon's desk to emphasize his last three words. "Nothing I do seems to work. And when they stop buying our toothbrushes, they stop buying our toothpaste. I'm a desperate man, which is why I'm here to put myself in your hands. Come up with one of your cockamamy schemes and I'm likely to give it a try." He pulled the finger from his ear and studied something on the tip of it. Whatever it was seemed to satisfy him, and a smile broke out on his face as he stood up and shook Simon's hand. "It's always been enough that a toothbrush is a toothbrush. Doesn't seem to be so anymore. I'm sure you'll think of something."

"Thank you for your confidence in me," said Simon, taking his hand. "I'll be back to you in a week with some ideas."

Mr. Lambert was nearly out of the office when he abruptly turned back toward Simon. "Phelps," he said, tapping the plate on the door. "Not a common name is it?"

"No, it isn't," said Simon, dreading what would follow.

"I knew a Phelps in St. Louis. Andrew Phelps. Was in the foot powder business. So long now."

That was unexpected, thought Simon with relief. His relatives were all named Filips. This Andrew wouldn't be one of them. Then, as he often did, he visualized the word. *Unexpected,* with its gullies and crisscrosses. And the word remained suspended in his imagination as he considered the problem before him: What could he offer a customer that would be unexpected and inexpensive and would make buying a toothbrush more appealing?

During these times, the idea of giving away something for free was an obvious one.

347

Simon was sure he'd be able to design the thingamajig; he just had no idea what it would be. As always, he brought his problem to the person who understood consumers better than anyone he knew: Flora.

"Whatever it is," he told her, "it has to be cheap, easy, and unexpected. And by that, I don't mean Seema." Simon flushed, uncomfortable with having made an off-color joke.

Flora looked startled. "Simon, you wicked man." She smiled, but Simon could see the parentheses of strain around her mouth.

This was no time to get distracted by thoughts of Seema, thought Flora. Whenever Simon asked for her help in business matters, she tried hard to be helpful and show him that there was more in her head than pretty hats and pocketbooks. She came up with two ideas immediately: a nailbrush and a small kit with samples of Lambert toothpaste, shampoo, and soap. They talked about doing a map of the stars or a guide to all the countries in the world and their capitals. Simon thought both seemed too ambitious for a freebie. "How about a chart with all the states of the United States, their capitals, and their populations?" suggested Flora. Simon wrote it down in his notebook. "Or how about a game of sorts?" That's

348

when he came up with the idea for a jigsaw puzzle.

"A jigsaw puzzle makes good sense," he said. "Right now, nobody has money to spend on movies or any other outside entertainment. A family can take days putting together a good jigsaw." It would be a great escape, he reasoned, and best of all, finishing it would give everyone a sense of accomplishment, something that was hard to come by with the unemployment rate creeping up toward 25 percent.

After some quick research, Simon discovered that the biggest problem with puzzles is that they were made of wood and they cost a fortune to produce. Each one had to be sawed by hand and it was tricky and time-consuming to manipulate those intricate patterns. Often the saws would break and it could take hours to complete just one of them. The cost of a 1,200-piece puzzle at one cent to one and a half cents a piece added up to as much as $18 a puzzle.

There has to be a cheaper way, he thought. For the next couple of nights, he stayed up well past midnight cutting out patterns from different thicknesses of paper and cardboard to see which would be the most pliable. When he figured out the right weight of cardboard, he found an automobile ad showing a magnificent maroon Packard whizzing around the corner beneath a snowy evening sky and a grove of cedars. He pasted the ad on the piece of cardboard and drew onto it the pattern of what would be a fifty-piece puzzle. Using an X-Acto knife, he cut out the pieces, and then fitted them back together.

When Lambert returned the following week, he again sat across from Simon in the too-small wooden chair. "So what have you got?" he asked, twirling his sideburn. Simon stood up in front of an easel and presented him with drawings he'd made of the nail-brush, the kit with the Lambert products, and the map with all of the capitals on it. Then he showed him the puzzle. "If we can figure out a way to stamp out hundreds of these at a time, rather than hand cutting them one by one," he said, absentmindedly running his fingers along the Packard's radiator, "this is the one that would cost the least to produce." Lambert bit his nail, then massaged the back of his neck with both hands. Simon wondered if he'd heard any-thing he said, and continued: "There you have it. I'm happy to answer any questions you might have."

"No questions," said Lambert, lifting himself out of the chair. He clasped his hands in front of him and cracked his knuckles. "You've got yourself a deal, Mr. Phelps. Just don't break the bank. I'll take a million of those puzzles."

The first thing Simon did was to commission a watercolor from Frances Tipton Hunter, an illustrator known for her endearing pictures of children. Her painting of a Rockwellian little boy brushing a startled bull terrier's teeth with a Pro-phy-lac-tic toothbrush painted in solid blocks and distinct images was perfectly suited to be chopped up into fifty pieces and put back together again. Simon brought the painting to the machinist at his shop. "All we have to do is figure out how to make a million of these at a time, and we're sitting pretty," he said. The machinist laughed out loud. But for the next few months, everyone at Phelps and Adler concentrated on little else. First, they photographed the Hunter painting and reduced its size. They lithographed the photo onto a single sheet of paper and pasted the paper by machine onto a thin piece of cardboard. The machinist devised something called a stamping machine. Instead of hand cutting the puzzle one piece at a time by saw, the machine pressed a steel die down onto the sheet, quickly cutting it into pieces. Because of that, the cardboard had to be exactly the right thickness and weight. Much as Simon had done at home, they experimented for weeks before finding the perfect cardboard. There would be workers, "cutters," they'd call them, who would figure out patterns in which to cut the pictures and then use electrically propelled but hand-guided jigsaws to do so. From those pieces, the steel dies were made. If everything went as planned, they figured they'd be able to punch out fifty thousand to sixty thousand puzzles of the same design in a single shift.

The Friday right before Labor Day, they were finally ready to try out the new equipment. That evening, everyone at Phelps and Adler stood around the pressroom waiting to see how it would work. After a run of about twenty sheets, the press jammed, and they had to shut it down in order to retrieve inky balls of paper. Then steel rules got too dull or broke. By now it was well past five p.m., when everyone would normally grab their bags and head out for the weekend. Nobody stirred. They stood silently, some with fingers pressed to their lips, others with arms folded, as once again the presses whirred and the stamping machine trembled and the first one hundred puzzles were born. The cutters did their job, and when Simon tried to fit the odd-shaped pieces together, the nubs and zigs and crescent-moon shapes locked in as smoothly as if they had never been parted. "Keep 'em rolling," shouted Simon, and a cheer went up as the first of what would eventually be a million puzzles rolled out.

What happened next made history. Mr. Fidget's sales skyrocketed 400 percent by December, and Simon got orders from big companies all around the country. The cardboard puzzles were so popular that Simon started the Every Week Jigsaw Puzzle, a line of cardboard puzzles that cost fifteen cents and were intricate and complicated enough to appeal to adults. Then came Radio Stars puzzles that, for only twenty-five cents, allowed customers to piece together the faces of people like Eddie Cantor, Rudy Vallee, or Kate Smith and get a brochure that told their life stories. In February 1933, the *New Yorker* ran a "Talk of the Town" column all about Simon's modernized factory that said the company had taken on between three and four hundred additional workers to turn out the puzzles. "It's a cheering sight in these times to visit the factory," the anonymous author wrote.

Everyone seemed to be pleased by Simon's success except for Simon. The long hours and constant pressure wore him out. He walked more slowly, talked less, and was so preoccupied that he'd often not hear what people were saying to him. But worse was his disappointment in himself. "It's unseemly to me that I am earning a fortune making puzzles when I can't even solve the real one in my own life," he'd say to Flora.

"When your family gets here, they will want for nothing," she'd say. But on this subject, he wouldn't be budged. And despite her soothing tone, she hardly believed her own words.

On a Tuesday afternoon, one week after the *New Yorker* ran its piece, Simon was working in his office, his head down as usual. There was a panel of glass in his office that ran from the ceiling to the floor and was about four feet wide. Although it was there for purely decorative reasons, there were those who thought that he had it installed so he could watch his employees. Nothing could be further from the truth. If anything, Simon could be faulted for keeping his door shut and not looking up long enough to know half the people who worked for him. But on this day, there was some commotion outside his door as a copy of *Time* was being passed around and read out loud. Someone in the art department painted a sign in crimson that said THE PUZZLE KING and tacked it up on Simon's door. Simon was on deadline creating an ad for Sapolin Paints, but he took time to look out at the hullabaloo. Several people noticed him watching through the window and gave him the thumbs up. Someone began chanting, "All hail to the Puzzle King," and the others joined in. Someone held up a copy of *Time.* There was a picture of Simon with a caption underneath that read: "Simon Phelps, America's Puzzle King." Simon recognized that this was a big deal; it was great for the company, great for him. He wished he could feel the excitement that everyone else did, but he would join in the celebration and make the effort. He pushed his chair away from his desk and was about to go outside when he spotted something that made him sit back down again.

A slim man wearing a coat whose hem had come undone and was ragged around the edge was walking toward him. The man's hair was thinning and he was so pale that not even his lips had color. He was carrying a paper shopping bag spilling over with envelopes, little boxes, and pages torn out of old magazines and newspapers. Something about the way the man moved and how his eyes kept shifting from one person to another as if he was worried about being noticed held Simon's attention. The man came closer and Simon could see by the way his skin seemed to melt around his chin that he had once been very fat. He walked with a slight limp, but that's not why Simon couldn't take his eyes off of him. He had a hunch that the man was there to see him, and when his secretary knocked on his door and said, "There's a gentleman here who says you go way back," Simon shook his head and said, "Of course, show him in," without knowing why.

The man stood before him. His eyes traveled the room, taking in the silver framed photographs on the desk and the leather-bound volumes on the shelf. As Simon stared at him, he peeled away age until he had excavated the face of a boy he once knew.

"I'll be damned. Aaron Eisendraft? Pissboy? Is it really you?"

"So it is," said Pissboy, who seemed an old man now, made older by some missing teeth and his tentative demeanor. "Forgive me for barging in on you like this."

"Don't be silly," said Simon. "After all

356

these years, I've often wondered what happened to you."

Pissboy looked away. "Yeah, well *there's* a story for *Time* magazine."

Simon waited for his old friend to continue. When he didn't, he knew not to pry. "Have a seat," he said. "Let me take your coat."

"That's okay," said Pissboy, "I'll keep it on." He was much smaller than Simon remembered and cut a curious figure, sitting on the couch wrapped in his shabby coat with the shopping bag on his lap. "Let me not take up too much of your valuable time. The purpose of my visit is twofold." He pulled an envelope from his bag and laid it on the coffee table that sat between them. "As you can see, I'm not a young man anymore. I could say that life hasn't been kind to me, but the truth is, I haven't been so kind to life." Here he paused to make sure that Simon caught his turn of phrase. "I'll tell you this, my friend, my past weighs heavy on me. I can't undo what's been done, but in the time I have left, I can try to make some of it right, if you know what I mean. Which is why I've brought you this." He handed Simon the envelope. "Go on, open it."

Inside the envelope were brittle pieces of

357

yellowed paper. Simon unfolded each sheet and spread them out on the table. His heart beat fast and he covered his mouth with his hand when he realized what they were: drawings of the Fatsos, of Strongman, of Mrs. O'Mara, his first-grade teacher. His drawings. They were exuberant and romantic and so filled with feeling. The boy who had drawn them had promise.

"Where did you get these?" he asked Piss-boy.

"You may remember that I had a certain, ahem, talent. I could pilfer 'souvenirs' from anybody practically right under their nose and they never knew. I took these from your sketchbook. I chose ones that were near duplicates because I thought you wouldn't notice. Guess I was right about that, huh? Anyway, that was then and now is now. Certain events have occurred that made me realize I no longer want to be in possession of possessions that are not rightfully mine. For the past few years my movements have been, shall we say, restricted, but now that they're not I'm making it my business to return every souvenir that I have, ah, borrowed. You were a cinch to track down. It helps that you're still alive." He pointed to his shopping bag. "I have all the articles that have been written about you. But finding all

358

the others?" He shook his head. "Believe you me it's not been easy. Know what I mean?

"The second reason for my visit here is of a less pleasant matter. To put it bluntly, I'm broke. I need a job. I don't have many skills but I have quick fingers and I'll work them to the bone. I'd rather not get into the particulars of my situation, but suffice it to say I'll take anything you might have."

Simon, overwhelmed by his drawings, and by seeing the down-and-out state of his old friend, raised his hands. "You don't have to say another word. Of course I'll give you a job. You'd make a perfect cutter." He explained the work of a cutter and Pissboy exercised his fingers as if he were playing the piano. "Sounds like just the thing for these nimble hands," he said.

Simon could see the uncertainty behind his friend's show of bravado and tried to reassure him. "Don't worry, it's not as complicated as it sounds. Oh, and one more thing," he said, desperate to lighten this impromptu reunion. "A puzzle isn't a puzzle without all of its pieces. So if one goes missing, and I find you've pilfered it?" He shrugged. "Know what I'm saying?"

"I get your drift," said Pissboy. "I promise I won't mess up. I owe you big for this."

"It's my pleasure," said Simon. "And you can keep the drawings."

That night, Flora was giddy when she greeted Simon at the door. "The King is home, long live the King. Does everyone in the world read *Time* magazine? I've gotten phone calls from people I hardly know. Say, if you're the Puzzle King, does that make me the Puzzle Queen?"

"It's good to be here," he said, taking her hands. His own were cold.

Lately, when Simon came home, all he wanted to do was to collapse into his leather chair, put his feet up on the ottoman, and read the paper. Sometimes he'd have a drink, but more often than not, by the time Flora brought it to him, his head would be inclined to one side, the paper would have fallen to the floor, and he would be fast asleep.

"Floramor, you will always be *my* queen, you know that." He held her hands tighter. "I am so very tired. Will you come upstairs and lie down with me?" He never called her Floramor except right after they'd made love, and then his voice would get childlike, as he lay curled up on his side with his arm around her belly and his head resting on her breast. "My Floramor I do adore her, do anything in the world just for her." He'd say it three or four times, like a nursery rhyme, and often those would be his last words of the evening.

They went upstairs and he fell onto the bed without bothering to remove his clothes. Flora pulled off his shoes and lay down next to him. He stared at the ceiling while she massaged his head. Simon had told her that when he was a little boy, his mother would rub his head before he went to sleep. She would tell him she was rubbing away everything bad so that he would only have good dreams and wake up with happy thoughts. Now, as Flora stroked her husband's graying temples and balding head, she hoped his mother was right. "Did something happen today?" she asked.

"No," he said, too worn out to tell her about Pissboy. "Today was a fine day. We made lots of puzzles and lots of money and we got a nice write up in *Time* magazine. Things couldn't be better."

"So then, it's life as usual. Right?"

"Life as usual, I guess. I'm just so tired I feel it in my bones."

"Well, then, maybe you need to get some sleep," she said.

"It isn't that kind of tired, Flora. Do you realize that in less than a month I'll be fifty years old? I'm probably twice the age my father was when he died. A half a century old. Does that seem possible? I'm not a young man anymore. I feel like I'm eighty. And for what?"

"Oh Simon, look at what you've achieved. More than you ever expected or imagined. I am so proud of you. Your family will be so proud of you." She kneaded the place above his eyebrows where she could feel the ropes of tension.

"I've made a lot of money," he said. "And don't get me wrong, I love how we live: our house, the beautiful clothes you wear. We have a wonderful life. But sometimes I feel as if we're living in a bubble. If all I do in my lifetime is make a million dollars and more puzzles than anyone else, what does that mean? I still have no idea what happened to my family. This country's in the pit of a depression, Europe is even worse, and I'm making premiums for toothpaste? This can't be all."

Flora stopped rubbing his head. She wanted to say, *You have everything in life a man could want, why can't you just be happy with that?* But she knew better than to try to argue with him when he got into one of these moods. So she lay next to him perplexed at how seriously he took the world.

They were different that way. When he was burdened, it was never about not being invited to one party or another or that there might be mice in the basement. It was more momentous than that. Her anxieties lived closer to home. Most of the time, she didn't even tell Simon about them for fear he'd find them silly.

Lately, it was Seema who shaped Flora's worries. Seema showed no signs of coming home and Flora feared she would be swallowed up by Germany. There were letters, typical Seema letters: "darling" this and "marvelous" that, but really, Flora had little sense of what was going on in her life. She knew there were men, maybe even one man, as she dropped "we" offhandedly: "We went to Berlin for the weekend. We were hoping to go to Paris for a few days, but there seems to be no time for anything but work, work, work" or "We simply love the opera." In one letter, Seema asked Flora to address her mail to Seema Glass from now on. "It's much easier that way and takes up much less room than big old Grossman. You were smart to get rid of it when you did."

Flora recoiled at the memory of having to tell Oliver that Seema wasn't coming back. He'd rung her up just after Christmas, the year their mother died. "Your sister's pulled a Houdini," he'd said. "Any idea when she's coming back?" When Flora told him Seema wasn't coming back, he laughed. "Of course she's coming back. Everything's here: her apartment, her jewelry, her clothes, me. She told me she was only staying a couple of weeks. Said she didn't think she could take more than that."

"Well, I'm telling you," Flora said, "she's still in Germany. She claims she's never coming back."

"That's ridiculous." His voice grew louder. "You're pulling my leg, aren't you? Oh, wait a minute. I get it, of course you are. She wants me to come find her, hunt her down? Okay, I'll play. But you tell that sister of yours that she's playing hide-and-seek with the big boys. I'll find her, and when I do, she's not getting away again. You tell her that for me, will you?"

"I'll put it in a letter," Flora said icily. To which Oliver replied, "You Glass girls are a hoot, you really are."

She never told Simon about that conversation.

Simon's mood stayed gloomy well beyond his fiftieth birthday in March. As they did every year, they went to Passover dinner at

Aunt Hannah and Uncle Paul's. Simon barely spoke through dinner, and afterward, when Flora and Hannah were doing the dishes, Hannah whispered to Flora, "Is Simon all right? He's unusually quiet tonight." Flora pressed her lips together and wondered how much to tell. "He's working like a dog," she said. "He worries about work, about the country, always about his family. About our family. You know him, he takes everything so seriously."

"Are you giving him enough attention?" Hannah raised her eyebrows to signify that this was a serious question. She was of a generation that believed there was a direct correlation between wifely duties and masculine woes. Flora took a deep breath, hoping her aunt would not repeat her favorite and oft-quoted piece of wisdom from *Good Housekeeping* magazine: "The woman who is as proficient in the kitchen as she is in the bedroom has a happy husband indeed." The last thing Flora wanted to do was to imagine Aunt Hannah and Uncle Paul in the bedroom, but what else was she supposed to think about when Hannah said things like that? Rather than risk hearing any more of her aunt's views, Flora volunteered, "I try to make him laugh. I've cooked him plenty of romantic candlelit dinners. We've gone out to the movies or a night on the town and it's always the same."

Flora shrugged, not knowing what more to say or how to describe the heaviness in Simon's step or the way his eyes would focus on something that seemed out of her sight. She didn't tell Aunt Hannah how she watched his moods and gauged his disposition, and how, when she'd ask him if he was okay, he'd say things like: "You read the papers, Flora. Nobody's okay." Nor did she admit that she and Simon had always had a playful and unrestrained sex life. Even when he worked long hours and they hadn't spoken much to one another, their lovemaking would always bring them back together again. But lately, even that seemed tired.

"Maybe we've just been married for so long that we know each other like old socks," she finally said.

"Time," said Aunt Hannah. "He needs to get away from work. You need to go away together. Go somewhere beautiful where there are few distractions, and stay for as long as you can."

That night, Flora told Simon about what Aunt Hannah had said. "I agree with her. You need a real rest and to be away from here and from work. And frankly, we need time together. We barely see each other

366

anymore. And when we do, well, you're so tired we don't do much of anything."

Simon heard the way Flora's voice got wispy when she said that. He wanted to argue that she was overreacting and if she'd only be patient, things would get better. But he knew that they wouldn't. Now that they were introducing a line of Popeye Games, and Jigsaw Puzzle Maker Kits, plus the Mystery Jigsaw Puzzles and novelettes, there would be even more work. As he thought about the months and years ahead, he could feel the weight of the steel die bearing down on him.

"So tell me," he said, rubbing the veins over his eyes with his thumb and forefinger. "Supposing we had all this *time.* Where would we go? What would we do with it?"

"I'll make a deal with you," said Flora. "You promise me the month of July, and I'll figure out the rest."

She found them a house to rent in the Catskill Mountains. It was on a lake and had a twenty-foot dock out the back. There was a flower garden filled with wisteria, zinnias, and dahlias the size of gramophone records. In the mornings they would swim in the lake and sit on the lawn reading their books. Sometimes they'd have a glass or two of wine with lunch. After that, they'd take a nap, and often they would make love. In the afternoons, they'd walk in the woods and come back in time for another swim before dinner.

In these daily rituals, they found their way back to each other. Simon told her about Pissboy and the drawings, and how he felt he'd lost touch with the eager creative child he'd been. She confided to him about Seema: "She uses people up, then throws them away like old lipsticks." They talked about how much they wanted Edith to come to America. And they fantasized about the children they might have had. "I would hope they'd have your humor and optimism and not my cloudy disposition," he said. "They would have to have your brains," she said. "And your looks," he answered. "Your startling and delectable looks."

At night, they would eat dinner by candlelight on a wrought-iron table in the backyard. While Flora cleared the table, Simon would stare up at the heavens. They were most likely the same stars he could see from their yard in Yonkers, but here he took the time to study their shapes and the intensity of their light. Sometimes, when he stood there long enough, he thought he could feel their heat through his clothes and in his heart, and it would make him think that it was his mother shining down on him and filling him with her warmth. And he would wonder if, somewhere in the world, his brothers and sisters were staring up at the same stars and thinking of their lost brother, feeling that he, too, was reaching down and trying to touch them.

Simon had other thoughts of a more practical nature during that July of 1933. He thought about time: *Time* magazine and his new fame, and time itself, how it shot by him yet pinned him down. Time wasn't his to take anymore. He'd put off so many plans for the future, and here it was. What was he waiting for? When it came to him, the decision seemed almost mundane in its absoluteness. Beginning in September, he would relinquish his day-to-day responsibilities as president of Phelps and Adler and become chairman of the board. After that, he would focus all of his attention on finding out who and what was left of his family, and on not letting Flora's family slip away.

PART 5

KAISERSLAUTERN:
1933

Tee-poo-peep-pa. Tee-poo-peep-pa. Tee-poo-peep-pa.

Seema stuck her head out the window. "Quit honking that horn, Karl," she shouted. "I'm coming."

She stopped in front of the mirror long enough to fluff her hair and check that there was no lipstick on her teeth. She ran her hands over her hips and turned sideways. Not bad. Her stocking seams were straight; there were no scuffmarks on her shoes. She grabbed her pocketbook. Karl hated to be kept waiting, but she would do a quick inventory anyway. Makeup. Hairbrush. Keys. Passport. Wallet. License. Police registration card. And now this, a *Sippen-blatt,* proof of pure Aryan ancestry, for which she had Karl to thank. You couldn't even leave the house anymore without an arsenal of paperwork. Politicians. What a bunch of clowns. Not that she followed politics all that much, but ever since the National Socialists had taken over a few months ago, there was all this rigmarole about what you could and couldn't do. All of a sudden, it was against the law to have dancing bears at the circus. And those poor Italian beggars with their monkeys on a string. They were so cute, those monkeys, the way they'd perch on their owner's shoulders and grasp the coins with their tendril-like fingers. Now, rather than risk being hauled off to prison for two years, the Italians and their monkeys were streaking back to Italy with their tails literally between their legs. It was a joke, really.

Despite all this nonsense, Seema loved Germany. It was true, she'd never thought she'd last more than two weeks in Kaiserslautern, and here she was, five years later, still living in the same room she and Flora had first shared at the Schultz farm. There was something about that room. It was small, yes, but it was perfect. Everything in it was beautiful. It made her feel contained and safe. Her New York apartment, easily eight times the size of this room, was cluttered with expensive furnishings, antique clocks, fine linen hand towels, and crystal wine glasses. None of these items reflected her taste, nor did she own any of them. Living among other people's belongings, she had begun to feel borrowed herself. She cherished the objects in this little room that were hers: a crockery set with handles shaped like cloverleafs; a bronze figurine of a German shepherd that reminded her of Lulu; the black onyx cross that hung above her bed.

So long as she kept the room clean and helped Frau Schultz with the housework, this would be her place, and no one would be watching how she lived in it or what she looked like when she did. Seema wasn't the sort to make promises to herself. Why bother if all that came of it was that she'd go ahead and break them? But there was one vow she took in her earliest days in Germany that she held on to for the rest of her life, and that was never to be financially beholden to any man again. At the time she made it she was broke and had no idea how she would earn a single pfennig. Once again, the neighborly Frau Schultz stepped in. She would talk to her sister, she said, who worked for the family that owned Schweriner, the only department store in town. Schweriner always needed good sales-people.

"But I know far more about buying things than I do selling them," Seema had argued.

"Ach," said Frau Schultz, making a dismissive motion with her hand. "What is there to know? You know what's pretty. You know what people like to buy. And look at you. You're a beautiful woman. People like beautiful women. They want to please them; they want to look like them. Whatever it is — girdles, gloves, bath salts — you'll have no trouble selling it. This I promise you."

Frau Schultz turned out to be right. Seema started in the perfume department but was quickly promoted to women's jewelry. She was equally at ease with the rich women who had all the money in the world to spend and the poor ones with their noses pressed against the display cases. In her life she had been both, and she regarded them all with the same sympathy and natural friendliness. And then there were the men who came in with pockets full of cash eager to spend it on something that would impress, convince, or prompt forgiveness.

When Seema lived in America, people thought her exotic because she was from Germany and spoke with a disarming accent. Now that she lived in Kaiserslautern, she cultivated Americanisms like chewing gum and calling people "kiddo," and the Germans found her as charming and exotic as had her friends in New York.

Karl said that when he first saw her, she shone so brightly he nearly had to turn away. "It was the hair," he said, "and the sparkling smile and the light in your eyes. Dazzling, like nothing I've seen before." She had just wrapped up a women's gold Patek Philippe watch for a man who had done far too much explaining. "For my mother," he'd said. "She turns seventy. It's a nice watch for a mother. It has value but doesn't shout out to be noticed. Nothing's too good for one's mother, wouldn't you agree?"

"One mother is all you get," Seema said trying not to think about her own. "Of course she should have the best that money can buy."

That's when she noticed Karl. He was standing over the man's left shoulder, smiling at her as if he'd known what she was thinking. With his salt-and-pepper hair and swimming pool–blue eyes, Karl was hard to miss. He had broad shoulders and wore a fine cashmere coat. His skin was slightly florid, as if he'd just enjoyed a stein of beer or come in from the cold. He was older and shorter than the men she usually found attractive, but there was something about his smile. It was personal and conspiratorial.

She wrapped the watch and handed the package to the man. *"Guten Tag,"* she said,

"Ich hoffe, da Ihre Mutter die Uhr geniessen wird." She hoped his mother would enjoy her watch. The man shoved the box into his coat pocket and stared at Seema as if trying to figure out whether or not she'd mocked him. When he was out of sight, Karl stepped close enough for her to smell his pine-scented cologne. "His *Mutter* my ass," he said.

Seema shook her head, knowing the effect her flickering hair had on men. "What a *Dummkopf.* Does he think I was born yesterday?"

"Men can be such idiots, particularly when it comes to beautiful women." He smiled.

It went like this for several weeks. Karl would show up every few days or so, usually late in the afternoon, with stories to tell about the customers Seema had waited on that day. She never noticed him watching, yet he somehow knew everything that had transpired. He'd describe the young woman who bought the diamond ring for herself; the old man who came in several times a week just to run a particular strand of pearls through his fingers; the middle-aged woman who thought, until the guards came, that Seema had not noticed her conceal an ivory brooch on the inside of her sleeve. In vivid detail, he could recall their outfits, their dialects, the coffee stains on their teeth, and the moles on their arms. He startled Seema one day when he said: "You speak German like a *Landsmann* who's spent a fair amount of time in New York."

"And you, Mr. Eagle Eyes," she answered. "Do you have nothing better to do than to spy on a simple shop girl?"

"There is a difference between being interested in someone and spying on her," he said. "I am interested, and I like to indulge my interests."

He came back the following week, early on a Thursday evening, just before closing. This time there was no banter or observations. Just this oddly formal declaration: "For many weeks now you and I have had an entertaining exchange, and yet I don't even know your name. I am Karl Emerling."

"Hello Karl Emerling. I'm Seema Glass," she said, surprised at how easily that name slipped out.

"Seema Glass. What a fortunate name. So I am wondering, Frau Glass," he said, as he stared at the finger where there would be a wedding ring should one exist, "would you like to join me for dinner tonight? I know a café not many blocks from here."

Seema stared back at his ringless finger:

"I don't see why not. I'm hungry and I like to indulge my hunger."

The air was raw and the temperature must have dropped fifteen degrees since Seema was last outside. With only a thin wool coat and no hat or gloves, she crossed her arms and tucked her hands under her armpits.

"You're shivering, aren't you?" Karl asked after a few blocks. He touched his finger to her nose. "Cold nose," he said. "Jewess nose."

"Broken nose."

"Your hands must be freezing," he said, and she wondered whether he was ignoring what she'd just said.

He went on: "You're a lucky woman because look at what I have." He pulled off his leather gloves. "These will do the trick. Go ahead, put them on." The gloves were too big but they were lined with cashmere and warm with the heat from his fingers. They walked the rest of the way in silence, the comment about her nose occupying the space between them. Seema thought about Oliver and how he'd made fun of her Jewishness. He made her feel ashamed of so many things that shouldn't have caused her shame. So what if she was Jewish? She didn't feel Jewish, didn't act it or look it, except for that crook in her nose. Besides, she was in Germany now. She was a German. She felt that more than anything else. Seema decided that if the subject came up, she'd say yes, she'd been born Jewish, but she was really a German who for reasons that she could never explain slept underneath a black onyx cross and wore a tiny gold one around her neck. As these thoughts came, she smiled imperceptibly.

"Something has amused you?" asked Karl.

"You don't miss a thing do you?"

"I try not to," he said.

When they got to the café, Karl ordered for both of them. "Champagne." He turned toward Seema. "I am correct in thinking you wouldn't mind sharing a bottle of Veuve Clicquot, am I not?" He didn't wait for an answer. "The duck flambé with the haricots verts? Yes, I think that we'll both have that, and some of your pâté to start."

Karl spoke imperatively, as if he were hammering the periods into the end of his sentences. He was as inquisitive as he was observant, and his questions were direct and unabashed. He asked Seema about her childhood, her sisters, her parents. Had she ever been married? Did she miss not having children? He had an intensity about him that could bend silverware. The way he stared into her eyes made it easy for her to tell him things she would normally keep to herself. When he asked: "Did you leave America because of a failed love affair?" she told him about Oliver. "He was very rich and very married," she said. She described the apartment on Park Avenue and the parties and jewelry that had come with it. "I had everything money could buy, except my freedom." She described the car accident to him and how, after she'd realized she'd broken her nose, Oliver had just handed her a handkerchief. He reached across the table and took her hand. His was large and muscular and as warm as the inside of his glove. He rubbed the back of her hand against his cheek and held it there. "Seema Glass, you are a mesmerizing woman." Then he kissed her wrist and placed her hand back on the table. "So tell me this, you are a Jew, aren't you?"

"Yes," she said. "In the sense that my family is Jewish. Grossman. That's my given name. I don't give a hoot about the religion one way or another. Same with America. I could take it or leave it. German is what I am." And then she told him about the crosses. "I have no feelings for Catholicism either," she said, pulling the little gold cross from under her sweater. "I just like the way they look and feel. I find them comforting.

Does this sound crazy to you?"

"No more crazy than the thoughts I have running through my mind," he said, moving his chair closer to hers.

They finished one bottle of champagne and a glass of cognac each. Under the table, they explored each other's bodies in ways that were barely permissible in public. Karl's house was only a few blocks from the café, and when they walked there embracing and kissing, their hands were too warm to bother with a pair of gloves.

After they made love, and after they made love again, they discovered each other with the tenderness that comes after the urgency. That's when he told her she was dazzling. "You have the look of someone fragile who might break apart," he said and laughed. "But when it comes right down to it, quite the opposite is true."

"There's more to me than meets the eye," she said, and laughed.

"I'll say there is." He leaned over her, pressing his thumbs into her collarbone, and kissed her hard on the mouth. He was as strong and definitive in his lovemaking as he was in the way he spoke, and in the days after, she would find small bruises on her body and smile at the memory of it. When she slept, he watched. She slept on her side with her knees bent and her hands tucked under her ear like a little girl. The gold cross rested on top of her breast and a wisp of hair fell across her cheek. The mind takes indelible pictures, and this would be the one of her that he would always carry.

When she woke up the next morning, she smelled him before she saw him. He smelled of male sweat, of her, and of the musky pine cologne he wore. The smell was sweet and foreign and she wondered if she might still be dreaming. They had no time to make love again because it was already past seven and she had to get home and change to get to Schweriner by eight. He opened the window and stuck his head out as she dressed. "It's cold this morning. I must insist that you wear my coat. That way, I know that I'll see you again because you'll have to return it."

"Okay, but next time I do the interrogating, Mr. Eagle Eye," she said as she slipped on her stockings. "I know nothing about you, not even if you are a respectable gentleman. Though after last night, I would guess that you're not."

He draped the coat over her shoulders. "Put your hand in the left pocket. See what you find." She dug out a blank envelope and held it in front of her. "Open it." Inside were two gray tickets to the Municipal Opera House in Berlin. "They're for Saturday night, *Turandot.* Come with me."

She made a sour face, remembering the one time Oliver had taken her to see *Tristan and Isolde.* It had been long and gloomy. She had gotten a splitting headache and fallen asleep twice. Oliver hadn't said anything, but he'd never invited her again even though she knew he had season's tickets. So she told Karl she had no use for opera. "All those people howling and carrying on." He told her that opera was like life that way: "Always the howling and carrying on. The trick is to find the beauty within."

"Sounds like a lot of bull to me," she said, trying to find her way into the sleeves of the coat.

"Berlin is a big city," he said. "Even without opera, I'm sure we can find things to entertain us."

She wiggled her arms through his sleeves and looked up at him with the most seamless smile she could muster.

When Seema came home wearing a man's cashmere coat and yesterday's makeup, Frau Schultz was in the kitchen scrubbing the floor. She looked up at Seema long enough to say, *"Guten Morgen."* The two women, though separated in age by nearly twenty years, had mutually agreed, without ever saying a word, that the only way to coexist in the small house they shared was to honor each other's privacy. Frau Schultz never asked about the cross over Seema's bed or where she'd been the night before. In return, Seema never questioned whether the older woman had any friends or family and why no one ever came to visit. For a German woman boarding a foreign Jew, it was better that way.

KAISERSLAUTERN:
WINTER 1934

Frederick pleaded with Margot to get out of the house. "If you don't talk to people all day, you'll get out of the habit of talking," he said.

"I see nothing wrong with that," she said, shrugging. Just the thought of bumping into a neighbor or, God forbid, a stranger, filled her with such dread that when she did go for a walk, she went early in the morning so that she was likely to be alone. If, as happened occasionally, she passed someone who innocently asked her how she was, she could barely find the words to answer.

With her mother gone and Edith off to school, Margot withdrew. People had died and disappointed her, and she found less and less reason to be among them. Instead, she doted on her geraniums. *"Meine hübsche Blumen,"* she'd murmur bending over them, confident that her whisper puffs bathed their leaves and nourished their roots. She'd pat the dirt and gently cup her hands around their petals while breathing in their spicy nutmeg aroma. Several times a day, she'd deadhead the flowers and carry the window boxes from room to room, making sure that they got as much light as possible. And grow they did, with shoots cascading over the edge of their containers, underscoring each window with a blaze of red. Because of Margot's geraniums, everyone knew the Ehrlich house from afar, though none were ever invited inside.

For company, she spoke to the porcelain owls, and they spoke back. Franz, the oldest, with a chip on his head and shiny black glass eyes, was critical of her appearance: *Your apron's filthy. You have flour in your hair.* Little yellow Anna, with her orange beaky nose, had nothing good to say about her cooking. *Not enough salt in the potato pancakes. Sauerbraten's too tough.* Thank heavens for Erich, the newest and dearest. He was always complimentary, sometimes even flirty. *That rosewater from Seema smells so sweet on you. Your hair is beautiful in this light. Go see for yourself.*

He was right. Sometimes, when the sun angled through the window in a certain way, light would swirl around her head like a burning white halo. The harder she stared, the more convinced she became that behind her, in the glare of the halo, she could see the shadowy outline of her mother's face. *Yes.* Erich agreed, *That really was your mutti come to say hello.* Brief though they were, these visits calmed Margot and reassured her.

After her mother died, Margot had suffered dizzy spells. Nervous exhaustion, the doctor had said; it was to be expected. But lately she was experiencing something far more frightening. It started two weeks after New Year's. Frederick had come home from work one night, pale and hunched over as if he'd just been slugged in the stomach. "What's wrong?" she cried, as he fell into a chair.

"It's nothing. Nothing to worry about," he said.

She knelt down next to him. "You're trembling." He turned his face away, but not before she'd noticed the tears. In all their years together, she had never seen Frederick cry except when Gilda died. She lay her cheek on his knees. In the same soothing voice he normally used when talking to her, she said: "My sweet Frederick, what is it? What is so horrible?"

He took a deep breath. In a strangled voice he told her what had happened.

"Ernst Licht. You remember him? Fat with the mustache and beard. We worked together until he opened his own store five years ago. Yesterday morning he's in his shop. A man comes in and asks for kosher brisket. So what does he do? He goes and prepares it for him. Three days after the government said there would be no kosher meat prepared in Germany!" Frederick never raised his voice but now he was nearly shouting. "We were all warned about this. Licht knew. Stubborn old fool. Of course, the customer turned out to be a member of the government. Just like that they closed down his shop. This morning his wife wakes up. He's gone. Can't find him. She goes into the backyard. There he is. Hanging from a tree. Hanging! Neck broken. Head resting on his own shoulder like he's napping. He hanged himself." Frederick shuddered and began to sob. "Can you imagine?"

"Come," said Margot, beckoning him to sit next to her. He slid off the chair and onto the floor, where she put her arm around him and nudged his head to her breast. She rocked back and forth, back and forth until she could feel his body slacken. When he was quiet, he sat up and patted her on the shoulder. "I'm sorry I let my tongue run on so," he said, trying to push the horror aside and assume his normal voice. "The times in which we live . . ." He paused and shook his head. "Thank God we have each other, right, my *Liebchen?*"

A week later, Margot was sweeping the floor as she did every evening, when suddenly it seemed to give way beneath her. If she hadn't grabbed onto the nearby table, she was certain she would have fallen.

Then, on a Sunday morning in early February, she went out for one of her walks. Fresh snow made the trees look white and ghostly. The closer she got to the trees, the more make-believe they seemed. Maybe they weren't there at all. She would touch them to find out. She wrapped her arms around one of them. It seemed substantial. But wait. The house! She was sure if she touched it, it would be like stroking air. She ran over to it and rubbed her hands up and down the cold stucco. She watched her arms move along the wall. The house seemed to be there. Then a greater panic set in. Her arms. Her arms were disappearing. She pulled up her sleeves and licked her forearm like a dog, desperate that the taste of her own salty flesh bring her back to reality. It was too late. She could feel herself slipping away.

Frederick, concerned that she'd been gone too long, went outside and found her lying in the snow. She was awake but confused and unsure of where she was. "What happened?" he cried. She told him about the tree and the house. "Then I felt as if the inside of me was emptying and I couldn't stop it. I was disappearing. That must be when I fainted."

He carried her inside and took off her wet clothes. He tucked her in under the quilt and made her some tea. When he came back to her, he sat at the foot of her bed, head in hands, and listened as she talked.

"I'm so frightened," she said. "Nothing seems real to me."

He rubbed the little mound on the quilt that was covering her feet. "My poor, scared Margot*schön*. Everything is real. No one is disappearing."

"Everyone is disappearing," she shouted. "Gilda. My mother. Edith. Now Ernst Licht. Everyone."

He shook his head. "This is my fault. I should have never brought my worries into this house. You are safe here, I promise you this. You are safe with me."

"Frederick, who is safe with anybody?"

"I could kick myself for telling you about Ernst. It's one of those things that happens, an isolated incident, I'm certain." But in his heart Frederick knew that in these times, in this place, being certain was nothing to count on.

Between her work at Schweriner and the time she spent with Karl, Seema rarely saw Frederick and Margot. Not that she'd keep their company even if she had more time. She felt sorry for Frederick. He had his hands full with Margot. And Margot, so strange and otherworldly. Seema had really tried with Margot. Taken her shopping, bought her nice clothes. Even got her a strand of pearls with her Schweriner discount two Christmases ago, thinking, mistakenly, that pretty jewelry would give her a reason to dress up and get out of the house. But Margot being Margot, she kept the pearls in the gift box wrapped in the original paper and put them somewhere for safekeeping, probably with all the other presents Seema had given her. For Pete's sake, there was only so much she could do for Margot.

If Edith were home, that would be different. Seema would be over there all the time trading gossip, sharing makeup and whatnot. She couldn't blame Edith for going back to the gymnasium as an assistant to the physical education teacher. If she were home, she'd be stuck caring for her mother. She was sure Edith had better things to do. But now that she'd introduced her to Werner Cohn, maybe Edith would find reason to come home more often.

She knew Werner and Edith would hit it off. He was no Clark Gable, but he was cute in an impish way, though less comfortable in his skin than Edith. Seema had guessed that he would find her liveliness and ease with the world appealing. Besides, since his father was one of the owners of Schweriner, Werner Cohn had money, and God knows Edith could use some of that. After their second date, Seema had asked Edith how it had gone. "He's funny," said Edith. "Different than other Jewish boys. He's more remote, harder to get to know." After their third date, Seema had asked if he'd kissed her, and Edith got all coy and giggly. "You're getting as bad as your boyfriend with all your questions. I don't have to answer everything you ask me," she said. "You don't have to answer anything," said Seema, laughing. "Your face tells me what I need to know. Remember the first time we met we went to see all those naked boys at the Metropolitan Museum of Art? How you ogled them and turned all pink, just like you're doing now."

"Aunt Seema," laughed Edith. "Just because your imagination is in the gutter doesn't mean the rest of us live down there with you."

"Maybe not," said Seema. "But tell me, how does Werner stack up next to those marble fellas at the museum?"

Seema enjoyed teasing Edith, something she couldn't do with her sisters. Even in her letters, Flora was so confident and combative; it was just no fun. And Margot? Well, what was the point? But she and Edith could go at each other day and night, both knowing that their vulnerabilities and secrets were off limits. When Karl pointed out to Seema that she had strong maternal instincts toward Edith, she laughed at him and said, "I wouldn't know a maternal instinct if it socked me in the eye."

"Say what you will," Karl had answered. "But you would lay down your life for that girl."

He was a wise man. Maybe that came from being older. In his late fifties, he was more than a decade older than she was. His perceptiveness was one of the things Seema found intriguing about him. That was his job, of course, seeing through people and second-guessing their motivations. As a newspaperman, he loved a good story, no matter how mundane or bizarre. When there was a fire at the zoo, or an infant was born with all of its teeth in its mouth, Karl was the first one there, pencil and notebook in hand. But he was also known as an intrepid reporter, unafraid to ask the provocative questions. His most famous interview had been with the actress Marlene Dietrich right after the movie *Der blaue Engel* came out in 1930. In one scene, Dietrich, who played a lusty cabaret performer, leaned back on a barrel, lifted her right leg, and wrapped her hands around her knee, exposing her garter-belted stockings. Then she sang, "Falling in Love Again." It was the most talked about scene in the film, and when Karl had asked, "Miss Dietrich, would it be fair to say that your beautiful legs are actually the star of this movie?" She answered, "Darling, the legs aren't so beautiful, I just know what to do with them." It made news from Berlin to Los Angeles.

That was the Karl who Seema had fallen in love with: funny, curious, charming. But lately he was different. More serious. Cautious even. On New Year's Eve they went to see prima donna Maria Mueller perform "Tannhauser" at the State Opera. Just before the intermission, Seema felt a draft on her shoulders and whispered to Karl, "All I'm wearing is this silk chemise. Not much underneath it. Mind if I borrow your jacket?" Karl kissed her neck and ran his hand down her back. "You certainly dressed lightly for a winter night," he whispered. She blew softly in his ear before murmuring back, "I didn't dress for a winter night, I dressed for a night with you." Flushed with the thought of what they would do after the opera, Karl wrapped his jacket around her shoulders and said, "This should keep you warm until then." During intermission, when he went to the men's room, she reached into his pocket to borrow his handkerchief and found the oddest thing. It was a flyer with a picture of Hitler and, underneath, the words "Gentle Hitler." It made Seema laugh. When Karl came back to his seat, she showed it to him and joked: "So is our esteemed leader now a contestant in the Miss Germany beauty pageant?"

Karl snatched the flyer from her hand, folded it carefully, and stuck it back in his coat pocket. "That's not funny," he said.

"But it is funny," she insisted. "A short ugly man competing for Miss Germany? It's very funny."

Karl whispered in fragments. "It's part of a national campaign. The German government. The Nobel Peace Prize."

"The Nobel Peace Prize?" Seema said in a startled voice. "Hitler?"

"Shh," urged Karl. "Do you want the whole theater to hear you? Yes, the handout is part of the Nazi effort to groom Hitler for the Nobel Prize."

"Hitler and the Nobel Peace Prize," said Seema in a low voice. "Now that is really funny."

"Enough," snapped Karl, as the lights dimmed and the orchestra began to warm up. "We'll discuss this later."

That night, when they got back to the hotel room, they seemed to have left the incident behind them. Karl was far more interested in what Seema wasn't wearing under her chemise and had his hands about her body before the door to their room had even closed behind them. He cupped his hands underneath her dress and carried her to the bed. He was hard and started to put himself inside her. "Wait," she cried and turned on her stomach, tucking her knees beneath her like a crouched animal. "Now."

Karl and Seema were proud of the pleasure they could give each other, and short of inflicting real pain, there were few things they wouldn't try or ask for. Their lovemaking nourished and surprised them, and within its life dwelled their secrets and trust.

When they were finished, Seema lay with her head on his belly. "Why were you such a grouch tonight?" she asked, stroking the hair on his chest.

"I wasn't a grouch."

"Well, you weren't very nice."

"Oh really. Judging from the sounds you were making five minutes ago, I'd say I was *very* nice."

"I don't mean that," she said. "I mean in the theater. About the flyer."

"Seema," he'd said, his voice turning serious, "there are some things even you can't joke about."

"I can joke about anything," she'd said, tickling his stomach, trying to sound light-hearted.

"I know you can. And you do. But sometimes it's not appropriate."

"Oh Karl, even you must think this business about Hitler and the Nobel Prize is funny."

"You know, Miss Wisenheimer, we need to talk. Being a Jewess is becoming risky business around here. I must ask if you've given any thought to going back to America?"

"Why on earth would I go back?" She folded her arms across her chest. "I am a

German woman in love with a German man. There's nothing for me in America. I'm staying right here."

"Come now, don't play naive with me. You know exactly what I'm talking about. Surely it's occurred to you."

"No, it really hasn't. This is my home. I belong here. Why should I leave?"

"Because," Karl said, sitting up in bed so abruptly it caused her head to drop onto the mattress. "This is not the place to be if your name is Seema Glass née Seema Grossman and you have a nose like yours. That's why."

She propped herself up on her elbows and stared up at him. "Are you trying to get rid of me? Is that what this is about?"

"Seema, don't be an idiot. I know you hate politics and you do your best to ignore what's going on. But look around you. Surely you notice all the Brownshirts in Berlin, the fact that Jewish stores are closing every day? I love you, but this is not a safe place for you. I can't help you."

Now it was Seema's turn to sit upright. "Help me? I never asked you to help me with anything. I'm staying and that's that."

Karl looked at his watch. His startling blue eyes were hazy now and the gray pouches under his eyes sagged into his cheeks. "You

400

are very headstrong and I am very weary. It's well after three and I have to be back at the paper tomorrow afternoon. We'll continue this conversation at another time." He held open an arm so she could lie next to him. "Come, let's get some rest." She curled up on her side and settled into the place just below his shoulder blade, which seemed to have been scooped out just for her. From there she could feel his heart beat.

In the rift between wakefulness and sleep, she'd become momentarily stranded on the paradox of their conversation. "You say I'm unsafe, yet right now I am safer than I have ever been." She tried saying the words out loud, but sleep stole over her before she could.

KAISERSLAUTERN:
SPRING 1935

When it became clear that Seema was not going to leave Germany, Karl finally dropped the subject. It wasn't until the first warm day in early March that it entered their conversation again. They were sitting at a corner table in the café near his house, drinking cognac, and leaning into each other, their heads almost touching. Seema was telling Karl about a woman who had come into the store and demanded to see a bracelet that was so expensive that the store guard had to stand by as Seema showed it to her. Somewhere in the language of diamonds and platinum, Karl's attention turned to the slip of the cross around her neck. He thought about how it fell onto one of her breasts when she slept and how sometimes, when they made love, it would dig into him like the nippy foot of a crab.

He smiled and would have liked to take her breast in his hand just then. Instead, he tugged gently on the cross as she continued on about carat weight and marquise cuts.

Then he interrupted her. "You ought to think about converting."

She screwed up her face as if she couldn't hear him. "Converting? To what?"

"You'd be a perfect Catholic." He continued to play with her cross. "You already have the equipment."

"Why would I convert from one religion I don't believe in to another?" she asked, raising the cognac to her lips.

"Because it could save your goddamned life," he said, jerking the cross so hard she dropped her glass, causing the drink to dribble down her chin and splash onto her yellow silk blouse.

"Oh no, we're not going to talk about that again!" she said, using her napkin to dab up the mess. "Shit. This is a brand-new blouse."

"Oh yes, we are going to talk about that again," he said, his chin jutting forward.

When Karl got angry, his voice had the timbre of two knife blades rubbed together. Like a good reporter, he stayed focused on his subject for as long as he needed to, and by the end of that long liquory night, the combination wore Seema down.

"So I'll convert," she said finally. "It's no big deal. And maybe then we could stop

403

talking about it."

"That's my sweet shiksa frau," he said, kissing her. "I promise from now on our exchanges will be nothing but scintillating."

Karl made all the arrangements and got the appropriate papers signed. She never got the cognac stain out of her blouse. Instead, she kept it hanging in her closet as a souvenir. They called it her christening gown.

Four weeks later, on an early afternoon in April, Seema decided to take her lunch outside where the tulips and daffodils had lit up the exhibition grounds. On this day, when every tree bud held a promise and the air was sweet with spring, deciding which bench to settle on or whether to sit facing the sun was the most grueling demand Seema made on her imagination. So she ignored the throng of people that swept past her. Midday shoppers, she assumed. But they moved so fast and made so much noise with their jeering and screaming. That and the bursts of guttural demands she could hear in the distance: *Mach schnell. Lauter singen!* Should she ignore the commotion and continue on to the exhibition grounds? There was something about those people: their rabid eyes, their contorted faces. They frightened her, yet she felt compelled to move with them. At first she walked, faster and faster until before she knew it, she, too, was running. She strained to catch her breath. Her heart drummed and a cold fear trickled through her. When they got to Lutherstrasse, she heard people singing the "Happy Birthday" song. Only it had no melody. It was being shouted in the imperative. The lyrics were different. She sorted them out.

Happy birthday to you.
Happy birthday to you.
Happy birthday, happy birthday,
Happy birthday, dirty Jew.

Seema let herself get pushed forward until she saw them. Six men, middle-aged and older. She recognized one of them as a dentist who had come into Schweriner a few months ago to buy his wife an opal ring for her fiftieth birthday. The men wore conical party hats with ruffles around the bottom and elastic bands under their chins. She thought of how the dentist had told her that when his wife saw the way the light refracted off the ring in the window of Schweriner, she said it looked to her like a globe. The party hats were green and purple and had red pompoms on their pointy tops. They were too small for the men and were cocked in crazy angles on their heads. She remembered the dentist saying that the ring was the perfect present for his wife because she was the world to him. The men held hands and danced in a circle while soldiers with guns stuck into their belts yelled at them to sing louder, dance faster. Seema put her hands over her ears and squeezed her eyes shut after one of the soldiers started shooting at their feet. Still, she could hear the other soldiers laughing. The dentist had told her that all three of his children were grown and lived in Kaiserslautern. The men were dancing and singing as fast and loud as they could. Two looked as if they might collapse. The other four clasped their hands tightly and nearly dragged them around the circle. There were more gunshots and there was more singing and then one body fell and then another and another and another and another and another until the men lay in the street, the party hats swimming in blood. Seema remembered the picture the dentist had shown her of his five grandchildren. The soldiers urged the crowd to go home. The show is over, one shouted, waving his gun. Then the soldiers dispersed, but not before a few of them bent over the fresh corpses, picking off their jewelry and searching their pockets for money.

Seema ran back to Schweriner and upstairs to the ladies room. She hadn't eaten lunch yet, and had only a piece of bread and butter for breakfast, yet she threw up as if she'd been feasting all morning. Small pieces of yellow vomit fell onto her shoes and the floor, and all around her was the sour smell. Her skin was clammy, and she was shivering and felt as if her legs might give way. The inside of her mouth tasted bitter and she held onto the walls of the bathroom stall for support. She thought about the lady with the opal ring and the man who had given it to her and how she was the world to him. It made her want to retch again, but there was nothing left.

For the first time since she'd worked at Schweriner, Seema went home sick in the middle of the day. Frau Schultz saw her come through the door. "You look terrible," she said, taking Seema's arm. "You're pale and shaky. Come, let's get you to bed." Seema let herself lean on the old woman's arm. She studied Seema's face "Oh my dear, you're crying. What is it?"

"It's nothing," Seema lied, falling onto her bed. "I must have the grippe." She would never tell Frau Schultz what she had seen. She would never tell anybody.

She lay in her bed thinking about Flora and Simon and how for so many years they'd been urging Edith to come to America. Maybe they were right. She thought about Margot and Frederick and what it would take to budge them from their home. Nothing would ever budge them. Nothing. And about Karl. Now there was a German through and through. He had no worries. He was a Christian, a newspaper reporter who loved his job. He'd never consider leaving Germany. And as long as Karl was here, this is where she would be. For the first time it occurred to her that she might put herself in harm's way by staying, but never mind. Life without Karl was unthinkable. Better to live in jeopardy than to flee back to America. To what? To nothing.

She wondered what had become of Oliver. He'd probably found someone else to install in that Park Avenue apartment. Had he lost all his money in the Great Depression? Was he still married? He wouldn't have aged well. He was probably balding and puny. Not like Karl, who was as vigorous in middle age as a man twenty years his junior.

But most of all, she thought about Edith. She remembered the hair pillow Edith had sent her and the story behind it. Edith seemed to be falling in love with Werner Cohn and was happier than Seema had ever known her. This was no place for Edith. No place for a young couple in love.

Falling in love made Edith jumpy. She had trouble swallowing her food and sleeping at night. Every time she thought about Werner, she lost her concentration and her head would spin. Sometimes she felt so over-whelmed by her emotions she thought she might topple over. That's when she'd close the door to her room, sit on her bed, and allow herself a good cry.

"You're in love with him, aren't you?" asked Seema a few days later, when Edith was home one weekend for one of her breaks. Edith tripped over her words as she answered: "He makes me laugh so much, and we talk about all sorts of things I never could talk to boys about. His parents never really wanted a child. His father works all the time and he never sees him. And his mother. She's a real social butterfly, out every night. He said he's never had anyone to talk to until he met me. Isn't that sad? And sweet? The other night, we both started singing 'Mack the Knife' in the middle of the street, and he started acting out the song, looking all sneaky and sadistic. It was adorable. And Seema, I know you'll want to know this. He is a great kisser," she said, her voice just above a whisper. "You know, some men have really soft lips. You wouldn't know to look at them, but . . . oh, and he has the strongest hands. Isn't it strange that we grew up in the same town and never met until you introduced us? Also, I like that he's older. Four years is a big difference. He's so much more sophisticated than I am . . . has so much to teach me."

Falling in love also made Edith beautiful. All the weight she'd put on at gymnasium dropped away. Her body was lean and athletic and, Seema imagined, as eager to play at sex as she was at any sport thrown at her. How could this boy not fall in love with her?

Late that same night, Edith showed up in Seema's room just after she'd come home from a date with Werner. "Seema, I have a big favor to ask of you." She held her hands folded in front of her chin. "Werner's coming to dinner at our house tonight. My mother's cooking." Seema had to laugh at the way she unintentionally rolled her eyes when she said this. "Please come. Bring Karl. Just come, please, please."

"Tell you what, I'll not only come to dinner, but I'll come early and give your mother a hand," said Seema. Edith threw her arms around her, kissed her on the mouth, and said, "I love you so much. What would I ever do without you?" So many people in Seema's life had done fine without her. That Edith felt she couldn't was one of the miracles of her life.

That night, Frederick brought home a piece of veal from the shop. Seema helped Margot fix dinner and get dressed. As she tucked some loose pieces of hair behind Margot's ears and put some rouge on her cheeks, she studied her face. Margot caught her sister staring at her and offered up a smile that obliterated the strain. "Of all of us," said Seema, "you are the real beauty." Margot shook her head and knotted her brow. "Nonsense. I've become an old hag. I know what I look like."

"Tonight you are beautiful," said Seema. "And your daughter is bringing home a man. Who knows, she may even be bringing home your future son-in-law."

Margot went inward for a few moments. *I mustn't do anything to spoil this evening,* she thought. "A reason to rejoice. Now wouldn't that be something!"

Karl brought two bottles of wine, as he had in the past. They drank them both as they devoured the roast, which Margot had cooked until it was moist and tender. Her potatoes were perfectly fried, and the dash of paprika she added at the end made them look festive. Through most of the dinner, Margot focused on her hands as if willing them not to blunder. Edith kept her eyes on her mother, praying that she not say anything inappropriate. Seema watched Edith and hoped she would quit chattering and answering the questions that were put to Werner. Frederick carved the meat, poured the wine, and made himself useful without saying much to anyone. Werner never took his eyes off Edith, and Karl never took his off Werner.

It was Karl who finally got Werner to speak for himself. "So, we've heard Edith's version of your life story," he said. "Tell us, what's yours?"

"Mine isn't the kind of life filled with stories," said Werner with a laugh. "My father works round the clock at the store, and I am working there now trying to learn everything I can. That's how I met Seema, when I was assigned to jewelry for a few weeks. That is my story, I suppose. My father wants me eventually to manage the store. I love to travel. I have spent several summers in Switzerland and, let me think, oh yes, one more thing. I love music, all kinds of music."

Karl leaned back in his chair. "So if you didn't have this *store* hanging around your neck, what would you really like to do with your life?"

Werner raised his eyebrows, caught off guard. "It's never been an option. I have no idea."

"Oh Werner," Edith couldn't help herself. "Tell them what a clever writer you are. He wrote for the school newspaper, and even drew cartoons like Uncle Simon."

"Ah, an artist at heart then?" asked Karl.

"Not really, I just draw silly things. And the school paper, well, Edith exaggerates a little." He turned toward her and smiled as if exaggerating was the most adorable thing anyone had ever done. "That was years ago and only for a little while."

"Werner got thrown out of school once, because he and some friends wrote up a whole newspaper making fun of all the teachers and the headmaster," burbled Edith. "He drew caricatures of all of them and even wrote some funny poems."

Karl laughed and clapped his hands together. "A subversive one. I knew it had to be something like that. People who say they have no stories to tell are the ones who have the best tales to hide. Do you still draw in your spare time?"

"No, that's all over with. I'm a businessman now," said Werner.

"A businessman with his head in the clouds," said Karl, not unkindly. "What does your father think of that?"

Werner shot Edith another look. "My father has his feet firmly planted on this earth. I think he'd be horrified by the notion that his son dwelled elsewhere."

Edith looked around the table. He was so clever, her Werner. Now it was obvious to everyone.

The other highlight of the evening occurred long after they'd finished the second bottle of wine and right before Karl and Seema said it was time for them to go. The conversation turned to Passover, which was only two weeks away. "You'll be coming to our house for the Seder, won't you, Seema?" asked Margot. Her words were memorable because they were the only ones she spoke that evening, and because of the response they provoked from Seema.

"I don't think so. I'm no longer a Jew. I've become an official Catholic."

They had accepted the fact that Karl wasn't Jewish, but this was something else. Margot folded her hands in her lap. Frederick lifted his eyes from the coffee he was pouring, and Werner kept his on his plate, not daring to look at anyone. Only Edith spoke up. "Why did you have to go and convert? Who cares if you're sort of Catholic or really Catholic?"

Seema turned to Karl, who cleared his throat before talking. "Surely you all know what the atmosphere is like these days." Margot and Frederick stared at each other as if Ernst Licht had passed before them. "In light of what's going on, and that she is seen in public with me and I am something of a known commodity in this town, we thought it would be for the best."

Seema was aware of how formal and jarring Karl's words must have sounded. She leaned in to the little group around the table, which, for better or worse, was her family. "We must all think about what to do," she said, urgently. "Frederick, who knows how long you will be welcomed at the shop. And Edith, there are some schools in Berlin that are already closed to Jews. Werner, your father owns a business. The chancellor frowns upon Jews who own businesses. I've been thinking about writing to Simon and Flora. You know, they have always wanted you, Edith, to come and stay with them. Maybe now is the time."

Edith looked from one parent to another. Margot stared down at her hands. Frederick, in an uncharacteristic flair of temper, pounded his fist on the table so hard that the dessert plates bounced, and everyone jumped. "Nobody goes anywhere," he said. "We are Germans and Germans do not desert their country just because it happens to be going through hard times. As long as I am the man of the house, that is that."

As her father made his pronouncement, Edith turned to Werner. *I am going nowhere without this man,* she thought. And from the way his eyes lingered on her, he seemed to be thinking the same thing.

Three days after the dinner, Frederick went to work at seven-thirty, as he had every morning for the past sixteen years. His boss, Gustave Reinhart, greeted him at the door. He spoke in a monotone as if reciting from a script: "Good morning, Frederick. I am sorry to inform you that this store, in accordance with the rules of the government, no longer employs Jews." He turned away from Frederick as he said the word "Jews." He was a short pear-shaped man who managed to block the doorway.

"I've come to work here every day for sixteen years," said Frederick. "Does that not count for anything, Gustave?"

Intentionally, Frederick had chosen to address his boss informally, although up until now he had always called him Herr Reinhart.

Reinhart's cheeks turned pink and his eyes darted away from Frederick's. "Please, don't make this harder," he said, moving aside so that Frederick could pass. "I am only doing what I must. You may gather your things. I have packed them up; you'll find them on your shelf in the back."

When Frederick went to retrieve his smock, his knives, and his knife sharpener, he found a large sack with his name on it. It was so heavy that he could barely lift it. It gave off a familiar bloody odor and Frederick feared that Reinhart had piled together a sack of bones in order to humiliate him further. But when he peered inside, he could see beautiful cuts of lamb and beef and pieces of chicken. He tried to catch Reinhart's eye to thank him, but Reinhart jerked his head and flicked his hand. "Go now," he said. "Quickly."

Only when he got home did he discover that Reinhart had also stuffed as many notes as he could between the breasts of chicken, loins of lamb, and shoulder cuts of beef. It was more money than he had ever seen in one place and, he figured, enough to keep them going until well into the new year. "You see," he said to Margot, who was not able to speak when he gave her the news. "They're not all bad."

YONKERS:
SEPTEMBER 1935

The letters came sporadically, but when they did they were terse and self-conscious. Even Edith's letters, usually sprawling with run-on sentences and funny little drawings, felt labored.

When Seema wrote, she never failed to mention Karl.

> Everyone in Kaiserslautern knows him for the wonderful stories he writes in the newspaper. He is the pride of our town. And those who don't know him for his writing recognize his beautiful German-made car with the unusual horn that goes, *Tee-poo-peep-pa, tee-poo-peep-pa.* Honestly, you've never heard anything like it.

She told them about the operas they attended, and in one letter she mentioned how she and Karl had gone to see Margot and Edith and Frederick after church one afternoon.

Edith is very excited about her wedding. So squirmy and filled with romantic plans. She never stops talking. Werner this and Werner that. She reminds me of you, dear Flora, before you married Simon.

Edith wrote of nothing but her upcoming nuptials.

The wedding will be on Sunday, September 22. My mother is working her fingers to the bone on the old Pfaff. She wants to make my dress long sleeved, but I want sleeveless with a matching shawl. More elegant, don't you think, Aunt Flora? There will be a reception in Werner's home. Have I told you about his house? It's one of the biggest in Kaiserslautern. It is built around a courtyard where the reception will be held. The floors are marble and there is a winding staircase that leads down to it. Can you imagine me as a bride? Oh, I wish you could be here. Even my parents are excited. Ever since my father retired, things have been very peaceful at home.

Werner's parents have been so kind. His father owns the department store here and works very hard. He is getting some rest after his journey, but I'm sure he will be back to work soon. Werner's mother takes me shopping at the finest stores doing what she can to make sure that her daughter-in-law is the model German wife. And then there's Werner. I can't wait for you to meet him. Uncle Simon, he's clever the way you are, and Aunt Flora, he has such wonderful taste. He bought me the most beautiful watch for my birthday. It's silver with little diamonds around the face. We will be taking our honeymoon for six weeks beginning in January. We start in Palestine then go to Venice, Paris, and finish in Marseille. Do you think there is any chance you could meet us in any of those places? Please think about it. That would be the most wonderful thing in the world.

They had only one letter from Margot announcing that Edith was getting married. She, too, mentioned Frederick's retirement and said,

Having Frederick around has done

wonders for the mood around here.

Simon would scrutinize each letter, searching for clues in what was and wasn't being said. There were plenty to be found. In the notebook that he kept about his family, he began a separate section under the words *Flora's People.* Each person had her own page. Under *Seema,* he noted:

The pride of Kaiserslautern. Why?
Beautiful German-made car. Why emphasize German-made?
Unusual horn goes "Tee-poo-peep-pa." Why bother telling us this?
Church!!! Flora says she remembers seeing a cross in Seema's suitcase when they went to Germany together. Related?
Filled with romantic plans. Probably just a pretentious "Seema" turn of phrase.

In his impeccable script, he wrote under *Edith:*

Why is she getting married on a Sunday?
Father retired?? Since when? Frederick would never retire! Still relatively young.
Things *peaceful* at home. Why bring it up?

Werner's father resting after journey. What journey?

Model Wife — doesn't sound like Edith.

Meet them on their honeymoon? Think about it.

And under *Margot* he jotted:

Again about Frederick's retirement?

What is *the mood* around here?

All this could mean nothing or everything. So far, despite his various trips to the State Department and the detective doggedly following through on every clue taking him to Baltimore, Charleston, and as far as Carson City, Nevada, Simon had still found out nothing about his mother, sisters, and brothers. Sometimes he thought that his family was like the characters he'd created on paper. One moment they were full of life, and then, with the turn of a page, they were gone. It frightened him to believe that the world was like that, and he was even more determined that Flora's family — particularly Edith — not meet the same transient fate. The news trickling out of Germany was alarming: Harassment. Arrests. Brutality. Rumors of camps. The Gestapo was becoming more oppressive.

Among the sisterhood at Beth David, there was much talk of the stringent immigration laws. Ever since the Johnson-Reed Act of 1924, the number of immigrants who could be permitted to enter from any country was only 2 percent of the number of people from that country already living in the United States. Now there was even more red tape involved in getting a visa, making it virtually impossible for Jews who wanted to leave Germany to find a place to go. Even if someone could secure a visa, there was the matter of the coveted affidavit of support. Normal immigration visas required proof of the LPC clause, that the applicant had enough resources so that he was not "likely to become a public charge." If they couldn't show proof of that, they had to have an affidavit of support from friends or relatives in the United States that promised they would be willing to provide for the applicant. For the past three months, the Beth David sisterhood had been going door to door in Westchester County circulating a petition that urged President Roosevelt to intervene on behalf of the Jews in Europe.

It was Flora's job to mail the two hundred-page document to Washington, but before she did, she brought it home so that Simon could see for himself what she and the sisterhood had accomplished. "The president won't know what hit him," she said plopping the hefty manuscript onto Simon's desk. "Take a look. Five thousand names from all over the country."

Simon put his hand on top of the petition and shook his head. "Flora, honey, it won't matter. Roosevelt doesn't care about the Jews in Europe. The Jews in America don't even care about the Jews in Europe. The last thing they want to do is call attention to themselves. Particularly now, when half of the country is blaming us for the Depression. You could have gotten a million signatures, but as long as people are scared that immigrants, mainly Jewish immigrants, are going to take away jobs here, no one's going to pay attention. I'm afraid that's how it is."

"Well then, what are we supposed to do?" said Flora. "Just give up?"

As soon as Flora spoke those words, she wished she could have swallowed them. For the past few months, Simon had been doing anything not to give up. Once a week he volunteered at the American Jewish Committee, where one of his jobs was to make public the names of missing Jewish people from all over Europe and Eastern Europe. Of course he hoped that somewhere in the reams of paper he'd come across his own family names, but so far that hadn't happened. And then there was the business. As quickly as it had exploded, the puzzle business dried up. All new ideas seemed stale and the old ones used up, and for a while it looked as if Phelps and Adler would disappear as new board games like Monopoly and the comic book *Famous Funnies* became the rage.

At the end of 1934, the Kellogg Company asked Phelps and Adler to create a premium for their Toasted Corn Flakes cereal. Their mandate: No puzzles. Puzzles were passé. They wanted something eye-catching, economical, and modern. For weeks everyone at the company brainstormed, but nothing seemed to work. In his new position as chairman, Simon had been coming into the office once or twice a week, but since the crisis he'd been there every day, tossing out suggestions, reacting to others. Privately, he worried that he'd run dry. "Maybe I've had every new thought I'm ever going to have," he said to Flora one night.

"That's nonsense, you're just exhausted," she told him. "You have so much going on in your brain, you just have to push it all aside to make room for corn flakes. Don't worry, it will come."

When it came, it did so in the sorry form of Pissboy, who walked into Simon's office one afternoon carrying a tube under his arm. "I hope I'm not bothering you, but I have something to show you," he said. "May I?"

"Of course," said Simon, still not used to his old friend's deference.

Even before Pissboy took out the brittle yellowed sheets of paper, Simon recognized them immediately. They were his drawings of the Fatsos, Strongman, and Mrs. O'Mara that Pissboy had stolen from him. Pissboy spread the pictures on the desk. "I think I might have an idea for the Kellogg project. Flip books. You know, you flip 'em quickly and if the drawings are right, they look like moving pictures. We use these characters to create a story around Toasted Corn Flakes. Of course, you'd have to do the drawings, but — I don't know, maybe it could work."

Simon remembered the primitive flipbook he'd created for the screaming little girl on the ship coming to America, Rita. She'd looked him up after the story appeared in *Time*. He'd taken her to lunch — nothing fancy — a local luncheonette. She'd been pretty in a frantic, excessive way but also charming and intelligent. What had unnerved him about that lunch was how she'd treated him like a famous man, a middle-aged famous man. He had had no thoughts about fooling around with Rita but would have enjoyed a flirtation or at least the recognition that she might find him attractive. It was stupid vanity on his part, and he never bothered to tell Flora about the lunch.

As he thought about Rita, he remembered how, with her at his side, he'd watched the ship's stokers and come up with the character of Strongman. It pleased him that now, after all these years, Strongman would make a comeback. He created a story for the flip book about Strongman rescuing a sinking ship at sea. In the last frames, all the passengers he has saved, still wet from their adventure, sit around a table with Strongman slurping up their bowls of Toasted Corn Flakes. The animated *Strongman: A Cereal Adventure of Bravery at Sea* turned out to be the idea that glued the company together again. The Kellogg Company ordered 1.5 million of them, and by Christmas, the story had been so successful, they placed an order for two million more for the spring of 1936. Now Simon spent his days sketching the characters he had created in his youth, long before he'd learned anything about the advertising business, selling toothpaste, or what it took to make a good premium.

One evening, after hours of drafting forty-two versions of Strongman, Simon said to Flora, "My drawings were more spontaneous and energetic forty years ago than they are today. It's ironic that the best I can do now is to copy myself."

"As ironies go," Flora pointed out, "that's not it. Pissboy's the one who put you back in business. And with the drawings he stole from you."

■ ■ ■ ■

PART 6

■ ■ ■ ■

KAISERSLAUTERN:
SEPTEMBER 1935

Edith and Werner's wedding took place on September 22, the third Sunday of the month that year. They were married at the Synagogue of Kaiserslautern, a grand Byzantine structure with four cupolas, Moorish archways, and sturdy ivory buttresses. The synagogue seated 620, and on that Sunday, every seat in the temple was taken. When the string quartet began to play the Allegro from the Brandenburg Concerto no. 4 in G Major, the setting sun spilled through the stained glass windows like watercolors and splashed across the stone walls. It was a wedding that few would forget; a marker between before and after, the last Jewish wedding in that venerable building.

Werner Cohn walked slowly down the aisle with a parent on each arm, his expression somber. His father had just been released from prison, where he served time for violating the government's ruling that no department stores be run by Jews. Many of the seats were filled with his current and former employees. As a man accustomed to containing his emotions, the elder Mr. Cohn found the presence of all these people so overwhelming that all he could do was stare ahead impassively. Werner's parents left him under the chuppah, where he stood and watched as Seema walked down the aisle by herself. He wasn't the only one who wondered why Karl wasn't beside her. Seema had told Edith that Karl had an important story he had to cover in Munich that day, but the way her voice dropped and the way she wouldn't look Edith in the eye when she said it made Edith think there was more to it than Munich. Seema and Karl had been fighting about the wedding since the day the invitations arrived. Karl had said as a Christian he wouldn't feel right coming inside a temple. Seema had said that was ridiculous, that there would be many Christians at the service. "They will be noticed," Karl said. "In my position, I can't afford to be." Seema had told him he was a pompous ass. He'd told Seema she was a spoiled brat and that she'd get along fine without him. And so it had gone, a bottomless argument that had laid the groundwork for many more to follow.

■ ■ ■ ■

When the Bach finished, the pristine notes from Handel's *Water Music* filled the hall. At last, Edith appeared at the back of the temple in a floor-length white organdy sleeveless gown. It was clear that, had Margot and Frederick not been by her side, she would have bounded down the aisle in great leaps.

It took more than a little urging, and even some pleading on Edith's part, to get her mother to appear in front of so many people. "I swear," she said, "you'll never have to do this again." The three of them walked with their arms around each other. Margot had a fixed smile on her face and kept looking at Edith. Frederick wore a tuxedo jacket slightly too large for him, and he'd allowed Edith to convince him to use pomade in order to slick back what was left of his hair. Edith's cheeks shone so hot and brightly, it seemed they might burn through her veil.

Later, Frederick would say that he thought he spotted his old boss, Gustave Reinhart, in the crowd, but he couldn't be sure. Margot remembered that her legs were shaking so badly that she thought she would fall down. Only Edith's strong arm around her waist kept her going.

YONKERS:
OCTOBER 1935

Late at night, after Flora was asleep, Simon worked on his paintings for the flipbooks. He had just finished a series of sketches of the Fatsos. In this one, they were launched in a rocket ship to the moon and the only thing they had to eat was cereal. The last animation was of the Fatsos in the rocket heading back to earth as the man in the moon winked and smiled a milky smile while seated atop a box of Kellogg's Toasted Corn Flakes. Tomorrow Simon would begin a flipbook based on Mrs. O'Mara and Pep Bran Flakes. It pleased him to visualize how he would draw her voluptuous form and use the persimmon watercolor for her hair. Preparation for his sketches took him back to when drawing was the only way he could express himself and being reunited with his family was a real possibility. While he painted, he was not the businessman who had made his fortune in puzzles and games but the young boy with the great talent who needed to use his head less and to find his heart. He could almost feel Mrs. O'Mara's white little fist gently rap him on the head. These were the moments in the hollow of the evening that lifted him above the sediment of his worries.

Lately, whatever spare time he had he spent at the American Jewish Committee in Manhattan. The names were piling up faster than he could sort through them. He felt desperate about what he couldn't do. What no one was doing. Last spring, he and Flora had gone to hear the physicist Albert Einstein speak at a dinner for the AJC. Einstein, who had emigrated to the United States from Berlin two years earlier, had a thick German accent, yet when Simon replayed the speech in his mind, his words were as clear and penetrating as if they'd been spoken by Franklin Roosevelt:

Learn from the destiny that has befallen the German Jews! Preserve your independence by the creation of an appropriate institution, which you will need in the hour of oppression. Do not trust that this hour will never come, but keep the international community of all Jews sacred and holy!

It impressed Simon the way Einstein was using his fame and power to help the Jews. As a part of the International Rescue Committee, Einstein had begun another organization to help the Germans who were being persecuted by Hitler. He was also calling for a plan of action on behalf of the German Jews and writing affidavits of support for a large number of them.

Lately, as he sat drawing Mrs. O'Mara, the glamorous movie star who eats her Pep Bran Flakes while men fall at her feet and duel for her honor, he found it almost impossible to daydream away the sense of doom that enveloped his corner of peace night after night.

On the drive back from a Sunday dinner at Aunt Hannah and Uncle Paul's, Simon said to Flora: "I wonder, do you have any idea how much money we have?"

She laughed off the comment. "Enough to keep me in hats and you in your Brooks Brothers suits, I presume."

"I'm being serious, Flora. Do you have any idea?"

"Well, I'm not the one who keeps the bank books and pays the bills around here, so no, I'd have to say I don't."

"All right then, let me tell you. We have more than one million dollars. One point seven to be precise. And what do we plan to do with all that money? We have no children. You know, I'd happily support Edith and any other members of your family if they were ever to come over here. And, God willing, mine. Even then, we'd have plenty left over. Does it not seem to you, as it does to me, that it is immoral for us to be hoarding all that money with all that's going on around us? If now's not the time to use it, then when is?"

"Oh . . . it's the letter, isn't it?"

Several weeks earlier, they had received a letter from Edith describing her wedding. The letter had a curious quality about it: smudged fingerprints too large to be Edith's, wrinkles in the paper, and words blacked out with solid, impenetrable strokes. These were the kinds of things Simon noticed as he held the paper up to the light. Edith wrote about her dress and described the flowers she carried. The next part, about somebody — a rabbi, Simon guessed — saying something, was blacked out. He had underlined the part where Edith wrote, "It's a good thing we all have our memories because there are no pictures of the wedding so we'll have to cherish those," and he scribbled this in his notebook: "Were there no pictures taken because everyone thought that to photograph a large Jewish wedding was as perilous as having one in the first place?"

But there was something else, a note he had written to himself underneath his question. "Exactly a week before the wedding, on September 15, 1935, the German government adopted the Nuremberg Laws. The laws distinguished Germans from German Jews and deprived the Jews of all their rights, including the right to call themselves Germans." After that, he'd added, "There's no going back now."

"It's the letter and everything else," said Simon. "I'm going to find it hard to sit around the table making chitchat with Aunt Hannah and Uncle Paul stuffing ourselves with turkey and sweet potatoes this Thanksgiving. Hard and frankly, outrageous."

"Now wait a minute. We give a lot of money to a lot of charities. I think it's safe to say that the Jewish Center of Yonkers wouldn't be standing without the generous donation of a Mr. and Mrs. Simon Phelps. So we're not that ridiculous."

"It's easy to write a check and give to charities," he said. "I'm talking about something more than that."

"And what would that be? Are you proposing we hire Al Capone to go over to Germany and shoot Mr. Hitler?"

"God, Flora, you can be such a . . ."

"Bitch. Go on and say it. I can be such a bitch. I know I can." Her voice relaxed. "I'm sorry, I don't see the world like you do. I like it here. I like our lives. I don't want anything to change. It scares me, the way you talk sometimes. I feel like you're going to go out and do something reckless and stupidly heroic just because you think it would be the right thing to do. You can't change the world, Simon. Even you can't do that."

"I'm not that much of an egomaniac," he said. "I know I can't change the world. But I can't sit by and do nothing."

"You're not doing nothing," her voice rose again. "You put in all that time at the Jewish Committee. What more are you supposed to do?"

"I don't know," he shook his head. "I really don't know. But we can't let them stay there. Not Edith and Werner. Your family. We really can't."

She stared out the window searching for the right words. "It's funny," she finally said. "Even though you're the practical, down-to-earth businessman, sometimes I think that between us, you're the romantic and

I'm the pragmatist."

"That's not it," he said. "The difference is that I see the consequences of things that are happening now and live with them. Don't get me wrong, Flora, I'm not criticizing you, but you have your version of the world and you won't be budged out of it. I envy you that."

"I like my version of the world. At least it's not filled with foreboding dark clouds."

And so it went, all the way back to Yonkers. Even as they readied for bed, the argument continued. "Think of it this way," he said after brushing his teeth. "They pass the Nuremberg Laws in America. Suddenly, we're deprived of everything: jobs, schools, even walking in the park. We can't even call ourselves Americans anymore. Picture that. Can you?"

Flora was exhausted from the drive, the constant bickering, the heavy meal. She lay back on the pillow and closed her eyes. "Please, can we take a break from this for just one night?"

"We can take a break from this forever if you promise me one thing."

"Anything," she answered.

"Promise me that we can go to Marseille and meet Edith and Werner."

She could do that.

"Yes, I promise. Now can we get some sleep?"

But just before she fell asleep, she thought about the Nuremberg Laws. What must that mean to a man like Frederick, so proud of his service in the war, so German in the way he carried himself and thought about himself? She really couldn't imagine.

KAISERSLAUTERN:
NOVEMBER 1935

No one could imagine how the news affected Frederick. Every day something else. The signs: JEWS NOT WANTED. The rules: "Jews forbidden to perform works by Aryan writers and composers." Old friends turned their heads and ignored him when he walked down the street. He and Margot were running out of money. He held himself in check when he talked about these things with Margot and told her, "Who we are is who we are and no one can change that with a bunch of laws." He would search her face for a reaction, but she would elude his glance and rush off to repot some geraniums or hang out some laundry. He envied how she could retreat into her flowers, her domestic chores, or even those silly glass owls, fussing over them as if they were her only world.

He had nowhere to go with his feelings. Even if Margot were up to hearing what was on his mind, whatever he would say would come out mawkish and foolish:

Yesterday I had two arms and two legs, now I have none.

The place that I have loved and cherished has thrown me out the door and put chains on the lock to make sure I never come back.

There once stood a man named Frederick Ehrlich. One day, a large boulder fell from the sky and crushed everything that was inside of him. Now, Frederick Ehrlich is like a character drawn on paper and the part of him that was a man is gone.

Part of him expected these Nuremberg Laws to be revoked. Expected any day he would receive a handwritten apology: *Frederick Ehrlich, devoted patriot, and veteran of war, you will always be cherished and beloved by the fatherland. Please disregard any news to the contrary.* And life, as it had been, would resume.

Round and round these thoughts went. Every day the same ones.

Lately, he'd wondered if he was the one with the nervous condition. Common sense told him that if ever there was a time not to call attention to oneself, this was it. Did no one else agree? Certainly not Mrs. Cohn, showing up at her son's wedding in that gaudy diamond-and-emerald necklace sprawled across her chest like a traffic jam. Or Werner's father, throwing that shindig of a reception, even after his arrest and his removal from the store. Or Seema and Karl, still unmarried but obviously sleeping in the same bed and riding around in that flashy car of his. And Edith. Over-the-moon Edith, who couldn't give a thought to anything but her Werner.

He was happy for her. Werner was a good man and would take care of her. But what kind of a future did this country hold for them? They would go on their honeymoon in January and when they came back, he would tell them they had to think about leaving. He and Margot were too old to go anywhere else, but Edith had her whole life ahead of her. If she left, it would break Margot's heart. The strain might be too much for her. Maybe things would be better by the time they came back from their honeymoon. But what if they weren't? *I worry too much,* he told himself. *I have too much idle time on my hands. Edith told me I was becoming an old fusspot. When I worked at the store, my thoughts were simpler, less fraught. I miss the people I worked with. I miss working. I miss making money. I miss my old life.*

ABOARD THE SS *AQUITANIA:* MARCH 1936

"A boutonniere for you, sir? A bouquet for the lady?" The offer was extravagant, and Simon and Flora exchanged puzzled looks. The ship's steward wouldn't be put off. "It is customary, when we pull into Marseilles, for the captain to give flowers to his first-class passengers, to show his appreciation," he said, making a slight bow while shoving the flowers in front of them. "Come now, you wouldn't want to insult the captain, would you?"

"No thank you for the boutonniere," said Simon. "Roses aren't my cup of tea, but I'm sure the lady would be honored to accept your bouquet."

Flora lowered her eyes, ashamed that Simon could see how they darted with excitement. Yellow roses in March: they were as lavish as the lobsters, the gilded headboards on the double beds, and the linen napkins folded to look like mountain peaks that had populated their world over the past two weeks.

Flora reveled in these luxuries and Simon took his pleasure by indulging her. That night, their last at sea, Flora and Simon were scheduled for the second seating at dinner. As he waited for her at the bar, he pulled a pen out of his vest pocket and began sketching on the paper napkin beneath his glass of champagne. He drew a picture of a ship filled with rotund ladies weighted down with fur and diamonds and pot-bellied men smoking cigars and sporting oversized pinky rings. The ship was forging ahead through the flames of hell that surrounded it. On its bow he'd written in large capital letters: THE SS *DECADENT.*

Simon had meant to crumple up the napkin before Flora came, but she had snuck up behind him. "It's that bad, huh?" she'd said, pulling up the stool next to him and draping her arm around his shoulder. "Sorry you've had to suffer so." She leaned over and kissed his cheek. She smelled like licorice and soap and a child fresh from its bath. "Oh, you know how I like to scribble." He tried to take in more of her smell. He could never get enough of that smell.

"Lucky for you, this hell will be over tomorrow morning," she said, "and then . . ." They stared at each other quizzically.

That night, they sat at the captain's table. When the waiter placed a small white plate with gold-leaf trim and a thistly artichoke in front of him, Simon looked to Flora to see how she was managing it. Simon disliked food that was complicated or messy and had managed to keep away from the unruly artichoke. Now he watched as Flora dipped the leaf in the butter sauce, scraped out the meat from the inside of the leaf with her teeth, and dropped the remainder into a small soup bowl. Simon only half-listened to the conversation she was having with the gentleman on her left. Conquering the artichoke took all of his attention. Only when Flora answered one of her dinner partner's questions did he look up from the spiky mound of leaves in front of him.

"Oh, our people are Jewish. My sister and I came from Germany almost thirty years ago," she'd said, dabbing some butter from her lips. Simon raised his eyebrows and stared at the stranger with the gold watch chain dangling from his pocket. Why, he'd wondered, had he asked Flora if she was Jewish. That was the kind of question no one asked unless there was trouble behind it.

Flora was never calculating in that way and answered every question put to her. "Every question deserves an honest answer," she'd say. As reserved as usual, in these times Simon was especially suspicious. But despite his reticence and odd formality, passengers on this crossing finagled a way to be seated next to him at dinner, and he was the one who got photographed for the ship's newsletter, "In the Same Boat." The caption read:

Dapper Simon Phelps enjoyed a round of shuffleboard on deck yesterday afternoon with his lovely wife, Flora. When asked why they were traveling from New York to Marseilles, Mr. Phelps answered, "There is so much to see and so many family and friends to visit."

These days, few people — particularly Jewish people — were taking pleasure cruises to Europe. Yet none of the first-class passengers wanted to talk about the unpleasantness, not when they'd paid nearly five hundred dollars to wash down their foie gras with French champagne. So on that night, they wrapped their arms around their partners and stared through half-closed eyes at the moonlight spilling into the black water while the orchestra played "The Way You Look Tonight." For those few moments they could believe that life was as sweet and rich as the music they were hearing, and they had already started to yearn with nostalgia for the time that was passing. The orchestra broke into a brisk version of "All of Me." Simon and Flora were dancing close enough to Flora's dinner partner, the man with the gold watch chain, to overhear him say to his wife: "The führer frowns on this kind of Negroized music." The wife nodded and said something that made him jerk his head back and make a disapproving tsking sound. As the two of them stopped dancing and headed back toward the table, Simon hugged Flora closer to him.

"What was that all about?" she asked. Simon hummed in her ear. "Keep dancing," he whispered, "and smile like you're having the time of your life."

The fog blurred the Marseille coastline as the ship pulled close to shore. Flora stuck one of the steward's roses into her lapel, another into the brim of her hat. The rest she held in both hands. "You don't think me frivolous for accepting the flowers?"

Simon put his hand around her waist and squeezed it. "If it were up to me, I would cover you in rose petals every morning and bathe you in them every night."

The early morning mist carried with it the briny air and burning fuel from the ship's engine. Even with the smell of roses wafting under his nose, Simon was mostly aware of the black smoke that huffed out of the funnels and settled heavy over them.

Whatever dread he was feeling, he kept it in check behind his steady gray-blue eyes and his wire-rim glasses. As she packed up the last of their shampoo and aftershave, Flora stared at the bunch of yellow roses that she had stuck into a water cup in the bathroom. "I wouldn't mind staying here a few more days, or forever," she said, rubbing her fingers across the polished mahogany shelf in the bathroom. "Who can blame you?" he asked, careful to keep the crease as he folded one of his shirts. He glanced up to see if she caught the falseness in his voice. But Flora was watching his fingers, surprisingly long for a man of his height. She still loved the way his hands were always busy — and usually ink stained. "Let's put all the necessary documents in the small valise," he said, picking up a white case with tan stripes and placing it on the bed.

He knew that Flora was apprehensive

about the days ahead, not knowing exactly what they held. If he hurried her along, she'd sense his anxiety, and there was no point to that. He wanted her to enjoy what time there was left, though time was the one thing he did not have to spare. He was ready to be off this ship and away from these people.

"I'll bet Edith and Werner have been waiting out there since daybreak," he said. They both smiled at the thought of Edith.

Flora took the roses out of the water cup and wrapped them in a white washcloth that had the words SS *AQUITANIA* embroidered on it in gold script. "I hate to leave these behind," she said, holding them up to the light coming from the porthole. "Edith will like them. Yellow's a good color for her, don't you think?"

"Yes," he said, "I'm sure she'll love them." There was a knock on the door as he snapped closed the smallest of their five valises.

The porter piled their suitcases on his cart in size order. They were each made of rich leather with the same brass rivets and snaps and two leather straps that secured them shut. Inside, they were lined with gray silk and had compartments where you could store everything from combs and socks to shoes and books. These were the kinds of things that gave Simon pleasure and served as markers in his life between the present and the past.

He took Flora's arm as they stepped into the morning air. His fingers were wrapped around her wrist, and he could tell how quickly her heart was beating. She was so beautiful in her maroon cloche with the yellow rose stuck in its headband, so alive in her gold-and-orange tweed coat and blue silk blouse, this lady on his arm with the smile that feasted on life. Heads turned toward her as they walked onto the deck and made their way down onto the gangplank. She was America: all porcelain pink and robust. He watched the mass of arms and faces below waving and hollering, and he searched to find the ones that were searching for him. This time, he was not alone. Not like the last time, when he was as alone as it is ever possible to be.

MARSEILLE, FRANCE: MARCH 1936

The first thing Edith noticed when she woke up in the morning was that the yellow rose petals had all dropped to the nightstand, leaving only the disrobed stalks in the vase. Flora and Simon. She smiled at the thought of them getting off the ship the day before: how Simon had taken Flora's arm, how he'd looked at her as if he still couldn't believe that he had this gorgeous woman by his side, how excited Flora had been to give Edith the roses she'd gotten onboard. "They remind me of you," she'd said. To the left of the bud vase was the royal blue Yankee hat with the white interlocking NY letters that Simon had given her. "You're still a Yankee fan, I presume," he'd said. "I am and I always will be," she'd answered, placing the hat on her head and refusing to take it off until bedtime.

She thought about how Simon had jumped to his feet and yelled "Attaboy,

Babe" when Babe Ruth hit that homerun at the game they'd attended. She remembered envying how much a part of the game he must have felt in order to shout out that way. She had been a lonely girl then. Just back from being sick, trying so hard to fit in, not being able to find her place.

It was different now. She looked over at Werner. In sleep his lips were slightly parted, and he made an airy whistling sound as he exhaled. She watched him and said his name softly. She wondered how many times in her life she would say *Werner*. Some things were impossible to count. The number of times a child calls for his mother, how often a person cries out "oh" in surprise. A whole lifetime with this man. The realization made her happy until she tried to picture what their lives would be like and no picture came. With things the way they were, she wondered what he would do when they got back. How would they support themselves? She pushed away these thoughts and retreated to her fresh memories, of the two of them feeding the pigeons in the Piazza San Marco, riding the mules in Palestine, nibbling escargot in Paris. Werner had promised her she would love the taste of escargots, and he had been right.

Lost in her daydreams, she didn't notice

that Werner had woken up. He rolled on his side, put his arm around her waist, and pulled her into a dozy sleep. When they awoke again it was 9:10. They had twenty minutes to shower and dress and meet Flora and Simon in the hotel restaurant for breakfast.

Simon and Flora were already sipping coffee when the two of them arrived, hair wet, arms entwined.

"Well, well, it's the lovebirds," said Flora. Simon put down the newspaper he was reading. He looked up and smiled at them. "I hope you're wearing your walking shoes. We've got two days to see this place, and I intend to see every part of it." That morning, they walked past the famous old fort and around the Quai des Belges, where Werner and Simon pretended not to notice the street girls. At lunch, they chose a fish house close to the port and ordered bouillabaisse. They laughed over the fact that none of them liked fish, but how could they come to Marseille and not eat the famous stew?

Simon ordered a bottle of dry white wine. After the waiter uncorked the bottle and they'd clinked glasses for a toast to the future, Simon pulled out a notepad. Edith could recognize his graceful script anywhere. On these pages, words were crammed together and there were places where he had circled a word or underlined a sentence so vigorously that the paper was punctuated with rips and holes.

"I have many questions about you and your family that I dared not ask in a letter," he began. He wanted to know about Frederick's "retirement." Edith told him that he'd been forced from his job. "What's this about Seema and church?" Werner and Edith exchanged looks. "Seema's a Catholic now," said Edith. "She's converted." Flora leaned forward and started to speak, but Simon shushed her. "Not now, Flora. We've got a lot of ground to cover."

"And what about this Karl fellow and his car with the crazy horn, *Tee-poo-peep-pa?* What's that got to do with anything?" Edith shrugged. Werner answered matter of factly: "Only government cars are outfitted with that horn."

Simon looked down at his notes and drew four exclamation points so hard that they too perforated the paper.

"And your wedding. Why did you have it on a Sunday and why are there no pictures?"

Again Werner spoke. "We were playing it safe. We didn't want to call more attention to ourselves than we already had."

Simon put down his notebook. He took a sip of wine and ran his tongue over his lips. "So how do you see your future? Werner, do you even have a future?"

Werner rubbed the place above his eye with the heel of his hand. "It's hard, Mr. Phelps, to know what the future will bring."

"I am not asking you kids this," said Simon deliberately. "I am begging you. Please come to America. Soon. We read the papers; we're involved with Jewish organizations." He held up the piece of paper with his notes and shook it in their faces. "Surely you're not blind to what is happening right before your eyes. You don't have time to see what the future will bring."

The table fell quiet. There was no place else for this conversation to go. Werner asked the waiter for more bread and Edith tapped his leg with her foot. He wasn't sure whether this meant she agreed with Simon or that she wanted him to break the uncomfortable silence. "It's not an easy thing for any of us to pick up and go to America, just like that," said Werner. "There are visas, and affidavits . . ."

"Yes, I know all that," said Simon impatiently. "And we are prepared to help you. As happy as we are to see you both, Flora and I didn't come here for a pleasure cruise.

460

You must know that."

"I thought that might be the case," said Werner.

"Hmm, I thought you came over just to see us," said Edith.

"We did," said Simon. "But we hoped you'd come home with us. Aside from everything else, our reasons for wanting you to come are selfish. You are family, the closest family that I have. Please, think about it."

They spent the rest of the afternoon walking around the port. The subject of America did not come up again. Instead, they wandered around to the covered markets and the town square, where the jugglers and fortune-tellers preyed on tourists and, for a few cents, promised a rosy tomorrow. They made small talk about the weather and the fashions in America. Edith and Werner were quiet, filled with sadness that their honeymoon would end the next day and with dread about what Simon had told them. Simon noticed that Flora was uncharacteristically uninterested in window-shopping, and Flora saw that Simon was tired and pausing to rest every few minutes. When, at her suggestion, they stopped for a late afternoon cup of coffee and piece of cake, he fell into his chair with a perceptible "ahh."

They had dinner early. The train to Frankfurt was leaving at six the next morning. The rain started as they walked back to the hotel. Flora and Simon packed up their bags, putting all the documents they would need in Germany in the small white valise with tan stripes that Simon had brought for precisely this purpose. She went through her wallet to make sure all her papers were there and found the piece of paper she'd been carrying around with her for nearly thirty years. By now, it was torn and faded and yellowed in the creases. "Look at this," she said, careful to unfold it. "The first drawing you ever gave me." It was a picture of the two of them, and underneath he had written: "Mr. Blockhead and the lovely Miss Chatterbug."

Simon had already taken off his glasses, so he squinted and brought the drawing right up to his eyes. "Why do you carry around this one?" he asked. "It's not even particularly well crafted."

"I like that you look goofy and I look young," she said. "And it makes me remember how happy we were."

"We *are*," Simon said, correcting her. "How happy we *are*."

■ ■ ■ ■

Although it was the nicest hotel in Marseille, the Grand Hotel was an old structure that couldn't keep out the cold and dampness that seeped through its mullioned glass windows. Even under the goose-feather quilt, they were chilled and Flora's feet were practically numb with cold. They lay in each other's arms, Flora's feet tucked next to his. The sound of the rain soothed them until they were warm and sleeping and breathing as one.

It was not yet light when Flora woke up the next morning. It was still raining and her arm was around Simon's chest as it was when they fell asleep. It was cold. He was cold. She carefully extricated herself. She looked at the clock. He had ten more minutes to sleep. She tucked the quilt around him as she went to the bathroom. When she came back, she sat by the side of the bed and placed her hand on his arm. "Simon sweetie, it's time to get up." She shook him gently and said it again. When she said it a third time, he still didn't move, and she became aware of how stiff his arm was. She checked to see if he was breathing. He was not. She shook his body and shouted his name. She heard the panic in her voice and felt an icy fear spread through the pit of her stomach. She ran down the hall and banged on Werner and Edith's door. She didn't wait for them to answer. "Come quickly, quickly. It's Simon," she shouted.

They gathered around his bed. Werner shook him. Flora cried his name again. A crazy thought ran through Edith's head. The horses. The *clock-clock* sound Simon made that time when he brought her to see the horses. They came to him. Maybe if she did that now, her tongue against the back of her palate, he would come to her. She did it so softly that no one heard. Werner called the front desk. Flora thought that just because someone understood how to run a fancy hotel didn't mean he would know how to bring another man back to life. The police were called; an ambulance arrived.

Flora sat in a red velvet chair in the parlor while the doctor examined Simon. Edith knelt down next to her and Werner stayed in the room with the doctor. When they came out of the room, Werner looked at Edith. The doctor took his time placing his stethoscope back into his bag. Then he turned to Flora. "His heart," he began. "I'm so sorry . . ."

Flora put her hand up in the air to stop

him from saying the words. He was wrong. She should have never let him in the room in the first place. He was old and fat. He wore thick spectacles and smelled like rubbing alcohol. Did he even know who Simon was? It was all a mistake. Simon would be fine; he was just tired. He needed more sleep. She went back to the bedside. The doctor had pulled the sheet over Simon's head. She stared at the sheet, waiting for it to move with his breath: just a puff, a ripple. She put her hand over where his mouth and nose were and waited some more. Nothing. "Oh God, no," cried Flora. "Please. No." Her legs went out from under her. Edith and Werner rushed over. Each took an arm and helped her out of the room.

For the rest of the morning, Flora let herself be led by the two of them. There were reports to be filed, authorities to be notified. When they told her to eat, she ate. When they said she should go with the body to the morgue, she went with the body to the morgue. But when they told her she had to sit down and try to catch her breath, it was the one thing she could not do. She was bent over and shivering, her arms folded across her chest. All the breath had gone out of her. Maybe she would die, too. It didn't seem like a bad thing.

Late that afternoon, the three of them walked back from the police station along the port. They talked about whether Flora should try to book passage on the next ship out of Marseille and take Simon's body with her. The fishing boats reeked with the odor of the day's catch. Yesterday, that smell was briny and romantic. Today, it made Flora gag. She was eager to get back to the hotel before she vomited in the street.

Werner went to see about booking Flora passage on a ship home. Edith took her to her room, where the two of them lay silently atop the goose-feather quilt staring up at the ceiling. Flora turned and looked at the tan suitcase with all of the documents that Simon had spent weeks assembling. She thought that if things were reversed and she was the one who had died, Simon would go on to Germany and do what they had come here to do. *But that is Simon,* she told herself, refusing to refer to him in the past tense. *He's the heroic one. I'm not.*

She remembered how they'd argued about coming to this place, how she would get so impatient with him whenever he talked about the sorry state of the world. Maybe her judgment bore down too hard on him, weakened his heart. After his long days at work, he should have come home to someone accepting and loving. She shouldn't have let him spend all that time on those stupid flipbooks. She should have pitched in at the American Jewish Committee. Should've helped him find his family. Should've been nicer, made him happier. He should've been a father. Her fault. Her bad blood.

The *should haves* and *shouldn't haves* were as persistent as the rain. If only it would stop raining. It was so cold in the hotel room, this dreadful hotel room. She got up and dug through the suitcase until she found one of Simon's sweaters. She pulled it over her silk blouse and her suit jacket. The sweater fit snugly and hit her right at the waist. She'd forgotten how small he was. Then she said the thing that made them all laugh despite the awful circumstances. "You never know a man's true size until you put on his clothes." The laughter freed them up to say other things.

"I can't stay in this room another minute," said Flora.

"We'll go downstairs, get something warm in our stomachs," said Edith. Flora took Edith's arm and they went to the lobby, where a piano player was battling a waltz as treacly as the odor of lilies trying to overpower the room. "Do they think if they play this schmaltzy music and fill the room with flowers that we'll forget that this is the worst weather in the history of the world?" asked Edith.

I love this girl, thought Flora, allowing herself be led to a corner table. If I leave tomorrow, I go back to Yonkers to what? To whom? She imagined walking through the front door of the house without Simon. His coat would still be hanging in the front room, his papers neatly filed at his desk. She thought about his slippers, his beautiful suits and handmade shirts standing at attention in his closet, and his mother's apron, the old ragged lady among them, all waiting for him to call upon them. Such a sad empty thought.

"Tea with rum and a little honey, the day calls for that," said Edith.

Flora was still lost in her thoughts. "I can't go back to our house," she said. "Not alone. I just can't."

"What if I go with you?" asked Edith. "I mean Werner and I? We could go back with you on the boat and stay for as long as you like."

"You would do that?" asked Flora.

"I would," said Edith. "I can't speak for Werner, but I think he would."

Grief sank, relief floated, and for the first

time since early that morning, Flora felt the weight ease. "Well, that would be, it would be, I don't know, I could . . ." Flora tried to collect her thoughts. "That would be wonderful but I think impossible. It's not easy for Jews . . . you remember what Simon said yesterday." The two of them cried at the thought that Simon was still part of their last twenty-four hours. They drank their tea and rum in silence, occasionally reaching across the table to hold hands. A few times Flora stroked Edith's cheek. "My sweet child, what would I ever do without you?"

And after their second or third cup of tea and rum, Flora put her elbows on the table and rubbed her swollen eyes. "I have to go lie down. Let's talk about all this tomorrow."

Edith took Flora up to her room and offered to stay the night with her.

"No, I'll be okay," insisted Flora. "You go, get some sleep."

Flora locked the door, relieved to be alone.

The hotel had made up the bed and left a single red rose in a vase on the dresser. Flora paced the room. She rubbed her hand along the freshly made bed and caught a glimpse of herself in the mirror. Her face was puffy and unrecognizable even to her. She ran her hands through her unkempt hair and kept walking around the room thinking if she stopped, she wouldn't know what to do.

She opened the closet door. Simon's suit was hanging exactly where he'd placed it the night before. It jarred her, almost as if he'd reappeared. She ran her fingers along the sleeve then pressed her nose to the suit's back hoping to catch a whiff of him. She took the suit from the hanger and laid it on the side of the bed where he had slept. She spread out the arms of the jacket and placed the pants beneath it. Then she laid down her back, on top of the suit, wrapping its arms around her, and fell asleep until long after sunset.

When she woke up, she felt calmer than she had since that morning. She washed her face and brushed her teeth. She picked the suitcase from its rack and placed it on the bed next to Simon's suit. She unpacked what was left inside, making neat piles of underwear, pajamas, and cosmetics. There was no reason to do what she was doing, yet she did it with purpose. She took the socks from the pockets, the medicines from the side compartments. She had no idea he'd packed all this: calamine lotion, witch hazel, Ben-Gay. Simon had thought of everything.

She took out the envelopes filled with some unfinished work from the flipbooks. She placed them next to the documents from the night before. When she finished unpacking, she turned the suitcase upside down to make sure she hadn't missed anything. She shook it and thumped it and could feel that there was something else inside. She ran her fingers along the silky inside of the suitcase. Then she felt it, the outline of a large envelope and the weight of a book. They were underneath the back pocket. She looked closely. The silk had been neatly cut and sewn back up again. Gently, she tugged at the stitches, wondering what it was that had needed to be hidden so carefully.

She slid her fingers inside the slit and felt the corner of an envelope, grasping it between her two fingers and pulling it out. The envelope was sealed and for a moment Flora wondered whether or not to open it. It was clearly something Simon hadn't wanted her to see. Would this be a betrayal? She thought she knew all of Simon's secrets. But this was no time for second thoughts.

She sliced through the envelope with the Grand Hotel letter opener. What she found inside were four sheets of paper, all written in Simon's beautiful cursive script. There

471

were lists of names, starting with Cohn.

Werner and Edith Cohn: 14 Eisenbahn
(businessman)
Artur and Erna Cohn: 32 Froebelstrase
(tailor)
Max and Hermine Cohn: 27 Bismarck-
strase (postal clerk)
Albert and Elsa Cohn: 5 Augustastrase
(furrier)

There must have been forty Cohns, each
listed with an address and profession after
the name. And then there were the Gross-
mans, another forty or so, same thing: name
address and profession, followed by the Ehrlichs, including Frederick and Margot Ehrlich (butcher). In all, there were more than
100 names.

There was also a book, a thick book with
a yellowish-beige cover and brown type.
She'd heard about this book.

Simon hadn't mentioned the book or the
list. She figured he'd picked up the new
book at the office, as he often did. The
names on the list must have come from the
AJC, all the Cohns, Ehrlichs, and Gross-
mans in Kaiserslautern, many of them relatives. She held the pages in her hand,
imagining Simon bent over his desk late at

night writing each name. She knew right away that the names on the list represented the people Simon was hoping to get out of Germany. His family.

But how? How could anybody get so many people out now?

Then she thought about the conversation with Edith and Werner the night before, and how Simon had become impatient when Werner mentioned the complications of Jews leaving Germany. "The visas, the affidavits of support . . ."

Simon had waved him away. "Yes, I know all that," he'd said. "And we are prepared to help you."

Flora stared at the sheets of paper. The affidavits of support. That must be what this was all about. He'd listed all the people he wanted to help, along with their occupations. He was going to ensure an affidavit for every one of them. That was what this trip was all about.

KAISERSLAUTERN:
APRIL 1936

It was the middle of the night when the train from Marseille crossed into Germany and lurched to a halt. Most passengers were sleeping, so the sudden stop caused books to fall from their laps and half-drunk bottles of wine to spill to the floor. Soldiers swarmed the train in darkness. The sound of them shouting orders and kicking various pieces of luggage added to the chaos. Flora, Edith, and Werner had chosen to stay awake. No doubt two German Jews traveling with an American Jew into Germany would be a cause for suspicion. They had rehearsed many times the part each would play: Flora, the arrogant American; Werner, the obedient German; and Edith, the new bride. And they wanted to be alert and fully in character when it came time for their papers to be inspected and questions to be answered. They were fortunate that Seema had a quick mind. When Edith cabled her to say that Simon had died and they were bringing Flora back to Kaiserslautern with them, Seema immediately wrote back: KARL EMERLING WILL SEE TO IT THAT YOU ALL HAVE A PLEASANT JOURNEY. It was the only reassurance they had that this part of the trip would go smoothly.

The officer who inspected their papers was brusque, licking his finger as he turned the pages of their documents. "Cohn," he said, looking down at Werner. "Yes sir, I am Werner Cohn, and this is Mrs. Cohn, my new wife." Edith lowered her eyes and bent her head. "We are traveling with my wife's aunt," he continued, "my Aunt Flora Phelps from America."

"What is the purpose of your journey?" snapped the officer.

"We are returning home from our honeymoon. Our aunt has met up with us so she can visit Kaiserslautern, where she will be a guest of our friend Karl Emerling."

The officer studied Flora, who was dressed in a mauve suit with a fur collar and matching hat. She sat straight and never looked him in the eye. "May I see your passport, madame?"

Flora looked as if she'd been inconvenienced by the officer's request. She rummaged through her purse, taking time before retrieving her passport. He took the passport, and again licked his fingers before flipping through its pages. "So, you have been to our beautiful country before," he said trying to make conversation.

Flora nodded and gave a weak smile. He handed the passport back to her. As soon as he turned his back, she pulled out a handkerchief and wiped where he'd touched the page with spit on his finger.

It took an hour for the soldiers to go person to person throughout the train, and by the time the engine began to chug forward, the sun was rising and the people in the train were talking loudly and laughing with relief.

It was late afternoon by the time they got to Frankfurt. Seema was waiting for them at the train station. Flora was the first to see her. Immediately she was struck by how much older she looked. She was still striking, that would never change, but her eyes seemed faded and smaller than she remembered. There were lines around her mouth, as if that area might cave in. Flora chided herself for noticing this. *You spiteful thing,* she thought. *You wouldn't be here except for her, and all you can think about is how she's aged.*

Of course, Seema was having similar

thoughts about Flora. Even in grief, she thought, her bearing was sturdy and regal. And of course she was dressed in one of her expensive suits. No one here dressed like that anymore. Seema drank in the sight of her sister's richly colored clothing and extravagant fur. She had become starved for color and style and women who didn't look drab and neutral. Flora looked so New York. It was the first favorable thought Seema had had about the city since she'd left.

Only when the two sisters embraced did Seema feel her sister's misery. Flora buried her head in her sister's neck and heaved with sobs. "Oh Flora," said Seema, rubbing her sister's back. "I'm so sorry. I'm so sorry."

"I know," said Flora "It's awful." They stood that way for a long while until the unmistakable sound of *Tee-poo-peep-pa. Tee-poo-peep-pa. Tee-poo-peep-pa* blared in the background.

"Karl's here," said Seema, her voice jumping. She dabbed her eyes and put on lipstick without bothering to look in the mirror. "He's going to drive us to Stuttgart." Flora stiffened and exchanged looks with Edith and Werner. They knew why Karl's horn made that funny sound. But they also knew that Karl was the one who had gotten them out of Marseille and into Germany, and how tomorrow Karl would smooth the way for Flora to get an appointment with the American consul in Stuttgart.

It was a windy, sunless morning when Flora, Seema, and Edith showed up at the American consul's office. Flora held onto her hat with one hand, and in the other she was clutching an envelope with the information that Simon had prepared, plus a package that he had brought along also for this day. The wind caught her skirt, and for a moment, it blew up around her knees, which gave the people around her even more reason to stare. She was still beautiful, this American woman, with her thick, curly, blond hair falling loosely to her shoulders. She was in no mood to worry about what she wore that day, but Seema and Edith had definite thoughts about what was or was not appropriate, and looking like a grieving widow was not what they had in mind. Instead, they chose a silk floral-patterned dress that clung to her body and accentuated her ample curves. And they made sure that the helmetlike raspberry cloche she wore was tilted in such a way as to emphasize her eager brown eyes. Vanities such as this had all but disappeared here and they wanted Flora to make an unforgettable impression.

The offices of the consulate were painted in an indeterminate gray, and Flora, Seema, and Edith were asked to sit with the others on folded wooden chairs. Edith pointed to the leg of her chair, on which someone had carved A.J. 1931. Flora thought about how empty this office probably had been in 1931. Not like now, with people desperate and sleepless who had clearly been waiting here for several days. The woman at the front desk wore her hair in a tight bun and never looked up when she called out names. She said them only once. If no one answered, she moved onto the next. So there was an unearthly quiet about this place, as everyone fixed their eyes on the woman's bun and leaned forward when it moved even an inch, just in case she was getting ready to speak.

When she called out, "Flora Phelps," she did so in a rounded tone and lifted her eyes to see who this woman was who had been jumped ahead of everyone else in line.

Flora stood up and gathered her things. She squeezed Edith's hand and glanced at Seema. Seema turned away and almost imperceptibly nodded her head no. Then, with all eyes on her, Flora wrapped both arms around the envelope and the bundle that was wrapped in brown paper and tied up with twine and clutched them to her bosom. She was led into a poorly lit room furnished with nothing but a desk overrun with papers and a wooden folding chair next to it. Behind the desk sat a man who looked as if he hadn't slept for days either.

"What brings you to this lovely place?" he asked, making no effort to conceal his irony.

They had all rehearsed the role Flora would play for him. No longer the haughty American, she would be sweet, vulnerable, and if called for, even flirtatious. She pictured Simon sitting in the back of the room, watching her and smiling the way he did when he didn't mean to. *You were born to do this, my Floramor, I do adore you.* Her eyes filled with the thought of him; through the mist she thought she could almost see him.

"I'm here to try and help some relatives come to America," she said lightly.

"Where are you from in America?" he asked.

She told him Yonkers. He told her that he, too, was from New York. "Upstate New York, Kingston. Have you heard of it?"

"Oh yes, I've been there often," said Flora, drawing from the summer she and Simon took a house in the Catskills for a month.

"The beautiful Shawangunk Mountains."

The consul brightened. "Then you must have gone snow shoeing there."

"Many times," Flora lied.

"Nothing like it," said the consul. "We used to set out at sunrise and not come home again until just before dark." He reminisced about Lake Minnewaska and Mohonk and the farms that were overrun with so many pumpkins during the autumn. Flora smiled and nodded, as if she, too, were nostalgic for the pumpkin fields. "You must be homesick," she said.

He shook his head. "This place is far from Kingston, that's for sure."

"I brought you something from home," she said, presenting him with the parcel she'd been holding so dear. "This is what everyone's going to be talking about in a couple of months." The consul kept his eyes on hers as he unwrapped the gift. "I wish it were a pumpkin from Kingston," she teased, "but I hope you'll like it anyway."

It was a book with a yellow cover and maroon type: *Gone with the Wind.* "The word is that America's going to go nuts for it," said Flora.

The consul held the book in his hands. "Heavy," he said. "Lots of pages. I can use something to read other than passport applications." He looked up from the book. "Thank you. Thank you for this. No one ever brings me anything but troubles. You are a kind lady. Now what can I do for you?"

Flora flattened her skirt and folded her hands in her lap. She told him how she'd been born in Germany and moved to America as a child. "I have so many relatives still left here. I'm here to sign affidavits of support for all of them."

He raised his eyebrows. "That's a lot of . . ."

"I know, it's a lot of money," she said, reaching into one of the envelopes Simon had prepared. "I can afford to do this." She pulled out a bank statement and passed it to him. "My husband, Simon Phelps, maybe you've heard of him. He was known as America's Puzzle King." She laid out Simon's kingdom, explaining about the puzzles, the toothbrush premiums, and the games. "So you see, we have the money."

"And how many people do you want to sign for?"

Now she handed him the list that Simon had prepared. "These people," she said. "All of them."

He whistled. "That's asking a lot. There's no way on earth I can possibly do this.

You've seen the lines." He pointed out the door.

"I've seen the lines," she said. "If you help me with my list, there'll be at least one hundred fewer people waiting."

The consul looked taken aback. "The people on your list, are they ready to leave?"

"I'm working on that," said Flora. "I think all of them will go except for my sister. But that's a whole other story."

Flora thought back to the conversation she and Edith had had with Seema earlier that morning. Then, as now, she'd fought to stay calm: "Can't you see? I need you to come with me." Seema had stroked her face. "I can't go to America. I belong right here with Karl."

Flora had heard the harshness in her voice when she'd said: "Men can't always save you, Seema. Sometimes they can't even save themselves."

Edith had watched silently until then. "For God's sake, Aunt Seema. You're still a Jew and they will kill you for it."

The three of them stared at each other blankly, trapped by Edith's words. Then Seema pulled a small item out of her bag: "Just promise me that you'll think of me every time you look at those Greek boys at

483

the museum." She winked at Edith then squeezed the item into her hand. It was the heart-shaped, hair-filled pillow that Edith had sent her after her trip to America.

Flora forced her mind back to the present.

"What about your husband?" asked the consul. "Is he with you?"

She took in a breath and waited until she was able to answer. "My husband died a few days ago."

"Oh, I'm so sorry." He started to reach for her hand, then reconsidered and patted it before pulling back.

Flora started to cry. "He came to America as a young boy. Left all his family in Lithuania and spent his whole life looking for them." She blew her nose. "Never found them. He didn't want that to happen to my family. He was the one who was supposed to come see you. I'm just here because he can't be." She dabbed her eyes.

"So if I can help you, how fast could you fill out all these forms?" He held up a stack of paper.

"I've got as much time as you need," said Flora.

"We're looking at six weeks, maybe two or three months even," he said, still holding the fistful of papers.

"I'll wait then," she said.

"Okay, let's begin." He took one of the many stamps from a cardboard box on his desk and firmly pounded each page with fresh ink. Then he moved the papers into a file on the right hand side of the desk. "This is the 'expedite now' file." He didn't look up. "You'll need to have these people get their visa applications to me as soon as possible, starting today."

The waiting took forty-five days. When Flora wasn't helping to prepare visas and visiting distant relatives trying to persuade them to immigrate, she was having futile fights with Seema. But Seema wouldn't be parted from her man or her country. Flora even tried talking to Karl, who, at first, sided with her but was eventually moved and even secretly pleased by Seema's intractability. Flora spent hours at the kitchen table with Margot and Frederick gently, and then less gently, trying to convince them to leave Kaiserslautern. Other nights she would dine with Edith and Werner at his parents' mansion. Most of the servants were gone now. Only one, a spindly woman named Kaetha, had stayed on, mostly because she had nowhere else to go.

During the waiting, Flora fought to stay

above the grief. It helped to have so much work to do, so many people to talk with. But she took her greatest solace from Simon. She envisioned him watching her and listening to her. Had he ever seen her this determined or fierce? She could feel his pride and it made her smile every time she thought about how surprised he would be.

On the last day of the waiting, when all the visas were issued and the papers signed, Flora went back to the consulate. She had lost weight since her first visit, and though her clothes were still stylish, they hung on her now. Her face was taut and without makeup, like the faces of all of the other women in the waiting room. This time, only Edith came with her.

"Thank you for all you have done," Flora said, taking the consul's hand. They forged a friendship based on New York and what they'd each left behind. "You've been so kind and generous."

"And you to me," he said, looking at the copy of *Gone with the Wind* on his desk. "Good luck with your voyage, and say hello to New York for me if I don't see you before you leave."

Flora nodded. "I leave next week. You can't imagine how I dread making that crossing by myself."

"Yes, that's completely understandable given the circumstances."

"I only wish Simon had lived long enough to know that our family would be safe," she said, her voice cracking.

"He knows. Somehow, I'm sure he knows."

Flora raised her eyes to the ceiling for a few moments then turned back to the consul. "Listen, I hope you won't consider me too forward, but I am going to ask another miracle of you. My favorite niece, who is here with me today, just got married. If you could see your way clear to issuing two more visas and approving two more affidavits so that she and her husband could accompany me back to America, it would mean the world to me."

"Are you kidding?"

"No, I'm willing to give you whatever it takes," she said reaching for her pocketbook.

He shook his head. "Money's not the issue. Frankly, the more people I can get out of here, the better. Let me see what I can do."

"I won't ever forget you," she said, rummaging through her bag. "Here, I want you to have this." She handed him a tattered envelope. "Go ahead, open it."

He pulled out the wrinkled sheet of paper

and laid it flat out on his desk.

Flora leaned over and pointed to Simon's old drawing of Mr. Blockhead and the lovely Miss Chatterbug.

"My husband made this picture many years ago," she said. "This is who we were."

EPILOGUE

Although this is a work of fiction, parts of it are based on family legend. Most of that family is gone now, and though I was able to learn much about the real Puzzle King from research, the rest of the story is lost, found again in my imagination.

What is true is that the real Flora did sail for America with her niece and nephew, and by the time the war ended, she had signed affidavits of support for hundreds of German Jews, saving their lives and assuring a future for them and the children who came after.

I am one of those children.

ACKNOWLEDGMENTS

Anne D. Williams, renowned puzzle expert and author of *The Jigsaw Puzzle: Piecing Together a History,* helped me with the first piece of this puzzle by answering my questions and generously offering up her own reference material.

The following institutions were invaluable in my research: the New York Historical Society; the YIVO Institute for Jewish Research; the New York Public Library; the Science, Industry and Business Library; the New York Society Library, and the Tourist Information Bureau of Kaiserslautern.

This novel and I would still be in many pieces without Kathy Robbins, Elisabeth Scharlatt, Lisa Grunwald Adler, Richard Cohen, Rachelle Bergstein, Karen Close, Miriam Brumer, and the watchful eyes of copy editor Courtney Denney. I am grateful to Brunson Hoole, Craig Popelars, Michael Taeckens, Christina Gates, Courtney Wilson, and everyone else at Algonquin for their extraordinary care and professionalism.

And always, Gary Hoenig, the final piece of my own puzzle, who urged me to tell this story and pushed me to get it as right as possible.

ABOUT THE AUTHOR

Betsy Carter is the author of *Swim to Me* and *The Orange Blossom Special.* Her memoir, *Nothing to Fall Back On,* was a national bestseller. She is a contributing editor for *O: The Oprah Magazine* and writes for *Good Housekeeping, New York,* and *AARP,* among others. Carter formerly served as an editor of *Esquire, Newsweek,* and *Harper's Bazaar,* and was the founding editor of *New York Woman.* She lives in New York City.